M000239363

REALM

A NOVEL

HL GIBSON

Bezalel
Media

Realm

Print ISBN 978-1-66788-636-7
eBook ISBN 978-1-66788-637-4

For William and Joshua

CHAPTER ONE

"FIVE . . . FOUR . . . three . . . two . . . one—*Happy—New—Year*!"

Cheers erupted as a couple hundred people, at least eighty past the maximum capacity allowed in the waterfront bar, wormed over each other, kissing and groping any flesh that came within reach of hungry mouths and seeking hands. A homemade sign blinked "3039" over and over and over again like an alarm clock from a bygone era, the bars composing the segmented red numbers either missing, dim, or flickering intermittently. Confetti made from shredded shipping labels and those torn from canned food rained down on people, sticking in their hair and clogging their drinks.

The clamor of raucous celebration and loud music vibrated the two plate-glass windows at the front of the bar, drowning out the screams and shouts of patrons who were being assaulted or pickpocketed. Not that anyone could or would come to the victims' assistance; the partyers were packed tighter than a can of sardines. They feigned ignorance for the sake of their own safety.

Someone had wedged a rock beneath the only door in or out of the bar that was jammed with just as many people trying to gain entrance to the party as those wishing to escape it. Rainwater from a three-day shower could not dampen the people's spirits, even as it trickled through the open door and puddled in the middle of the uneven concrete floor. The humidity intensified the odor of stale alcohol, vomit, sweaty bodies, sex, drugs, and cigarette smoke, leaving the wafer of debauchery from one's fellow celebrant to linger on the tongue. The horde swilled synthetic beer and wine in an attempt to rinse the flavor of social corruption from their mouths.

Waves of music and conversation rose and fell throughout the bar, crashing unintelligibly on ears and diminishing as it reached a back room, where six card players huddled around a table. Their positions had been determined by their order of arrival. The otherwise empty room offered breathing space for twenty or more revelers, but everyone knew better than to approach the poker game about to take place. One simply did not saunter in to watch this particular game, and any drunk unfortunate enough to stumble across the threshold would be shot without mercy. All festivities led up to and stopped at the door of the room.

As important as this game was for those involved, they opted for the third-rate bar because of the seclusion it provided. All participants trusted their collective reputations would keep spectators at bay. The seventh person for whom they waited entered without requesting permission and placed a briefcase on the table.

A white wimple and black veil framed her triangular face, accentuating her cheekbones as well as her pert lips. Her large, brown eyes peered from behind the frameless, round lens of her glasses. An ample chest and derriere thrust her long-sleeved black habit in all the right directions, enough to satisfy any man's fantasies. It would surprise no man present to discover she had a Glock strapped to her shapely thigh for protection. Yet for all her beauty and curves, Sister Mary Joy was the real deal.

The nun assumed her position at the head of the table. She blinked slowly, her eyes lingering as she looked the men over, pausing at their faces. The small but faithful order to which she belonged had been without a priest for years, so Sister Mary Joy had had the privilege of hearing confession for each of the six players. Against the rules, the nun often conversed about her own life, sharing painful details and offering words of comfort. She used her own issues to draw comparisons between herself and the gamblers, eventually earning their trust. When they discovered her passion for poker and abilities as a dealer, they issued an invitation to deal their games.

Five pairs of eyes glazed over at the sight of the battered briefcase the nun held. She rolled her eyes at the men, expecting them to salivate at any minute. Only the tall, dark-haired man with gray at his temples seated two places to her right remained calm upon seeing where she kept the buy-in. He held a toothpick in the corner of his mouth and rolled it gently across his bottom lip with his tongue.

"Rogue," she whispered against her will, blushing when he lowered his eyelids once in acknowledgement.

The nun wished she had not spoken his name, hoped that he would have understood it as a teasing insult. A quick flick of her thumbs released the catches on the briefcase, and Sister Mary Joy removed a fresh pack of cards, distracting the men from her discomfort. She placed the briefcase on the floor behind the chair she took, pulled the empty chip tray from the center of the table toward her, and held the unopened pack of cards aloft before breaking the foil seal on the cellophane. It was time to dole out a dose of the only religion these men practiced.

Fingers tapped the table, hands clenched and unclenched, and bodies shuddered as if charged with electricity. The sound of cards riffling through the nun's hands tantalized the gamblers' ears. Abundant stacks of chips sat in front of all six players. It would be at least eight hours before any of them left the room, including Sister Mary Joy. Amenities were limited to a toilet without the benefit of a stall and drinks delivered to the door by a dark-haired boy with small, downward-angled eyes set in his round, ruddy face, who sat just outside the room to receive their orders.

The nun availed herself of the boy's presence and ordered a Manhattan. AI servers used to staff every establishment in every Quadrant, but when even roaming soda machines became sentient, the powers that be decommissioned all artificial intelligence across the planet. They did not want to deal with the potential threat of something they could not control. Besides, humans bred faster, were cheaper, and one did not become as attached to them when they expired. To prove his worth, the boy returned within five minutes with the drink.

So began the annual game the gamblers jokingly called The Rite of Passage. The outcome determined who possessed preeminence for another year in transporting stolen goods along legal modes of shipping. Honor among thieves ensured they adhered to the results as law. The process of elimination from the game equated to drawing straws to settle the order of who chose first the when, where, and how he moved his preferred illegal cargo. For this reason, no one wanted to be eliminated too soon.

The buy-in consisted of slips of paper printed with shipping routes and contact names of personnel employed by established, legal companies who were willing to turn a blind eye to smugglers. The information on the paper was worth more than the cred-coin encrypted on the players' HoloCom devices, worth more than the lives of the men who wagered them just to get in the game. Millions in gold coin could be made utilizing this information, as every man present bought in with his best sources. It could be dangerous in the hands of the wrong person.

Rogue intended to win the pot regardless of whether the others thought him worthy or not. He held a particular interest in two pieces of paper bearing the routes and contact info of the people used by crime boss Frank Blast when shipping illegal goods from Quadrant One of the Northern Hemisphere. They alone equaled all the other pieces of info, especially if using them meant people believed Rogue had aligned his business with Blast's. It never hurt to lend the appearance of hobnobbing with the rich and powerful, even if one had to take care not to end up in the canal with a slit throat.

The only concern niggling Rogue's mind was how Red Humphries had secured the invaluable knowledge of who Blast used. Not that it really mattered as long as the information was accurate, or Rogue would be the one making sure Humphries learned how to hold his breath through a slashed windpipe. For the sake of keeping the peace while playing, he decided to extend the benefit of the doubt to the spindly redheaded with an apple-sized goiter. Besides, the thought of cutting through that monstrosity turned Rogue's stomach.

The first rounds were played cautiously as the men observed each other with side-eye glances looking for tells and gauging styles. Few chips passed hands, and the columns remained as tall as when the game began. Two hours in, Sister Mary Joy yawned and ordered another Manhattan, shooting a look at the men that conveyed she would pray for forgiveness later. The nun moaned over three hearty sips and plucked the cherry from the glass. She held the bright red fruit delicately between her teeth, pulled the stem away, and chewed languorously before returning her attention back to the game. The men sat mesmerized throughout her performance.

Impatience, arrogance, or inexperience finally pushed Jax Herrera to bid aggressively on mediocre hands. The other five allowed him to win for a while before they took advantage of his apparent stupidity. Like sharks on a wounded dolphin, the gamblers ripped through the stack of chips in front of Herrera until beads of sweat broke out on the coppery skin of the young man's forehead. Herrera reined in and performed like a seasoned player, so much so that it was Terry Li Fang who found himself without any chips at the four-hour mark.

Fang stood, impeccably clad in a blue pinstripe suit, and bowed to each of the remaining five players, although he scowled at Herrera, who thumped his foot and swayed to the music seeping from the front of the bar.

When Fang resumed his seat, several players barked drink orders at the boy asleep against the doorframe. Pawn shop owner Si Cohen's request raised several eyebrows, but nothing was said until he carefully pushed the glass of milk he ordered over in front of Fang.

"A little something to soothe the sting, perhaps, Fang?" Cohen said.

Everyone understood the insult of a weak drink for a weak player. Sister Mary Joy slammed the deck of cards on the table and flashed her index finger skyward, held inches from her face.

"One more stunt like that, Cohen, and so help me—you're out of this game."

Fang picked up the glass and consumed the milk in a single, long swallow. He slammed the glass on the table, sending a crack snaking up the side. If Fang's gray hair did not already stand at attention from his signature buzz cut, Rogue swore it would have stood on end from the lightning flashing through his dark eyes. The nun skimmed cards across the table in the direction of the remaining five players, luring their attention back to the game. Rogue chewed the toothpick at the corner of his mouth as Fang resumed his seat according to the unwritten rules of their game.

Hours five and six saw the elimination of Cohen as well as restaurateur Chow Chow Roberts. By then the bar had switched staff, except for the owner, and served free coffee to any partyer still present. Real eggs, toast, and black-market bacon could be purchased at a hundred dollars a plate; otherwise, it was Nutri-Synth, the wholesome food equivalent laden with vitamins and minerals that Earthlings had been eating for the last five hundred years. At least it looked, tasted, and felt like real food even if one could not say exactly what effect it had on the body.

Jax Herrera tried in vain not to swagger at still being present in the game. Even if he went out third to last—which he did—he played for another hour and a half like a man on fire. Being third from the top ensured that his smuggling business would not experience any disruption. He celebrated with a plate of real food, smashing the eggs and bacon between the toast to make a sandwich, and raised a glass of milk to Fang, making a deal right before everyone's eyes. Rogue chewed the toothpick in his mouth, unfazed.

A bathroom break—during which Sister Mary Joy used her long, black habit to provide a modicum of privacy—and a fresh round of drinks put everyone in a decent mood. Rogue and Red Humphries each had skyscrapers of chips separated by color in front of them. Although the other four gamblers retained their original seats per the rules, it was obvious who Chow Chow, fingering his cornrows and shooting glances at Humphries, wanted to win. Cohen, also making his desires known, offered to purchase Rogue's next drink. Herrera and Fang already felt secure in their private deal.

Rogue eyed Chow Chow peripherally and inserted a new toothpick between his lips, the last having been chewed to splinters. Sister Mary Joy dealt the next hand and complained about the single fluorescent bulb, which had begun to shimmer as it burned out. The light cast a greenish glow about the den of thieves, hampering the vision of red-rimmed eyes. Rogue thought the effect was not unlike being inside a lightning bug. He was so confident in his hand that he chewed his toothpick and allowed his mind to wander further, trying to remember the last time he had seen a lightning bug.

Nine o'clock sunshine and a fresh round of drinkers entered the bar. In the dim back room, neat stacks of chips disintegrated into twin piles, shifting back and forth between Humphries and Rogue. Another two hours of time sandblasted their way through the hourglass. When the lanky redhead beat Rogue with three queens, Rogue asked for a fifteen-minute break. Humphries consented, earning a glare from Sister Mary Joy for trumping her authority at the game. She punished Humphries by ordering a round of drinks and putting it on his tab.

Rogue stood as he yawned and stretched, exposing his stomach muscles, much to the delight of the nun and Jax Herrera, before plunking down on the hard chair he had sat in since before midnight. He reached forward, the sleeves of his black leather jacket inching up to reveal the beginning of well-muscled arms. A neck roll finished his improvised exercises, and he leaned back in his chair with a satisfied groan.

"You good?" Humphries drawled with a thick accent sure to grate on the steeliest of nerves. "Because we could get a yoga mat up in here if you want."

"I'm good," Rogue grunted.

And then the hammer came down. Rogue chewed through a seemingly endless supply of toothpicks pulled from the inner pocket of his leather jacket as he worked his way through Humphries's chips. The four players already eliminated sat rigid with hands clasped and shoulders hunched. Their eyes grazed the faces and cards of Rogue and Humphries, looking for traces of uncertainty in a chewed cheek or trembling hands. The nun's lips moved as she silently prayed. Everyone jumped when a blast of music and the screamed request to turn that crap down emanated from the front of the bar.

When Humphries's chips totaled fifty thousand, Sister Mary Joy asked if he wanted a break. The ginger-haired freak, as Rogue began calling him mentally, rubbed two black chips together, creating a cricketing noise that irritated everyone. His eyes bored into Rogue's. The ungainly, ill-dressed gambler swallowed hard, making the apple-sized goiter in his neck bob in a way Rogue found revolting. Without being told, the eliminated gamblers knew the next hand would be the last. Cards were dealt with precision, swaps were made judiciously, and music and conversation drifted back to the room where fates were being decided.

Raises were not quite as aggressive as they had been the last hour, until Humphries noticed Rogue rolling his toothpick along his bottom lip. The man smiled and raised the bet with more verve. The toothpick rolled back and wobbled as if about to fall. Rogue's right eye twitched like a flame caught in a soft wind. His comrades noticed the mistake—some grinning, others wincing—all knowing Rogue would not want to look at his cards unless he needed reassurance of the strength of his hand. But he knew his hand. It was the same one he had been holding for twenty minutes. Again, his tongue rolled the toothpick dangling from his lips as he calculated which cards he had let go and which cards better than his own Humphries might possibly have.

"It's your move, Rogue," the red-head said, pushing his sweat-stained, straw fedora to the back of his head.

Rogue took a deep breath. "All right. I'm putting you all in."

Humphries startled then smiled when Rogue's toothpick began traveling back across his bottom lip. With his eyes never leaving his opponent's face, the redhead snapped his cards on the table one at a time face up. A king, another king, a jack, another jack, and a five. Sister Mary Joy moaned softly deep in her throat.

"That's a pretty good hand," Rogue said, his voice flat. "But it ain't damn good."

The five cards Rogue fanned across the table included three sevens not even in sequence. Humphries jumped up, knocking his chair backward, arms windmilling. Rogue scooted his chair back, his fingertips grazing the handles of the knives he kept tucked in his jump boots. Sister Mary Joy's Glock made its first appearance.

"You sorry dog—what the hell is that?"

"I believe that's called the winning hand. Sit *down*, Humphries," she said.

Instead of complying, the second-best gambler of the day stormed from the room, stepping on the fingers of the boy who took their drink orders still sitting in the doorway. The other four gamblers shuffled out with nods of approval or lips curled in contempt. The nun holstered her gun, providing Rogue with a glimpse of her long leg in black hosiery, the sight of which prompted another roll of the toothpick across his lip.

"You are one cool customer," she said, pointing at his toothpick.

"Worked, didn't it?"

A black chip flew from Rogue's fingers to Sister Mary Joy's fist where she snatched it out of the air.

"Why don't you let me kiss those sexy lips of yours, Sister?"

"Rogue, I'd have let you frisk me for ten."

She placed the briefcase on the table within his reach and left the blushing man with the sound of her laughter heard all the way from the front of the bar.

CHAPTER TWO

ANGLED RAYS OF SUNLIGHT SLICED through the front windows of the bar and accentuated spiraling clouds of cigarette smoke. Rogue contemplated the tarnished light from his seat at the table in the back room. The haze crept into his tired mind to blend with the thrill of winning and the memory of hunger. His stomach growled, rebelling against almost twelve hours of heavy drinking and no food. Against his better judgment to bolt with the briefcase, he allowed himself time to enjoy the pleasure of his win. His fingertips rested on the faux leather exterior of the case before him as if he touched a holy relic. The air expanded around Rogue and just as suddenly collapsed into the reality of how his life was about to change.

For a few moments, he was no longer the orphan abandoned by the cruel hand of fate that had mired him on a dying planet. He had managed to play a better hand than the one life had dealt him. Now, the bio-domes where all humans lived due to centuries of over-polluting, his lack of family and friends, his depression, and even his unfulfilled desires took a back seat to the golden opportunity resting beneath his hands.

The profit he would make from utilizing this opportunity would put him closer to reaching his goal of the five million in gold coin required to exit this death trap known as Earth. The ranks of the wealthy who had exchanged the sentence of an unwholesome existence for the salvation of clean living would soon include another member. All his life, Rogue had dreamt about buying a place on the transport that arrived once every decade to deliver fresh filters and scrubbers for the bio-dome ventilation systems and remove any soul fortunate enough to have accumulated the purchase price to paradise.

Moon Base Tarigo, named for the scientist who had designed the lunar settlement and led its construction, was the nearest place colonized by humans with Mars Base Algernon a close second. Rogue could have settled at either community quite happily, but his heart was set on one of two space stations orbiting past the edges of the known galaxy.

Interactive 3D signage for Vista Station and Eden Station had tortured the gambler for the last nine years since they were first plastered all over Sector 17. Bright-eyed, young couples with perfect teeth glowed with the luxury of health as they smiled and beckoned from the holographic advertisements. Children who had never known hunger laughed and frolicked in the background. When the father in one such display had reached a vibrant, ghostly hand out to Rogue, the gambler extended his hand in return. Rogue's fingers passed through the hologram's hand, grasping the air in desperation. Those standing closest laughed in understanding, and one man clapped Rogue on the shoulder.

"Wait 'til you try the holo-home tour, buddy. You can do it right here on the sidewalk. You'd think you were in the house with 'em."

Rogue had shrugged the man's hand off and stalked away into the night. His mood descended an alley darker than the one through which he walked. The transport ship would depart with anyone lucky enough to have purchased their way off Earth, but if he was not among them, he could not have cared less. Rogue, only one and a half million short, tried to beg, bribe, and barter with the captain of the crew. But the captain, some jerk whose name he forgot the second the transport's engines flared for takeoff, was unwilling to permit Rogue a place on the ship with the promise to work it off upon arrival at the space station.

The incident—combined with a particularly bad season of storms darkening the already smoggy skies outside the bio-domes—sent Rogue into a depression tailspin. He succumbed to a weeklong drinking binge, used a sledgehammer to redesign the wall of the bio-dome, earned a month of hard labor in prison, paid a corrupt judge five hundred thousand to get out two weeks early, and was still no closer to escaping Earth.

Guilt prompted an act of restitution for the panic he had caused. Another one hundred thousand of Rogue's cred-coin found its way to the black market where new filters for bio-domes in disadvantaged Sectors were purchased and delivered anonymously. Such Sectors had at least one orphanage in it with a high rate of children suffering from breathing problems due to bad filtration. Greed and callousness kept the children from gaining access to bio-domes with up-to-date systems where they could receive treatment. In the opinion of many, orphans were even more expendable than a reconditioned filter.

Rogue had come to accept that he could not save every parentless child. He did what he could, but now it was time to take care of number one. His attention returned to the briefcase and away from Earth's ozone-depleted atmosphere, unpredictable weather, and pollution-seared landscapes. Chipped UV glazing on bio-domes, suspected Nutri-Synth side effects, and inadequate filtration systems would soon plague his every waking thought no longer.

Whether on Vista or Eden, Rogue believed he could have the life he always wanted. During rare yet hopeful moments, he allowed himself to fantasize about a wife and children. But now was not the time. Nor would he revisit the memories of his life in Mother Jean's Orphanage, which amounted to nothing more than a kindhearted woman with a three-story house and the willingness to hound the local government for funds. Even Mother Jean could not tell him who his parents were. Rogue was the storybook baby left on the doorstep.

Heaven help him, he needed to rein in his focus back to the briefcase and the new life he envisioned building. His first plan of action was vacating the premises. By lunchtime the drinking crowd had swelled to fill the bar to bursting through the corrugated steel walls. The drone of people should have been deafening, but for some reason the noise had fizzled to the soft buzz of a radio stuck between stations. His gut told him a dangerous current had entered the hum coming from the bar. He heard feet shuffle and sensed the crowd parting as if by the unseen hand of God. He moved to the side of the room farthest from the door where he knelt, opened the briefcase, and began jamming the slips of paper into the pockets of his camo cargo pants. Rogue cringed inwardly as a hand—not God's but still rather powerful—compressed his shoulder from behind.

"Hello, Rogue. I thought I might find you here."

The gambler slammed the briefcase shut and slid it across the floor where it crashed into the table legs, knocking over empty glasses and rattling chips. He jumped to his feet and shook off the restraining hand before turning to face his unwelcome visitor.

"Hello, Raine. You had no idea where I'd be."

"That hurt, Rogue. You have so little faith in my ability to find you."

A slow smile creased the oval-shaped face of the woman standing before him, radiating warmth, although her eyes held ice. Rogue would not know this because he refused to look into Jessica Raine's eyes. He looked everywhere else—at her ash-blonde dreadlocks held in an elastic band, her lean figure jumpsuited in the red and gray of the Global Enforcement Agency, at the armor beneath the TechMesh bodysuit accentuating her thighs, calves, and biceps, even her delicate hands with spidery fingers that should have been sliding over the keys of a grand piano but instead rested on the holster of her weapon—anywhere except her eyes.

He had looked once when they first crossed paths five years ago, and it nearly undid him. Her eyes, as green as poison, shot through with gold like sparks off hammered metal, never left his face as she questioned him during a murder investigation in which he had been a suspect. He assumed the direct eye contact was an intimidation tactic she learned in basic training. Perhaps it had been the youthful enthusiasm of a new agent looking to make her mark. Either way, it left him in a trance-like state throughout the interview and ticked her off to the point that he swore he could see flames passing through her eyes.

Rogue dodged the murder rap, as he knew he would, but his encounter with Raine left him shaken in a way he could not quite define. His business activities and chronic insomnia ensured they met several more times. Every occurrence unsettled him a little bit more. He watched her accompany victims to medical centers, comfort the loved ones of those lying under white sheets at crime scenes, and sit all night with druggies coming down from highs until they were able to give their statements. Raine participated in Sector cleanups and donated to clean air projects. She even gave drinks from her personal water bottle to emaciated children running around the streets.

Head shakes were all he had for the Good Samaritan GEA agent who anchored herself and those around her with the ridiculous notion of hope. There was no hope on Earth. Rogue decided Raine needed to grow up, and fast. She needed a lesson in the cold, hard facts of survival. That lesson came the day her brother, also an agent, was killed during routine surveillance. Rogue had been the object of that surveillance.

He had been aware that he was being watched; his survival depended on always knowing who had their eyes on him. Theo Raine, on the other hand, had no idea that he had picked up a tail in the form of a rival smuggler determined to put Rogue out of business. He led them directly to Rogue's operation. The rival occupied himself with the elimination of Theo Raine's unit, giving Rogue time to escape during the fighting. When he returned to see how much of his stolen goods had been confiscated by the GEA, what he witnessed settled his feelings about Raine.

The young woman cradled her brother's bloody head in her lap as he took his last breath. Even as his bullet-ridden, laser-charred body was zipped in a black bag for removal to the morgue, Raine was picking up his weapon and directing her fellow agents in an investigation of events. Her brother's lieutenant insignia now shone proudly from her chest, placed there by Raine herself because she knew the poorly run GEA would not question her actions. They would be happy to have a replacement for Theo so quickly.

Her eyes had glowed, not with hatred or grief, but with an optimistic quality that made Rogue shudder. The gambler barked a laugh, almost drawing the agents' attention as he melded into the crowd behind the yellow tape securing the scene. So Raine had a little steel in her backbone. So what? He knew then he had been right to suppress his feelings for the beautiful, strong young woman, and from that moment forward, he had shut his emotions down cold.

"Did you want something?" Rogue asked.

"Yes, the location of the . . . what do you smugglers call it . . . the Rite of Passage annual poker game?"

Raine laughed as she would at little boys playing cops and robbers in the streets.

"I have no idea—"

"—what I'm talking about. Yes, Rogue, I figured as much. What's in the briefcase?"

"Check for yourself, princess."

"I'd rather search you—I mean . . ."

Now it was Rogue's turn to laugh, and he threw back his head to maximize Raine's embarrassment. Heat rose in her cheeks, and she took a step backward, fingers flexing on her weapon.

"Look, loser—I know the game took place here, and if you're the last one around, that means you won. So why don't you make this easy on both of us and just tell me what I want to know."

Through chuckles meant to tick her off, Rogue said, "Yeah, I played poker here last night—ask anybody—and I won big." He removed a HoloCom from his jacket pocket and flashed the cred-coin rating on the screen. "But as we both know, gambling isn't illegal, babe."

Rogue's movements to remove and replace the HoloCom on his person revealed an article of clothing beneath his gray t-shirt. Raine tugged on the black TechMesh.

"Since we're talking about what we both know, just admit you never wear this unless you're planning on getting knifed," she said, tossing the ball back in his court. "And since no one except the high-rolling scumbags who attend the prestigious Rite of Passage would be brave enough to entertain such a thought . . . well, you see where I'm going with this."

"Raine, sweetheart, unless you have a warrant to search my body or you're arresting me on the usual trumped-up charges, I suggest we go for breakfast then head back to my place where you can frisk me all day and all night."

A front snap kick to the stomach erased the smug grin from Rogue's face and knocked the wind from his lungs.

"Yeah, okay . . . not my idea of foreplay, babe," the gambler groaned as Raine stormed from the bar.

"I'll be watching you," she called back.

Rogue straightened and brushed the dusty footprint from the front of his t-shirt.

"You stink at women, boss," said the boy still seated outside the door.

"What the hell are you still doing here, you miserable whelp?"

"Waiting for tip. Other cheapskate leave without paying Ping."

The six-foot-two gambler folded his long frame into the space before the boy so he could look directly at his face. The boy pressed himself against the doorframe. Rogue took in the dark circles beneath glassy eyes, the tracks up his arms, and ribs standing out against a threadbare t-shirt. Synthetic heroin—all the mind-blowing effects without the addiction—had taken its toll on the kid. Ping, who could have been anywhere between thirteen and nineteen, had the face of a forty-year-old who had lived a hard life. If for not addiction, Rogue could not imagine why people kept using.

As if reading Rogue's thoughts, the boy said, "It take mind off being hungry so more food go to many little brother and sister."

Per government directive, medical centers handed out synthetic heroin for free. Earth's population knew it was a method of controlling the masses for whom there was not enough food on the planet. It also meant the need for fewer GEA agents. Until a better solution of crowd control presented itself, the synthetic drug would continue to be shipped from the Southern Hemisphere where it was produced, and the poor would slowly starve without feeling the pain.

"Doesn't the bar owner feed you?"

"That skinflint? He too stingy. Give Ping one bowl food for one day work. He pay to bring my family here and promise freedom. But he treat me like slave."

Rogue groaned through clenched teeth as his hand, of its own accord, withdrew the HoloCom from his inner pocket. He stood abruptly and threw the clear device at the boy's hollow chest. Ping scrambled for it as it bounced off.

"Go on, you stray cat, go get yourself something to eat."

Holding the device as if it was the Holy Grail, Ping said, "Now I buy food for family."

Ping scurried from the bar with his hands clutched at his chest, making Rogue shake his head. Obviously, the boy had something he did not want to share. His actions would attract attention but hopefully not before he had the opportunity to buy food. Rogue wondered if he had done the kid a favor or set him up to be killed and robbed. Since it was too late to withdraw his generosity, the gambler finally left the bar and began the long walk back to his apartment. The January cold braced Rogue against the exhaustion saturating his body.

Upon arrival, he ran up the rough-hewn granite steps of his apartment building, skipping every other one. Any elegance in form began and ended with the stone slabs outside. Rogue ducked left and right through mismatched sections of construction cobbled together from the best of condemned buildings. He jumped down a flight of six wooden steps that rose as twelve metal ones leading to another level. Hallways meandered in no discernable pattern, some ending in doors closed over brick walls.

He ducked under ductwork and stepped over plumbing that bisected the maze of hallways, working his way upward. Somewhere between the ninth and tenth floors rested Rogue's single-person unit complete with a twin bed, shower stall, and portable cooking element. He ate every meal alone or on the move. The twelve-by-twelve room provided a place for him to crash when he was not out making deals.

A window over his twin bed had been painted black to prevent him from seeing into the family-sized unit on the tenth floor. Not that he had ever seen anything except feet going by and occasionally a red-cheeked baby licking the glass. The paint guaranteed his privacy and ensured that no one saw his boots, the two knives stashed within them, and the converted 9mm that matched GEA weapons energy blast for energy blast hidden in the nightstand beside the bed. Gold coin and heavy weaponry were wisely kept offsite. Mrs. Zehner, who lived in the unit above him, washed his clothes when needed. Otherwise, the only additional possession in his room was a guitar.

Rogue fell on his bed without removing his clothes. His body begged for sleep, but his mind would not shut down. With eyes closed, he felt for the guitar beneath the bed, bumping the instrument on the legs of the furniture and making it thrum. He hugged the guitar to his body, allowing his hands to explore the curves and tease the strings. Just the way Manuel had taught him.

The old addict had lived in the garage behind Mother Jean's Orphanage. When his hands were not shaking from the need for pure heroin, the disgraced GEA agent could seduce notes from his guitar with the promise of turning them into climactic music. As a child, Rogue slipped out each night to listen to Manuel play, begging to learn how to compose songs. The former agent complied, pleased when his pupil demonstrated natural talent. The lessons lasted until the day thirteen-year-old Rogue found Manuel with his head bashed in and white residue dusting the floor around him. A drug deal gone wrong. Rogue paused for half a second, picked up the guitar, and left the orphanage forever.

Several melancholy chords resounded in Rogue's small room, blending into an unrehearsed melody. The silhouette of a woman arose in his mind. She stood looking away from him, her body shaped like the guitar he caressed, taking on color and flesh. Her face turned slowly to look at him over her shoulder, and just as her green eyes met his—

"Son of a—," Rogue said through gritted teeth, thrusting the guitar away.

The need for sleep lost out to a cold shower as Rogue peeled off his clothes. He leaned out the hexagon window once belonging to a mansion and yelled for Mrs. Zehner who lowered a basket from her window to receive the dirty garments.

"No starch in the underwear, Mrs. Z."

The older woman cackled at their joke as she pulled the basket back up.

"How else still will you keep it stiff, Rogue?"

"If you only knew, you old bat," he muttered once the windows were closed. "If you only knew."

CHAPTER THREE

RAINE STALKED AWAY FROM THE bar, her arms rigid at her sides, fists clenched. Her lips moved with silent curses meant for Rogue as she plowed through the crowds on the sidewalk. The growing storm lashed her cheeks, red with the heat of frustration. People yielded to the crazy GEA agent muttering to herself, shaking her head, and occasionally shouldering one of them out of the way. They jumped into doorways and businesses more to escape her bizarre behavior than the frigid rain. Her marching did not slow when the weather intensified, sending a shower of near-frozen drops down the back of her jumpsuit.

"Damn environmental hacks," she yelled. "Stupid artificial clouds. Couldn't you idiots coordinate some snow for winter? It is freakin' January. It's not like we don't have crappy weather outside the domes. Do we have to have it inside, too?"

What had started as a good day with a strong lead on the Rite of Passage poker game had turned into three arrests for smuggling, the breakup of an unregistered prostitution ring, and the confiscation of ten thousand pounds of toxic shellfish illegally harvested off the coast. Still a good day, but not the fish she had hoped to catch.

"Make your mark, make a difference. That's what you said, Theo, and that's what I'm trying to do."

Raine's habit of speaking aloud to vent her anger used to make her brother laugh. He would never know that most of her conversations were directed at him as she tried to keep the promises she made when she joined the GEA. Promises they had both made to their retired GEA agent father to remain humble by never seeking their own fame, to serve the community by placing others first, to stay loyal to the mission statement outlined in the GEA handbook, and other such mantras meant to keep his children from giving in to the temptation of corruption.

The Raine siblings were branded naïve idealists among their fellow agents. They were also the ones everyone depended on when a situation turned dangerous. Yet, there had been no one for Raine to turn to the year her father died from lung cancer and Theo was killed during routine surveillance. She dredged her own soul for a source of hope the way her father had when he lost Raine's mother to a hit and run accident. There were days when she wanted to surrender to the tragedies that had piled up in her twenty-eight years of life, especially when combined with the dire conditions of life on Earth. Only her brother's words as he lay dying kept her from giving in.

"We can save them . . . only one at a time, Jess . . ."

But Rogue had not been Raine's choice for redemption. She believed her obligation was to her brother, not the smuggler. Ever since the day she first met Rogue, when he had stared at her with as much interest as a high schooler being bawled out by a principal, he had gone out of his way to belittle her chosen profession. He showed his constant disrespect by calling her babe, princess, and—the one that ticked her off the most—sweetheart.

"Well guess what, *sweetheart*—it's just you and me now," Raine declared to the domed skies. She turned her face into the iron sheets of semi-frozen water drenching her to the skin. "And so help me, you make one wrong move, I'll crush you under my boot heel."

* * *

FAT DROPS OF SLUSHY SNOW smacked the windows of Frank Blast's office like sloppy kisses. The fire cast honeyed light about the room, creating dancing shadows of the room's occupants along the walls. Blast's hand moved across the thick, cream-colored paper on which he insisted his contracts be printed, the tip of his pen scratching furiously as he made edits. His signature, written with the illegible flourish of a movie star, took up the bottom one-third of the page. He rocked an antique blotter across the scrawl and pulled his gold pocket watch from his vest pocket to check the time. The delicate gold hands indicated it was a quarter past two in the afternoon. He snapped the watch shut and slipped it back into his pocket.

Blast rolled his head to stretch his neck muscles and paused to appreciate the music piped through the sound system of his building. A voice that sounded heavy, as if drugged, crooned about something called a White Christmas. Historical documents showed this event once took place during the winter months. He deemed the song appropriate for the time of year as well as the small potted pine in the corner. Gold stars and silver snowflakes bowed its tender branches. Blast nodded, pleased with the whole effect.

Unfortunately, sobbing from the blonde woman seated in the Queen Anne chair by the fireplace ruined the pleasant atmosphere of the moment. Blast glared at her, his pen held aloft, as she sat there in her scarlet, satin slip without shoes on her feet. Her filthy hosiery had ripped across her knees from hours of kneeling on a hard cement floor. The apples of her cheeks bore plum-colored bruises, and her eyes—mere slits from repeated slaps to her face—leaked tears. Two of his thugs stood behind her, holding her in place with their presence.

Further killing the mood was the wench's incessant claims that she promised to find a way to pay for the gram of pure heroin she had stolen from him, that she had done a good job managing his prostitutes and keeping them healthy because nobody likes a sick whore. As if he needed reminding.

He wished she would just shut up. That she had overdosed on the heroin. That the two thugs had thought to gag her with her own panties. Her sniveling ruined the next song about roasting chestnuts.

When Blast's eyes returned to the papers on the desk, he noticed a blot of ink marring the middle of one page. He examined the tip of his fountain pen, humming softly and shaking his head. The girl could not tell whether his displeasure was directed toward her or the drop of ink that fell from his fountain pen onto the pristine paper. He stood and whispered, "Such shoddy workmanship these days."

He approached the crying woman and placed his fingers against her cheek, his thumb beneath her chin, and lifted her face to meet his. Expecting a reprieve, she did not flinch. Her eyes widened as Blast stanched the flow of dripping ink by thrusting the pen up to the gold clip into the side of her lovely neck. Her body jerked, her arms and legs thrashed, but at least she had shut up. Blast returned to his desk. When she quit moving, the man standing to the right of her said, "What should we do with the body, sir?"

"Drop it on the front steps of the GEA with a card printed compliments of Frank Blast and Company."

Blast's flat, black eyes beheld the man until he said, "Huh—good one, Mr. Blast. We'll take her where we do the others."

"Very good, Mike."

"Mark, sir."

The second man elbowed his companion and nodded toward Blast, whose chin now rested in his hand, fingers pressed against his lips. His dark eyes penetrated the two men, seeing nothing and everything. Finding the perfect balance of loyalty and intelligence had become an almost impossible standard to meet.

"Don't roll her in the Persian carpet. Cleaning it costs more than your combined salaries. Get a bag from housekeeping."

"Yes, Mr. Blast."

After complying with the suggestion, the men hefted the body across their shoulders, one standing in front of the other, to carry it from the room.

"One moment, please."

"Yes, Mr. Blast?"

"Make sure the internment service spells her name correctly on the headstone."

"You want a marker for this one?"

"She was a niece or cousin or . . . something. You may go."

Calm resettled over the darkened room as Blast returned to his desk and tore the ruined contract in two. The fire devoured the expensive paper, burning through the middle and curling the edges. Per request, his secretary promptly delivered a new copy and a fresh fountain pen from his collection. Before she could exit the room, the man Blast had been waiting for rushed in.

"Well?"

"I followed her like you said, sir."

The secretary scurried from the room, pulling the door closed behind her so as not to hear a single word of the conversation between her employer and one of his many contacts. This one wore the uniform of a GEA agent.

"And what did you see?"

"After she left the bar where the game took place, she wandered around like she was all ticked off or something. Muttering to herself."

"I'm sorry, perhaps I don't understand. Was the game over by the time she arrived?"

Blast leaned back in his desk chair as he listened to the GEA agent explain how Raine had not been led to the game as early as expected, how she had not died in a shootout between Red Humphries and the other gamblers who would have been spooked. The agent rambled on about Rogue winning the buy-in, which included information on Blast's smuggling contacts. Information entrusted to Humphries because he assured Blast that he could use it to lure Rogue to the game and kill him as well as Raine in the conflict he hoped to generate.

Somewhere between the excuses the agent made for losing Raine in the storm and Humphries not being as good a poker player as he bragged, Blast stopped listening. Now he had another dead body on his hands—a GEA agent this time—and they were always so much harder to dispose of than the general population.

He stood at the large picture window of his office, clasped hands behind his back still palming the antique .380 Ruger. The small gun felt comfortable in his grip. It tucked nicely into the inside pocket of his suitcoat. Most of his contemporaries, and there were few in the Northern Hemisphere, eschewed the weapon for newer, showier pieces. But Blast always favored quality and efficiency over making an impression. He wondered if the GEA agent had been impressed.

They were made of poor stuff, these Global Enforcement Agents, held together by nothing stronger than their dreams of glory and a chest full of easily earned medals. Low pay and no guarantee of retirement benefits made them easy prey. They practically vied for positions with him just as he had done with Manuel.

General Manuel Ojeda of the GEA had worked for one of two crime bosses who operated drug smuggling rings in Quadrant One. Corporal Frank Blast knew he would never climb high enough or fast enough in the GEA, but his intelligence, ambition, and resourcefulness caught the attention of his superiors, specifically General Ojeda. When Manuel dropped the hint of large cred-coin payouts for guarding illegal drug shipments, Blast had grabbed the golden apple from the General's outstretched hand and bitten hard. But wealth was not enough for Blast. He craved control as well.

In the classic style of exceeding his mentor, Blast not only surpassed Manuel in the eyes of their employers, but he also sold him out to the GEA's Internal Affairs, eliminated both crime bosses, consolidated their businesses, and assumed control of Quadrant One. Memories of General Ojeda occasionally drifted into Blast's mind, but like dousing a flame with water, he could snuff out any thought of his guitar-playing acquaintance who had outlived his usefulness. Addicting Ojeda to the heroin he guarded had been a sheer stroke of genius. So was paying the head of Internal Affairs to erase any permanent record that Frank Blast had ever served in the GEA.

A long, deep inhale cleared his mind, and he drew the drapes on the window, making a mental note to call Environmental about the snow he had requested. Freezing rain did not quite put him in the mood he had hoped to achieve, but then neither did dead whores and GEA agents. Blast glanced at the dead man on the carpet, filing another mental note regarding the disposal of the body. And one to get the Persian carpet cleaned. He returned to the contracts at his desk.

Dead bodies. They stacked up like cordwood around Blast. His hands no longer trembled at the sight of them and had not for decades. Not even the ones he did himself. They were objects to be discarded like a used toothbrush. And while they stayed dead, their offspring had an annoying habit of appearing at the most inconvenient times.

Take GEA Agent Arthur Raine's children for example. Arthur performed an enormous favor for Blast when he died an early death due to lung cancer, but just like the trooper he was, he left behind two progeny champing at the bit to fill Daddy's shoes. Blast always knew those cigarettes would be the death of his former nemesis. He owned the plant responsible for manufacturing Arthur's favorite brand. What were a few added carcinogens between enemies? Even Arthur's wife warned him against smoking. Helen, that was her name. What a beauty she had been. What a shame to have her killed in a hit and run to expedite Arthur's slow demise.

Brother Theo had stepped up to fill the role of head of the family, guiding his younger sister, Jessica, through their shared grief. Then, he made it his personal mission to crack down on smuggling operations in Sector 17, where Blast located his headquarters. How could he not take it personally? Yet the bigger affront to Blast had been Theo's mistake of thinking he could reach him via Rogue's smuggling business. Only an absolute idiot could believe he would associate with a scoundrel like Rogue. The man possessed no class, no finesse.

So, Theo had to go and Rogue with him. The proverbial killing of two birds with one botched operation. People died, just not all of them. Rogue, with his usual eel-like qualities, slithered away unscathed. Not so Theo Raine. Surely Jessica would curl up and die like a hothouse rose left out in the cold. This rose, however, had thorns.

Blast shuddered with hatred for the Raine family. They kept crawling from the cracks like cockroaches unnaturally drawn to the light. At least Jessica was the last. Recent mishandling of Agent Raine's death required he become personally involved with measures concerning the matter, but as always, he had an alternative plan. Patient observation provided the means by which the young woman would die.

The crime boss's eyes widened at the knowledge he possessed over the usually self-aware Jessica Raine. The simplicity of the situation forced a laugh from his throat, the sound strange and coarse to his own ears. A good surprise never failed to improve his mood, and nothing could be timelier than the one he had orchestrated for the lovely Agent Raine.

Blast stopped writing and opened the center desk drawer. He removed a small cardboard box without a lid. A tiny glass vial lay on a wad of blue velvet to keep it from rolling around and breaking the wax seal around the stopper, spilling the golden liquid within. Extreme caution kept Blast from touching the vial. Having it in his desk drawer made him edgy, but he kept it there to remind himself to stay vigilant. Death was always right around the corner.

* * *

RAINE KNEW SHE HAD BEEN followed to the poker game. What she had not expected was that the tail was a GEA agent. Tears of frustration mixed with those of anger, and yet again she cursed Frank Blast for the depths of his depravity. Maybe he was not responsible for her father's death, but the suspicious circumstances surrounding her mother's and brother's deaths left no doubt in her mind that she was his next target.

She, Theo, and her father had been instrumental in curtailing a large portion of Blast's drug smuggling operation in Quadrant One and throughout the Northern Hemisphere. Their efforts had also put a crimp in the flow of the crime boss's other businesses, and by doing so, they had made a lethal enemy out of a powerful man. She believed that among those trying to battle Blast and others like him, her family had been singled out for this reason. It seemed as if cold rain and warm tears would be the hallmarks of her life until she brought Blast to justice or killed him. Or he killed her. Or both.

Enough sulking, she told herself. If the agent responsible for patrolling the neighborhood where the Rite of Passage poker game took place was in Blast's employ, then the outcome of the game had probably been manipulated. Yet, why would Blast allow Rogue to win when he posed the biggest threat of competition to Blast's operations? Surely Rogue could not be so credulous as to believe he would align himself with Blast.

Stranger thoughts had guided smarter men, leading them to failure, torture, and death in that order. But Rogue was shrewd as well as smart. Raine also knew that he had become desperate. Desperate to get off Earth no matter what the cost. It was making him reckless to the point that he was possibly playing right into Blast's hands. Maybe this was not about her after all. Maybe the whole point of this year's game was to destroy a rival smuggler and absorb his thriving business.

Panic squeezed Raine's heart. She swayed and reached for the building beside her to steady herself. The sense of void she had experienced when she watched Theo's coffin being loaded into the incinerator swept over her. She could not lose another person she cared about. The thought jarred her out of her misery and left her wondering where it had come from. Theo's voice came back to her.

"It would be so much easier to hate Rogue if he wasn't so damn handsome."

Raine had punched her brother in the arm. He punched her back. She swept his legs out from under him and the wrestling match began. A lamp and end table took the brunt of their roughhousing until their father yelled, "Knock this crap off in the house. You're too dang old to be acting this way. For Pete's sake, you're GEA agents. Have a little respect for the uniform if not your dying father."

Strength of will tamped her feelings deep within her consciousness, bypassing her heart. Arthur Raine had warned his daughter against thinking with her heart. He just never got around to telling her how to accomplish that.

CHAPTER FOUR

ROGUE TURNED UP THE COLLAR of his leather jacket and jammed his hands in his pockets. He kicked every filthy pile of frozen slush between his apartment and the diner where he had an appointment. For the past week since winning the poker game, the artificial skies of Sector 17 had dumped hard pellets of snow by the truckload followed by a freeze of extraordinary severity. Almost everything in the city had shut down except the GEA and medical centers, the bars and a few eateries.

The shipping lanes froze over within two days with the unprecedented amount of cold. Rogue had not even had the opportunity to evaluate the quality of the information he had won, let alone use it. Three days of pacing his apartment like a kid who could not ride his new bike because of bad weather drove him and the neighbors crazy. All day and night his feet pounded the thin flooring between the levels of the rattrap apartment building. Finally, Mrs. Zehner yelled down for him to go to sleep or get the hell out. So, he did. He walked the streets for another two days, occasionally stopping to refuel with coffee and food or to catch a safe nap in the corner booths of bars where he conducted business.

The message to meet at Larry's Diner came on day ten. A boy wearing a hooded coat delivered it to Rogue as they crossed the street from opposite directions. An unrehearsed shoulder bump with all the skill of an amateur actor preceded palm pressing palm as the crumpled note transferred hands. *Sloppy and unprofessional*, Rogue thought to himself. He put his hand in his pocket and sought a safe place to read.

He headed for the wall of the bio-dome. Because tall buildings could not be erected along the curve, it had become a natural place for homeless people and stray dogs to congregate. One of the tasks assigned to the GEA had been to keep vagrants from sleeping in the tunnels connecting the bio-domes blistered across the landscape. Another had been to patrol the air locks between the domes and the world outside, also a favorite place to seek shelter. Rogue stepped carefully over bodies, asleep or possibly dead, lying under crusty blankets, and stood beside the wall to peruse the note. Cold radiated from the filthy, fogged glass obscuring the view beyond.

There was nothing peculiar or threatening about the message written on a greasy page torn from an order pad. Rogue turned it over, looking for anything that would alleviate his boredom and anxiety. He gave up and threw the wad of paper at a passing cat. Then he rubbed a spot on the wall of the bio-dome with the sleeve of his jacket. Environmental Services maintained a strict schedule with a rotation of artificial daylight, nighttime, and seasons. Time within the bio-domes matched what should be going on outside if one could see the sun, moon, and stars through the blanket of pollution obscuring the view. Rogue's brow lowered as he observed a soft, white glow in the sky outside that he assumed was the real moon. How could that be?

He pressed his nose to the cold glass wall and cupped his hands around his eyes to block light spilling from the few streetlamps in the park behind him. Rogue concentrated as if by mental prowess he could make the moon appear. He did not have to focus very hard to see the pearlescent custodian of the cloudy night sky. It was clear even through the death shroud of pollution breathed from the lungs of long-dead factories. The harshness of his own laugh startled Rogue, and he stepped back from the wall, glancing around to see if he had awakened anyone to his discovery.

No one inside the domes had seen any of the celestial bodies for centuries. True, there were people who maintained the domes from outside, especially over waterways, and the lucky few who traveled in enclosed ships across the oceans. But if any one of them had seen something in the skies over Earth, surely the news would have been reported worldwide. All efforts to clean up the skies had been abandoned long ago.

He looked one more time and shook his head to dismiss the notion trying to take root in his mind. No matter. Once Rogue left Earth for the greener pastures of space, he could not care less what orbited the dying planet. He toed the blanket closest to him, lifting it to seek anything of value, and headed for the diner to keep his eleven o'clock meeting. Maybe he would celebrate his gambling victory and bid farewell to Earth at the same time by treating himself to a real hamburger and fries. The idea cheered him considerably.

Rogue's eyes swept Larry's Diner upon entering. The typical riffraff hiding beneath hats and hoodies occupied booths and barstools throughout the restaurant. A few looked up from cups of cold coffee and glasses of flat beer, but he did not know any of them. One empty booth midway along the left wall of the diner looked about as good as anywhere for the meeting about to take place. He headed for the seat when he felt the rush of cold air across his back from the open diner door. Hopefully his mysterious host had arrived, but Rogue did not turn around to confirm this in case he gave the impression that he was there for any reason other than a meal.

He sensed the new presence following him to the booth. Rogue always sat facing the door of any building he was in; it allowed him to see who came and went, and the practice had saved his life more than once when enemies could not get the drop on him. His habit required him to face whoever had requested the meeting.

"Oh, damn . . . not you again," the smuggler groaned as he turned.

Raine slipped into the seat facing Rogue. She pointed to the bench across from her and waited as he threw himself down, sighing like a deflating tire, and slid over with exaggerated effort. They sat in silence for several minutes. She scrutinized every inch of his face, testing her motives for coming. He stared slightly above her head to avoid making eye contact.

"Pretty risky coming here in uniform, Raine."

"I have a coat on."

"As if everyone in here doesn't know you're wearing GEA-issued boots."

"Forget my boots, Rogue. I didn't come here to discuss fashion with you."

A skinny waitress with dirty brown hair trying to escape from the ponytail sagging at the back of her head interrupted and took their order. She returned with two cups of lukewarm, oily black coffee and left before Raine could ask for cream. Rogue swirled his spoon in his cup, stirring in nothing but killing time.

"Okay, fine. I asked you to come here because I think your life may be in danger."

Rogue nodded with what looked like sincerity until an amused grin split his face. In a mocking tone he asked, "When is my life not in danger? I'm touched that you care—really—but if you're just now sensing danger, then you haven't been paying attention, sweetheart."

"Don't start with me, jerk off. I don't have to be here saving your sorry hide."

"Keeping up Brother Theo's good works, are we?"

Raine's body tensed as she jerked backward. Her breath came in shallow gasps as heat flushed her face.

"What are you talking about?" she whispered.

"I knew your brother was keeping an eye on me for some misguided, altruistic reason. It was actually kind of funny to discover I'd become his pet project. I mean, when Theo—"

Their coffee cups and spoons rattled when Raine slammed her fists down on the table.

"Don't you speak his name to me—*ever*."

Every head in the diner turned to watch the GEA agent grill the man she was with. They did not know him—Raine had purposefully chosen a location with which Rogue was not familiar—but they recognized him as one of their own. If the argument escalated, they would come to his assistance, not hers.

"Take it down a notch, Raine. You don't want to attract attention in here."

His voice maintained a conversational level yet carried a tone of caution; she had overstepped her bounds. The smile on his face, the slow blink of his eyes, indicated something for which Raine was not prepared. She looked around the diner, meeting the glares peering from beneath hats and hoods, sensing the criminal aspect around her. Rogue alone stood between her and them. She was shocked to realize that he would.

"Please look at me, Rogue."

"I am looking." His downcast eyes took in her reflection on the surface of his coffee.

"I think you're being manipulated into believing you won the poker game. I think Blast might be setting you up for . . . something."

Rogue rested his chin on his thumb with two fingers on his temple and two in front of his mouth. Raine could hear his whispered reply, but no one else could read his lips.

"Be careful, princess, whose name you toss about in places like this."

"Okay. So, you believe me?"

"I believe you think you know something worth sending you out in the middle of the night to warn me. But I have to tell you, I'm just as concerned that it's you setting me up."

"Me? No . . . not this time. I wouldn't do that."

"Wouldn't you?" He did not give her time to respond, instead enjoying her blushed cheeks, and finished with, "So why do you suddenly care so much what the hell happens to me?"

Except for the glaring light hanging over their booth, the rest of the diner darkened and receded from view. Nothing and no one existed beyond the cube of space Rogue and Raine occupied, separated from each other by the greasy Formica tabletop. The air between them crackled with all the things she wanted to say. All the things he wanted to hear. She turned her head and read the menu board behind the counter and a posted notice from the Health Department with thirty-one violations.

"I was followed after I left you at the bar, after your poker game last week. I know the person because he's a GEA agent, or at least he was. His body turned up in the canals a few days later, so I poked around to see what I could find. Long story short, he was on the payroll for a company with distant ties to Frank Blast."

She mouthed the last two words per Rogue's directive.

"That doesn't prove anything."

"The tipoff about the poker game came from this guy in the first place."

Rogue shrugged his shoulders and said, "There are a lot of crooked GEA agents out there. I'm sure he's not the only one working for our mutual friend."

"Well, thank you for that glowing assessment of the GEA. But that's not all. Don't you find it the least bit suspicious that the weather changed drastically the minute your fortunes took a turn for the better?"

"What's the weather have to do with it?"

Raine pushed her coffee cup aside and leaned across the table, hoping Rogue would follow suit.

"C'mon, Rogue. If anyone in this Quadrant had the power to request bad weather, it would be Blast. You hadn't even had the chance to use the information you won before the weather took a dump. Shipping lanes are closed, and air transport vehicles are grounded."

"First of all, what are you talking about? Blast has his fingers in everyone's pies, so yeah, he could influence the weather. Secondly, we played for cred-coin, Raine, remember? I showed you my HoloCom that night."

"Look, idiot, I'm not trying to trick you into telling me what was in the pot. I already know, and it's because I know that I'm here to warn you. I admit I was going to keep an eye on you, catch you at using the info, and bust you for smuggling. But now I think you may be in some serious danger, and that a certain crime boss is behind it."

"On what do you base this? I'm going to need something more than your gut feelings. And again, why the hell do you care? Smugglers die every day, taken out by the competition. Besides, I'm a legitimate businessman."

Raine chewed the inside of her cheek and rubbed the back of her neck.

"Okay, how about this? Wouldn't you like to see Blast removed from the game and be the one who helped do it?"

"Are you appealing to me for help?" Rogue asked, laughter punctuating his words until he could not contain it. He threw back his head and laughed, his whole body shaking. "You're dreaming, Raine. It's like you've been—I don't know—tiptoeing around the Realm or something."

She blew out her lips and shook her head. "Don't be a jerk, okay? Damn, you can be so juvenile sometimes. The Realm? Really? I honestly don't know why I give a crap."

Urban legends came and went over the millennia but none as controversial as the Realm. When humans achieved advances in space travel in the mid-2000s, tales of aliens visiting Earth for the express purpose of probing drunken hillbillies went by the wayside. People expected to find truly awesome and marvelous wonders once they breached the bounds of

Earth. First the moon and then Mars was colonized, but Earthlings did not encounter extraterrestrials the way they anticipated.

Scientific organizations collaborated with governments and prominent universities to create programs with the intention of connecting with other lifeforms in the universe. Their efforts kept alive the dream of becoming part of an intergalactic community. Satellites, probes, and messages in various languages and codes shot across the cosmos. The hardware was often lost, and the communiques never received a reply. The dream slowly died.

Then in the late 2800s, a single encounter between a retired, octogenarian English professor and what he described as benevolent beings of human-angelic hybrid spurred a resurgence of belief that life beyond Earth existed. The professor went on to establish a religion based on his experience and brought many to faith. He described a place he branded The Unknown Realm. His cult grew mostly because he insisted that all were welcome at absolutely no cost. He preferred to peddle enlightenment and hope. When he could not repeat the incident where he crossed over to the alleged alternate state, the group dwindled to a few pockets of faithful followers living in the bio-domed deserts of Sector 29.

But the damage had already been done, and those looking for an excuse to dismantle the failing space project jumped on the encounter, although unprovable and unrepeatable, as justification for doing so.

Because these so-called aliens visited Earth instead of being discovered out in space, the scientific community experienced major setbacks, leading to a reassessment of the need for space travel. Funding for the programs was reallocated to the space station project. It made more sense to keep humans alive and then worry about finding and connecting with alien lifeforms that may or may not actually exist. Further condemning space exploration was the particularly annoying trend every fifteen to twenty years of encounters between Earthlings and the off-world beings.

As a result, many employed by the space travel programs bailed to find work on the moon or Mars and assist with the development of Vista Station and Eden Station. They were welcomed with open arms as were intellectuals in all fields and artists of every type who would be among the first to inhabit the heavenly oases. The mass exodus of intelligent and creative people left Earth with the dregs of humanity and spawned the creation of the GEA.

It also relegated the Realm to nothing more than an insult. The minute an otherwise level-headed person began acting or talking crazy, he or she was accused of having been in the Realm.

"I swear, sometimes it's like I'm talking to a high school punk," Raine said.

Rogue pointed at himself with both hands. "Hey, babe, I'm not the one suggesting absurdities here. Either you're shooting synthetic heroin, or your head has been in the Realm. There is no way I'm going to help the GEA take down public enemy number one. I might as well paint a target on my back."

Raine steepled her fingers, pressing them to the bridge of her nose. She searched for the right words to reach Rogue.

"I can't make you tell me about your business, what you intend to do. All I'm asking is that you scrutinize every single piece of information you have, every action you anticipate taking. If anything—*anything*—appears remotely suspicious . . ." Raine paused to sigh. "If you won't call me, then at least protect yourself by not going forward."

The skinny waitress, dead on her feet from a twelve-hour shift, returned to top off their coffee.

"You ain't drank any yet," she complained and shuffled away.

The GEA agent and the smuggler sat in silence in their column of air, unaffected by conversation and customers milling about them.

"All right then. There's really nothing more to say," Raine said.

"You could tell me one thing."

"What's that?"

"Why don't you go by your first name?"

Raine rolled her eyes. "That's what you want to know? Why?"

"Just curious, I guess. Is it a bad first name? Don't you like it?"

"What about you? What kind of mother names her kid Rogue? Or did you assign yourself that moniker because it sounds cool?"

"I never knew my mother. Or my dad. Grew up in an orphanage."

"Oh . . . well, somebody had to name you."

"People called me Rogue for as long as I can remember, and hearing it every day, I never thought to ask who started it."

Raine looked at the gray tabletop beneath her splayed fingers.

"When Theo died, other agents started calling me Raine. I always assumed they did it subconsciously. I guess they were trying to emphasize the fact that someone with that name still existed."

Rogue nodded and pulled two cred-coin markers from his pocket. He placed them on the table and stood, patting Raine's shoulder as he left.

CHAPTER FIVE

A REPRIEVE IN THE WEATHER came when the precipitation in the biodome's artificially controlled atmosphere changed to palm-sized clusters of snowflakes, which drifted like ash over Sector 17. Fresh snow coated the layers of frozen terrain, warming the city by a couple degrees and luring children outside. Rogue sat on a bench in the park, watching them mold snow into forts and barricades for a friendly game of war. Their alliances were as malleable as their loosely packed structures.

He rubbed his hands together and blew on them as he watched. His leather jacket had a liner, but age had stripped the fabric from the pockets and left creases on the inner elbows. The luxury of gloves lost out to the nuisance they presented when Rogue needed to calculate cred-coin quickly during a transaction or grab a weapon hidden on his person. Besides, there was always a warm fire made by a homeless person, burning in a barrel or tucked in an alley, over which he could defrost his hands.

Rogue pushed off from his seat in the park to resume wandering. He had been awake since six that morning when his mind could no longer withstand Raine's words boring into his brain. It had taken him hours to drift off in the first place, and just as he felt himself slipping into unconsciousness, the idea that Blast had orchestrated the weather to hinder his smuggling operation robbed him of sleep. He lay for two more hours, becoming increasingly agitated, before he donned his clothes and left.

The assault on his mind was a two-front battle. The second prong of attack was his old friend insomnia. It had worsened in the three days since his conversation with Raine and deepened the depression always hovering below his desire to leave Earth. Both conditions fed off each other, and at its worst, it resulted in his knives carving new scars across his wrists. It had been over nine years since he last cut himself, the practice held in check by the promise of the transport due to arrive from Vista Station within the year.

The early morning walk could not rid him of the nagging idea that Raine might be right about the weather. The tactic was brilliant in its simplicity, and no one would believe it to be a nefarious plan directed at one person among millions. The ease with which Blast could execute the strategy impressed Rogue; it was what he would have done if he possessed that kind of influence. Or maybe he was just giving in to sleep-deprived paranoia.

Either way, the break in the weather provided the perfect opportunity to inspect the warehouse employing one of Blast's shipping contacts. If the man proved capable—and Rogue had no doubt he would—his next stop would include a bar three streets over. From there he would participate in the bidding on a shipment of high-tech computer components.

Rumor on the street was that the hardware originated across the ocean in Sector 48. Every competent smuggler knew Sector 48 was one of the healthiest on Earth with a rate of lung disease far below average. Quality hardware and software running the bio-dome filtration systems accounted for this as did the fact that Sector 48 produced their own supplies rather than purchase them from Moon Base Tarigo. Add in policing of the government and local GEA by citizen task forces, and Sector 48 enjoyed a level of stability much coveted by fellow Earthlings.

Backing up the rumors of the hot components was a news report issued from Sector 48 expressing outrage at the theft of the hardware. The judicial system of Sector 48 was famous for capturing and punishing those who committed crimes against their residents. If all the Sectors on Earth functioned as efficiently, life might not be so dismal. And Rogue would have been out of business.

Luckily, the goods were located somewhere in Sector 17, waiting to make him rich. The cred-coin required to win the bid would put a serious dent in his funds, but the return on selling the stolen goods along faster, more secure shipping routes to better clients would replace the investment three times over. Sector 48 had no jurisdiction beyond their own borders and was further impeded by being located in Quadrant Three of the Northern Hemisphere. Cooperation between Quadrants was rarer than a sighting of the sun. But then, the sun did not shine like the gold coin Rogue trusted this transaction would land in his coffers.

A thirty-minute walk deposited him in the warehouse district beside the canals. He roamed between buildings as if he worked there, despite not sporting the traditional insulated coveralls worn by warehouse and dock workers in the winter. Accents and languages from every Quadrant on Earth melded into a diverse soup of conversation with everyone understanding each other because of the employment of HoloCom devices. Rogue tuned his ears to the audible translations for any scrap of information regarding the Sector 48 hardware.

He moved in and out of the clusters of workers, often stopping to unload a few boxes or lend a hand hoisting a particularly large drum for an outfit without the benefit of a crane. Rogue drank coffee with those on break standing near heating vents and ducked and dodged forklifts whose operators screamed at him to get the hell out of their way or get run over. No one questioned his presence during his slow progress toward the building he sought. Despite all his efforts, he failed to learn anything about the hardware from Sector 48.

Rogue's mouth turned down when he saw the condition of warehouse 13A. Chunks of mortar fell into the stagnant water of the canal next to the building. Years of neglect meant the concrete blocks had shifted, lending a serpentine fluidity to the outer walls. Ice-covered, broken pallets stood in twelve-foot stacks against the warehouse. Rogue hoped appearances outside did not reflect the quality of business within.

He walked through one of the open bay doors on the short side of the warehouse and called the name of the contact with feigned familiarity. The inside of the building belied its outward appearance; freshly painted steel racks rose to the ceiling and stretched as far as he could see. New boxes sealed with clean tape and pallets of shrink-wrapped goods occupied every square inch of space on the racks. Fluorescent lighting illuminated the place like an interrogation room.

A short warthog of a worker with more hair in his ears than on his head approached him, pulling off a grubby glove so he could shake Rogue's hand. When the man smiled, his four missing front teeth made his eye teeth look like tusks. Two days' worth of mud-colored whiskers completed the look.

"Good day, sir. Welcome, welcome, you must be my new *employer*." The contact's sing-song voice disintegrated into laughter at his pitiful joke. "Come this way, and we will discuss terms."

There was no way this man could have guessed Rogue's identity seeing him for the first time, even if he was dressed for the street and not the warehouses. A thousand ways to play this raced through the smuggler's mind. Other warehouse workers went about their business, and Rogue stood close enough to the bay door to escape if needed.

"Why don't we talk in there," he said, pointing at a corner office right inside the door. The empty room had windows on two walls facing inward.

The warthog shrugged. "Yes, sir. Very good, sir."

Rogue followed the man into the brightly lit room to make sure the warehouse worker did not close the door behind him. He watched as the man opened a filing cabinet and pulled something from the drawer. From behind, he could not discern what the warehouse worker was doing. A gust of heat rushed over Rogue. He stepped back, swaying, and looked up at the lights which swam before his eyes. A soft click behind him signaled a warning, but he could not coordinate his mind and body to respond.

"It's kind of hot in here," the smuggler said.

"Yes, sir, the heating system is on because of the cold weather."

The worker's muffled voice came from down a long tunnel. When he turned to face Rogue, he wore a respirator that covered his eyes, nose, and mouth.

"Aw, damn it," Rogue said.

The table and chairs in the small office skidded across the floor when Rogue crashed into them. He groped along the floor for a few feet as his eyes registered multiple copies of objects in the room. Unable to force his body to respond, he flopped to his back, his line of sight falling on the windows looking into the warehouse.

A handsome yet pockmarked face with flat black eyes stared down at Rogue. The sentinel scarecrow, devoid of all expression, stood rigid as he watched the smuggler slip into oblivion. He tipped his head in greeting when Rogue mouthed the word *Blast*.

* * *

NOT ALL HIS SENSES HAD returned to him. Rogue felt himself traveling through the tunnel he had experienced earlier, this time coming closer to the voices he heard. He labored to breathe warm, moist air and realized that he was bent double and wore a hood. Strong hands held him in place, and links of chain dug into his wrists and ankles, arms and legs, waist and chest. As if through a mist, his vision returned but did not clear entirely. He strained to see through the fabric of the hood.

"He's awake."

Experience taught Rogue to keep his eyes tightly closed when the hood came off, a fact he would have found funny under different circumstances. A sunburst of red, yellow, and orange fireworks exploded through his eyelids, intensifying the hammers pounding his temples.

"Take a moment to collect yourself."

"Can I have some water?" Rogue asked.

"No. It will make you throw up."

"Can I at least sit up?"

Rogue had been staring at Blast's black wingtips, straining against the hands that held him forward in the chair to which he was bound.

"Allow me to explain a few things, after which you may decide for yourself whether or not you would like to sit up."

A yank to the hair on the back of his head brought Rogue's face up to meet Blast's. He had never been this close to his rival and could not help but feel impressed by Blast's immaculate gray suit, diamond tie tack, and gold watch.

"You are positioned in the chair in such a way that allows you about two inches of movement backward. Behind you is a syringe filled with venom from a snake found in Quadrant Two of the Southern Hemisphere. A rather unassuming snake, but its venom is fifty times more toxic than a cobra's. It is a neurotoxin with a spreading factor that increases the rate of absorption.

"The venom in the syringe would normally take about forty-five minutes to kill you. Scientists in my employ have sped up the lethality of the toxin by a process which I would explain, but you would only be more confused than you are at present. Leaning against the syringe will inject the venom and kill you in about five minutes. Do you understand?"

"Wait a minute . . . this is because I won a stupid poker game? It seems a little overkill."

"No, Rogue, this is because you foolishly believed you could compete with me in business."

"I was just trying to get off Earth—"

"Shut up."

Blast, his voice never rising, backhanded Rogue, raking his diamond ring across the smuggler's cheek. The thugs holding Rogue in place kept him from lurching away from the strike, and the full force of the hit nauseated him.

"I have spent thirty years building my empire in Quadrant One and expanding across the Northern Hemisphere. You have experienced some *luck* with your ventures, and I commend you. However, when you start to step on my toes and foolishly believe you can align yourself with or overtake my business, you must die."

"Cut me some slack, Blast, that's not what I'm doing. I just want to get off this stinking, dying cesspit."

"I am tired of waiting for you to acquire enough gold coin to leave the planet and die."

"Wait—what? What are you talking about 'leave the planet and die'?"

The crime boss waved away Rogue's question and tugged at his shirtsleeves beneath his suit coat, then straightened his gold cufflinks.

"The building is wired to blow starting at the back and moving forward in fifty-foot increments. Detonation takes place every five seconds, and you're approximately sixty feet from the bay door. I'm uncertain about the length of this particular building or I would do the math for you. You may spend your remaining moments figuring out how long you have, not considering that the whole thing will probably collapse once the structural integrity is compromised, negating the need for any further explosions."

"So, I get to decide if I want to die fast by poison or slowly when the building comes down? Damn, you're dramatic."

"That's amusing, Rogue, really. It is your choice, but I thought perhaps you would want to say goodbye to Agent Raine. She's on her way here now."

"Why on earth would Raine come here?"

"Looking for you. She knows how eager you are to use the information you won, and I know how deep her desire is to save you. She entered the warehouse district a few moments ago under the guise of a GEA inspection. My contacts are outside now directing her to the warehouse where someone fitting your description was seen."

"Leave her alone, you animal. She isn't involved with whatever you believe is going on between you and me."

"You see. There it is."

A single accusing finger hovered in front of Rogue's face. He leaned against the hands and chains restraining him in a futile attempt to reach Blast. Rage contorted his face like putty. His eyes watered, and he ground his teeth against the stinging sensation.

"I owe you my gratitude for providing the method for how I will destroy Agent Raine, thus removing the last real annoyance in my life. It is because she refuses to quit interfering in my affairs that she will die. It was her choice. She could have stopped when I had her family killed."

"I mean it, Blast—you stay the hell away from her, do you hear me?"

"How desperate you are to save her in return. Who could have predicted the two of you would share such deep feelings for each other? Well, not I. Anyhow—goodbye, Rogue. I would like to say it's been a pleasure knowing you, but I hate to lie."

The two men holding Rogue released his shoulders, but the smuggler still leaned away from the back of the chair. He watched Blast and his men remove a few files from the cabinet in the office, turn off the lights, and walk from the warehouse as if heading home to the wife and kids.

"Wait a minute—*Blast*—damn it, come back here. Please, you've got to stop Raine from coming here. She doesn't deserve this. Blast!"

Rogue watched the three men slip into a black limousine and drive away. Tomb-like silence swallowed him once the vehicle rounded the corner. No voices reached him in the darkened warehouse, and he knew all the workers had been sent away. Through the open bay door, he watched snow falling across the orange glow of the security light outside. It had probably come on as the skies continued to darken with an unusual amount of snowfall courtesy of Frank Blast.

His mind scrambled to figure out what Blast had been babbling on about. Whatever had been used to knock him out earlier still clouded his thinking. He swallowed three times to keep the panic and bile from rising. Sweat trickled between his shoulder blades even as frigid air blew through the open bay door. The cold chilled and calmed him, and finally his mind sank lower into the warped world of Frank Blast. Clarity surfaced like a shark in dark waters.

"Oh, no," Rogue moaned.

Without leaning back, he raised his head to scan the corners of the building. His eyes had adjusted to the lack of light, and in doing so quickly spotted the pinpoint red light of a functioning security camera mounted high on the wall. Blast was watching, waiting, to see if Rogue would take the coward's way out and die quickly while Raine tried to save him. The man trusted in the fact that she would not leave him, even as the explosions came closer every moment she lingered.

Rogue jerked forward in the chair, but he only managed to scoot about an inch. He strained against chains held in place with welded locks, groaning until he screamed. A few seconds of rest, and then he repeated the whole process, achieving another three inches of movement. His lungs burned with cold air and futile effort. Blood dripped from his nose, and small vessels in his eyes burst with the strain of his next attempt. There was no way out save one.

Steady footsteps crunched the soft snow, coming closer to the warehouse. Rogue froze, afraid that the noise he had made had attracted someone, specifically Raine. He thought of calling to her, warning her, but that would only serve to bring her within range of the danger. Blast was right. Raine would never leave him.

The smuggler sat immobile, careful not to lean back into the syringe. His head dropped when he heard footsteps on the concrete floor and a female voice call out, "Hello? Anyone here?"

The camera on the wall moved, and the first explosion detonated.

CHAPTER SIX

THE FIGURE SILHOUETTED IN THE bay door did not move, even as the back of the warehouse collapsed. But it sprang into action the very next second by running both hands over the inside walls of the dark warehouse. A flood of fluorescent light blinded Rogue as the bank of switches was thrown all at once. Raine turned to run toward the unknown, halted in stride by the sight of him chained to a wooden chair.

"Hey, princess. We gotta stop meeting like this."

The second explosion—or was it the third? He had already lost track—rumbled toward them with the threat of death, but only Rogue understood what was taking place. Raine crossed the ground between them in a matter of seconds, and another explosion shook the building. She knelt before him, hands supporting his head from off his chest, wiping away blood and sweat.

"What kind of trouble have you gotten yourself into?" she asked.

"I think you might have been right about Blast. Is it too late to change my mind?"

"Stop joking, and let's get you the hell out of here."

Raine pressed her hands gently against Rogue's shoulders. A flash of relief crossed his mind until he arched his back and yelled, "No—wait!"

She withdrew her hands as if shocked and said, “What’s wrong?”

Rogue’s answer was lost to the sound of steel girders groaning and cinder block crumbling. He knew he had five seconds to explain before the next detonation.

“Look behind me—*look*.”

“What the . . . what is that thing?”

“It’s a—”

His response could not compete with the further destruction of the building. Raine did not require an explanation to realize he was in danger. Her fingers went to work on the chains, seeking space beneath the links to loosen them from his raw wrists. When that failed, her hands scrambled over his body like scurrying rats, trying to free him from captivity.

“This isn’t working. The chains are too tight, and the locks are broken or something—”

Explosions came closer, fire and smoke visible from the doorway. The odor of burning boxes and pallets surged forward on the cold wind. Rogue’s body sank a fraction of an inch; his mind kept him from relaxing against the needle positioned behind him.

“Raine—”

“If you could lean back just a titch—and I mean *just* a titch—then I think I could work this one chain over your shoulders—”

“*Raine—*”

“C’mon before the next—”

Dust and debris rained down on them with the next blast. He curled around her head buried against his stomach, the only way he could shield her. Neither sat up, and they shuddered at the next explosion. When she raised her eyes to his face, tears of understanding rimmed the edges.

“Let’s do this, we can do this. *Now*, Rogue.”

“Raine . . . sweetheart . . .”

She clawed at the chains, raking her nails over his chest and breaking them on the iron links. Her attention returned to the syringe, but he yelled at her not to touch it.

"I could break the needle off."

"Don't touch it. There's poison inside, and I don't know what happens if it gets on your skin."

"I'll pull you out—drag you out of here . . . from the front, maybe, so you don't . . ."

She screamed over the explosions, trying to make him understand. The ebb and flow of her words could not break his resolve, and she stopped speaking when she sensed him not trying at all to escape the situation.

"Why aren't you helping?" she yelled, her voice ragged with fear.

He smiled and laughed at her statement. He probably would have kissed her then if his arms had been free to draw her forward. The stillness of his body penetrated deep within his core, and he closed his eyes. His breathing returned to normal. When he opened his eyes, he looked directly into Raine's.

"This has all been planned for Blast's entertainment, but I don't really feel like—" They trembled with the next shockwave coursing through the building. "—like playing this game anymore."

"I can get you out of here if you'll just listen to me."

"No, you can't. That's the whole point."

Fire snaked along the edges of boxes in the next section of building set to blow. Rogue felt waves of heat even though the building had been torn wide open. Like rushing waters, the wall of flames cascaded over everything in its path. Snowflakes evaporated before they touched the ground.

"Blast means for you to die trying to save me, Raine. He wants us both dead, but it doesn't have to be that way."

"That's because we're both getting out of here."

"No, sweetheart . . . we're not."

"Listen, you jerk—I haven't trailed you all over the city to let you die in such a pathetic way."

Back-to-back explosions indicated that the fire had progressed faster than the five second intervals Blast intended. Heat damaged the wiring and triggered a succession of detonations that rocked the building. Rogue leaned his forehead against Raine's, and then slammed his body backward as hard as he could.

Tingling replaced numbness as he waited for the pain that never came. He knew Raine was speaking. He watched her lips moving, but no sound reached him. Bursts of orange from behind intermittently lit up her tear-streaked face as the last row of lights lost power and blinked out of existence.

Rogue's eyelids drooped and his head bobbed. He knew that his lack of response to Raine's words and actions would keep her in the warehouse until it was too late. He struggled to mouth the words *go, now, please.* Large portions of burning roof fell around them. Fear released the grasp it had on his mind and body as he watched her stand and back away from him. He urged her to leave with his eyes, never taking them off her own. He jerked his chin upward, and she looked over her shoulder to where the bay door descended, controlled by the man who had orchestrated this charade. She shook her head, still refusing to leave.

Rogue read impending death in Raine's widened eyes when she stumbled backward, tripping over burning debris. She jumped up and took a few more steps back. Her open mouth screamed words he never heard. Her hands reached for him even as she backed away. His vision shimmered at the edges as the next explosion sent her sprawling, rolling toward the door. He felt nothing.

Raine pushed herself up on weakened arms, struggling to lift her own weight. She drew herself up on her knees and paused. Then with lightning quickness, she sprang forward and sprinted for the door a foot away from closing. A feet-first, baseball-style slide saved her life. Her head whipped back for one last look at Rogue as the eight hands of death pulled him from consciousness toward oblivion.

* * *

THE HEAT OF REMEMBRANCE FLUSHED her singed cheeks. The odor of burnt hair filled her nostrils. Her chest pounded with a cold void where her heart used to be. Her feet hurt from walking, and salt stung the burns and scrapes on her face.

Raine did not know how many cycles of artificial daylight and nighttime had passed since she escaped the warehouse. The yellow haze beaming down through snow flurries meant nothing to her. She could not see it. Nor could she see people on the streets rushing past her as she walked upstream against the crowds. Buildings receded from view. The soundtrack of the bustling city fell on deaf ears.

For the first few hours that had literally been true. Safety did not exist immediately outside the bay door, and Raine had to remind herself to continue running away from the danger about to burst forth. She was still too close when the explosion occurred. It slammed her against the adjacent building, knocking her senseless. The shrill ringing in her ears sounded like the final note of a bad opera. Now she chose to keep from hearing the living world around her.

She could not see anything beyond the endless loop repeating in her mind's eye. Fire provided the backdrop and lighting on the stage where a bizarre comedy took place. Raine did not know what else to call it. She had to laugh at what she had witnessed or lose her mind to the truth of the situation. But in a situation such as she had experienced, the truth was a little more fluid.

And so, she kept walking until she could accept or reject what she had seen as fact or fiction. She wanted answers, needed them, but none were forthcoming. Raine prayed for guidance, for release from her wakeful nightmare. *Speak to me*, her brain screamed at people jostling and shoving her along. She shrank from all contact. Knots of muscle in her jaws kept her from speaking aloud, although she longed to describe the scene that roiled her stomach. The acid of it encroached upon her throat. If only someone could clarify what she had seen. More likely, they would cart her away to a mental facility.

And so, she kept walking with her arms wrapped tightly around her body. Shivering in the snow turned to rain. Awake and unconscious in her demand for answers. Ignorant of where her wanderings deposited her. A door set within two larger doors opened. Golden light puddled on the dirty snow. The nun beckoned to Raine with both hands. The GEA agent stepped inside and collapsed at Sister Mary Joy's feet.

* * *

"YOU DON'T HAVE TO TALK about it until you're ready," the nun said.

"Talk about what?"

"Whatever it is you came here to tell me."

Raine worked a towel over damp sections of her dreadlocked hair that still smelled of smoke. Her GEA uniform was unzipped and pushed to her waist. Her tank top could not hide the bruises branding her arms and shoulders, evidence of the violence she had endured. Much to her relief, Sister Mary Joy noticed the purple shadows were not in the shape of gripping fingers. Still, the injuries were more than a GEA agent should have suffered unless a full-scale operation had taken place, and there had been nothing on the news about it. Whatever happened had been suffered by Raine alone.

"Do you believe in heaven, Sister?"

"Why do you ask?"

"And hell?"

"I believe in spiritual states of reward and punishment."

"What about angels and demons?"

The nun took a sip from the porcelain teacup gripped in her hands and nodded toward the one sitting beside Raine on the long table. The GEA agent took a drink of green tea and held it in her mouth. The presence of a stronger liquid warmed her as she swallowed. Lights in the dining hall hummed above them.

"You've seen something." Sister Mary Joy paused as clouds of indecision stormed across Raine's face. "You're not questioning whether or not you have, but whether or not you believe in what you saw. That's why you came here."

The GEA agent looked as if she would cry but jumped up and vomited in the trash barrel by the door. Volcanic heaves brought two other nuns running. Sister Mary Joy sent them away with a head shake and a hand wave as Raine subsided into panting. From where she sat, the nun could see Raine trembling, her already pale skin bleached to whiteness.

"Come sit down before you pass out. Lean over, that's it, and let your head rest between your knees. No, don't sit up yet."

From her bent position, Raine's voice echoed off the tiled floor.

"I should have died in that explosion, too."

"What explosion? And what do you mean 'too'?"

Details of the events gushed forth from Raine much like the bile from her stomach moments earlier. Sister Mary Joy stopped her when she could tell certain parts were being left out.

"I don't understand. Was this a GEA operation?"

"No. I just went there to look for my . . . friend."

"And this 'friend' was in trouble when you arrived?"

"Yes."

"I don't know what to make of this. Who would do this? Who could have the power to set up what you're describ—"

Frank Blast's reputation and animosity toward any GEA agent not under his thumb answered the nun's question. She shook her head in reproach of the young woman.

"And how, exactly, did you manage to fall on Frank Blast's bad side?"

"It's the point of my job to get on Blast's bad side, *Sister*."

"I'm sorry. I didn't mean that like it sounded. I just thought—"

"You thought like everyone else that every GEA agent can be bought off whenever it suits a criminal's purpose. That we're all corrupt and self-serving."

The nun pursed her lips and joined Raine on her side of the table. Once seated on the bench, she placed a battered metal box between them and opened it, removing bottles and packets with handwritten labels. Powders and liquids combined to make a thin salve with a camphorous aroma. Sister Mary joy used the homemade concoction to treat Raine's injured face and hands.

"Who was the other person?"

"Would you believe he's a smuggler? Was a smuggler."

"Why in the world would a GEA agent try to save a smuggler? I understand that you must arrest them, bring them to justice, but you called this person your friend. Clearly, you're upset at his death.

"Maybe friend is too strong a word."

"Does this smuggler have a name?"

"Rogue."

The answer jolted through the nun's body like electricity. Her hands faltered, and the cotton ball of salve dropped to the floor. Raine did not have to ask if the nun knew him, and she was not at all surprised that she did. Even the most hardened criminal needed a merciful port in the storm from time to time. Raine leaned toward Sister Mary Joy, searching her face for clues to her unexpected reaction.

"And you're sure . . ."

"Yes, Sister. There was no way he could have survived that."

"Is there anything else you want to tell me?"

"Bless me first."

"What?"

"Bless me, and then I'll tell you. I don't want this going any farther than the two of us."

"You want to confess something?"

Raine took Sister Mary Joy's long fingers in her own and squeezed them. The nun nodded and stood to close the doors to the dining hall. She closed the one to the kitchen as well before returning to her seat. Raine swallowed twice and began, already forgetting that she had requested the conversation be conducted as a confession.

"It all happened so fast, but I see it clearly. The bright, steady glow like the blue of a candle flame appearing behind him. It lightened to an almost blinding white, and . . ."

"Go on."

"It became like glass, transparent. I could feel wind all around me, but it wasn't from outside or from the fire."

"The wind blew out from the brightness?"

"No, it rushed past me as if being sucked into the light."

"Then what?"

"Something or someone leaned forward in the open space. I saw land behind them."

"One something or many?"

"There were four of them. And they were huge."

"What were they?"

"People, I guess. Maybe angels or demons. That's why I asked earlier if you believed in them. I don't have much expertise in that field, so recognizing one is kind of beyond me."

The nun chuckled, easing the tension drawing lines on Raine's face.

"There isn't a handbook on that sort of thing. Just a few salvaged pages from an ancient manuscript and many, many stories handed down verbally. Were the beings fiery or winged?"

"No. They were tall and pale with white hair."

"That could be an angel, I suppose. Were they aggressive?"

"No, that's the weird part. Their faces looked anxious, like they were there to save . . ."

"Go on, please."

Raine rolled both lips inward and held them shut with her teeth. She inhaled until her lungs begged for release and expelled air against her will, forcing her mouth open.

"I won't say anything to give myself false hope. What I saw—it wasn't real."

"I don't know what you saw. I couldn't say."

"I'm telling you; it wasn't real."

"Then why are you here?"

Staccato breaths preceded Raine's tears. "Because I don't want Rogue to be dead but telling you what I saw isn't going to change that."

"Then just forget it. Let's get you out of these wet clothes and into a warm bed. There's an open one on the second floor where we take in homeless women for the night. Don't look at me like that. We delouse them before they come in and the linens are clean. I oversee that myself."

"You don't want me to finish?"

"You don't want to finish."

"That's not true."

Sister Mary Joy stood and placed her hands on the table. "So, finish."

"They put their hands on him, on his shoulders, and lifted him chair and all into wherever they came from. Then the light shimmered and disappeared. That's what I saw as I slid under the door right before it shut."

CHAPTER SEVEN

SILKEN FINGERS OF COOL WIND blew across his face. A comforting weight pressed down on his body—a blanket perhaps, but soft and shifting like fur. The luxurious feeling of waking from a long and peaceful sleep surged through his limbs, and he wanted to yawn and stretch. Sounds of movement nearby prevented him from acting on his desire. That and the crackle of burning wood. A change in the direction of the wind brought the smell of food within reach of his senses. His mouth moistened at the scent of smoky meat.

Through closed eyelids, Rogue sensed an expansion of darkness. Night and another stealthy presence visited him. Unsure of his ability to move at all, he could only hope the presence would do him no harm. Shushing noises of a mother soothing a child and the fragrance of smoldering herbs followed him back into sleep.

* * *

AGAIN, THE SENSATION OF COLD greeted him first. The thickness in his arms and legs weighing him down dissipated with the last stars. Even as he watched them disappear, he wondered if his eyes were open or if he imagined the bright pinpricks of light. Turning his head to the right did little to convince Rogue that he was awake and alive. Neither did the four figures bundled under furs positioned around the campfire. An avalanche of white hair fell from every head, but their faces were turned away from him.

For the next few moments Rogue tested which parts of him still worked. Toes and fingers wiggled, arms and legs stretched. He rolled his head from side to side and shrugged his shoulders to loosen his muscles. When he arched his body to reach an itch on his lower back, he discovered he was naked. How he had missed that fact before eluded him, but the thought was lost in importance to the cause of the irritation prickling his skin. Poison. Surely, he was dead.

The sound of rustling among the figures around the fire kept him from contemplating this further. One by one, four pairs of gray eyes turned toward Rogue, each conveying a different emotion as the figures sat up, raised themselves on arms, or leaned on elbows. His own eyes dropped to the fire. He was more curious than afraid. Still, he decided to let one of them make the first move.

An upturned mouth pressing cheeks into eyes presented the start Rogue had hoped for. He welcomed the familiar sign of friendliness and smiled in return. The figure pushed back the fur and stood, revealing signs of womanhood beneath clothes made from skins. She took two steps toward Rogue.

"Nish."

The male's voice carried the weight of authority, and the woman dropped to one knee and bowed her head. She reached her hand, palm up, toward the broad-shouldered man. He approached her, then pressed his palm on hers. The act conveyed willing submission without the fear of reprimand. More like a custom, Rogue decided as the man helped the woman to her feet.

From the ground, Rogue's point of view made the two standing beside him look inordinately tall. He did not know whether to focus his concentration on their person or conversation. He opted for physical details as the purring tones of their voices blended in discussion, sounding like a slow recording of warped voices. Somehow this seemed appropriate for people with lavender skin.

In all other ways, they resembled humans. A face with two eyes, two ears, a nose, and a mouth. Two arms with five fingers per hand and two legs. Rogue assumed they had ten toes within their leather footwear. Nothing elongated or superfluous appeared on their bodies. Except for differing shades of skin, they all had gray eyes and white hair, unusual characteristics for them all to share, but perhaps they were family.

Rogue continued to watch the pair as they stood facing each other. Their conversation dwindled to silence. The female's head tilted up to look into his eyes; his expression conveyed caution and something Rogue could not discern. When the woman smiled and looked down at her hand still clasped in his, a fierce plum blush spread across the man's face. He dropped her hand unceremoniously, stepping back and turning his eyes from her.

The other two members of the group sat up from their bedding and began the routine task of folding it into transportable rolls. All talking and movement ceased when Rogue sat up. The group of four stared without any trace of emotion on their faces until one of them, a willowy figure with a youthful visage, laughed and resumed working. The last member, slower and with a more grizzled appearance than the others, often grabbed his knees or lower back as he worked his way upright.

The desire to make something happen prompted Rogue to insert himself into the situation. He needed to know if he was dead or alive, a prisoner or a guest, and where, exactly, he was. He clutched a fur around his body and stood on rubber band legs. The top of his head did not reach the female's shoulder and came nowhere near that of the male standing next to her, nor of the young man who joined their group. Even the elderly fellow hobbling over with his back still bent looked down at him through watery eyes. Rogue's hands gripped the fur, and he shuffled backward to put more space between himself and them.

The old fellow followed Rogue the few steps he took, bending his face down until they were nose to nose. He sniffed hard at the top of Rogue's head, holding him in place with gnarled hands to his shoulders. Rogue submitted to the examination with an uncertain smile on his face, but he almost stumbled as his unknown inspector whisked him around and ripped the fur from his grasp.

"Hey—"

"*Debos fero*," the man said with what Rogue recognized as the authority of age.

"*Debos kralgtor, Mir-Talj*," the female said. She patted the air in front of her to reassure Rogue that her friend meant him no harm. Then to Rogue, "*Nuat debor goase est. Nu tae ke harbato*."

Rogue's first reaction had been to shield his body from the woman; his second was to swat the older man's hands away as the long fingers began kneading his shoulders, working their way toward his lower back. He grabbed the fur from where it had dropped and wrapped it around his waist. Then he turned to confront the confused old man and pointed his finger up toward his face.

"I don't know what you're saying or who the hell you are, but I do not appreciate—"

Not so much as a twitch preceded the sweep that took Rogue's legs out from under him. He did not just tumble to the ground; his feet reached the height of his backside, ensuring a long, hard drop to the earth and a jolt that shook him to the top of his head. Thick words growled in the throat of the tallest member of the group as he stood over Rogue.

"*Ket stres zorlo Mir-Talj pestra dit wahl. Podtrefil sieth s'gradol. Mis ileba-a goljatbi tae lieme debora pu ite sot*."

Clearly, this man was the Leader of the unusual band. His size alone prompted Rogue to curl up into a ball in case a thrashing followed his harsh words. A few seconds of heated glare from his cool gray eyes preceded a shower of dust from his foot kicking the ground beside Rogue. Then, the tall one turned and walked away. The old one and the young one followed, and all three resumed packing their bedding.

Only the female remained. She crouched beside Rogue and touched him lightly on the shoulder, speaking softly.

"*Tae blau ke emtresa Bialig. Tae debos lieme nez obo forl, hahk nuat debor remt jaduse Bialig nuat rotera.*"

Rogue unrolled with the shyness of a pill bug beneath a child's fingers. The female's tone let him know he had at least one person still willing to tolerate him. He eased up on his elbows, dragging the fur across the middle of his body.

"*Felkes hel uma wotshel bian. Mi ke laeme ontos nez zhe vasti pulat hel ithig onoden,*" the tall one said.

The statement issued forth as a command, and the female rejoined her companions. She and the old one and young one began rooting through their packs, each pulling out a garment of clothing, holding it up, and shaking their heads. Finally, two pieces were settled on, and the female returned to where Rogue still sat on the ground. She held up a long, linen tunic from her own stash and a pair of leather leggings from the young man's.

With a grateful smile and sigh of relief, Rogue stood and accepted the clothes. He looked around for a rock or tree behind which he could dress, but the barren landscape offered nothing. A wind-twisted stump no thicker than Rogue's leg stood about a hundred yards away and clumps of thigh-high grasses dotted the dun-colored land. The female dropped her head and returned to the group affording Rogue all the privacy he would receive.

The tunic reached below Rogue's knees and the leggings past his feet. As he rolled up the sleeves and pant legs, the old one hobbled over, his hands extended before him with a long piece of fabric draped across his palms. His already bowed head dropped further in nodded encouragement. He grunted and motioned toward Rogue's waist. An uneven smile inched its way upward, and for the first time Rogue observed a jagged scar among the wrinkles mapping the aged face. The injured half could not match the working side, no doubt due to nerve damage.

As Rogue wound the too-long sash three or four times around his middle and tied it off, the others loaded their packs and bedding onto their backs. The three men waited as the female shoveled dirt over the embers of the dying campfire. She mixed the earth and ash then spread the mixture around to safeguard against a flare up after they left. Rogue dug his toes into the sandy dirt, becoming more aware of the desert-like atmosphere of his surroundings.

"*Debor quorotag erpe*? *Rotey baso aelsey*," the tall one ordered, and the others fell in line behind him.

The old one walked immediately following the Leader, falling behind as his staff sought purchase in the soft ground that his sluggish legs could not, dragging them forward as he stabbed at the terrain. The Leader outdistanced his comrade in a few long strides, then turned and waited. The woman took slow steps so that she did not overrun her elderly friend, her hand slipping beneath his pack to lighten it on his weary shoulders unbeknownst to him. The young one did not even start moving until the three in front worked out a steady pace for the benefit of their wizened companion. He looked back as Rogue, uncertain if he should follow, watched them.

"*Uhrshues*," the youth said with a summoning wave in Rogue's direction.

Something in the way the four regarded each other sat uneasy in the pit of Rogue's stomach. He assumed respect dictated the order in which they walked. The younger members could have held the old one's arms, supporting him from the side, but they patiently offered him the gift of dignity and allowed him to set the pace. The scene generated a familiar longing in Rogue, one from his earliest memories that he used to embrace but had abandoned through the years.

With one last glance over his shoulder, the young one set off after the others. A few jogged steps caught him up as he joined the slow trek. Rogue's hands fidgeted at his sides; his jaw worked a toothpick that was not there. He felt like a choice needed to be made, but the power to make the decision had already been removed when he ended up here with these people. The mystery of who, what, where, why, and how would only be solved by following them, and Rogue hated to have his hand forced in that way.

He trailed behind the young one a good twenty feet and received a smile from the youth for deciding to follow. Hopefully, there would be an explanation in that smile at some point. As to how they would communicate, Rogue could only guess. For now, he would concentrate on keeping up with his long-legged companions, a feat that required him to trot occasionally. At least the sandy ground beneath his bare feet cushioned his steps.

Rogue's thoughts absorbed his concentration quicker than the dirt sponged up the brief rain shower that began falling from charcoal-colored skies. He shivered a little in the cool winds that never stopped blowing, thankful that the rain had ceased before he was truly soaked. The other four had pulled rain-resistant hoods over their snowy heads when the drizzle began, and now they flipped them back over their shoulders. Rogue envied the small amount of warmth the hoods-turned-capes no doubt provided.

Bitterness took root in his mind when none of them looked back to make sure he still followed. His resentment flared at the Leader, who he dubbed The Lion for the mane-like effect of the man's white hair framing his broad face. His petulant thoughts worked through the many ways he would make The Lion pay for attacking him without provocation. Rogue hated not being in charge of his own fate, and although there were four of them, he chose to direct his anger specifically toward the Leader.

All day Rogue entertained himself with plots of revenge against the tall man. When the four stopped briefly for a shared meal, lessening their portions to make sure he had enough food, he would not lift his countenance or say thank you. He used the lack of communication as an excuse to justify his behavior.

Negative thoughts continued to distract Rogue during their resumed walk, and he did not notice when the four ahead of him gave a slight berth to an area of land circled by knee-high pyramids of small rocks. Deepening thirst added to his irritated state of mind as well as being winded from jogging and falling farther behind. By the time he refocused on the four ahead of him, they appeared directly before him as if never having skirted the rocky pyramids. Rogue ran straight through them.

Torrents of sand and rocks pelted Rogue when the ground gave way beneath him. His arms, legs, and head banged against the sides of the narrow hole into which he had fallen. His feet and hands scraped the crumbling sides as he tried to halt his descent. He twisted an ankle trying to dig in, but finally managed to grab a tangle of roots. With his other hand and foot, he braced himself across the hole and took several deep breaths through his mouth, inhaling dust that made him cough. He spat and tried again through his nose, more slowly and deeply to calm himself.

Nothing more than a gasp had escaped his lips when he felt the earth give way, and he wondered if the others even knew he was gone. He bowed his head as dirt from the edges of the hole rained down on him. The opportunity allowed his eyes to focus in the darkness of the pit; he could not see the bottom, nor could he sense how far down it went. Icy winds blew up from below and a damp smell permeated his nostrils. His ragged breaths left silver mist in the air in front of him.

More dirt sifted down upon Rogue. He looked up to see if the hole was collapsing in on him. Four anxious faces peeked over the edge and a flurry of language followed as each offered solutions on how to extricate Rogue from the shaft. A small amount of relief bolstered him until a low hiss from below silenced the people above. No one and nothing moved for half a second, and then the four above disappeared from view.

Rogue knew he was in trouble when gusts of warm, moist air replaced the cold winds. They came in large bursts as if panted. He could still hear the four above, shouting and scrambling about. Scraping noises joined the hissing and brought the warmth closer as well as the stench of rotten flesh. Rogue sensed another presence in the pit, one that opened and closed a mouth large enough to smack wetly with what was undoubtedly hunger.

A flurry of activity took place in the narrow circle of fading light above Rogue. He heard something fall and identified it as a coarse rope when it slapped him in the face. His limbs had begun to shake under his own weight, and he did not trust letting go to grab the rope. The youth's head appeared over the hole.

"*Vutdaes—mano! Pyras hel sitha*," he called.

Rogue understood the urgency if not the language. He let go of the side of the pit, maintaining his grip on the roots with his other hand as he wound the rope around his free hand. Then he clamped the lower portion between his feet, wincing from the pain shooting up his injured ankle. The snap of teeth persuaded him to let go of the roots.

"Pull me up," Rogue shouted.

Grunts from above accompanied his progress out of the hole. He swayed in the small space, hitting the sides, and loosening more sprays of dirt to fall on whatever it was he left behind. The top of the hole looked larger the closer he came, and finally Rogue was able to reach the edges as four hands grabbed him, pulling him out by limb and clothing. He collapsed in a heap with the woman and the young man. The Leader stumbled backward from slack in the rope looped around his waist, but he recovered quickly.

"You fool! Did you not see the stones around the *bargelnelo* pit? How stupid could you be to walk right into their hole?" the Leader yelled.

"*Mir*-Bialig, now is not the time for—"

The woman's words died to the sound of claws scraping over the edge of the pit followed by a forked tongue testing its grip around Rogue's ankle. The youth stomped on the black tongue, and the creature roared in pain. The Leader dropped the rope still tangled around Rogue and reached for two spears from his pack. He tossed one to the wide-eyed youth who hesitated a moment before an elated grin nearly split his face. Together they circled the creature's red, sinewy head poking out of the hole. The other two dragged Rogue from the animal's reach.

Waves of nausea passed over Rogue as the two men speared the creature repeatedly in the eyes and head, careful not to let it pull the weapons from their hands with its strong jaws. It did not die easily, but when the creature's claws slipped in its own thick blood, it fell to the depths of the pit to provide food for the others lurking below.

The Leader and the young man leaned heavily on the spear shafts, hard breaths fogging the cold air. The woman and the old one tended them with sips from drinking skins. When the Leader righted himself, his eyes fell to where Rogue sat rubbing his injured ankle. He stalked toward the prone man with his weapon raised to his shoulder but halted when Rogue spoke.

"Why the hell didn't you tell me you speak my language?"

CHAPTER EIGHT

A CONCOCTION OF BITTER HERBS and sweet flowers brewed in a water skin with rocks heated in the fire provided relief from the pain in Rogue's ankle. The mixture reduced the swelling and bruising, then put him to sleep after his first horrible day with his new companions. He awoke to ashen gray skies and a trio of unpolished jade moons slipping toward the horizon. The ever-present wind drew mauve-colored clouds across the disc of a star close enough to be called a sun but too far away to warm the air for Rogue's liking. He pulled the fur over his head.

He remembered the woman and the youth half carrying, half dragging him away from the hole of the lizard-like creature that had tried to make a meal of him. In words he understood, the Leader informed the group that they could not camp near the pit for the night because other creatures would surface to repair the sand trap over the hole. Once they made camp, they served a light dinner of dried meat and something that passed for bread. Then, the old one brewed the drink and gave it to Rogue, and he fell into a sleep muraled with vivid images both fantastic and frightening.

Rogue owed these people his life, yet he could not relinquish his resentment for being kept in the dark about his situation by their unwillingness to speak his language. If he had been back on Earth, a few well-placed words and a weapon would have produced the results he wanted.

But he was not on Earth, and he did not know how to approach the matter without further offending them. Especially the Leader, who he believed disliked him.

Cooperating on someone else's terms was a skill Rogue lacked. So was working as a team. He feigned sleep, peeking from beneath his fur to watch as the four worked in harmony to prepare for the day. Without spoken requests the appropriate items were passed from hand to hand as if intuited. Rogue wondered if they were telepathic or if familiarity bred this level of efficiency. His head turtled beneath the fur when he saw The Lion's legs approach where he lay.

"You may join us for food at the fire or lay there all day pretending to be asleep. The choice is yours."

Disgust tinged the Leader's words, spoken in a voice rich with an accent that rolled an R and softly buzzed an S. Heat rose in Rogue's face, and he cringed for having been exposed. Never in his life had anyone mistaken Rogue as being lazy. He could not say why he cared that this man thought well of him when he had never given a second thought about another person's opinion.

The foursome sat around the fire with long legs crossed and wooden bowls held in their laps. The old one's left leg stuck straight out; his constant massaging of the knee indicated the soreness of age or injury. Rogue walked over and knelt between the woman and the youth, looking down at his hands hanging empty and hoping they would understand his plight. The woman pulled a small bowl from her pack and handed it to him. He had no idea what he was supposed to do next or what was permitted.

"Everyone works together to survive, *uma*. If you want or need something, you must ask. We cannot read your mind."

The Leader did not look at Rogue as he spoke.

"May I . . . share your food?" Rogue asked.

"There is a knife. Meat is on the spit, and Nish made bread, vegetables, and herbs. We have eaten. There is enough for you."

Rogue helped himself, carving slices of dark red meat from a long carcase skewered on a pole and balanced between two rocks holding it above the embers. From a platter he took what he assumed were the other food items mentioned.

"And something to drink, please?"

"Here," the woman said as she poured water into a tall cup. "You did not drink all day yesterday. You must be thirsty."

"I am, thank you."

The edge of the cup felt strange to Rogue. He doubted it was plastic, probably bone or antler, and he shivered in revulsion. Fortunately, none of the others witnessed his reaction as he downed the water in one gulp. Thirst overrode his desire for food, but when the woman continued eating, he carefully picked up her skin bag and poured for himself. Three more cups barely took the edge off his thirst.

"I'll refill your bag for you if you tell me where I can get more water."

The woman smiled and nodded at him, her eyes shining like a mother's when her child has learned manners. She finished chewing and pointed at herself.

"I am Nish."

Rogue chewed slowly to give himself time to appraise her. Even seated, she was taller than he was kneeling. A long, pearl white braid draped over her shoulder, suede hides formed her short-sleeved top and knee-length skirt, and parentheses creased her heart-shaped face beginning at her nose and ending below her narrow lips. The last effect accentuated her plump cheeks when she smiled and lent the appearance of kindness and wisdom. He was already used to the large gray eyes, but the lavender hue of her skin made him stare at her exposed neck, legs, and arms.

"Rogue," he said.

"That is your name?"

"Yeah, just Rogue."

She pointed across the fire to the wide-mouthed youth with a broad nose, whose skin was duskier than the others and said, "He is Misko—"

"Hello."

"—and this is Talj."

The old one grunted and continued gnawing meat from a long bone held by each end. The pause that followed possessed an air of expectancy. Nish waited for the silence to draw the Leader's attention. She contemplated him with a tilted head and teasing smile when his gray, almond-shaped eyes slowly rose from his bowl to gaze back at her from across the fire. Sharp cheekbones, steeply angled eyebrows, and a strong jaw with cleft chin contrasted with his full lips, the only part of him to appear easygoing. Understanding crackled between them, and Nish released a breathy laugh.

"And this? This is Bialig, our *Natamos*."

"I'm sorry . . . your what?"

"You would say Leader."

Rogue would have preferred to continue calling him The Lion, and letting him know exactly why, but a force unknown checked him, and he dipped his head once in greeting. Bialig's eyebrows flickered just short of rising in surprise. He looked around as if searching for the correct response, standing quickly to divert attention.

"The *bargelne* have probably finished spinning the web for their sand trap, but I do not want to stay here another day. They sometimes hunt outside their hole."

The statement ended the meal. The foursome cleaned up the remains, scrubbed out their bowls with sand, and packed their belongings. Rogue remembered Bialig's directive to ask for what he wanted.

"I could use some shoes and maybe a coat or something. The winds are cold, and I have splinters in my feet from the dry grass."

"The weather is as it should be for the season. That is why we are traveling. Heavier clothes will be obtained from other Clans during our journey."

"Yeah, well, maybe it's warm for you, but I'm freezing. Could I wrap one of the sleeping furs around my shoulders while we walk?"

Bialig's face bore the patience of a parent for a demanding child. "You are thin-blooded, *uma*, but we will not allow you to freeze." He emphasized the last word in a harsh manner that Rogue thought was unwarranted.

Misko offered a piece of worn leather that he cut in two pieces, then tied around Rogue's feet with lengths of fibrous twine.

"I keep my *slele* wrapped in here, but since the weather is good, I think it will be fine as long as the strings do not get wet."

Then the young man slung a long-necked instrument over his shoulder that Rogue took to be his *slele*. As Rogue had nothing to carry, he was ready first. Nish dealt with the fire as the others lifted their packs to their backs. The four fell in line the same as the day before with Rogue trailing Misko. They traveled for about thirty minutes before Rogue broke the stillness. His winded words pounded out with the pace required to keep up with the others.

"Where are we going?"

"To the *Avboeth s'hel Dohne s'Ima*," Nish called back.

"I don't know—"

"It is the Assembly of the Groups of Four," Bialig barked over his shoulder.

"Sorry I asked," Rogue snapped back. "What's going to happen there?"

"We will meet with other Groups of Four from all the Clans to learn and share," Misko said in a lilting voice. "We gather every five cycles of the moons and meet at the base of the *Shaleh* Mountains when the three moons align."

"Okay, that's interesting, but do you think anyone there might have an idea of how to get me back to Earth?"

Talj crashed into Bialig's back with a roar of complaint when the Leader stopped midstride, his powerful legs planted firm like pillars. Nish and Misko did not respond in time, and they accordioned into the others. Rogue jumped sideways to miss the collision and scrambled farther from the group when Bialig pivoted back in his direction. But not fast enough. Bialig had a handful of his tunic and held Rogue several feet off the ground.

"You useless *gradol*, are you so ungrateful to us for saving your life that you want to go back and die? And no—you will not be seen at the *Avboeth* to find out if anybody knows how to send you back. I can send you back when I choose, and you make me sorry I ever brought you here."

Nish gripped the arm from which Rogue dangled, her hands barely spanning Bialig's bicep, unable to lower his rigid limb.

"Bialig—*Mira*—he does not understand. The *umane* do not know of the sacred *Avboeth* or how the time here moves differently than in their world. Tell him the truth, *Mir*-Bialig, explain, and he will know."

Rogue flew through the air and landed in a heap a short distance from the group. He sprang up with fists primed to do whatever damage he could if attacked, heedless of the fact that his head did not reach the middle of Bialig's chest. Talj shuffled into the center of the tension and placed a hand on Bialig's shoulder, his presence a balm to the friction of personalities.

"Come, *Mira*, let us form the *chute*," Talj said in a rusted voice much in need of oil.

The big man's shoulders relaxed as he muttered, "We will never make it to the *Avboeth* on time if we keep stopping."

Close acquaintance and common knowledge imparted grace to the foursome's movements as they settled into place around Rogue. He scooted to the edge of their circle, every muscle taut with a fight or flight response. Nish whipped up a small fire in no time, the spark jumping from two stones she struck together. Misko cradled his *slele* and strummed his long fingers from the neck of the instrument down to the bowl-shaped base, coaxing forth a song.

"*Mira*-Bialig," Misko said, repeating the term of affection Nish and Talj had employed. It had a soothing effect on their Leader. "Speak the ancient words. Let us begin the *chute*."

Bialig drew himself up to his full height as he knelt before the fire and breathed deeply. The other three followed suit. Rogue repositioned his legs to kneel as well. He sneaked sideways glances at Nish and Misko, who had closed their eyes. Misko's fingers never stopped plucking the strings of his instrument; the sharp twang resonated for a long time with melancholy and mystery.

"*Rotey baso jumy hel chute*."

The other three waited for Bialig to say something more, but Rogue sensed this would be an abbreviated ceremony for his benefit probably because Bialig was still irritated with him. Talj nodded once, twice, three times, and began speaking. His tarnished voice grew in strength, taking on a singsong quality.

"This is your story, Rogue of the *Umane*."

The old man swayed with delight as he settled into telling the tale.

"On the day Nish the *Jiltraos*, the Gatherer, used her second sight to see into Earth, she saw the man called Rogue in trouble and the evil men who meant him harm. She saw the woman who came to free him and the dwelling on fire, and Nish requested of her *Natamos*, Bialig, to save the life of the man called Rogue.

"But it is forbidden for *umane* to come to this world and has been for almost as long as Talj has been alive. Talj remembered *umane* and how some of them were good, and he also asked his *Natamos*, Bialig, to open the door between the worlds to save the man called Rogue.

"And because our *Natamos*, Bialig, is compassionate, he allowed that which is forbidden to save the life of the man called Rogue. At his order, the members of the Group of Four, the *Doh s'Ima*, joined hands and opened the door between the worlds. With joined hands the *Doh s'Ima* pulled the man called Rogue into their world, and he alone came because nothing that did not come from our world can enter.

"And now Rogue of the *Umane* is here, but he does not understand our world. He must know that Bialig is *Natamos* and is to be followed—trusted—at all times. He must accept that Bialig has risked his place, and that of the other three members of the *Doh s'Ima*, with the High Council of Elders just to save the man called Rogue's life. Have respect and appreciation for the position in which Bialig finds himself on behalf of Rogue of the *Umane*.

"Talj the *Thedanos*, the Healer, will find a cure for the poison that moves through the body of Rogue the *uma*. It is he who tells the story of Rogue of the *Umane* and will remember his story to tell future generations. Talj has time to find the cure because even though the poison is of Earth and should not be here, it moves slowly in this world as does all that is on Earth.

"And so, the *Doh s'Ima* of the *Shlodane* Clan travels to the *Avboeth*, and they must be careful not to run into other *Dohne s'Ima* also traveling because Rogue of the *Umane* is with them, and it is forbidden for him to be here. Do you understand?"

"Wait—what?" Rogue looked to Nish first for an explanation. "Can I ask questions now?"

Bialig rolled his eyes at Rogue. Nish and Misko chuckled softly, more forgiving toward their friend's lack of knowledge regarding the storytelling circle. He was like a child to them, learning with each new experience. Misko livened the tune he played to match the mood Rogue brought to the circle. Even Talj smiled beneath his beard now that the seriousness of the story had ended.

"Okay, first of all, what the hell is an *umane*?"

"They are your people," Bialig said. "How can you not know this?"

Rogue scratched his head and said, "I've been around people on Earth all my life, and I've never heard any of them called *umane*."

"*Umane* is many people. You are an *uma*," Nish said. "This is the way the word has been pronounced since contact with your people was made many cycles of the moons ago. Perhaps we are saying it wrong?"

"Humans? Are you trying to say humans?" Rogue fell backward with genuine laughter, holding his stomach and taking advantage of the situation. When his amusement wound down, he sat up and said, "That's a really poor translation considering you all speak pretty good English otherwise." His eyes met Bialig's directly.

"Okay," he continued, "let me get this straight. I came over naked because nothing from Earth can come here, right? That's why the chair I was chained to disappeared?"

"That is correct," Nish said.

"And all my wounds and injuries?"

"Have been healed by Talj."

"That's some impressive medicine you all have. Okay, next question: where the hell am I, exactly?"

"This is our world."

"Yeah, I get that, but what planet is this?"

"Planet?"

"You know, like the other planets revolving around the sun up there with the stars? Or is this—I don't know—heaven or something? Are you guys angels? Am I dead?"

"Did you feel dead, *uma*, when you fell in the *bargelnelo* pit? Or when we fed you? Or when I threw you?" Bialig asked.

"But Talj said there's poison in my body, and based on what Blast told me, I should be dead."

"Time in our world moves differently than on Earth. Usually, nothing from Earth comes to our world, but perhaps because the poison is inside your body, it somehow came over, too. We think this is why the poison moves slowly without killing you. It will give Talj time to find a cure. But we cannot send you back."

"Because if you do?"

"You will die immediately."

CHAPTER NINE

WHAT ROGUE REALLY WANTED TO know was how much time he had. The question plagued him as he and the foursome traveled toward the Assembly of the *Dohne s'Ima*. For two days he contemplated his situation, silenced—much to Bialig's relief—by the knowledge that he really had not cheated death. He had been given a reprieve when the four brought him to their world. Yet a death sentence still hung over his head because Talj did not know exactly how long it would take the poison to work. The old Healer was banking on the fact that it would continue to move slowly in the . . .

Realm.

Rogue finally had to admit to himself where he was. It mattered not that the four friends had no name for their world, or that they may be on another planet in another galaxy, both concepts beyond their understanding. For all he knew, he was in another plane of existence altogether, an alternate timeline. But whatever the case, the descriptions of this place that he had heard growing up on the street matched what he was experiencing firsthand.

All he ever wanted in life was to escape the hellish conditions on Earth, but his current situation was definitely not what he had in mind. Yet when he inhaled deep breaths of fresh air, when he remembered that he was no longer trapped in a bio-dome, when he saw herds of animals thunder across the land, when he plunged his hand into an amethyst-colored river and drank deeply, when he fell asleep beneath the triple moons and awoke to the porcelain sun—no description existed for what Rogue felt every time he experienced these wonders.

But as amazing as this world was, he could not rid himself of the indifference he felt for the risk Bialig had taken in bringing him here. Then there were his feelings about leaving Raine behind to die in the warehouse, emotions that made his heart feel like it had been burned in the fire. Talj had spoken of a woman in the story circle, but he never said what happened to her, and Rogue dreaded what he would be told if he asked. The most disturbing fact was that more than anything—more than getting the poison out of his body—Rogue wanted to return to Earth to find Raine if she was still alive. He shivered at the notion that he cared so much about the GEA agent.

He kept these thoughts to himself. In the two weeks following the story circle, Rogue watched Bialig cringe every time he opened his mouth to ask a question during a meal. Silence reigned supreme as they traveled, and he wondered if other groups followed this unspoken rule or if it was just Bialig exerting his authority every chance he had. He knew Nish had approached the Leader on his behalf to plead leniency toward him, but so far Bialig kept ignoring him.

By the third week after the story circle, Rogue's survival instincts overrode the shock of being in another world with a lethal poison trapped in his body. The gambler decided to play the hand he had been dealt. Already he had revealed his vulnerabilities with his questions. He retracted his emotions to a safe place as he observed these strangers among whom he was forced to live. Unbeknownst to them, he did not intend to stay long.

Despite what the gambler had been told, skepticism and the superior quality of medicine in the Realm made him doubtful about the seriousness of the poison in his body. He believed Talj would find the cure quickly, and when he did, Rogue must be prepared to detach from the group and return to the exact location where he first woke up, the place where he was sure he could return to Earth on his own.

Any plan to hasten his departure had to be executed flawlessly; he did not want the four to keep him against his will. Not that he was clear on their intentions toward him. Would they express concern or experience relief when he disappeared? Uncertainty prompted Rogue to interact with them as he did business associates on Earth, filtering their words and actions through his overly cautious nature.

He stayed on the edge of the group, only coming close to request food and water per Bialig's directive and at night when he needed to be near the safety of the campfire. His tactics lasted two days before he realized he would need to engage the group directly.

Nish seemed the obvious choice for attempting a liaison. Her request had resulted in Rogue's presence in the Realm. Under the guise of watching her prepare food, Rogue managed to slip a hand-sized stone blade from among her cooking utensils and tuck it in his makeshift footwear. Twine from packets of dried herbs found its way beneath his sash. The discarded pole upon which she roasted meat served as a charred walking staff and would double as a weapon. The items Rogue swiped were of little importance, but they lent a sense of security to him as if he had regained a small measure of control over his own life.

Further opportunities to steal more items never presented themselves. Rogue had no idea what he would do with them anyhow, as he was completely ignorant of any threats he might encounter once he broke away from the group. Without a pack of his own, he lacked a place to stash stolen goods. His constant plotting caused him to miss the strained glances between Nish and Bialig every time an item disappeared. With pleading eyes and a head shake, Nish kept the Leader's reactions limited to grinding his teeth and snorting in disgust.

Rogue misunderstood Talj's actions when he surrendered extra lengths of twine from parcels once the contents had been used. The old Healer showed him how to weave them together, creating stronger sections that could be braided into rope. The gambler was also oblivious to Bialig flaking chips of stone from a larger piece as he created a new blade for Nish to cut food. And when Misko shortened Rogue's staff, carving designs into the charred ends thus making it useless as a weapon, Rogue could only stare with an open mouth and blank eyes.

It never occurred to Rogue that the four were not threatened by him or that they were completely aware of his self-absorbed thievery. The more reserved he acted, the more patient they became. Their actions disturbed him, especially when Bialig started including Rogue in his barked orders regarding the routines of the camp. Small tasks, such as clearing brush from the campsite or finding rocks to ring the fire, fell to Rogue. He did not resent the chores. Rather, he smiled inwardly and believed his hosts had foolishly given him the chance to nick whatever he deemed necessary for his escape.

This emboldened Rogue to further insinuate himself into the group. He trailed Talj into a stand of thorn trees as the old one picked leaves and scraped bark into his medicine bag as a potential cure for Rogue. When Misko wrote new songs on pieces of vellum, Rogue peered over the youth's shoulder until Misko welcomed his input with the music. Rogue began to develop an admiration for the group's unity that accentuated their individuality. His confidence grew with every encounter.

One morning he tried to stoke the fire before the others woke up. He succeeded in catching the edge of Bialig's sleeping fur on fire. The big man threw his covers off and stomped them to extinguish the smoldering fur. Nish intervened by declaring it a day for washing clothes, bedding, and bodies in the river they had been following.

In his ignorance, Rogue overstepped the bounds of even a Leader by joining Nish in the river as she bathed. He assumed the opaque water would provide enough privacy, and Nish did not have anything he had not seen before despite her larger proportions. Bialig waded in fully clothed and removed Rogue from the river with his hand clamped around the gambler's neck. He dropped Rogue buck naked on the sandy shore without breaking stride as he returned to camp. Misko spared Rogue further embarrassment by showing him how to shave the stubble that had been growing since he arrived.

Rogue's worst transgressions occurred as disruptions during the weekly day of rest. His nervous energy prevented him from sleeping in like the others, and there was only so much meditating and singing he could endure. He thought the whole process was a waste of time, and he fidgeted and sighed when Talj read from the ancient writings in the Language of the Realm. When he broke the commandment to not work by gathering kindling, Bialig banished him from camp. A night away from the safety of the group drove home the point that rest truly meant rest.

Rogue gave up on acceptance by the group and concluded that something was fundamentally lacking in his nature. Nish knew better; she sensed in Rogue a strength of character hidden beneath his inability to use his talents for the benefit of others. With a little luck—and the right circumstances—she trusted Rogue would rise to the occasion.

After another two weeks of the dull routine of eating, walking, and sleeping, Misko came to Rogue's rescue. The youth walked last in line and often trailed behind to fall in step with Rogue, encouraging his human friend to walk beside him. The young man taught him the names of the sparse shrubs and wind-blasted trees, the naturally camouflaged birds and lizards, the jagged mountain ranges and river carving the land. Bialig would look back over his shoulder when he heard them talking, but to his credit, he never interfered.

When they stopped that night to make camp, Rogue helped Nish collect firewood. In return, she showed him how to arrange the wood and stuff it with grasses twisted into coils. She handed him her striking stones and mimicked the movements to produce a spark. It took Rogue several tries before a decent spark landed on the dry grass. In his enthusiasm, he forgot to gently blow on the spark to encourage the grass to catch.

Once he finally had a decent fire going, he guided Talj to his furs and fetched whatever the Healer pointed at. Rogue realized that beyond the story telling circle, the old man used gestures and grunts to communicate. He coached Rogue, often with his large, gnarled hands covering Rogue's own, as they ground ash and a sticky substance together. Then they heated the mixture in water over the fire. Their work resulted in a small pot of smooth, black fluid. Talj dipped a carved stick with a sharpened point into the murky liquid and unrolled a piece of vellum.

Mir-Talj, we made ink," Rogue said.

Bialig's head snapped up at Rogue's use of the respectful term. Reflected flames danced like fireflies in his steady gaze. Peripherally, he saw Nish nod with approval while she seasoned the food over the fire. Tonight's meal would be all vegetables and herbs; the game herds had moved on since the *uma* showed up. Bialig finished restringing his bow and quietly began sharpening his hunting knife.

The group ate the simple meal, and Rogue sand-scoured his eating bowl and utensils as well as those of Nish, Misko, and Talj. Bialig told himself it was because he finished first that the *uma* did not offer to clean his. He pushed the thought from his head when Misko pulled his *slele* onto his lap. The youth's music always soothed his nerves, but a couple of plunks on the instrument revealed the need for new strings. No amount of tightening would save them.

"I am going hunting," Bialig announced without preamble.

"What? Now? The moons are hidden tonight, and we have not seen the herds in days," Nish said. Her delicate brow wrinkled, and her jaw tightened.

"We ran out of dried meat quicker than expected and cannot wait for the herds to find us. The *elopa* I killed four moons ago was the last fresh meat we have had. Besides, Misko needs new strings and another skin to wrap his *slele*. It must be tonight."

Nish stood and pulled Bialig's outer coat across his chest, fastening the single clasp at the top. Then she placed a small packet in his pocket and handed him her drinking skin.

"Mine is smaller and good for quick travel. There is *chelpi* for you to eat if you get hungry. Do you have your knife? Are you taking your bow? What about rope to drag the animal back?"

Bialig chuckled and said, "Yes, yes, and I will probably clean the carcase on the plains. *Mir*-Nish, this is not my first hunt."

Then he turned and disappeared into the scrub and the darkness. The crackle and gust of the fire bid him farewell. Night insects and distant howling welcomed him into their presence. Nish stood longer than necessary watching the direction in which he left before she finally rejoined the group at the fire. Misko blew softly into another instrument, his fingers covering holes bored along the column of wood, producing hollow, sweet sounds.

"He said that because of me, didn't he?" Rogue asked no one in particular. "Bialig said you ran out of food quicker, and that wouldn't have happened if I hadn't come along."

Nish dismissed him with a *tsk* and a wave. She pulled a garment from her bag, a sliver of bone, and thread. A jagged tear received steady, even stitches until one could no longer see where the fabric had been ripped.

"His concerns are many since your arrival," she said without looking up. "As our *Natamos*, Bialig not only leads, but he also protects and provides. There is much weight on his shoulders, Rogue, now that you are here. He is responsible for you, do you understand?"

"I can take care of myself."

"No, you cannot. The *bargelnelo* pit proved that. If you should die, Bialig must admit to the High Council that he broke their ruling by bringing you here, and he must atone for your death. The poison in your body weighs heavy on his mind. And so, we walk in silence to give him time to work it out. We trust him completely as we have done since our *Doh s'Ima* was formed."

"Explain that."

"It is our Group of Four. Every Clan has one. There is always a Leader, a Healer, an Artist, and a Gatherer taken from among the families. We do not know who will be in this group, and it may take many cycles of the moons before one emerges, but once the group is formed, they serve the families and represent them at the *Avboeth*."

"How do you choose who gets to be in the group?"

"No one chooses. By one's skills it becomes obvious that a person belongs in a group. When my ability at second sight developed as a child, my family knew that I would one day join a group. Bialig was proving himself as a natural Leader, and Talj already had the art of a Healer. We three waited until an Artist arose among the families and were not disappointed when Misko's talents became apparent."

The youth stopped blowing into the wind instrument. An awkward smile crossed his face.

"So what did you do before Misko came along? I mean, Talj is really old—I'm sorry . . ."

The old Healer grunted and shook with laughter at Rogue's comment.

"We waited," Nish said. "It can be a very unsettling time for a Clan to not have a *Doh s'Ima*, to not be represented at the *Avboeth*. But age does not determine who joins a group."

"Wasn't another group serving? Or couldn't one of you fit into the group that served before yours? I'm assuming there was one."

"There was, but when a member of a group dies, the bond is broken forever. You cannot simply put another person in that place. The remaining members either go back to their families or they stay at the *Avboeth* forever, teaching other members and passing on wisdom and knowledge. It is a very sad time to lose a member of the *Doh s'Ima*. The ability to open the door between worlds is lost, although the other skills remain."

Rogue shot a glance at Talj. If nature took its course, he would pass before the others.

"That hardly seems fair to the youngest and last person to join," Rogue said.

"It is not about fairness; it is about living life to the fullest every moment we are together by serving others."

Misko's hands and instrument fell to his lap. A noise of exasperation escaped his throat. The youth looked away from the fire, staring into the shadows where Bialig had disappeared. Nish sewed and Talj's stylus scratched across the vellum. Rogue waited in the abrupt silence, sensing an incongruity in the usually cohesive group.

"I, Misko, am the Artist, *Paten*. I bring joy to our *Doh s'Ima* with song and music. The sights we see are recorded in the artwork I create. I teach the dances of our people. Nish is the Gatherer, *Jiltraos*. She grows our food and prepares it, provides our clothing, makes a home for us. She sees into the other worlds with the second sight. Talj is our *Thedanos*, our Healer. He knows all the secrets of medicine and healing of the body and mind. And Bialig is the Leader, the *Natamos*, who guides and protects us, whom we trust blindly, and who enforces all the rules."

The young man recited the formal introduction with no passion in his lilting voice, earning a scowl of reprimand from Nish for his altered version.

"You know that is not all, Misko," she added with counterfeit lightheartedness. "What binds us together is our ability to open the door between our world and the other. Only when four who possess our talents can do this is the *Doh s'Ima* formed."

Rogue thought for a moment then said, "You mean there are no other Artists or Healers or people like you and Bialig in the Clans?"

"There are, and in the different roles of Second, Mentor, or Student, they contribute to keeping the skills alive to ensure the wisdom and knowledge goes forward with each generation. But there is a power within those who form the *Doh s'Ima*, and that ability—when their hands are joined in harmony—opens the door to your world. Finding this combination takes time."

"Can you open doors to other places? Other worlds?"

"The Second Sighted uses their abilities to see into wherever they are directed."

Rogue's eyebrow arched at the imprecise comment.

"Any clue as to why time moves differently here?"

"No, but we do know that our days, nights and . . . what do you call it . . . years are longer than those on Earth. Perhaps this is why time on Earth seems slow."

Nish tied off the sewing she had completed before she bit the thread near the fabric to cut it. Then she stowed her supplies and banked the fire for the night. Her actions signaled that it was time for sleep, and the three members settled in their furs. Rogue's head still spun with questions he wanted to ask. He positioned his sleeping fur so that his head would be near Misko's.

Talj snored within minutes, and Nish's even breathing indicated that she had drifted off. When Rogue turned to face Misko, he startled to see the young man's large eyes staring in anticipation, his chin resting on folded arms. His long, white hair flowed free of the bands that held it in a segmented ponytail during the day. The locks cascaded over his thin shoulders.

"I guess you can't sleep either," Rogue said.

"What did you think of the things Nish told you?" Misko whispered.

"I've learned a lot about your family."

"We are not family. Not in the way you think."

"I get that you're not blood relations, but Nish and Bialig are obviously together."

"We are all together. We take care of each other."

"No, I mean they're married."

"Where did you get that idea?"

Misko buried his face in his arms and pulled his fur over his head, and still Rogue thought sure his laughter would wake the others. The young man explained in a chuckled whisper, "No ceremony has been performed joining them."

"Why not?"

"I believe the law prohibiting marriage between *Doh s'Ima* members is written somewhere in the ancient writings. Talj pesters me to learn them, but the study is long and hard. Besides, the only hope of any real happiness for *Doh s'Ima* members is the death of . . ."

Acrimony rasped the edges of Misko's statement, but he did not finish his thought. Rogue rolled to his back and contemplated Misko's words.

"I don't think I understand the purpose of the *Doh s'Ima*."

"Don't worry, Rogue, I will explain whatever you want to know."

"How come we haven't seen any other people?"

"Our Clan lives the farthest from the others. Bialig is taking a little-used route so we do not run into other *Dohne s'Ima* traveling. You must not be seen."

"Speaking of The Lion, where is he?"

Misko paused for a second before he understood Rogue meant Bialig. Real concern for the Leader shadowed the young man's face, and he leaned up on his arms to peer into the blackness beyond the fire.

"I do not know. It is not unusual for him to return while we sleep. Bialig is capable, and there will be meat in the morning."

Misko and Rogue stopped talking, their eyes grew heavy, and sleep overtook them. Nish's eyes stayed open. Her face was turned away from the others; they did not know she had heard their conversation. Worry kept her awake throughout the night as she listened for Bialig's return.

CHAPTER TEN

AFTER MORE THAN FIVE WEEKS in the Realm, Rogue had become accustomed to the dove's breast of padded sky slipstreamed with mulberry clouds and etched with the silhouette of birds. He tried not to overthink the strange colors of the world or question the science of nature that produced them. As he awoke each day, he took a deep breath of clean air, feeling mild surprise that his body tolerated real food even if it was from animals and plants he had never seen before. Not that he had encountered much of the real stuff in a life sustained by Nutri-Synth.

This morning, he performed a quick headcount to make sure his companions were still present before he rolled out of his sleeping fur to get the day started. He spied two bodies huddled beneath their bedding. The gear grinding snores of one told Rogue that Talj had not awakened, but Misko, lying beside him, began to stir. Rogue sat up and looked around the dying fire. Nish's furs were packed for traveling. He was pretty sure Bialig's, still strapped to his pack frame, had not been unrolled for use last night.

Rogue stood and scanned the area for Nish, locating her in the near distance. She paced along an outcrop forming a natural shelf on the landscape. Her attention focused on troops of feeding omnivores below. Rogue was no hunter, but he assumed the calm actions of the foraging animals indicated the lack of a predator among them. Specifically, Bialig. His observations drew Misko's curiosity. The young man nodded when he saw Nish's nervous vigil and Bialig's unused bedding.

Talj awoke and the three remaining men took it upon themselves to restore last night's fire as well as concoct a simple meal of tea and porridge seasoned with items from Nish's stash. The three called to Nish, still stalking short distances in search of their missing Leader. She declined with a smile and a wave. Rogue took his cue from Talj, who appeared the least worried. Besides, he wanted to ask Misko more questions.

With the sweetened porridge packed in his cheek, Rogue asked, "Are Gatherers the only ones with second sight?"

"Yes. Gatherers keep members safe by scouting locations where the portal can be opened without being seen."

"So you can return to the same location more than once?"

"Of course," Misko said. "The building where we found you was a favorite site because it was never used. Imagine our surprise when Nish saw into your world to see the building on fire and you in trouble."

"If the building is gone, how will I get back?"

Misko sensed more to Rogue's question than the gambler expressed.

"You don't have to return to the exact same place. Once Talj has cured you, Nish will scout a safe place to open the portal."

"So, we don't have to be in the exact spot where you brought me to?"

"Of course not, Rogue. The portal is not restricted by location. If it were, the members of the *Dohne s'Ima* would not be able to travel as freely as they do. In fact, we do not have to be the ones to send you back. Any *Doh s'Ima* can do that."

If Rogue had had a toothpick in the corner of his mouth, he would have rolled it across his lower lip, but Misko still would not have recognized his pleasure at the carefully dropped information. The youth could only hope his new friend had picked up on what he was being told. Rogue smiled and continued.

"Talj said something during the storytelling circle about remembering humans who were good. Does that mean you've encountered bad ones?"

"That was before my time. Some *umane* who came over welcomed the opportunity to share knowledge and wisdom. It is said others tried to exploit our world and people. They supposedly brought ideas and practices that were considered hostile. Even though they could not stay here forever, their ways were considered corruptive to the teachings of our Clans. The High Council of Elders determined that their philosophy was bad for our people and our culture, and the law forbidding *umane* from crossing the portal was put in place."

Misko's downcast eyes darkened as he relayed the story, and he sucked in his cheeks as if to stop himself from speaking. Rogue finished his breakfast and scoured his bowl and spoon clean.

"What would it take to get some kind of backpack for me?" he asked. "I appreciate the borrowed stuff, but I need my own things for however long I'm going to be here."

"Bialig will have a new skin when he returns. If it is large enough, we can make a cover for my *slele* and a pack for you. Unless Bialig already has a purpose for it, but he will share if you help him prepare the hide."

Rogue's stomach turned at the thought of handling a fresh skin, but he agreed to Misko's proposal rather than have the youth discern his revulsion. Another offer of breakfast for Nish was met with the same response, so the men undertook her duties as well as they could and prepared for travel.

As they packed, Rogue asked, "Why do Realmers come to Earth? It's not like you can take anything back."

"Who?" Misko asked.

"You know . . . people from your world."

"Is that what you call us?"

"Yeah, well, there was this guy hundreds of years ago who had been over, and he kind of labeled this place The Unknown Realm, so your people became known as Realmers. It's not meant as an insult."

A blush crept up Rogue's neck at the lie. Misko pursed his ample lips, considering the term and humming his acceptance.

"We Realmers come because the High Council is still interested in making a connection with *umane* who want to receive knowledge, starting with those interested in saving your dying world."

Deep offense darkened Rogue's face. "What could Realmers possibly have to offer humans?"

His comment produced surprise in Misko and muffled laughter from Talj. The old Healer was several words into his explanation by the time Rogue realized he was speaking.

". . . ruined your world by polluting the air, the land, and the water. When the Second Sighted were first directed to see into Earth, it was not too far gone. We sought to help *umane* by teaching them methods of purification, better ways to sustain life. But most of them were only interested in escaping the problems they had inflicted upon your world. They wanted to make a profit by demanding payment from other *umane* for the right to live in our world. These reckless people refused to accept responsibility for what they had allowed to be done on Earth. And it was never the High Council's intention to be overrun by a people who would spoil their own world. What would keep them from doing the same here?

"But worse than what *umane* did to the Earth was what they did to themselves. Acting upon their unstable emotions, they abandoned rational thinking and chose to embrace all manner of perversion, incorporating it into their society until the lines between good and evil, truth and falsehood were blurred. Then they raised up their children in it.

"There are those who understand our desire to help, and it is to these *umane* that we continue to reach out. But we must take care not to be seen when we cross over and leave the scrolls telling the ways in which Earth can be recovered and people restored."

"Wait—you leave things behind for us?"

Talj nodded slowly, and said, "There is one place where certain *Dohne s'Ima* cross over and have had success dealing with people from your world. The Elders knew it was worthwhile to contact them when the Second Sighted saw them trying on their own to make a better life."

"Where?"

"We do not know the name of this area, but the people there speak a deep, throaty language that was difficult for *Dohne s'Ima* to learn."

Life as a smuggler on the docks gave Rogue the opportunity to learn tidbits of many languages. Although he was not fluent, the description of the language spoken by the people the Realmers had visited, combined with his knowledge of a Sector on Earth experiencing a better quality of life, tipped off Rogue's suspicions. His mind flew to those jerks in Sector 48 who had an annoying habit of keeping things under wraps. Now he knew why.

"So other Realmers can speak different Earth languages?" he asked.

"Yes, and it is odd to us that you need so many. It makes communication difficult."

"Don't you learn Earth languages at your *Avboeth*?"

"That lesson takes place in the Clans," Talj said. "The *Dohne s'Ima* attend the *Avboeth* because it is commanded by the *Liabish Tag*. It is a time of rest during which our energies are restored so that we may fulfill our purpose of serving the Clans by teaching them to serve each other."

"Who is this *Liabish Tag*? Another Realmer?"

"No. Your language renders the words Infinite One."

"And the Groups of Four are the only ones who benefit from going to the *Avboeth*?"

"There are appointed times for the Clans and Elders as well, and, of course, the Infinite One is accessible to everyone who comes to faith."

"So, he's some kind of god?"

"He is the only living God."

"And you jump when He says come?"

A low rumble crept up Talj's throat but never passed his pursed lips.

"He is with us at all times, in all places. But there are certain times when He requests our presence at a particular place, and who are we to tell Him no? That is not convenient for me? Rather, I will meet you at another date and location?"

"Yeah, okay. And how exactly do you access this living God?"

Talj inhaled slowly and studied Rogue's face, looking for signs of true interest, testing to see if he would mock.

"We read His truths written in the stars' songs."

Rogue gazed upward, searching the daytime sky of the Realm for evidence of Talj's words.

"What's in it for you to come to Earth?"

"We come because we are obedient to the Infinite One's commission to encourage *umane* toward seeking Him."

"You mean there are stories in the stars for us?"

"There is codified instruction to guide you. The very mind of the Infinite One written down."

"What are you guys? Our conscience? Priests? I've never seen or heard of anything like what you're talking about."

Exasperation drew Talj's crooked mouth into a tight frown, but patience softened his words.

"The *Dohne s'Ima* are responsible for directing Clan members in daily physical and spiritual activities. The Elders oversee our efforts. When these are in balance, we learn how to relate to each other and, more importantly, the Infinite One. How *umane* respond to the influences upon their conscience is a matter of exercising free will. But make no mistake, the written instruction still exists for one to hear and obey."

"How can you be so sure?"

"Because it is a living document. If it were not, we would not have been sent to encourage you to find and return to it."

"And you guys learn about this living God through the ancient writings?"

"Our ancient writings are commentary by the High Council of Elders. Only the stars are His instruction to us."

Rogue tried to sort out everything Talj told him. Guilt overrode his desire for more answers when Nish stepped into his peripheral vision. She alone kept watch for their missing Leader.

"We better check on Nish. She hasn't eaten anything. Is there any tea left from breakfast?"

"There is a cup, but it is cold," Misko said.

Rogue accepted the cup from Misko and walked to where Nish stood with her arms wrapped around herself. Rogue, cold himself, knew her posture was not due to the weather. He recognized her stance as that of a woman mired in apprehension. She jumped at the touch of his hand on her arm.

"Rogue—I did not hear you approach."

"I figured that when you almost sent the cup flying out of my hands."

They shared an uneasy laugh, both hesitant to address her concern.

"What do we do, Nish?"

"We wait."

"Has he ever been gone this long before?"

"It can take a few days when the herds are far away, but Bialig always signals us to let us know his plans."

"Signals how?"

"Bialig uses different substances in a fire to make colored smoke. The color tells us if he will travel far, is in trouble, to come where he is, or other such things."

"Okay, but what if he's . . ."

The statement died in the air between them, and Nish cast pleading eyes on Rogue to not finish. Even though he was not fond of Bialig, Rogue did not wish him any ill. At least not for Nish's sake.

"I know your group waits for Bialig to say jump before you ask how high, but I'm not the kind of person to sit around waiting."

"Rogue, we cannot travel without him. We cannot leave him behind to wonder where we are."

"No, I'm saying I'll go look for him. And before you protest, I know what the markers for a *bargel* pit looks like."

"I must insist that we stay together. I know things are difficult between you and Bialig, but trust me in this even if you cannot yet place faith in him."

"But that's just it, Nish. I don't have a role in your little group, so I won't get in trouble with the big man if he returns before I do. Besides, I'm not as helpless in your world as you think. I did a pretty good job taking care of myself on Earth. Well, up until that last thing with Blast. I'll take my staff and that little knife I swiped from you, and I'll be back before you know it."

Nish's cheeks warmed with pleasure at Rogue's confession. His face reddened because he knew what a jerk he had been. Both turned at the sound of Misko's footsteps.

"What has been decided? Do we wait or travel?" the young man asked.

"We wait," Nish said, surprise and irritation mingling on her face. "Rogue was saying that he needed a role in our *Doh s'Ima*."

"No, I'm pretty sure that's not what I said—"

"What kind of role?" Misko asked, his eyes alight with interest. "*Umane* are too small to be of any real use in The Unknown Realm."

"Unknown Realm?" Nish said.

Misko explained Rogue's label for their world as he and Nish literally talked over his head.

"I suppose that is one way to define where we live, but we must find a place for our own little *uma* in our *Doh s'Ima* for as long as he is in the Realm," Nish concluded, placing her hand on Rogue's head.

"What about a water bearer? Four skins plus his own would be heavy, but the little *uma* has muscles. It would not hurt him to build up more strength for the next time he challenges a *bargel*."

"I do not know if our *umalus* can start with such a heavy chore. What if he carried the bands we use to tie our hair? He could use both hands."

"Hello up there," Rogue said, "I can hear everything you're saying about me."

Rogue did not join the laughter, but he allowed the teasing along with friendly head pats. The trio continued chatting until Talj's labored progress toward them and urgent, coarse voice drew their attention. They were momentarily stilled as the old one's arms flailed above his head. When he stopped and pointed to a commotion scattering the animals on the plain and coming toward them, his odd movements gained clarity.

"*Sojabosne*?" Misko asked in a whisper.

"No—not now when Bialig is away."

The fear on Nish's face sent chills through Rogue. His first thought flew to Bialig, and he assumed the word Misko had spoken was the cause of the Leader's delay. An explanation would have been helpful. He did not have a chance to open his mouth before Nish pushed him down to the ground by his shoulders. Misko also flattened himself on the rock ledge. Talj, bending over to appear smaller, shuffled back to camp.

"What the hell is going on?" Rogue asked, his face pressed into the dry turf covering the rock.

"Be quiet. The sound of your voice carries on the wind, and we might have been seen," Nish said.

Misko edged away on his belly from the other two.

"Where are you going?" Nish demanded.

"To get Bialig's spears. Rogue should come with me, and we will confront them before they reach our camp."

"What difference does it make if you attack them here or there? There are too many for you to overcome. You are not trained to use a weapon, Misko, and Rogue does not have one suitable for making war."

"This is not war, Nish, this is self-defense, and I have proved myself with a weapon at the *bargelnelo* pit."

"Would somebody please tell me what is going on?" Rogue asked again.

"The *sojabosne* are coming—"

"I heard that part, Nish. What are they?"

"People who have abandoned the Infinite One, their families, and Clans. Sometimes their *Doh s'Ima*. They are the ones corrupted by the bad *umane*, and they seek travelers on their way to the *Avboeth*."

"Not all of them are bad, Nish," Misko said. "They just have different ideas—"

Rogue silenced Misko with a hand directed toward the young man's face. "Tell me why they're looking for travelers."

"To plunder their camps, steal from the goods they carry." Nish hesitated. "They kill all who resist them and those who refuse to join them or accept their flawed ways of thinking."

Temptation to ask more questions rose like bile in Rogue's throat, but he suppressed the desire and shook his head. It was not the first time he had been in this situation, and usually he could extricate himself. This time his enemy not only outnumbered him, but they also had size and strength in their favor. He would give anything for a GEA blaster or a gun with bullets. As much as he hated it, retreat looked to be their only option.

Rogue motioned Misko and Nish back toward camp. The trio crawled on their stomachs. When they reached Talj, they hurried to collect their gear and seek shelter behind one of the rock formations dotting the landscape.

"We have the advantage of surprise, Nish, if we attack the *sojabosne* first," Misko said. "Let us hide the packs and Talj, and then together with Bialig's spears and your knife, we could defend ourselves."

"Defense is not to attack first. It would be suicide to go against the *sojabosne*, and you know that. Why do you persist in this line of thinking?"

"Because I am sick of living in fear and always running—"

"It is not our way to seek conflict," Nish hissed. "Do you want to become like them?" She pointed over her shoulder at the band of people who had disappeared the nearer they came, hidden by the rock overhang. "We do not live in fear because Bialig and other *Natamosne* keep us safe—"

"But Bialig is not here, is he?" Misko spat back. "And we find ourselves helpless because we adhere to the rules of the Infinite One, never learning the skills of the other members, because if we did, we could defend ourselves against any threat."

Misko slashed the air in front of him with his hand, finalizing his dissent.

"There was no threat before the *umane* tainted our world," Nish said. "I will not debate this issue with you now when our lives are in danger. Why, *Mir*-Misko, do you continue to think as the *sojabosne* do with their violence and their disregard for law and order?"

The youth stood with shoulders slumped, pack at his feet, straps in hand. Struggle twisted his face, and he opened his mouth several times before speaking.

"Because I agree with some of their beliefs."

The gasp escaping Nish's lips could have been caused by Misko's comment. It could have been caused by the *sojabosne* casually strolling into camp with weapons raised. Only when he awoke much later did Rogue realize she had gasped at the sight of the person standing behind him about to hit him on the head.

CHAPTER ELEVEN

SINGING ACCOMPANIED BY THE RHYTHM of percussion instruments penetrated Rogue's senses first. The sound of a large fire roared in his ears. Only because the two did not go together did he realize he was still in the Realm and not in a burning warehouse.

Grit pressed into his cheek. His body felt contorted, restrained. From this he understood that he was bound and lying on the ground. He tried to move his arms but could not even feel them. A tingling in his shoulders told him they had gone to sleep probably from resting at an odd angle. His legs, too, were not positioned correctly.

Cold prickled his skin. He was beyond the reach of the fire's heat. His eye closest to the ground worked its way open to assess his situation. Darkness layered upon darkness with flashes of red, yellow, and orange; it was night, and many people moved in front of the fire. Rogue lay in the shadows.

Cocooned in the icy stillness, he sensed a presence with size and mass close to him. He bent his head forward and succumbed to the spinning and throbbing about to burst through his skull. A soft groan escaped his lips, and he made a mental note to kill whoever had hit him in the back of his head. When the nausea passed, he looked down the length of his body and could not see his legs past his knees.

His mind struggled to work out the configuration of his body. Slowly it came to him that his hands were behind him and tied to his feet, legs bent at the knees. He had two options: stay as he lay or roll to his stomach. Neither appealed to him. Instead, he opened his other eye.

This time he tilted his head back hoping to minimize the dizziness. His eyes teared up, but through the haze he saw Talj tied up in the same position as he was. Rogue's heart lurched at the sight of the old man's aged body bent against its will in such a cruel fashion. A dirty rag had been wound around his head, passing through his slack mouth.

Rogue considered rolling over on his already numb arms to see if he could find Misko and Nish. There did not seem to be a guard watching him and Talj. Something about that fact disturbed him, and his fears were confirmed when he heard Nish's voice beg in a panicked scream. The heat of rage flushed Rogue's body. He strained against the ropes incapacitating him.

Suddenly, a giant, leathery palm appeared in front of him, covering his face and muffling his cry. An arm snaked between him and the ground, encircling his chest and holding him in place. Rogue tried to thrash his head and body but gave up when he almost fainted from the pain. A calm whisper in a familiar voice commanded him, "Do not move, *uma*. You will attract unwanted attention."

The hot gust of breath seared Rogue's cold panic, and he relaxed in Bialig's grip. His dead weight was nothing for the big man to lift with the care of a parent for a child, and he almost yielded to his relief until he remembered Talj. A few grunts encouraged Bialig to lighten his hand over Rogue's mouth.

"Talj." The word fought to escape the desert of Rogue's throat.

"I know. He is not so easy to move as you."

Rogue allowed himself to be carried far from the bonfire and dancing people. When he and Bialig were safely behind a dam of weathered rocks and desiccated tree trunks in a dry riverbed, the Leader set his charge down and freed him from his bonds. Rogue rubbed blood back into his cold arms, stretched his legs to limber his muscles. His first good look around revealed a terrain dotted with boulders, explaining the twisted path they had taken to escape and why no one had seen them leave.

"I need your help," Bialig said.

"I need a weapon."

The Leader of the *Doh s'Ima* smiled and nodded, pleased that Rogue did not back down from a fight despite minor injuries and an enemy greater in size and number. He placed a short sword across Rogue's lap. The carved wooden handle required Rogue to hold it in both hands.

"You can handle my hunting knife," Bialig said.

The comment humbled Rogue: a sword proportionate to Bialig's size would have been impossible to wield.

"We need to get Talj out of there. His breathing seemed shallow, and he is too old to suffer this torture much longer," Rogue said.

"We must free Nish and Misko first—"

"So, you're just going to leave Talj to the whims of those animals? He's not as strong as the other two."

"I am aware of the strength of our *Doh s'Imalo Thedanos*."

"But—"

"*Kidreth!*" Bialig exhaled through his teeth, growled softly in his throat. "You make too much noise, *uma*, and you waste too much time. I will do this without you if you continue to endanger my *Doh s'Ima*. This is not a matter for debate, and I do not have to seek your approval. If you continue to interfere, I will restrain you myself."

With his final warning, Bialig retrieved his bow, quiver with arrows, and spears he had hidden among the rocks. Tucked in his belt was a knife like the one he had given Rogue. He draped a leather strap across his chest and shoulder, taking care to adjust the scabbard at his back. Then Bialig unrolled an oil-darkened cloth to reveal the broadsword within. Moonlight flashed along the blade held aloft as if baptizing the weapon for combat.

"In their lust for prisoners, the *sojabosne* neither stole nor destroyed my weapons."

"You can't use those all at once," Rogue said. "What are you going to do?"

"Kill as many as I can from a distance with the bow. I can remove at least five before they realize their comrades are not succumbing to intoxication and another five before they retrieve their weapons."

"Then what?"

Bialig motioned for Rogue to follow. The two men trod carefully to avoid dislodging small rocks or breaking twigs. They walked with their knees bent and torsos parallel to the ground in case a lookout had decided to scale one of the boulders. Sounds of revelry reached them before they were in sight of the bonfire, and Bialig led them to the left of where he had found Rogue and Talj. From behind a rock formation creating a natural wall, he explained his strategy.

"After I kill the first group, the others will run toward the place from where they believe the attack came. For this reason, I will work my way around the perimeter to misdirect them. When that happens, you must slip into the camp and free Nish and Misko with the knife I gave you. At the same time, I will make my presence known to draw them away from you."

"Do you have any idea how many there are?"

"Thirty, more or less. You must lead Nish and Misko to Talj, free him, and help carry him out of the *sojabosnelo* camp to the riverbed. There is a cave a short distance beyond the fallen trees. Hide there."

"What are you going to do? Take on the last twenty crazed killers alone?"

"Please, *uma*, this is not the time—"

"My—name—is—Rogue."

Bialig's grip tightened on his bow, and he exhaled with more patience than he felt.

"Look, big guy, I know I can't go up against these jerks like you would, but if I can inflict some damage, that will help Nish and Misko escape."

"I do not want to have to save you twice, *Rogue*."

"Don't sweat it. I'm going to sting these guys like a wasp, and they'll never see it coming because of my size."

Humor and interest eased the tension lines on Bialig's brow.

Rogue continued, "Your general makeup looks similar to mine, and if I'm guessing right, a slash to the back of the ankle will disable these losers permanently."

"Yes, that is true. They will be unable to walk."

"Perfect, because most of them have removed their footwear. I'm no stranger to down and dirty street fighting. I figure a little ducking and rolling, and I'll be able to take out at least five to eight of them."

"Whatever this 'dirty street fighting' is, do not get stepped on."

"Just take care of yourself, and leave it to—"

Screaming from Nish silenced the men's conversation as raucous laughter scrabbled over the rock wall toward them. They peeked above the edge to see her with her hands tied in front of her. She was pushed from man to man as they groped her body. A handful of hard-looking women encouraged the depravity. Rogue could not understand their language, but he recognized the raw tones of bitterness and malice from the women.

One man with an eyepatch grabbed Nish's braid as she spun away from the last man trying to fondle her. He yanked hard on her hair, baring her neck for a kiss that started at the base of her throat. His tongue and teeth raking her skin brought strangled protests from Nish and harsh words of condemnation from another woman in the crowd.

Red ink tattoos scrawled across the woman's arms, looking like open wounds on her pale lavender flesh. She was shorter and stouter than

Nish with unkempt, frizzled white hair framing her round face. With her chin thrust out, she stepped forward to challenge the man with the eyepatch. It was clear from the woman's jabs to the man's shoulder that she was displeased with his conduct. An argument broke out between them and ended when the man pushed the woman away from him. Hurt and betrayal swirled like oil and water on the woman's face when she landed hard on her backside, and her eyes blazed as only a scorned lover's could.

Misko thrust himself into this fray with what sounded like words meant to placate. He strummed the loosened strings of his *slele*, producing a warbling song. His captors did not appear to mind. The miscreants slapped him on the back, threw their arms around his shoulders, and swayed and crooned drunkenly. His playing refocused their attention on drinking and dancing. Rogue found it curious that the youth was not tied up.

But all was not settled between the woman and the man with the eyepatch; humiliation drove her to pull her knife from her pack. The next time Nish lunged in her direction to escape another grasping hand, the woman seized Nish's braid and sliced the knife through her hair, sheering it close to the base of her skull. Cheers of congratulation, even from the man with the eyepatch, erupted as the woman held the plaited trophy high. Already the thick sections had unraveled at the cut end.

The man with the eyepatch laughed and pulled Nish onto his lap by the rope around her wrists as he sat by the fire. She squirmed to get away from him when his pelvis thrust upward several times, grinding into her body. More laughing from the group accompanied the man's vulgar actions. The woman who held Nish's braid tossed it into the flames, joining in the laughter now that she understood what her man intended for Nish. Bialig could stand no more and started over the top of the rock wall.

"Whoa—where do you think you're going?" Rogue whispered as loud as he dared. He dragged on Bialig's arm with all his weight.

"That filthy *gradol* must be made to suffer for putting his hands on Nish."

"Then he dies first, okay? Okay?"

The Leader closed his eyes to dispel the sight and nodded vigorously.

"At least we won't have to free Misko," Rogue said.

Bialig bared his teeth and said, "It is time to make our move. They are getting drunker and will be easier to kill."

The men slid off the rocks. Rogue went toward the right along the wall where he could leap over a low portion once the arrows started to fly. Bialig stole to the left, nocking the first arrow as he sought the best vantage point from which to begin his assault. His mind and body melded with the beat of the drums that had joined Misko's music. The four-beat rhythm repeated twice, and on the ninth beat, the arrow found its mark. The first body to drop tripped several dancers, delaying the group's notice when bodies two through five also fell. Only the man with the eyepatch sat straight and still.

Keeping track of ammunition was always a challenge in a fight; one rarely took the time to count shots fired. But Rogue's wits never left him as he tallied the fallen. He almost cheered when Bialig took out seven more *sojabosne* before their leader shoved Nish to the ground and jumped up. Twelve motionless bodies with arrows through their chests brought laughter from the intoxicated dancers and a demand for silence from their leader.

Three more bodies fell as the drumbeats died out to shouts of confusion. Three of the dancers knelt beside their fallen friends—one of them the woman with the tattoos—and howled their outrage. Their cries turned to death throes. The remaining ten scrambled for their weapons, and Rogue leapt the wall to attack the one closest to him.

His victim erupted like a cornered lioness when she turned to lash out at Rogue with a flanged mace pulled from her pack. He had not quite hit his mark. Ducking and dodging her poorly aimed swings, he managed to tackle her around her knees and finish off the tendons in both ankles. She sent him flying backward when he forgot about the Realmers' extended reach. She knocked the breath out of him and infuriated him; a suicide run at her throat ended her life.

Bialig abandoned his bow in favor of his knife and spear. He charged the group running toward him and swept the legs of the first to reach him, then thrust his spear into the man's stomach, causing him to bolt upright into the slash of a knife across his throat. The next two were removed in a similar fashion.

"Misko, Nish—get the hell out of here," Rogue yelled.

Nish ran toward the sound of Rogue's voice but was halted by the rope around her wrists. The man with the eyepatch wound the rope around his own hand, dragging her back to him as she dug in her heels. His arm curled around Nish's neck, lifting her to her tiptoes and pressing her close to his chest. He backed away from the fighting and into the shadows, his one good eye scanning the cyclone of bodies whirling around the fire, looking for the presence he sensed but could not locate.

Misko stood with mouth open and eyes blank, his instrument useless in his hands. When he found the courage to move beyond his shock, his pleading words fell on deaf ears. He tried to stop the fighting but was knocked to the ground by the *sojabosne* as they attacked Bialig and Rogue. Horror sealed the young Artist's eyes when he fell into blood-soaked sand near the fire pit, unable to push himself away fast enough.

Five bloodied and injured *sojabosne* encircled Bialig and Rogue who stood back to back. They thrust their weapons toward the two men, never coming within range to truly engage. False bravado produced sneers on their bruised and bloodied faces, but fear still lingered in their twitching eyes. If it would not have left Rogue undefended, Bialig would have lunged at two or three of the fools and finished them off.

Instead, he called out, "Let the others go. This is between you and me."

"Bialig—*Mira-Natamos*—please. End this conflict now. These people are not our enemies," Misko said.

"What the hell are you talking about, Misko? They attacked and kidnapped us," Rogue shot back.

"You do not understand, Rogue. This is not your world, and these people simply want the chance to be accepted the same as you."

"I'm all for acceptance, my friend, but violence and coercion are not the way to achieve it."

"Please listen to what they have to say. Their ideas are good and worthy to be incorporated into our belief system."

"Are we seriously going to have a philosophical debate here?"

A decrescendo of laughter seeped from the shadows. Rogue's muscles retracted at the strangled sound. Behind him he felt Bialig shudder. Neither took their eyes off the *sojabosne* still pacing a nervous circle around them.

A voice dry as death called out, "For one who is supposed to uphold the law, you have failed in your duty, Bialig."

Rogue peered into the darkness beyond the fire trying to identify the speaker whose mouth raked every word with claws of contempt.

"You speak the language of the *umane* as if it was your own, and you bring one to our world against the ruling of the High Council of Elders?"

"I will not justify my actions to you, Kolbian," Bialig said.

"Oh no, highly favored one, I would not expect you to do so. You alone may act outside the laws governing our people. But tell me, how is it that the *uma* takes your side while Misko understands the path of the *Kidtiana Tagne*?"

"No one abandoned you. You chose corruption over lawfulness and embraced ideals that threatened our way of life. You were free to go away and practice your evil, but you chose to stay and disrupt life for everyone."

"And why should we be forced to leave our families and Clans?" the voice snarled. "It is time for a new order to be established. The old no longer serves our needs."

"It is not for you to decide."

"Could you not tick off this guy any more than he already is?" Rogue hissed.

Bialig spun slowly with his back to Rogue, turning to face his accuser. He heard Nish whimper in the darkness. Her gasps tore at him.

"Face me, Kolbian, and let the others go."

"You are not in charge here, Bialig. I choose who lives or dies."

Nish emerged first from the cloak of night, held as a shield in front of the man taunting them. Visible over her shoulder was the damaged face of the person Bialig distrusted more than anyone. The smiling mouth and one dancing eye belied the wrath within fueling the man's hatred.

"Hurt her and I will blind your other eye as I did the first," Bialig said. "I should have killed you when I had the chance."

"Greetings, brother," Kolbian said.

CHAPTER TWELVE

TALJ RESTED DEEP WITHIN THE recesses of his mind. The old Healer had slipped away as soon as the *sojabosne* put their hands on him, roughing him up with shoves, yanking him back and forth. The ropes came out and Talj disappeared. He timed it to land on the soft sand and sparse grass, faking his faint in a place that would leave the fewest bruises on his time-worn body. He figured he would have a few when he awoke, but at least he would be spared the causes if not the effects.

The skill would not help anyone but him, but it was the only way he had to save himself and hopefully preserve the *Doh s'Ima*. He could not defend himself or the others with combat skills the way Bialig could, and he was not as young and sturdy as Nish and Misko. So, he turned his thoughts inward in such a way that took his consciousness deep within his mind. Deeper than ordinary people could go, deeper even than other *Thedanosne*.

From this safe place, Talj maintained a slower rhythm of breathing and heartbeats. His body cooled with his lowered pulse, and he could not be woken. He was fully conscious inside his own mind, living in hopes and desires, revisiting memories and dreams, skirting fear and heartbreak. Sound from the outside came to him as an echo from across a great divide. This was how he knew Bialig had returned and rescued Rogue. Now the clash of metal upon metal assailed his senses, and behind his closed eyes he could feel the flash of light from the crashing blades.

The tearful voice of Nish beckoned Talj from his self-imposed slumber. Her hands felt cool and soothing on his face, his head in her lap. Rogue cut through the ropes around his hands and feet, trying to be careful, apologizing every time he nicked Talj's skin. Misko straightened his legs and helped him sit up. He heard, he saw, he felt. Groggy but relieved to have his loved ones around him, Talj's asymmetrical smile reassured his friends that he was going to be all right.

"Bialig?"

Talj's question drew more tears into Nish's voice. "We must go, *Mir*-Talj, to the cave where all our things are hidden."

"I don't like this," Rogue said. "I'm not okay with leaving him here to fight these people alone."

Rogue's statement told Talj more than Nish's had. No one said anything more as they helped him to his feet. Nish and Misko made a seat by holding each other's forearms. Talj lowered himself and hooked his arms around their necks. They labored a little but managed to lift him. Rogue led the way as he was the only one who knew where to find the dry riverbed.

"What of the others?" Talj asked.

"Bialig killed most of them. Those left received many wounds." Nish's voice was strained from Talj's weight. She and Misko shuffled their feet so as not to trip.

"We could go back to help once Talj is safely in the cave," Misko said, his voice winded.

"Shut up and conserve your energy," Rogue said. "I don't trust that the five we didn't kill won't break the agreement and come after us. I don't like this any better than you, but it's what Bialig said to do."

Uncertainty wavered Rogue's voice. He ran ahead of them, stopping often to hurry them along with harsh words, occasionally running back the way they came to ensure that no one followed. He still had Bialig's knife tucked between his arm and body. It was of the utmost importance that he returned the weapon to the Leader.

After many stops and starts, Rogue led them to the edge of the waterless riverbed. Nish and Misko panted hard, and Talj insisted on walking the last part under his own power. The younger two wanted to set their companion down; their arms felt stretched beyond limits, but they did not trust his poor eyesight and tottering gait, especially when their own feet stumbled over the cracks in the fractured earth.

Rogue left the knife with Misko and ran ahead to find the cave Bialig had spoken of. He scrambled down the side of the deteriorating bank, assuming a cave big enough to hide Realmers would be obvious. He called back to the other three to wait above and rest until he found it, all the while wondering how they would get Talj down the steep sides.

He ran along the left side of the deep channel, expecting to see the cave at any moment. For the first time, he noticed the lightening gray skies, and fear gripped his heart at the thought of failing his friends. His search followed the course of the extinct river, taking him around a bend and out of sight of the others. He stopped when the barren waterway ended at a vertical drop, the bottom of which he could not see.

The darkness below pinned Rogue to the dry land, sucking him downward, and miring him in defeat. His chin dropped to his chest, and he swore under his breath. He wanted to fall forward and end this nightmare, but his own irrational thoughts angered him. His frustration breathed new life into his determination to protect Misko, Nish, and Talj. Thirty more seconds passed in which the smuggler tried to align his thoughts with the course of action Bialig would have taken. The only problem was, Bialig knew the exact location of the cave and did not have to improvise.

Dawning came with the sun over the horizon, and Rogue laughed to himself. Of course, Bialig knew where the cave was because it actually existed. He would not have sent Rogue on a foolish pursuit to hopefully find some place to shelter his *Doh s'Ima*. Rogue returned the way he had come, but this time he explored the right side of the riverbed, sixty feet across the channel of cracked earth and becoming more visible in the increasing light.

"Where are you going?" Misko called as he watched Rogue run along the far side.

The gambler threw a hand upward in response and continued his exploration. Ahead, Rogue spied a fold in the rock wall forming the right side of the arid river bottom. He rounded the bulge, expecting to find the mouth of the cave. His hands smacked cold, dry stone as he came to an abrupt halt. Refusing to concede the quest, Rogue raised his eyes to the precipitous cliff.

"If down doesn't work, try up," Rogue shouted over his shoulder to Misko as he began climbing, dislodging loose stones, and sending purple lizards with topaz eyes scurrying.

Rogue ascended the water-hewn bank, his hands and feet finding purchase on staggered layers of rock too perfect to have been cut by the river alone. As he climbed, he realized the pleat extended above what had been the surface of the vanished river. Hidden within the rock wall's stony creases was a cleft big enough for a Realmer to enter. Past the opening crevice a cave expanded as if giant lungs had blown air into a balloon. How Bialig knew this existed amazed Rogue. All that mattered was getting the other three inside.

"It's here, over here," Rogue shouted, jumping and waving his arms.

He descended and traversed the parched ground to guide the others to the place of refuge. Helping Talj navigate the downward climb landed all four in a heap at the bottom, but the promise of safety kept them pressing forward.

From a distance, Rogue could see for the first time the steps he had climbed to reach the cave high above, concealed in plain sight because they were meant for the stride of a Realmer. As if speaking the gambler's thoughts, Talj said, "Our ancestors must have used this river for immersion. Incense and anointing oil would have been stored in the cave."

Rogue, too thirsty and anxious to inquire, assumed Talj spoke of some ceremony. His only concern was to get the old *Thedanos* up the steps and within the cave.

Once inside, Nish and Misko propped Talj against one wall and collapsed on either side of him. Rogue kept bouncing between his friends and the opening to keep lookout. When she finally caught her breath, Nish crawled to where their packs had been stowed and found her skin bag. She offered a drink to Talj first, then Misko.

"Here," she said to Rogue as he stood guard, "take a drink."

"I'm fine. Take care of the others."

"I did. When was the last time you had any water?"

"What about you? You first."

Rogue guided the opening toward her mouth, cradling the weight of the skin bag in both arms.

"There you go, easy now. See, you were thirsty, too," he said.

The tight lines around Nish's eyes relaxed as she drank. Rogue watched as exhaustion crept over her frame, dragging her shoulders down and bowing her head. He quickly capped the bag and set it down, bracing himself in case she fainted. She leaned her arms heavily on his shoulders, touched her forehead to the top of his head. He called for Misko when he felt her tremble, and together they guided her toward Talj. The old man opened his arms to receive her, and each fell asleep in the embrace of the other.

"We should use Nish's striking stones to start a fire," Misko said.

"No, the cave isn't quite big enough. We'd choke from the smoke in no time. Besides, once it reached the top, it would slip out the opening and attract someone," Rogue said.

"Oh, I had not thought of that." Misko's brows knotted several times, drawing his features into a tangle of anxiety. "What if we took the knife Bialig left you and went back to—"

"No—no, we can't. Bialig specifically said that we should stay here, and that's what we're going to do."

"But what if he is dead?"

The question whipped Rogue's head from the opening where he had been shielding his eyes from the rising sun, watching for Bialig's silhouette to appear.

"He isn't dead. How the hell can you even ask something like that?" Rogue peeked around Misko to where Nish sat sleeping. "You can't think like that, all right? I'm doing my best to keep the three of you safe because that's what Bialig wanted. Please don't make this any harder."

Misko pressed his fists to his temples, sliding his hands around to grind the heels into his eyes. He chose his words carefully as he said, "You have to know that Bialig is outnumbered, and even for a warrior as capable as he, there is no withstanding Kolbian and five other *sojabosne*."

"You think I haven't thought of that?"

"Then if you think there is no point in going back to help, let us gather our things and—"

"—we're staying put—"

"—travel on to the *Avboeth*—"

"I said *no*."

Rogue's command repeated off the cave walls with fading strength, disturbing Nish's and Talj's slumber. He grabbed Misko below the elbow and led him from the cave. They stood in the shadow of the folded rock in case an enemy was on the lookout.

"Listen, kid, I like you, but you have got to stop stirring the pot, okay? And I don't know what was going on with you back there at the kidnappers' camp but leave it alone. You can't always be in charge, or maybe ever because of the way you guys are, but that's not the point. You have to follow directions in a bad situation, or you just end up making it worse. Believe me, I know. I'm trying to come up with something that will keep you guys safe and only then will I go look for Bialig."

"Why do you get to go?"

"Seriously? Do you not get it, Misko? You guys are too special to run the risk of getting killed."

"But Bialig may already be . . ."

"Yeah, I know, but that's the other thing you're missing. He made the sacrifice so that you three could live. I don't know, maybe your *Doh s'Ima* is already screwed, but if not, I am absolutely not putting your lives in jeopardy. I will not dishonor him that way."

Misko flinched as if punched, thrusting his jaw and looking away. Rogue softened toward the youth and said, "I'm expendable in a way you're not. I get your enthusiasm—really—and how you want to cross-train and explore new ideas, but you must do it in a way that's right for everybody, okay? Now is just not the time, Misko."

Another chin thrust from Misko signaled the end of the conversation, and he slipped back inside the cave. Rogue did not know if the Artist's actions were in agreement with or defiance of his request, but it surprised him to find that he actually cared. He would make it up to Misko somehow, maybe find his lost *slele*. For now, Rogue pushed all other thoughts aside in the hopes of coming up with a plan to find Bialig. He kept coming back to the only option of returning to the *sojabosnelo* camp.

"The sun is up, so I've lost the cover of darkness," Rogue began by way of an explanation to the others.

Nish and Talj nodded, their heads clouded with sleep. Misko sat silent with his arms draped over drawn up knees.

"What I'm saying is it doesn't make sense to waste any more time sitting here. I'm going to look for Bialig back at the kidnappers' camp. I'll be careful not to give away your location or get myself caught." He paused, kneeling before the others and drawing his fingers through the sand on the cave floor. “If I don’t come back or Bialig doesn’t show up in a reasonable amount of time, I suppose you can assume the worst. I’m not your Leader, but my advice is to stay here and rest until night. Then get yourselves to the closest Clan. They’ll know what to do.”

Talj’s arms tightened around Nish, stopping what would probably have been her protest of Rogue’s departure. Misko turned his head toward the back of the cave and stared into the blackness. Wanting to say something more, and yet knowing there were no words to lessen their worry, Rogue stood and left the cave without looking back.

The three sat in the cool silence with their ears straining to hear the sand and rock shift beneath Rogue’s feet, the sound fading the farther he walked. When nothing but the song of birds and wind whispered in the cave, Talj eased away from Nish and crawled toward the opening. He did not exit the cave but rather plunked himself down where the most light came in. His knotty fingers explored the surface of the walls, pausing over patches of scaly, sage green moss.

“Nish, my knife.”

She complied and sat next to Talj as the old Healer scraped pieces of the moss from the walls into his palm.

“What is it, *Mir*-Talj?” she asked.

The old Healer paused to face the younger woman. His face twisted with a sympathetic smile as his eyes grazed the shag of hair framing Nish’s face. She blushed under his intense gaze and turned away until he drew her face back with a hand to her chin.

“I believe it is the cure for the poison trapped in Rogue’s body.”

* * *

ROGUE WAS HALFWAY BACK TO the *sojabosnelo* camp before his emotions transitioned from worry to anticipation. Despite his diminutive size—a fact that did not lend much confidence—he promised himself he would find a way to exact revenge on the kidnappers. Especially the one called Kolbian who, he just remembered, was Bialig's brother. At least that was how he had addressed Bialig. Whether or not Kolbian meant it as a taunt between Leaders, Rogue could not say. But he did not care.

The noise of a skirmish sent Rogue ducking for cover behind one of the many boulders wedged into the terrain. He eased himself around the circumference of the massive rock with Bialig's knife held in front of him. The ground sloped downward sharply into a natural basin, and several tense minutes passed before Rogue saw the heads of two Realmers who were fighting. He did not have long to observe the scene before the one with a lion's mane of white hair thrust his sword into the stomach of the other.

"*Bialig—*," Rogue shouted.

The *Doh s'Ima* Leader gripped his opponent by the hair, holding the dead man in place until he withdrew his sword and dropped the body. In a single move, Bialig turned and swept Rogue behind the boulder with his arm around the smaller man's waist, winding Rogue from the force of impact.

"Do you always make so much noise, *uma*?"

Rogue pushed the big man's arm away and punched him feebly in the stomach.

"I'm just glad to see you're still breathing. I'm sick of babysitting your *Doh s'Ima*."

"They are alive?"

"Of course they are. What did you think I'd do? You said go to the cave, so that's what I did."

Bialig leaned against the boulder and slid into an awkward sitting position with a great sigh. For the first time, Rogue took in the blood and bruises mottling his face, the clothing torn by weapons leaving behind more cuts and gashes on the big man's arms, legs, and torso. He knelt beside the Leader, wishing he had thought to bring Nish's water skin.

"The *sojabosne* held to the agreement to fight me one at a time, and as I was killing the third *sojabos*, Kolbian sent the remaining two after you and the others," Bialig said.

"I'm surprised they didn't jump you all at once."

"Kolbian wanted me distracted with worry while I fought."

"How did that go?"

The muscles in Bialig's jaw quivered as he moaned softly.

"I'm sorry," Rogue said.

"I did not think I could beat him. He was strong and skilled and so full of hatred. But I did not kill him."

"What the hell do you mean you didn't kill him?"

"My brother . . ." Bialig paused to allow Rogue to absorb the information. ". . . fled before I could deliver the killing blow, so I turned my attention to stopping the *sojabosne* coming for you and my *Doh s'Ima*."

"He ran and let you leave?"

"I now believe it was his intention all along. Kolbian's mind does not work like yours or mine. I have no doubt he orchestrated this encounter from the start."

"What makes you so sure?"

"Shortly before you arrived, Rogue, I saw flashes of light from the mountains—people signaling to each other. And there were footprints that did not belong to my *Doh s'Ima* around a watering hole where I hunted. And Nish heard the cry of an *olate* on the wind."

"So what? People can signal for all sorts of reasons, the footprints could have been old, and I don't even know what an *olate* is."

Bialig sighed. "The coded flashes of light signaled an imminent attack, water was still seeping into the footprints, and *olatene* do not live in this region."

"Oh, crap," Rogue said. "You didn't tell your *Doh s'Ima*, did you? No, of course you wouldn't. That would worry them. So, what about the last guy? I saw you kill one, but isn't there another?"

"No, Kolbian's *sojabosne* are all dead."

"Then we're in the clear. It doesn't matter what they did before. They were sloppy and got their butts handed to them."

Bialig tentatively pressed his palm to the cut on his cheekbone, wincing when he touched the blood crusted in the wound. His gray eyes rose from the desert floor to meet Rogue's.

"We are being hunted."

CHAPTER THIRTEEN

THERE WAS NO LEANING ON Rogue as Bialig walked to the cave where his *Doh s'Ima* hid. The best the *uma* could do was to shoulder the burden of Bialig's spears. To his credit, Rogue did not flinch at the sight of the bloodstained weapons. The Leader carried his sword and two knives. His bow had been damaged beyond repair when he used it to break the neck of a *sojabos*, and the threat presented by Kolbian prevented the return to the *sojabosnelo* camp to retrieve arrows from the bodies of the dead.

Even under the weight of Bialig's two spears, Rogue appeared comfortable walking in the bright sunlight. Bialig's clothes showed dark stains down his chest and back, beneath his arms. The Leader panted and kept reaching for where his drinking skin would hang had they been traveling. He saw Rogue watching him peripherally under the guise of shifting his grip on the spears.

"I want to thank you for helping me fight the *sojabosne*. Especially the one woman you killed," Bialig said between dry, hard breaths. The dignified tone of the comment contradicted the words and made Rogue smile.

"Would you like to lie down before you pass out from the non-existent heat of this world and your minor wounds? Maybe take a nap before the last five steps that put us at the cave entrance?" Rogue replied.

Bialig's snort and Rogue's chuckle drew the heads of Nish and Misko from the cave opening. Shock painted their anxious faces. Nish melted into tears of relief while something indefinable crept into Misko's eyes at the sight of their injured Leader. Rogue recognized it as the look in Red Humphries's eyes when he realized he had lost the Rite of Passage poker game.

Talj joined the others at the entrance as they guided Bialig to a place within the cave where he could rest. The old Healer and Nish sprang into action, removing the blood and sweat-stained clothing from their Leader. Rogue brought the drinking skin and raised it to Bialig's mouth. Only Misko hung back, sitting across the cave with his back to the wall, long arms circling his knees on which he rested his forehead.

As Talj's and Nish's hands rushed to wash and stitch cuts, to apply balms and bandages, to encourage sips of a medicinal brew, Bialig's eyes never left the top of Misko's bowed head. When the youth finally looked up, Rogue wondered again if the Realmers were telepathic. The wordless transaction he witnessed between the Leader and the young Artist reawakened a familiar longing.

Instead of anger and judgment hardening Bialig's expression, his gray eyes were soft and liquid with a quality unfamiliar to Rogue. It was the look he would have liked to receive from the older kids at Mother Jean's orphanage when he had screwed up. The look he would have preferred to the head smacks given by other young street toughs as he made a name for himself.

Talj and Nish worked swiftly, missing what passed between Bialig and Misko. Nish interrupted Rogue's observation when she knelt in front of Bialig, breaking the connection between the Leader and the Artist. As if seeing her for the first time, Bialig's breath caught at the sight of her jagged tresses. He quickly realized his mistake and leaned forward to place his hand on her blushing cheek. She turned her face toward his palm, closing her eyes as Bialig's fingers slipped into the white shag framing her face.

Tell her she's still beautiful, Rogue thought. Still unsettled from what had transpired between Bialig and Misko, Rogue did not know what to think of the scene between the Leader and Gatherer. He could not explain his anger when Bialig withdrew his hand from Nish as if he had been burned.

"We will camp here tonight," Bialig said to cover his embarrassment.

"I thought you said we're being hunted," Rogue replied.

The other three Realmers looked at Rogue first, and then to Bialig for answers. The Leader groaned and pushed himself up from the ground. He rummaged through his pack for fresh clothing, allowing Rogue's question to hang in the air.

"We are safe here. There is plenty of wood in the riverbed to build a fire and prepare food, *Mir*-Nish. I regret I was unable to take an animal before the *sojabosne* . . ."

Bialig finished dressing without further comment. As before the kidnapping, all four fell into the comfort of routine. Nish and Misko exited the cave first, carrying all four packs. They started setting up camp in the dry riverbed. Talj performed a final inspection of Bialig's wounds, patted him on the shoulder, and followed his younger companions. Rogue stood with his arms rigid, fists clenched, waiting for Bialig to say something.

"I thought you said we're being hunted. I assumed you meant by Kolbian. That is what you meant?"

"Rogue, you need to show more caution, more tact when speaking with people."

Rogue barked a cynical laugh and said, "You mean lie to them creatively? I don't think so. If there's one thing I've learned on Earth, it's—"

"And what have you learned in our world?" Bialig's words echoed off the cave walls, his slate-colored eyes frozen over with the glaze of protectiveness. "Yes, Kolbian will track us. He probably knows where we are this very moment, but I know his methods, and he will not strike tonight."

"You're sure about that?"

"Yes, Rogue, I am. My brother prefers to keep me guessing, worrying as I wait for him to decide when and where he will launch his attack. But first he must regroup with other *sojabosne* and convince them to join him in this foolish mission."

"What does that word mean anyhow?"

"*Sojabosne*? Thieves."

"Because they steal stuff?"

"Because every crime they commit is a form of theft. Against us and ultimately against the Infinite One."

"What's the deal with your brother? Why does he hate you so much?"

A cloud of pain shadowed the landscape of Bialig's face at the word "hate." He shook his head to banish the memory, but he could not erase the lines of stress at the corners of his eyes.

"Kolbian lost his way when he accepted the beliefs of the corrupt *umane*," he said, his voice softening. "No writings exist of their beliefs, yet the younger generations have been deceived by their behaviors and thoughts which are whispered among our people. The High Council hoped to stop this problem before it affected the Clans, but it is a battle we fight every day."

"What does that have to do with him hating you?"

"Walk with me," Bialig said, leading Rogue out of the cave and away from the camp. He threw a wave in the air to Nish when he saw her sit up and watch them out of sight.

"Kolbian had hopes of being a *Doh s'Ima* Leader. Our Clan believed Talj would be a member, and Nish proved her abilities with her second sight. My older brother displayed potential as a *Natamos*, and I respected him enough to serve him as a *Fayos*, a Second, to follow his direction.

"But Kolbian was impatient. He tried to force a *Doh s'Ima* with a young woman whose skill as *Paten* looked promising. The four could not open the portal when they joined hands. Kolbian was furious; he blamed Talj, especially when he found out Talj had doubted the young woman's abilities all along.

"Talj tried to calm him, but my brother believed that he had missed his chance to lead. He tried to lure Nish away. I did not know then that he wanted her for a *nosem*."

Rogue shook his head at the word.

"A wife," Bialig continued. "Talj remained vigilant in his search for a *Paten* to join him, Kolbian, and Nish. But then, at the behest of a Clan Mentor called Eben, Talj's focus shifted, and he began to include me in discussions concerning the *Doh s'Ima*. The whole Clan waited, led by any remaining Seconds and Mentors appointed by the former *Doh s'Ima*. It was many cycles of the moons before Misko demonstrated the requirements of a *Paten*. Shortly after, Talj invited me, Nish, and Misko to his dwelling. I suspected his intentions by then.

"As soon as we joined hands, I sensed something unlike anything I had ever experienced. Nish used her second sight to see into Earth, the portal opened, and we crossed over. We stayed only a few moments as Talj was excited to return to our world and inform our Clan that a *Doh s'Ima* had been formed."

"How'd your brother take it?"

"How do you think? When we repeated our unified abilities for the Clan, he became enraged and attacked Talj immediately upon our return. My first act as *Natamos* was to defend our *Thedanos*. Kolbian lost an eye in the fight. It seemed fitting for the one he had cost *Mir*-Talj. My second act as *Natamos* was to exile my brother forever from our Clan.

"Kolbian lived on the fringe. He became a bad influence, as he spoke highly of the dishonorable *umane*, demanding that anyone be part of a *Doh s'Ima* whether they could open the portal or not. He believed the members should have the right to charge for their services instead of working for the good of the Clans. He set up secret camps where cross-training of skills took place."

"And this is bad because?"

"The command to not pursue skills outside of those revealed to the individual by the Infinite One maintains the purity of our abilities. This helps us recognize *Doh s'Ima* members early in life. Obviously, Nish can use a knife, I could draw a picture, Misko can apply a bandage, and Talj can build a fire. There is limited crossover so that life goes smoothly. But it is when we choose not to embrace who we are as created by the Infinite One and perform what we are called to do that chaos ensues.

"To some degree, every Clan member has a calling that falls under the organization of Leader, Gatherer, Artist, or Healer. Peace is achieved when members work in harmony."

"So your God assigns your roles?"

"No, Rogue. But we closely align ourselves to Him and accept His guidance in all areas of our lives. Why anyone would willingly walk away from such perfect union is a mystery to me."

"But the cross-training didn't make any of them truly *Dohne s'Ima*?"

Bialig hummed at Rogue's proper use of the plural.

"No, it only served to frustrate those who chose that path. The ones who were already dissatisfied with their lives became bitter and turned to the use of mind-altering substances to fake the experiences they sought. They tried to exert their will by forcing their way into roles where they possessed no skill. They refused to work together, to take responsibility for their own actions, and to abide by the instruction of the Infinite One."

"Then you were right to kick him out?"

"Yes, but Kolbian still has influence within our Clan."

Bialig turned back toward the camp.

"You're talking about Misko," Rogue said. "I noticed he was rather chummy with Kolbian's crew. How old is he anyway?"

"Two hundred and thirty cycles of the moons."

"You're kidding."

"That is young for our people. He is old enough to be on his own, but too young to consider marriage. When he first joined the *Doh s'Ima*, he was excited and proud. Over time, the commitment and responsibilities have weighed on him. He sees his friends living what he believes to be a freer life, and together with the teachings of people like Kolbian, his mind becomes confused, his heart divided."

The two men finished their conversation as they returned to the camp. Nish had food and drink prepared. She served everyone, taking pleasure in managing her *Doh s'Ima*. The group ate in silence and contentment despite the threat hanging over their heads. All except Misko, who gulped his food and requested permission to take a walk.

"Just over the edge of the riverbed, please *Natamos*," the young man said. He kept pulling at the long sleeves of his tunic.

"Stay within sight," Bialig replied.

Rogue knelt a short distance from the fire and scoured out his eating bowl. He lifted his eyes but not his head as he watched Misko remove something from his pack and tuck it in his belt. If he had not been looking for it, Rogue would have missed Misko's furtive actions. But he had seen, and so he watched to see where Misko went.

Following Bialig's instructions, Misko did not stray too far. Rogue could see him over the edge of the riverbed, and he made a mental note to walk in the same direction if the chance arose. The gambler recognized Misko's actions as those of someone trying to discard something. While he did not exactly mistrust Misko, he felt compelled to keep an eye on him for his own sake. After a few moments in one place, the young man ambled off in the opposite direction, pretending to be interested in the rock formations. *What an amateur*, Rogue thought.

"I don't want to cause undue alarm, but how are we supposed to defend ourselves tonight?" Rogue asked.

"We will post a guard throughout the night," Bialig said.

"By 'we' you mean you and me?"

"And me," Nish added.

"No, *Mir*-Nish, you need to rest after your ordeal."

"And what about you, *Natamos*?"

Nish's voice carried a depth of concern, not defiance, and Bialig's chest swelled with more than admiration for her courage.

"What about Misko?" Rogue asked. "He was pretty handy with a spear killing that lizard."

"I am reluctant to put a weapon in his hands right now when he is so confused about his role in our *Doh s'Ima*," Bialig said.

"True, and he's not expendable like me."

"We never thought of you that way," Nish said. She helped Talj settle on his sleeping furs and covered the old Healer. The two made eye contact, and Talj nodded. "Rogue, I have good news for you. Talj believes he has found the cure for the poison in your body."

So much had happened in the brief time since Rogue had crossed over to the Realm that he could not quite process what Nish had said. When his problems became bound up with those of the Realmers, he had forgotten the matter as well as his return to Earth.

"Oh, okay."

"I will make it into a paste and put it in your food," Talj said. "If I am right, the medicine is strong, and it will make you sick in your stomach. Maybe dizzy or tired."

"Then there's no hurry to take it."

All three Realmers looked at their human friend with the same scrutiny they would an unknown species.

"I thought your sole desire was to be healed and leave our world," Bialig said.

"It was—it is . . . it's just that if I'm needed on guard duty tonight, it probably wouldn't hurt to wait until we're all somewhere safe. I don't want to be tossing my cookies should Kolbian . . . you know."

Bialig nodded his approval and understanding. He was cautious but hopeful of Rogue's selfless actions, but the strain in his shoulders returned when Misko walked back into camp. The young man had several small items in his hand, tossing them lightly and inspecting them.

"What do you have, Misko?" Nish asked.

"*Mochenne* for grinding and mixing with oils to create my paints."

"You will have quite a scene to paint at the *Avboeth* this time."

"Do you really think I should record what happened with the *sojabosne*?"

"Is that not part of the *Patenlo* role? To capture the good with the bad?"

Bialig watched Misko, his mouth a taut line. If Nish knew what he suspected, she would not have persisted in this line of questioning. The Leader did not want any of the unprincipled beliefs of the *sojabosne* represented in the murals at the *Avboeth* for fear that it might generate questions from other young *Doh s'Ima* members.

"Why don't you do something about Nish's hair?" Rogue said to Misko.

The Realmers enjoyed a more discreet approach to sensitive matters. They were still unused to Rogue's directness, and they winced as if he had slapped Nish across the face, then laughed. Sensing his social gaffe, Rogue pulled out the hand knife he had stolen from Nish and offered it to Misko. Bialig exhaled slowly, his frustration with the *uma* rumbling in his throat as a groan trying to punch its way past his lips. Once again, Nish met the Leader's eyes with a gentleness of expression and a pleading shake of her head.

"Why me?" asked Misko. "I have never cut hair."

"Because you're the *Paten*," Rogue said. "And I'm on guard duty."

"Wait for me," Bialig said, heaving himself from the ground where he had been resting.

"Shouldn't you take it easy a little longer? You're still pretty banged up."

The Leader shifted a couple bandages on his arms to show Rogue the cuts beneath were already healed and turning into pale scars.

"Damn," Rogue said. "What the hell kind of medicine did Talj put on you?"

"The same medicine he used to heal the gash on your cheek when we brought you over. The same cures the *umane* from long ago wanted to sell to those suffering on Earth."

Rogue's fingers drifted to the long-forgotten cut on his cheek from where Blast had hit him in the warehouse. He did not have long to consider what his own scar looked like as Bialig grabbed his sword and stalked off toward the other side of a dam of fallen trees and rocks across the riverbed.

"Hey, do you mind if I bring one of these along?" Rogue asked as he picked up one of the Leader's hunting knives midstride and jogged to catch up. Bialig replied with a two-finger wave over his shoulder in the direction he was walking, so Rogue assumed he had permission.

Nish watched the two men assume post on top of a large boulder from which they could see danger coming in any direction. Then she banked the fire for the night, checked on the already snoring Talj, and presented herself to Misko for the first haircut she had ever had in her life.

"I can sharpen the edge if it needs," she said.

"I do not believe Rogue had the chance to use it, so the edge is still quite sharp. I apologize now for how this may turn out," Misko said as he settled Nish before the fire and sat behind her, his fingers combing through her shortened hair.

"It could not look any worse than it already does. I can feel a hole at the back of my head where Sheliza cut my braid."

Misko let out a small gasp. "You knew her?"

"Yes, *Mir*-Misko, I knew her from long ago when she was a skilled *paten* who designed her own skin art, developed her own ink."

Misko began pulling the knife through small sections of Nish's hair to even up the length. He paused and asked, "How did she end up with Kolbian and the *sojabosne*?" His hands resumed cutting.

"She left her Clan when her skill was not enough to secure her a position with their *Doh s'Ima*. She was always a restless spirit, impatient and unwilling to take instruction as a *Fayos*. She believed the lies Kolbian told her about forming a new kind of *Doh s'Ima*. In time, her heart followed another path, and they became *pumalosne*."

"What transpired between them was not love."

"Well, no. Everything he did was for selfish reasons, but Sheliza was blind to that, too. You witnessed how hard the *sojabos* life was on her. On all of them."

Conversation ceased as Misko trimmed Nish's hair around her ears, leaving short locks in front of them, and created a thatched fringe of bangs. The back of her hair could only be repaired by cropping it closely to the curve of her head. At least he was able to leave it longer on top.

Finally, Misko asked, "Did Talj put medicine on Rogue's wrists when he first came over?"

"No. I saw the scars, too. I do not know what they are from, but I do know a deep cut there should have killed him." She paused. "I hope that was not his intention."

Misko nodded, understanding Nish's implication. When he finished the haircut, they crawled into their sleeping furs and fell asleep. Rogue watched them from the top of the boulder where he sat back to back with Bialig.

"I'm going to walk the perimeter," Rogue said.

Bialig nodded, and the gambler slipped over the side of the boulder. It took him a few minutes to locate the spot where Misko had wandered earlier, but he found it when moonlight glinted off what looked like broken shards of pottery coated with metallic paint. Rogue fitted the pieces back together to form a small disc. The type of item one would use to signal with flashes of light.

CHAPTER FOURTEEN

BIALIG NUDGED ROGUE AWAKE AS ice cold, saucer-sized raindrops pelted the boulder on which the two men sat. Rogue recoiled from the splash of water, wondering if everything in the Realm was bigger than on Earth. This thought quickly gave way to embarrassment at having fallen asleep on guard duty. He thought his insomnia and experience with the *sojabosne* would have kept him wide awake, yet a measure of peace had melted many of his anxieties, leaving him with a growing sense of strength and purpose.

He and Bialig climbed down the sides of the massive stone and headed for the camp, where the other three were already packing up. The fire hissed into extinction; the deluge pummeled the aroma of burning wood into the dry ground. The parched riverbed drank the shower as fast as it fell, but not fast enough.

"We need to get to higher ground before we are caught in a flood," Bialig shouted over the storm. His words died to the competing symphonies of lightning and thunder.

The Realmers jammed their arms into coats they had brought only as a precaution and threw their hooded capes over their heads. Packs found their way over one shoulder or were carried in front by both hands, and

Bialig grabbed Talj's pack. Misko draped his cloak around Rogue, who tucked Bialig's spears under his arms to drag them to safety.

"Leave them—run for the high ground," the Leader said as the water at their feet began flowing past.

"*Natamos*—the cave," Nish said.

"There is no longer a bridge between the two sides. We would be trapped when the water rose."

The floor of the riverbed welcomed its old friend water and turned into slick mud, hindering their efforts. Climbing up the sides required Misko and Rogue to pull Talj by his arms as Bialig pushed from behind. Nish ran ahead to scout a place where they could collect themselves, giving Bialig time to decide their next move. She stood about twenty yards away, waving both arms above her head.

The four men hastened to her location. No shelter existed among the boulders dotting the landscape. The few trees and wiry shrubs barely concealed Rogue, let alone four Realmers. Yet somehow, Nish managed to find a hollowed-out section in a large rock formation that required them to climb. Less than a cave or overhang, the patient hands of wind and rain combined to strike the gritty surface in a way that scooped out a bowl-shaped depression, giving the five travelers a place to shelter.

Talj and Nish stood closest to the rock wall, but Rogue could still feel the cold radiating toward him. It crept over him with another familiar but unwelcome presence. All five panted from their exertions, clearly aware that their situation was far from ideal. Rain coursed over the craggy surface outside the shallow cavity, threatening to run in and pool at their feet. Harsh winds slapped the rain into their faces, and Misko and Bialig turned their backs to the weather. Their belongings were shielded within the makeshift circle.

Rogue could not tear his eyes from the undulating sheets of water sweeping across the desert landscape. He had never witnessed a natural force of this magnitude, and it humbled and terrified him all at once. He watched the sides of the once-dry riverbed crumble and rush away, dislodging boulders near the edge as if they were marbles swept into a gutter. The voice of the storm raged for supremacy over the roar of water swelling in the riverbed.

Into this nightmare flew winged creatures Rogue could see congregating over what had been the *sojabosnelo* camp. They descended with such ferocity that he recognized them for the scavengers they were. He shuddered at the thought of the feast taking place. Nish misunderstood and pulled him into a soggy, warm embrace, tucking his head under her chin. With her head tilted downward, Rogue trusted she would not see the horror in the distance.

When the Realmers started to tremble, they instinctively drew closer to Rogue. Cold weather for them could be perilous for an *uma*. Rogue tucked his hands into his armpits and rested his chin on his chest. He chuckled to himself when thirst nagged his senses. Nothing could make him leave the shelter of bodies to open his mouth to the bounty falling from the blackened skies. Instead, he stood for what seemed like an eternity until the steady rain lulled him into a cold and restless slumber.

* * *

A NUDGE IN HIS LOWER back roused Rogue from his shallow sleep. He tried to stretch in the cramped space, rolling his neck and stamping his cold, wet feet. No sunlight penetrated the fleece of black clouds covering the skies, and he could not tell what time of day it was or how long they had been standing in the shelter. The rain had lessened but not enough to make traveling safe or pleasant.

Without bending, Nish pulled her pack up and plunged her arm to the bottom until she found the item she wanted. She opened a small, leather drawstring pouch and handed out handfuls of something granular. Rogue received his portion in both hands and sniffed at the dried berries and grains in his palms. Everyone chewed greedily but with contentment; they had not had time for breakfast. The snack did little to take the edge off their hunger, but they were grateful to Nish all the same.

Rogue savored the sweet and savory flavor, but the concoction scratched his throat when he swallowed. He did not mention the raw burn he felt with each satisfying yet painful bite nor the ache radiating into his ears. After consuming the meager meal, there was nothing else to do but continue waiting out the storm.

* * *

A RUSH OF HEAT OVER his body woke Rogue from a place where fire and water coexisted with flashes of light and the sound of explosions. The fingers of the dream slid over his face, replaced by fever, as they dragged the images back into the recesses of his mind. His senses slowly returned, and he knew that strong arms held him upright. What could only be the beat of a giant heart pounded in his ears.

"He's awake," Nish whispered.

The acknowledging grunt from Bialig told Rogue in whose arms he reclined. Still, his eyes remained closed, giving way to the earthy scents of damp rock, wet leather, and metallic rain. He ached all over, but his body lacked the energy to shiver. A taste like rust lingered on his tongue, and he tried to swallow, wincing from a sore and swollen throat. He turned his head away when icy water trickled over his lips.

"Try again," Bialig said, encouraging Nish to lift her drinking skin to Rogue's mouth.

Painful sips could not override Rogue's need for water; he gulped until he coughed. The chill woke him a little but not as much as Nish wiping his sleep-sticky eyes with a wet cloth. Rogue pushed away from Bialig and tried to stand without assistance. There was nowhere to go in the cramped space, and his legs buckled beneath him. Eight hands reached out to grasp him all at once. Dizziness danced between Rogue's temples, and he missed much of the mumbled conversation between the Realmers.

* * *

THE NEXT TIME HE AWOKE, Rogue felt his body bound to something. For a panicked moment, he believed he was back in the warehouse about to die. Movement refuted his erroneous assumption. He paused in his thinking, his agitated brain struggling to comprehend the situation, and understood the rhythmic sway was the pattern of great strides being taken. The rain still fell, darkness in the form of a fur blanket engulfed him, his arms and legs hung limp, and his head rested against a lion's mane of white hair. Despite his fever, he worked out that he was strapped to Bialig's back.

The decision to leave the shelter of stone had been made while Rogue dozed. Bialig planned to use the cover of rain to travel a more open and direct route toward the *Avboeth*; no other *Dohne s'Ima* would be foolish enough to travel in such weather. But the others had probably not been waylaid by a vengeful brother, the need to find better shelter for a sick *uma*, or were traversing a circuitous route because of the presence of an *uma* in the first place. If Kolbian wanted an opportunity in which to exact revenge on his brother, now would present the perfect scenario.

The *Doh s'Ima* Leader vacillated between trying to rectify the situation alone or seeking help from the *Jutimar* Clan, which was a one-day walk away. His friend, Eben, now resided with his wife's Clan, having married and moved. Would the old Mentor of the *Shlodane* Clan be pleased to see his former protégé, or would anger forge his bony features into a mask of disapproval when he learned what Bialig had done? Surely Eben had not lost the deep compassion he showered on Bialig when he first noticed the youth's abilities.

But no definitive answer came to Bialig as the group plodded on. He walked with his eyes cast downward, failing to notice the change in landscape from the soaked and shifting sands to the leaf and needle-strewn earth beneath his feet. He did not see Nish walking beside Talj and holding the old Healer's arm to steady him. He missed the fact that Misko had eased his way to the front of the line, leading them to who knew where. All Bialig registered were the ropes binding Rogue to his back cutting into his shoulders and torso and the waterlogged sleeping fur dripping down his neck.

Bialig's toe caught the edge of a hand-sized rock peeking through a layer of rusted needles from the boughs high above. He crashed to the ground without a sound except his breath being knocked out of him as he landed flat on his stomach, both arms thrown out before him. Rogue's weight added to the force of impact. The drumming rain kept the others from hearing him; they walked on for the time it took their Leader to gather himself.

Bialig leaned on his forearms to lessen the weight on his back and to gulp air into his lungs. He pushed up on both abraded and stinging palms and drew one bruised knee beneath him. Finally, he pulled his other leg forward, wincing as pain shot through his ankle. When he raised his head, his *Doh s'Ima* was veiled in a curtain of gray rain.

"*Migraes*," Bialig called, halting the others.

All three turned to look back. Nish's and Talj's faces bore expressions of surprise. Misko thrust his chin forward and observed Bialig's state through narrowed eyes. Then the young man sighed and trudged back to where the Leader knelt. He grasped Bialig by his upper arm and jerked him to his feet. Bialig staggered three steps before regaining his balance, moving his shoulders to reposition Rogue and making sure the ropes were still tight.

"*Mi tae weve*," Bialig said, nodding his appreciation as well. Misko grunted and turned to continue leading the *Doh s'Ima*. "*Tro, Misko. Bas yomeyo lieme zorlothiep.*"

Again, the young Artist stopped and scrutinized his Leader. Then he looked around to assess the quality of the location Bialig had chosen for camp that night. The branches of the trees swayed in the wind, providing no relief from the rain. They had not traveled far enough into the forest to lessen the effects of the storm. Misko turned his head away and shrugged.

Nish, however, pulled her ax from her pack and began trimming fallen branches for a frame. The *Jiltraos* motioned for Misko and Talj to help. In no time she had adequate shelter for them to weather the storm. Bialig flung the sleeping fur off and began working at the ropes binding Rogue to his back. He twisted his torso and lowered his shoulder so Rogue would slip forward, landing awkwardly in his waiting arms. Nish settled Rogue farthest from the opening, and then prepared to build a fire.

Her hands moved with artistry and grace for what she would call a simple task. And yet the substantial fire she built to warm and protect them through the night brought a wave of gratitude surging through Bialig's chest. The Leader nodded at her, amazed at how quickly Nish could create a home for them. Talj finished tending Rogue before joining his friends around the fire for a simple meal.

As they settled in for the night, Nish glanced at Misko, who had fallen into a deep sleep, and Talj, who sat upright, snoring softly with his head bowed.

"*Mira*, there is something I need to tell you about our *uma*," she said.

Bialig smiled at her from across the fire; she had claimed Rogue as the possession of their *Doh s'Ima*.

"When I held Rogue close as we huddled together, I sensed something about him that I never experienced before."

"Explain what you mean, *Mir*-Nish."

"You know I can share my second sight with members of the *Dohne s'Ima* by simply touching them when I am seeing where the Infinite One directs me. It is how you scout safe locations for us to cross over to Earth."

The Leader nodded even as his skin prickled at what he suspected was coming.

"While we waited for the rain to stop, I recalled the woman we saw in the building that was on fire. I searched for her in the rubble using my second sight. I remembered her face clearly, and as I did so, Rogue became quite agitated. It was as if he witnessed what I saw and thought about."

"Are you quite certain? He is not part of a *Doh s'Ima*. He is not even one of us."

"I have described for you how I am aware of the presence of others when they are sharing my second sight. It was the same with Rogue. I could feel him in my mind, seeing and remembering with me."

There was no point in telling Nish that the scenario she relayed was impossible, and Bialig knew she would never fabricate such a tale. In truth, he really did not know what to say about it.

"Please keep this to yourself until I can determine if there is any importance to it."

"Of course, *Mir*-Bialig."

For all his weariness, Bialig could not fall asleep. He would have enjoyed one of Misko's soothing songs, but he spent the night listening for sounds incongruous with the steady rain, anything to indicate his brother's presence. By morning, the rains had abated, and small animals and insects added their voices to the still, saturated dawn. Nish, already awake, had the fire stoked and gathered edible greens outside their shelter. Bialig packed quietly so as not to awaken the other three. He slipped out with rope for a snare.

Talj awoke and checked on his patient. Rogue's red-rimmed eyes opened. His grimace indicated pain and understanding; he willingly swallowed the doses of medicine the old Healer gave him. Doses meant for a child of the Clans. It concerned Talj that he had never tended a sick *uma*, that he was unsure of the correct amounts to give Rogue. Too much might kill him, and too little would be of no effect. Once Talj had Rogue's fever under control and had healed his swollen throat, he would think about mixing the medicine meant to cure him of the poison in his body.

Misko awoke much later in the morning. From his tousled bedding he watched the three *Doh s'Ima* members and Rogue eat a *wadlo* Bialig had snared. Hunger rumbled his stomach, but resentment kept him pinned to his bed.

"Come, *Mir*-Misko," Nish said when she saw his open eyes. "I saved the legs for you; they are your favorite."

The young Artist threw back his covers and stretched, sighed, and sat up. He scratched his head, his back, and his arms before he crawled to where Nish sat with her hands extended, a full bowl of food within.

"It is cold," Misko said after his first bite. "And tough."

"Tastes pretty damn good to me, kid," Rogue said in a hoarse whisper. "Better than Talj's medicine."

Much laughter and nodding flushed the old Healer's lavender cheeks plum as he coughed, trying to speak around a mouthful of food. He pointed a gnarled finger at Rogue and said, "You will thank me for the bad tasting medicine when I cure you of the poison, *uma*."

This is how it should always be, Bialig thought as his *Doh s'Ima* laughed with ease and slipped back into the give and take that came naturally to them. The Leader smiled when he realized he had included Rogue in his observation.

Two long limbs from the shelter were lashed together and covered with a sleeping fur as a stretcher for Rogue. The gambler resisted at first, assuming he would walk now that he was awake, but Talj urged him to rest a few more days to build up strength to withstand any side effects of the cure he had yet to take. Rogue did not know what to make of the attention he received, especially when he still considered himself a constant source of irritation to the Realmers.

Rogue snuggled under the furs as the Realmers threw off their outer wrappings and settled into a comfortable pace, walking deeper into the forested landscape, with Nish at the front and Misko at the back of the stretcher. Talj planned it this way.

"*Mira*," the old Healer said as he walked next to his *Natamos*. "What were the first things Eben taught you when you accepted his invitation to instruct and guide you?"

Bialig straightened at the mention of his former Mentor. Had Talj noticed the direction they almost took?

"He spoke of the responsibilities of a *Natamos*, how he or she would best meet the needs of the *Doh s'Ima* by serving. He told me a good Leader was the first to confront danger and the last to withdraw. We worked with many tools and weapons to improve my skills. He included me in hunting parties and games meant to strengthen my mind and body. But he did not encourage any fantasy about becoming something I might not be."

His last comment was for Misko's sake in case the young man listened.

"And when you think back farther, my friend, to the time when as a child you sat on Eben's lap watching him sharpen his sword?"

Bialig's face flushed when he could not discern which lesson Talj wanted him to recall.

"All the instructions we follow in our Clans and our *Dohne s'Ima* are meant to sustain us, but they are not so rigid as to prevent us from preserving life," Talj said. "You did not break the Infinite One's commands by bringing the *uma* here, *Mir*-Bialig. You honored them by protecting his life. Whether or not the *uma* stays is another matter, but do not ever think that you were wrong to save him."

Talj's words fell like a reprieve on Bialig's conscience. Precise adherence to the instructions was one of his strengths, and while he did not lack compassion, he learned a new lesson in how to apply it where the commands were concerned.

"Also, being a good Leader does not mean that you have to do it on your own," Talj concluded.

CHAPTER FIFTEEN

SCENTS BOTH PUNGENT AND SWEET assailed Rogue's nose, and sunlight through the mesh of tree branches dazzled his eyes, leaving sparks behind when he closed his lids. The stretcher on which he lay swayed with the rhythm of Nish's and Misko's strides as the group traveled farther into the forest. The air became even cooler beneath the canopy of leaves, but Rogue inhaled every breath as if receiving the gift of life.

He obediently swallowed the medicine Talj administered during the three days it took his fever to break. Nish also plied him with special foods to restore his strength. Bialig performing the tasks he had formerly assigned the gambler finally drove Rogue from his sick bed.

Rogue loaded his arms with firewood, careful not to get bits of bark or dirt on the sleeping fur draped around his shoulders. He fetched water for Nish to cook and leaves for Talj to turn into medicine. Perspiration dotted his forehead, yet he shivered beneath the fur in the cooler climate of the Realm. Nish removed stones from his hands for a fire ring and guided him back to the stretcher she had moved into a leaf-dappled pool of sunlight.

From his horizontal position, he satisfied his need to contribute by observing the mosaic of foliage and shadows for signs of movement indicating an imminent attack. He had witnessed Bialig doing the same as they journeyed, always with a weapon in hand when the Leader was not otherwise engaged.

In this fashion, two weeks passed as they walked through the primeval forest en route to the *Avboeth*. Rogue knew that time passed differently, seemingly faster in the Realm than on Earth, but he was still shocked to learn that it would take at least an Earth year to reach the Assembly of the Groups of Four.

"This is why we only go every four cycles when the three moons align," Bialig explained.

This knowledge warred with Rogue's desire to take the cure and return to Earth versus stay with the Realmers, enjoy their way of life, and travel to see the *Avboeth*. His old nemesis depression, the sensation he registered in the shallow cave during the storm, threatened to thread its way into the fabric of his thoughts. He battled his melancholy by making a new *slele* to replace the one Misko lost at the *sojabosnelo* camp. Keeping it a surprise from the young Artist, although difficult, further lightened Rogue's mood.

He began by cleaning the shell of a long-dead aquatic animal he found near a stream. It would make the perfect body for the new instrument. He borrowed tools from the Realmers to fashion the neck and turning pegs. When it came time to assemble the instrument and add the strings, he admitted his plans to Bialig.

"I need your help with the strings. I know they'll come from some animal, but I don't have any experience with that sort of thing."

Bialig nodded and woke Rogue early the next morning for his first hunting trip. A forest-grazing animal was taken, and the Leader coached Rogue through field dressing the carcass. In the following weeks, he helped Rogue prepare the skin and the intestines as a covering and strings for Misko's new instrument. The process delayed Rogue from taking his cure.

"I did not think the *uma* would vomit every time we worked with the animal," Bialig confided to Talj.

The old Healer chuckled and said, "We will give him some time to allow his stomach to settle."

Misko watched Rogue and Bialig's furtive actions throughout the lengthy process, his face flushing every time the pair walked away to confer before working together. The Artist's jaw clenched when they did not invite him, especially when he noticed they slipped away when he was engaged elsewhere. He refused Nish's offer to walk the forest paths or explore small streams. That night around the fire, Rogue presented the new *slele* to Misko.

"It's kind of plain, without the painted carvings your other one had, but I tuned it myself, so the sound is pretty good. At least I think it is. You be the judge," Rogue said.

Color drained from Misko's face, leaving his dusky lavender visage a washed-out gray. He swallowed twice, his fingers grazing the taut strings of the instrument resting on his lap.

"This is beautiful. I did not know you possessed knowledge of music or instruments."

"Yeah, well, I fool around with a guitar back on Earth, so I figured I'd give it a try."

Mention of Rogue's musical ability shot through Nish and Bialig like lightning. They sat straighter and glanced at Talj, whose critical observation never missed anything. That night and the next morning, Misko again witnessed more private conversations that did not include him. The three Realmers failed to notice when he took his *slele* and wandered off to compose. Nor did they hear his day spent playing sharp chords in contrast with the melody of forest life.

With Bialig's permission, Nish approached Rogue at dusk and invited him on a walk. Large, moth-like insects with bioluminescent wings lit their trail. Nish held her arms in the insect's flight path for them to land softly on her hands and wrists.

"I noticed we spent today in one place. Did you bring me out here to talk about Kolbian? I know Bialig thinks I'm too blunt, but I can see you're all on edge."

"We are cautious, but no, that is not why I asked you to come."

"Then is this about me not taking the cure because I do have a reason, you know."

"No, Talj said you would take the cure when you were ready. We understand."

"So what's—"

"*Rogue*—I have something to show you."

Nish dropped to a cross-legged position, crunching leaves from another season beneath her. Rogue followed suit and sat facing her. Her long fingers enveloped his hands as fire and ice shot through his brain. He felt himself plunged beneath crashing waves of thoughts and memories not his own. Rogue sucked air into his lungs like a drowning man and felt Nish's grip on his hands tighten. Through what he could only describe as shimmering water, he saw Jessica Raine standing before him.

"What the—am I back on Earth?"

"No, Rogue. Listen. You are seeing through my second sight into Earth. I can find the woman from the warehouse wherever she is because I have seen her once."

Nish's voice came from across the cosmos. Rogue could feel her touch, sense her presence, but he could not see her. He took a step forward until Raine's face was inches from his own. Until he looked directly into her emerald eyes.

"So, I'm not really here?"

"Not in body. She cannot see you."

"Why isn't she moving?"

"Because time on Earth moves differently than where we are."

Rogue stepped to Raine's right and continued until he was standing behind her, seeing what Raine saw in the mirror before her. An oval face no longer framed by ash-blonde dreadlocks stared back at both of them. Frozen time immobilized liquid and salt on the rim of her eyes. Coils of hair littered the sink, and tiny pieces clung to her ears. One delicate hand held the silenced razor that had wrought the destruction. The palm of the other rested on the quarter-inch stubble crowning her head.

"Oh, Raine, what have you done?"

Rogue did not know how much time he had. He searched the bathroom for clues to her behavior. His eyes landed on the vanity and a HoloMir tablet projecting blueprints for Blast Tower. A precise red line marked a path in the 3D image from the basement to the suite at the top via elevator shafts and vacant offices. As his mind tried to comprehend what he saw, iridescent light wavered at the edges of his vision.

"No—*Nish*—please wait," Rogue yelled.

Nish pulled Rogue to his feet as his consciousness returned to the Realm. He felt like a fool for having screamed his plea directly in her face, but he did not have an opportunity to regret his actions.

"Listen," she said.

Shouting and the clash of weapons reached them where they stood. Smoke drifted toward them on the breeze. In the distance, a sound familiar to Rogue inched its way closer. A strange glow among the trees accentuated wraith-like shadows in the dark.

"Fire. Coming this way. *Kolbian—*," Rogue said as he took off running toward camp.

Nish and Rogue reached the camp in time to see Bialig kill a *sojabos* about to run his spear through Talj. Two other dead bodies lay in the brush.

"They are trying to burn us out. Run," Bialig shouted, pointing in the direction from which Nish and Rogue had just arrived.

There was no time to pack. Hands grabbed randomly at bedding, a weapon, a tool, an instrument, before Rogue and the Realmers escaped the ring of fire slowly encompassing the perimeter of the camp. Behind the encroaching flames walked the members of Kolbian's *sojabosne*.

The panicked group forced branches out of their way, stumbled over fallen limbs and rocks, and plowed through low bushes. Bialig feared they would become separated in their flight as they ran through the smoke-filled blackness. He kept a firm grip on Talj's arm, half-dragging, half-guiding the old Healer through the woods.

Misko and Nish quickly outdistanced the others with Rogue not far behind. When the threesome breathed cool, fresh air, they realized they had run far enough to stop and assess their situation.

"Where . . . where are . . . Bialig and Talj?" Nish asked between pants.

Misko's answer also came between ragged breaths as he bent over with his hands on his knees, head hanging.

"I do not know. I have not heard their footsteps for some time."

"I don't see them," Rogue said. He scrambled up a large outcrop and looked back in the direction of the pulsing orange glow.

"I will go back and look for them," Misko said.

"You can't do that," Rogue said. "That fire could change direction any moment, and you'd be trapped."

"I am not asking for your permission, Rogue. You are not the *Natamos*."

Nish's sharp intake of breath matched Rogue's own.

"Kid, I'm just saying—"

"I am not a child," Misko shouted. "I do not need to wait for your decision. You do not always know what is best for us. You are not even one of us."

Rogue jumped from the rock and took Misko's wrist.

"I'm not trying to tell you what to do—"

"Let go of me," Misko said, raising his arm and flinging Rogue off.

In the second Misko's upraised arm was caught in the light of the approaching fire, Rogue saw a small, red tattoo on the underside of his forearm where his sleeve rode up. His observation failed to register.

"Look," Nish shouted. She pointed to where two shadows moved among the dark tree trunks.

Rogue was afraid she had given their location away to the *sojabosne*, but in the next few moments, Talj and Bialig came into view.

"Kolbian and the others are waiting for the fire to die down to see if we are among the dead. We must go quickly and quietly," Bialig said in a voice singed by smoke.

"Can we outrun them?" Rogue asked.

"We must try."

All present understood the message. They moved as one into the deeper shadows of the forest and away from the blaze behind them. No path existed and all sense of direction had been lost. Nish led with Rogue and Misko immediately following while maintaining a strained distance from each other. Bialig brought up the rear, encouraging Talj with a rapid pace.

They made decent progress and managed to find a forest stream where they drank deeply and washed their stinging eyes. Talj sat on a rock to rest, their few rescued possessions at his feet.

"We should have stayed and fought," Misko said to no one in particular.

Rogue splashed through the stream and climbed up the embankment on the other side, stopping at the crest. The triple moons backlit his silhouette; Nish could see his balled hands on his hips, his head shaking. She chose not to tell Bialig what had transpired between Rogue and Misko.

"We did not have enough weapons, *Mir*-Misko," Bialig said. "And they were so many."

Even in the darkness Nish sensed weariness in Bialig's shrewd answer.

"Hey," Rogue called in a hoarse whisper. "You guys need to see this."

Bialig motioned for the others to stay put before he ran up the embankment to where Rogue stood pointing.

"Will that ravine take us through the woods?" Rogue asked.

Bialig squinted as clouds obscured the three moons.

"I am not as familiar with this forest as I am our usual route to the *Avboeth*. I honestly cannot say where that would lead."

"Couldn't we find shelter there to hide from Kolbian?"

"Hiding means staying in one place, and that is not an option. We should explore this path if for no other reason than to keep moving."

A meandering descent punctuated with tense moments of slipping hands and misplaced footing finally ended with the group of five safely at the bottom of the ravine. They walked between cool rock walls, away from the thrashing sounds and angry shouts of Kolbian and his *sojabosne* searching the forest. Their lack of coordination and proper leadership emboldened Rogue and the Realmers in their escape.

Quiet permeated the ravine, and they were sorely tempted to stop for rest if not sleep. Bialig pressed them on from the back of the line; his whispered encouragements gently pressured the others to keep placing one foot in front of the other.

Exhaustion hampered their steps as the first dim rays of morning caressed the edge of the narrow passage. Rogue, who had slipped into the lead, turned to look at Bialig, walking last to hustle Talj along. The Leader nodded once, and Rogue slumped against the cold stone for support before he slid into a heap. Nish and Misko, nearly asleep on their feet, took a few more steps and collapsed with sighs of relief.

Bialig helped Talj into a more dignified position than his comrades. The old Healer leaned hard against his Leader's shoulder, but sleep eluded them both.

"Permission to speak, *Mira*-Bialig?" Talj asked in a creaky whisper.

"Of course, old friend."

"You cannot outrun Kolbian forever."

"I will never allow him to harm my *Doh s'Ima*." Bialig's words came with a soft growl of warning.

"I know, but even if Kolbian killed us, he would still pursue you to until the end of days."

Golden fingers of sunlight penetrated the dense forest and crept down the jagged, moss-covered stone. It would be a clear day, and the canyon passage would no longer afford them seclusion or safety. It could become a trap if they delayed much longer.

"Are you saying the only way to stop Kolbian is to kill him, *Mir*-Talj?"

"Sometimes our enemies are closer to our heart than we care to admit."

"You think I cannot deal with my brother?"

"I know you will. But there is no way to prepare for that time when it comes."

Longing to stay in the ravine and sleep for the day teased the edges of Bialig's mind. Resolve to keep moving came from an unexpected source.

"There they are. Below us." The cry rang out from the top edge of the sheer walls.

Many faces joined the one peering over the edge, but not until Bialig looked up into the scarred face of his brother did he acknowledge fear colder than the stone against his back.

"Nish, Misko," Bialig yelled as he hauled Talj to his feet. "Wake up now. Rogue—we are in danger."

Bialig's tone breached the safety of their dreams, rousing them into action. They moved with more efficiency than he would have thought possible after the night they had endured. The few items they had salvaged from their camp were swept up on the run as they fled. Their pursuers prepared to rappel into the passage using thick vines pulled from the trees above. The weary group made it a hundred yards before the first *sojabos* landed.

Only because Rogue fell behind did he see the crevice in the rock walls. He skidded to a stop and called to Bialig, pointing frantically and waving the group back. Already out of options, the Leader retraced his steps with Talj, Nish, and Misko following. Rogue disappeared into the fissure and ran freely along the narrow path. The Realmers had to flatten themselves between the walls, shuffling sideways and bending backward with the curve of the steep sides.

At least Kolbian could not attack them directly. His only choices were to follow them into the crevice or try to outrun them to the end of the passage and cut them off. Bialig counted on the fact that his brother did not know where the end was. But then neither did he. They might have sealed their own fate; a fate in which Kolbian could take his time disposing of his trapped quarry.

Light in the passage diminished as the seam in the rock above closed over them. The Realmers reached a point they could not travel beyond. Rogue called to them from the darkness ahead.

"We can go no farther," Bialig called back as loud as he dared without revealing their situation to Kolbian.

Rogue felt his way back along the wet stone; he, too, had to flatten himself in order to pass. The first Realmer he saw in the shadowy light was Misko. Nish stood beside him, then Talj, and lastly Bialig.

"I don't think they followed us," Rogue said, trying to offer some comfort. "Do you have your sword, Bialig?"

"We dropped everything as we ran."

"We are trapped without weapons?" Misko shouted. "We will die now, *Natamos*. They will kill us without mercy. Why did you not make peace with them when we had the chance?"

"There is no making peace with animals like Kolbian," Rogue shouted back. "There is only destroying them or outsmarting them."

"I suppose you have an idea on how to do that? You have been trying to lead us for so long. Go ahead, Rogue, tell us your brilliant plan."

Rogue directed his answer to the Leader.

"You have to go to Earth, Bialig. It's the only way to save your *Doh s'Ima*."

"What about you?" Nish asked.

"I can't return because of the poison."

"No—to abandon you—"

"It's your only choice. Go to the warehouses near the place you saved me. There are many deserted ones where you can hide from humans. Then return to a safe location in the Realm."

"We cannot leave you," Bialig said.

"Kolbian doesn't know I have to stay here. He'll think I went with you. I can hide until it's safe. Just tell me where to meet you."

A heartbeat passed, then Bialig said, "Walk in the direction of the rising sun. That will put you on the path to the *Avboeth*. Nish will locate your position with the second sight, and we will come to you. Now—Misko, give me your hand."

The Realmers took each other's hands, and Bialig and Misko completed the circle by reaching over Talj's and Nish's heads. The dim light shimmered around them, a gust of icy wind rushed past, and they disappeared.

Rogue was alone in the Realm.

CHAPTER SIXTEEN

RAINE GATHERED THE TWISTED LOCKS into a pile and considered making a funeral pyre out of them, so much so that the odor of smoke escaped her mind and entered her nostrils. The first to die upon the blaze would be Frank Blast. Of this, she was sure.

In the twenty-four hours since she had sneaked away from Sister Mary Joy's convent, she had obtained a download of blueprints for Blast Tower. Her source, another GEA agent in Blast's service, was more than pleased to believe she had finally convinced Raine to align herself with the crime boss. She had died with a smug smile on her face, and the guilt of having eliminated a fellow agent still roiled Raine's stomach.

Working in Raine's favor was the fact that Blast believed she had died in the warehouse fire along with Rogue. He would never see her coming. News stations ran reports of the unfortunate death of GEA Agent Jessica Raine, who died inspecting the warehouse district for illegally shipped goods. The fabricated accounts detailed Raine's encounter with smugglers who blew up the building and escaped the Quadrant. Memorial services would be held tomorrow at the GEA Headquarters, concluding with the addition of her name to the plaque already bearing her father's and brother's.

Wet warmth trailed down the sides of Raine's face, meeting beneath her chin and dropping to the floor. She missed her father and brother, but these tears were not for them. Whatever Rogue may have been, he did not deserve to die the way he had. She only cared because she hated to see another human die so unjustly. It had nothing to do with Rogue sacrificing himself to save her, and it sure as hell had nothing to do with the unresolved feelings agitating her heart.

Raine rubbed her hand over her face and newly shorn head, blowing upward to dislodge any remaining bits of hair. Her GEA uniform lay at her feet. She stepped away from it and into the shower. Afterward, she donned a black TechMesh bodysuit with built-in body armor stolen from the GEA barracks and her GEA boots. The dead agent's hooded sweatshirt completed the transition from law enforcement to vigilante.

She tucked Theo's knife in her boot pocket and strapped her GEA blaster to her thigh. A sawed-off shotgun hitched a ride across her back beneath the sweatshirt. Into a drawstring knapsack she stuffed a BioMetric Duplicator Card used to copy an image of the dead agent's retinas and her HoloMir tablet with the blueprints for Blast Tower. She looked around a final time and closed the door behind her.

Raine was alone on Earth.

* * *

A METHOD FOR CALCULATING THE time difference between Earth and the Realm did not exist. If it had, Rogue might not have spent every moment of his self-imposed solitude wondering where the Realmers were and regretting his suggestion that sent them away.

At least recalling his escape from Kolbian brought a smile of satisfaction. Staying still in the dark crevice was all that was required to lose the disorganized, impetuous leader and his followers. Kolbian's rage upon discovering his brother had escaped him—combined with a lack of understanding as to how—echoed off the ravine walls. Several *sojabosne* lost their lives due to incompetence.

Rogue had crept from his hiding place as the triple moons reappeared for the night. He searched for Bialig's sword in the hopes of returning it; he could never have wielded it. All he found was a dirty sleeping fur and one of Nish's small stone knives. It would have to be enough.

It took Rogue ten days to walk out of the forest during which time he lamented the loss of Misko's new *slele*. Plans to make another wrestled with the realization that once he took the cure, there would be no opportunity to construct another instrument. Thoughts on how to survive without his friends suppressed both contemplations. Forest streams supplied the water he needed, and a repetitious diet of the edible plants Rogue recognized staved off his hunger. He would have enjoyed some meat, but the stone knife would never be adequate for killing a large animal, and he did not know how to make a snare.

Still, he managed to hold desperation and depression at bay. He slept well and experienced no fear from Kolbian because he knew he was not being hunted. The only precaution he took was toward the wildlife of the Realm and other Realmers traveling. He did not want to be eaten by one or seen by the other.

The forest emptied onto a plain of grasses reaching Rogue's waist. A miserly distribution of trees, their limbs bent and twisted by the iron will of the wind, reminded Rogue of Talj's ancient hands pointing him in the right direction. Birds called to each other, and herds of ruminating animals watched him pass. Respect for Bialig's wishes kept Rogue from seeking the company of other Realmers.

Except for loneliness, he enjoyed the four days he traversed the grasslands. On the fifth night out of the woods, he chanced lighting a small fire using stones similar to those Nish employed. Pleasant memories arose at the ritual of making camp; he wished someone had been present to compliment his fire building skills. He lay on the soft grass near twin trees and drifted off counting the myriad stars visible in a sky unobstructed by artificial light.

* * *

THE VOICE OF THE WIND carried the shush of grasses and murmurs of conversation. Last night's fire crackled afresh as flames lapped at grease dripping from roasting meat. His mouth watered, but he snuggled a few more minutes under his sleeping fur, sensing movement around him. Probably Bialig coming to nudge him with the toe of his boot. He was just about to throw his covers off and declare himself awake when Rogue remembered that his Realmers were on Earth.

His eyes snapped open to seven amused faces watching him as they ate meat from a spit over his fire. Rogue scrambled backward, practically inching his way up the tree behind him. The faces split with grins and laughter. The Realmer closest to him patted the air and spoke soothing words. She stood and walked toward him, choosing each step as if she anticipated a snare.

"Jedla," the woman said when she stood before him. She pointed at herself and waited to see if Rogue comprehended.

A quick assessment put the woman within range of Bialig's height. Round, ash-colored eyes stared at him from a face the shade of wisteria. Her full lips and broad nose reminded him of Misko. Her leather jerkin and short skirt showed the swell of toned muscles on her bare arms and thighs. A segmented, alabaster ponytail began at the top of her head and hung over her shoulder. Leather bracers adorned her wrists, and suede boots laced above her knees. Rogue did not see any red tattoos on her body.

His eyes scanned the other six—four men and two women—who were also hearty in stature and similar in dress. Rogue guessed they were older than Misko but younger than Nish. Every one of them wore at least two knives visibly and had either a spear or bow within reach.

"*Sojabosne*?" Rogue whispered.

The men of the group jumped to their feet, spitting what could only be a stream of expletives at Rogue's comment. Jedla glared at the remark but held her ground between them and Rogue. She spoke harshly to them, silencing their tirade. Rogue breathed easier at the thought of a woman in charge until she stepped closer and grabbed a handful of his tunic.

"Rogue—my name is Rogue. I'm a human—an *uma*—and I know Bialig, *Natamos s'hel Doh s'Ima*."

Jedla gasped and released him. The others gathered closer; their gray eyes widened with wonder. Whether at his knowledge of their language or familiarity with Bialig, Rogue could not say. They conferred among themselves, voices rising, until Jedla again silenced them and turned to Rogue.

"*Gedal debot Bialig, uma*?" Jedla asked. She shrugged her shoulders and raised her upturned palms, pretending to look for the Leader.

Rogue thought for a few moments. He stepped toward them, and although they dwarfed him, they parted for him as he neared the fire. With a quick sweep of his foot, he drew ashes from the edge of the pit and spread them across the ground. He used his finger to draw a scene where many people attacked him and four others who were much taller. One man mumbled something that included the word *Paten*, and laughter followed. Rogue understood they were enjoying a joke at his expense.

"*Sojabosne*," Rogue said.

The seven Realmers nodded, but again Jedla asked, "*Bialig*?"

This time Rogue shrugged his shoulders and shook his head. A small lie, but how could he ever explain where his friends were?

"*Gedar debos tae lieme*?" Jedla touched Rogue's arm and indicated everything around her. It took him a few minutes to figure out her question.

He swiped his hand across the ashes and drew a circle with a stick figure in the middle. Then he drew another circle with four taller stick figures. Between the two circles he drew a straight line. Jedla's brow knotted, so he mimicked opening a door and being pulled through. She barked a laugh when she realized Bialig had opened the portal between Earth and their world.

"*Gedar, uma*?" She pressed Rogue for understanding.

Rogue frowned at his lack of artistic ability. He sketched a *bargel* with huge fangs to depict Frank Blast and the poison in his body. The Realmers recognized it as representing danger. The tone of their words held praise for Bialig and his decision to save the *uma*. They clapped Rogue on the back, making him stagger, and invited him to join in their meal.

Close inspection of Rogue's ragged clothing resulted in the bestowing of a new pair of leather pants. He was amazed at how quickly the man presenting the gift altered them to his size. One woman offered a tunic not unlike the one he wore. The best contribution to his new wardrobe was the custom-made boots with real laces and thick soles. Jedla looked on with pride at her group's efforts.

"*Natamos*?" Rogue asked her.

More laughter and head shaking answered him.

"*Chejasosne*," Jedla replied, her arm sweeping the circle of Realmers.

The gambler deliberated the meaning. He decided with all the weapons, leather, fresh and dried meat, and the packs they carried that they must be hunters. He searched his mind for another word.

"*Shlodane*?"

"*Bado*," Jedla exclaimed, her face brightening.

Rogue understood their connection to Bialig; the Leader had probably taught every one of them how to hunt. His knowledge of their *Natamos* was enough for them to accept Rogue as part of their Clan. For the remainder of the day and long into the night, they ate, drank, and worked through their language barrier with hand signs, laughter, and drawn pictures, finally falling asleep under a sky milky with stars.

In the morning, Jedla gave him one of her own knives. The others had fashioned a small pack complete with dried rations, a skin bag for water, and a new sleeping fur. They ate a final meal together and broke camp. Jedla motioned for him to follow them. Rogue shook his head and pointed at the sun.

"*Avboeth*," he said.

Jedla sighed, still not understanding the *uma* or his peculiar mission.

"*Olosti, Rogue s'hel Umane. Nulpes leveth.*"

Goodbye in any language always hurt. The seven Realmers pressed their fists to their chests then swung their arms in the direction he would walk, palms forward. Rogue turned from them with their final blessing still hanging in the air. He refused to look back when he heard them lift their packs and walk in the opposite direction, their pleasant chatter drifting toward him on the wind.

Once again Rogue was without friends in the Realm.

* * *

"HEY, PRETTY LADY, WANNA BE friends for the night?"

Raine spat at the drug dealer with the singsong voice and pulled her sweatshirt hood tighter around her face but not so tight as to reveal the shotgun strapped to her back. She flipped him off with both hands to show she had no fear. To ignore him would be to invite him to follow her which would lead to an unfortunate incident in a back alley.

The sidewalk in front of her disappeared under the midnight snowstorm. Her only concern now was how long she had before someone discovered the dead GEA agent in her apartment. White embroidery spelled the name Arusi Bakshi on the navy sweatshirt; Raine could not have chosen a more unsuitable candidate to impersonate.

None of that mattered now. All she had to do was soldier on until she reached the parking garage where Arusi's vehicle waited. Get in and drive to Blast Tower. Use the BioMet Card to gain access to the garage, the lobby, and the elevators that would take Raine up the first twenty stories. Toss a wave at the security guards at the front desk. No need to sign in when you are Arusi Bakshi, Frank Blast's trusted informant and sometime whore.

Numbness pervaded Raine's body as she stood in Arusi's office on the twentieth floor. The blinds on the inside windows had been lowered before she arrived. She moved through darkness to the twenty-inch HoloMir hover-locked vertically over the desk and sat with her back toward the outer windows. Electronic billboards on buildings surrounding Blast Tower cast a greenish glow about the room, advertisements flashing everything from toothpaste to porn. Raine simulated Arusi's retinal scan and synced her HoloMir with Arusi's.

She could not resist scrolling through files detailing the transfer of illegal funds to GEA agents in Blast's employ. Agents who had graduated from the Academy with her father, Theo, and herself appeared on the screen. She closed the file and opened another tracking people in Quadrant One who were close to buying their way off Earth. Raine did not recognize anyone on the short list of names. Professions such as engineer, biologist, and physicist were interspersed with journalist, writer, and historian. The occupations did not match, and yet there was something about their dissimilarity that unified them. It pained Raine to see all the intelligent and talented people fleeing Earth.

She scrolled through a few more files before locating one labeled Security. The ease with which Raine downloaded the codes giving her access to the next twenty floors made her feel as if she was being set up. For all Blast's paranoia, he had not chosen well for his head of third-tier security. He would probably thank Raine for killing Arusi.

Before leaving the office, Raine accessed the security cameras on floors twenty-one through forty as well as those in the elevators. She recorded and uploaded a ten-minute loop of cleaning people working and taking elevators to different floors into the cameras for the benefit of the guards in the lobby. Then she slowly made her way upward, maneuvering between banks of elevators and sending cars in random directions so as not to alert the guards that someone was headed for the top suite where Blast lived and worked. She expertly avoided the few people on each level.

Two hours had passed since Raine left her apartment. She stood in an elevator paused at the fortieth floor, hoping no one would request a car before she synced her HoloMir via the control panel to the computer system running the whole operation. Arusi's security clearance did not go past this point, but it proved useful in overriding the elevator sensors detecting Raine's presence via her weight and body temperature. It also kept all other cars engaged while Raine waited for a member of the cleaning crew on the forty-first through sixtieth floors to request a car. She did not have to wait long.

Raine jumped when the elevator rotated to the right and began a swift transition through the tracks that would take it inward and upward to the next tier of Blast Tower. She tugged the sweatshirt hood forward in case security had figured out they had been watching the same video for over an hour. The elevator stopped at the fifty-seventh floor, a retinal scan was performed outside the car by someone with the appropriate clearance, and the doors opened.

There was no reason for the young man backing onto the elevator with his cleaning cart to suspect Raine had no right to be there. She looked like any other dirty GEA agent on her way to see her handler. He smiled at her, never expecting the arm she used to hold the doors for him would wrap around his neck and break it. Raine scanned his retinas with the BioMet Card and used it to continue to the sixtieth floor.

When the doors opened three floors later, Raine stepped out onto thick, red carpet that swallowed up her boots. Potted palms lined the entire hallway, and recessed lighting glowed off black marble walls. Some of the highest paid criminals in Blast's empire lived and worked on these floors. None were present at two in the morning to question the new girl struggling to push a cleaning cart with something bulky stuffed in the garbage can at the front.

Raine parked the dead man's cart in the ladies' room. Then she dumped his body and borrowed jumpsuit down the disposal chute where they landed atop a pile of rubbish on a conveyor belt headed for the incinerator. She entered the ventilation system above the last toilet stall and followed the route plotted on her HoloMir until she was over the office of Campbell Hastings. Her good luck held until she peered through the vent looking down into Hasting's office. Blast's right-hand man for conducting business in Quadrant One was hosting a private party, complete with lines of heroin on the glass coffee table and a prostitute grinding on his lap. Raine lay trapped in the ductwork and waited out their depravity.

Two hours later, Hastings and the hooker were stripped to their underwear and passed out on the floor. Raine deactivated the motion sensors on the vent cover, removed it, and lowered herself into the room. She replaced the vent cover then turned to pick her way past their bodies and empty liquor bottles to the adjoining room where Hastings kept his computer. Her heart skipped a beat when she looked directly into his half-open eyes, recovering only when she realized he was out cold. A quick scan with the BioMet Card meant she would not have to waste time hacking the computer.

Raine kept the lights off as she employed Hastings's retinal scan to sync her HoloMir with his. Thirty minutes later she still had not found the security codes for floors sixty-one through eighty. In desperation she searched for a ghost drive, using every skill Theo had taught her about how criminals hide information digitally. Her jaw clenched until her teeth ached before she finally discovered what she had been looking for.

She would take her time sorting through all the downloaded information once she was back in the duct work. The line across the bottom of the screen read eighty five percent when she heard a retinal scanner for the outer door to Hastings's office beep. Someone shoved the door into the arms and legs of the two people heaped in front of it. Their struggle bought Raine a few moments, but she had to desynchronize the computers at ninety five percent complete and duck under the desk.

"Sorry, Mr. Blast," said one of his thugs, kicking an arm out of the way.

"Are they dead?"

"Yes, sir. Looks like it."

"I don't want to know what it looks like. I want to know that the man who conspired against me is dead."

The second bodyguard knelt and placed his fingertips on Hastings's wrist.

"The poisoned heroin did its job."

"Retrieve his computer and bring it to my office."

Blast left with the first bodyguard while the second entered the office where Raine hid. He leaned across the desk to disengage the HoloMir's hover-lock without coming around to where she crouched in the space for a desk chair. In the reflection of the windows, Raine watched him tuck the thin, clear screen under his arm before he turned off the lights in the outer room and left. She held her breath until she heard the elevator in the hallway ding and the doors close.

Self-reproach burned her eyes with angry tears for allowing Blast to escape.

CHAPTER SEVENTEEN

THE HOLOMIR SCREEN GLOWED IN the tomb that was Frank Blast's office. He sucked a deep breath through clenched teeth, held it burning in his chest, and released the air as a powerful hiss. His leather gloves creaked with every grip of his fists as he stared at Hastings's computer, the screen frozen in the middle of an interrupted download.

Someone—some unauthorized person—possessed ninety-five percent of the information regarding Moon Base Tarigo, Mars Base Algernon, and Vista and Eden Stations. Or rather, this fool who had inserted himself into Blast's operations had ninety-five percent of nothing. Because that is exactly what Tarigo, Algernon, Vista, and Eden were. Nothing. Oblivion. False dreams for sale.

The crime boss's eyes widened at the thought of the sheer stupidity prompting a person to cross paths with him. He stood and removed his outer coat and scarf, hanging both in the mahogany wardrobe behind his desk. Then he peeled off his gloves, tossed them on the desk, and tapped the intercom icon on his computer.

"Clarice. I will not be traveling to the Southern Hemisphere today."

"Shall I cancel your passage altogether, sir?" the secretary asked.

"No. There's simply someone I need to find before departing."

"Who shall I summon for you, Mr. Blast?"

"I'll do this one myself."

A hollow pause in the open call preceded, "Yes, sir, Mr. Blast."

Blast touched the clear screen again, ending the conversation. The predator within considered how to stalk the quarry that had walked into his domain.

* * *

A DOLLOP OF SUN MELTED on the horizon, shimmering and smearing the air above, but Rogue shivered and drew his sleeping fur around his shoulders. He turned from the setting sun, willing every last ounce of light to illuminate this path. He had been traveling across the endless carpet of the grasslands for two weeks since encountering Jedla's hunting party. Herding animals, birds, lizards, insects, and the occasional solitary tusked monstrosity to which Rogue gave a wide berth provided his only company. At least he had not seen a predator. Strange growls echoed throughout the night as well as the cries of animals succumbing to the ensuing attacks. Yet, the more aggressive animals remained hidden beyond the light of his meager fires.

Trees became a rare sight, and some nights Rogue could not gather enough grass to keep the fire going for much more than protection. He was sure Bialig would know a way to overcome this, but the Leader had not returned from Earth. If he and the others were back in the Realm, Rogue feared they had missed each other in their travels. He shook his head to erase the thought only to have it replaced with an equally pressing concern. His skin bag hung limp at his side; no more than a mouthful of water sloshed inside. Anything green had fled with the last stream he had seen two days ago.

The triple moons rose before him as the sun blinked out behind him, its disappearance revealing stars tossed across the velvet night. Rogue should have already stopped, but he stumbled toward the spot on the thin, gray ribbon of horizon where the sun had come up that morning, determined to put himself one step closer to the *Avboeth* or at least the copse he thought he had spotted. Rogue's steps disintegrated into shuffling, and he wished for the sound of voices, laughter, even Talj's snoring to break the monotony of buzzing insects. In his exhausted state, the gambler thought he saw several trees detach from the ground and glide toward him. His hand moved to the knife Jedla gave him tucked at his waist.

Rogue peered into the layers of night until his eyes watered. He crouched before the whisper of dry grasses bowing to the oncoming threat and the discordant thunder of running feet. Against so many, with nothing but a knife, he would not stand a chance. There was nowhere to run, nowhere to hide. Their cries reached him first.

"Rogue—you are alive," Bialig exclaimed with admiration. The big man yanked Rogue upright and shook him by his shoulders. "I thought for sure you would be dead by now."

Nish laughed and clasped Rogue to her breast while Talj delivered rough pats to the top of Rogue's head and grunted his satisfaction. Misko hovered close enough to add his forced laughter to the celebration but far enough to not engage in the reunion.

"Where the hell have you guys been?" Rogue asked, his voice wavering.

"Let us move to the safety of the trees where we can build a fire and talk," Bialig said, eyeing Rogue's clothes, footwear, backpack, and skin bag.

Once they were settled around the fire, reclining on woven mats of dry grass fashioned by Nish, Rogue told his tale of survival complete with escaping Kolbian's *sojabosne* and meeting Jedla's hunting party. Talj pressed him for details of the terrain over which he had traveled. Misko asked him nothing.

"So where did you guys end up?" Rogue asked. He noticed his friends fidgeting and looking around warily.

"Nish directed us with her second sight to the warehouses where we used to cross over," Bialig said. "We immediately sought shelter in an abandoned building to escape the snowstorm."

"Yeah, but how long were you there?"

Bialig poked a stick into the embers, releasing a swarm of sparks to join the night insects.

"We arrived on Earth, found a place to hide while Nish located you, and returned to the Signal Tree toward which you were walking."

Rogue chewed on a piece of roasted root and the information the Leader had given him. His hand waved several times as if he reasoned with himself. Finally, he said, "So for you it's only been a few moments since you left here? Is that why you guys keep looking around like Kolbian is going to jump out any minute?"

"It feels that way for us. For you, it must have been an eternity," Bialig said.

Rogue deflected the comment with a shrug. "It's had its ups and downs, but I haven't seen Kolbian or the *sojabosne* since you guys left. We're safe now, and what's more, we're all together."

Talj looked away from Rogue, his grizzled head bent under the need to confess. There would never be a good time to speak what would surely sound like a curse. The old Healer seized on Rogue's last comment to deliver his news.

"Yes, my friend, and together we will search for another source of the specific *yorit* to make the cure that will rid your body of poison."

A hailstorm of understanding crashed down on all of them. No one had had the opportunity to think about all they had lost during the flight from Kolbian. Bialig rested a large hand on Rogue's shoulder. Misko raised his palms to Talj asking when and where, but the old Healer had no answer for any of them.

"So, we're back to square one," Rogue said. His eyes could not meet Talj's.

"No," Bialig replied. "Now we know what we are looking for."

Rogue stood and kicked the turf, spraying the fire with a shower of dirt. Words he longed to say died between his grinding teeth, and he stalked away from the others. Nish reached for him as he brushed past. Bialig caught her hands, pressing them between his own, and shook his head.

The Realmers listened to their friend pacing in the darkness beyond the fire, muttering his frustrations. They blinked with the effort to stay awake and watchful. Talj succumbed to sleep first with Nish and Misko quickly following. Bialig rubbed his thumb across each eye, having turned away from the firelight to hone his focus on the restless silhouette conversing with the stars.

* * *

THE LEADER'S CHIN RESTED ON his chest, his back against a tree. Fire pulsed within the glowing embers, and the ashen dawn crept upward with the rising sun. Downy clouds covered the speckled green moons refusing to yield the sky. A lone figure ghosted back to camp. Rogue knelt next to the remains of the fire and hugged himself, rubbing his arms to generate heat. Bialig's head rose, yet he remained silent.

"I'll gather some wood to get this fire going." An emotion Bialig could not discern padded Rogue's voice. "There's enough dead on this tree to pull down and get it going."

"Or you could conserve energy and not wake the others by using grass," the Leader whispered.

"I figured you'd know a way to use the grass efficiently." Rogue paused and rubbed a piece of cold ash between his finger and thumb. "I didn't take the cure because I wasn't ready to go back to Earth. It's so peaceful here. And healthy. I was trying to find the courage to ask you to let me stay, but now that the cure is lost, I think I'd rather have a few moments on Earth with Raine than die slowly in the Realm."

Frustration was the quality Bialig heard in Rogue's tone. He made a mental note to teach the *uma* as much as he could in case catastrophe struck again.

"Bring your knife and come with me."

Together the Realmer and the human cut fistfuls of tall grass that they twisted and folded into tight bundles. Bialig held the ends as Rogue used another piece of grass to tie them off.

"They will not burn as long as wood, but they burn more slowly than grass scattered over a fire. You would need a pile this big to make a decent fire," Bialig said, indicating how high with his hand.

When they completed about thirty bundles, they carried them back to camp and stoked the fire. Nish used the last of Rogue's supplies to make breakfast, which they shared, cooking and eating out of the bowl given to him by a member of Jedla's group.

"Where did you get the water to make the porridge, Nish?" Rogue asked.

"From the tree. I filled your skin bag, too."

Before annoyance could knit Rogue's brow, Bialig led him to a tree with delicate, mottled bark. He pointed at the diagonal slashes Nish had made with the stone knife Rogue had recovered. Each cut dripped liquid faster than a leaky faucet.

"The sap is thin and flavorless. We use it when traveling in places where water is scarce."

Misko observed Bialig teaching Rogue survival skills, pointing at edible insects, mimicking tasks, and demonstrating fighting techniques. It was everything Misko yearned to glean from his *Natamos*, everything he was forbidden to know. He took comfort in the thought that perhaps Bialig would yield to his desire to cross-train in light of all the unusual circumstances they had endured. Already the Leader had softened to Rogue's presence, crossed over to Earth to save the *Doh s'Ima*, and withheld anger when the *uma* admitted to seeing other Realmers. The youth decided to broach the subject at the right time.

When they finished eating, Bialig surprised the others by saying, "We will travel toward the mountains where the *Damirg* Clan lives. There we will find the assistance and supplies we need to resume traveling toward the *Avboeth*."

"How long will it take us to get there?" Rogue asked.

"Three days. Your water skin will provide enough for each of us to have one drink a day."

"The grasses are beginning to go to seed, *Mir*-Bialig," Nish added. "We can chew them when we are hungry and eat the eggs of ground-nesting birds."

"And *Mir*-Talj can search the caves at the base of the mountains where he may find another source of *yorit* for Rogue's cure."

The Leader ran his hand over strange carvings in the bark of what he referred to as the Signal Tree. Then he looked in the direction the marks indicated and led his *Doh s'Ima* toward the black mountains slashed across the landscape.

* * *

THE JOURNEY TOWARD THE *DAMIRG* Clan provided Rogue the opportunity to make amends with Misko. At first the gambler walked last in line, willing Misko to turn around, drop back, and talk the way they did when Rogue first entered the Realm. The attention he garnered came from Bialig, who barked at Rogue when he thought he was dawdling; Nish, who could not mask her desire for peace within their ranks; and Talj, whose guilt-ridden countenance over losing the cure made Rogue wince. Their observations provoked sighs from Misko who was painfully aware that everyone wanted him and Rogue to patch things up. He walked with his head down, hands gripped at his side.

Evenings around the campfire crackled with false cheer and sparse conversation. Their lack of activities added to the tension, and all turned to sleep as a means of escape. Searching for food as they walked should have lessened the friction between Rogue and Misko, especially when the gambler shared everything he found with the youth. Misko interpreted Rogue's actions as patronizing and ignored his growling stomach rather than accept anything from the *uma*.

Rogue's attempts at small talk pushed Misko farther away when he joked about the young man's nervous habit of constantly pulling at his long sleeves. Rogue wondered aloud and quite innocently what he had under there and offered his sleeping fur in jest, teasing Misko that he must have some human in him if he was cold. His reward was a pursed-lipped scowl.

The night before they arrived at the *Damirg* Clan, Rogue tried the last thing he knew to do before giving up and seeking advice from the others. Nish built a fire and roasted eggs from a clutch she had discovered earlier in the day. Talj and Bialig settled on the mats of braided grass. Rogue waited until Misko sat cross-legged on his mat before placing his own beside him. The gambler did not really understand the role of a *Paten* in the *Doh s'Ima*, but he knew how to flatter someone by emphasizing their passions and abilities. It was a trick he used on Earth to lure marks into trusting him before he eliminated them.

But Rogue did not want Misko gone. He wanted the carefree, friendly Misko he had first met to return. Knowing that the request he was about to make could go either way, he breathed deeply and said, "Hey, Misko, how about a song?"

The question underscored the fact that the young *Paten* was completely without instruments. Half a second after posing the question, Rogue realized he probably should have requested a story. Instead, he had virtually asked Misko to paint without a brush, carve without a chisel, and write without a stylus. He had also touched the young man at a core level, drawing from the deep wells of an Artist who longed to create.

Misko tugged at his sleeves, and Rogue's stomach knotted. Then the young man unbound his hair and loosened it with his long fingers. Again, Rogue thought he had overstepped his bounds and pushed his friend too far. What he could not know was that he had reached back in Misko's memory to remind him of why he had joined the *Doh s'Ima* in the first place. Everything they had endured for the past weeks fell away when Misko closed his eyes and tipped his head back.

The pure, clear note expanded in the air before Misko reined it in to decrescendo with the fluidity of a stream falling over smooth stones. Softly, without losing the thread, seemingly without drawing breath, Misko's voice lured images and emotions from all present and blended them into a wordless ballad. His song unmasked vulnerabilities and secrets as it grew with the power of storm clouds rolling across the sky, finishing with the lightness of mists after the rain.

Moments passed before the insects and a lone hunter rejoined with their own night music. Bialig gazed at Nish, whose eyes brimmed with tears. She blinked once, her affection spilling over her lashes. Talj rocked back and forth, his rough voice caught at the base of his throat, a clear indication that he consulted and answered himself. Rogue sat motionless, overcome by memories of Raine. Just as a true Artist should, Misko remained invisible to them; his was not a performance but a gift.

As the young man leaned forward to pull a frond of smoldering grass from the fire, his sleeve rode up, and he alone saw the red tattoo on his arm. More recent remembrances spread like blood in water, the poison of Kolbian's influence tainting the honor of the *Doh s'Ima*. Misko looked at his companions still adrift on the waves of their own thoughts. He crossed his arms and legs, retreating in on himself.

"Without food, medicine, or weapons, I finally become useful," Misko said.

All warmth had drained from his voice, causing the others to shiver.

* * *

BIALIG INSISTED THAT ROGUE HIDE while he and the others approached the *Damirg* Clan. Misko started to protest that Rogue had already been seen by Jedla's hunting party, but the Leader headed him off.

"I must still obey the rulings of the Elders, even if they were broken at a moment to save Rogue's life, and I must respect the *Damirgne* who may not want to associate with an *uma*."

Bialig shot a glance at Rogue who shrugged and held up his hands.

"What about searching the caves for Rogue's cure?" Misko asked.

"Talj will have time to do that while we gather supplies."

"What about compensation?" Rogue asked.

"I do not understand," Bialig replied.

"We need to replace everything. Are they going to do that for free?"

Shock registered on the Reamlers' faces.

"That is not our way," Bialig sputtered with indignation. "We do not make a profit when people are in need or hurt or sick. If we did, we might find ourselves requiring assistance and without a form of payment."

"I'm sorry. I didn't mean to offend," Rogue said.

Nish put her hand on Rogue's shoulder. "Remember how Jedla gave you everything without asking for anything in return? There have been times in all our lives when we needed, so we received, and when others needed, so we gave. We do not keep track of the things in our possession that come and go, but rather the quality of Clan members' lives."

"But what if you want something?"

"We work for what we have and for what we want. We do not resent it if someone has something we do not. We are happy for them, for their good fortune. Good things happen to all of us, and we share the experience just like we do when something bad happens. In this way, our joys are more and our sorrows less."

"You can't begin to imagine how perfect and impossible that sounds to someone like me," Rogue said.

"Yes, we can," Bialig said. "It is what *Dohne s'Ima* battle every day since our Clans were corrupted by *umane* unwilling to live for others, who take more than they need, leaving people in want. Who refuse to accept responsibility for their actions. It is this greed that drives Kolbian and those like him."

Rogue walked away a few paces and sat in the long, dry grass. He looked at the Leader and tossed his head in the direction of the mountains where his friends would find the help and supplies they needed. His knowledge that they would return for him regardless of any difficulties suppressed his uneasy sense of dependency. He breathed deeply, laid back, and watched the sun's rays penetrate thick, plum-colored clouds.

CHAPTER EIGHTEEN

ROGUE COULD TELL BY HIS friends' faces that a cure had not been found in the mountain caves of the *Damirg* Clan. Their disappointment hid beneath a veneer of enthusiasm for the many gifts received from the *Damirgne*, whose own *Doh s'Ima* had left for the *Avboeth* many moon/sun cycles ago. Their generosity made it seem as if no disasters had befallen the travelers. The greatest honor came when the Second to the *Damirgnelo Natamos* bestowed her own sword on Bialig.

The group of five resumed the journey toward the *Avboeth* without discussing Rogue's predicament. Bialig fluctuated between leading the line and driving it from behind. His eyes never stopped scanning for indications of Kolbian's presence; he knew his brother would not abandon the hunt. To help normalize their journey, he led them in the routines of setting up and breaking camp.

Misko's stride lightened, and he beamed like a child at having received three new instruments from the *Damirgne*. Possession of what he loved most improved his mood, and the gambler looked forward to nights of music and song around the campfire to help keep his anxiety at bay. Yet after five days of walking, Misko still had not played for them.

As they broke camp the next morning, the gambler sidled up next to Nish and asked, "Is Misko still mad at me or something?"

"I am worried about *Mir*-Misko. When he received instruments from the *Damirgne*, he did not express the gratitude one would expect from a *Paten* of the *Doh s'Ima*. We were all embarrassed for him as he nodded his head and walked away from the woman appointed Second in service of their *Paten*. He did not join her and the Mentors for a time of fellowshipping, and he offered nothing in the way of instruction to the Students."

"What did Bialig do?"

"You know *Mir*-Bialig would say nothing in front of the *Damirgne* to embarrass Misko. I have noticed him seeking Talj's counsel on how best to approach the situation."

With night came the return of Misko's music, but the young Artist did not share his talent with the group. Rather he walked a short distance away, enough to have privacy but stay within sight of the fire. Bialig knelt at the blaze and watched him from the side of his eye. He stayed crouched, groaning softly, when sharp, discordant notes drifted back on the listless wind. Misko's talents provided a gauge for his emotions; clearly something bothered him that he had not communicated to anyone in his *Doh s'Ima*.

Into this mix of tension and disquiet, Rogue presented his request. He waited until the group had hiked for several miles the next day, secure within their personal columns of silence, before he dropped back a few paces to walk beside Bialig.

With head bowed and a hand extended palm up toward Bialig, Rogue said, "Can I ask you a question?"

The attempt at formality humored and pleased the Leader; he pressed his palm to Rogue's.

"Is there any chance you'd let Nish show me into Earth again?"

Bialig hummed deep in his chest, nodded. "You are worried about the woman called Raine?"

"You know her name?"

"Nish told me. Is that acceptable to you?"

"Yeah, that's fine. Do you guys know what's going on with her?"

"We had never seen her before the day we saved you. I understand there is concern for her safety."

"Raine was headed for a place of danger. I know where she's going because I've broken in there myself." Rogue looked away at the mention of his criminal activity, baring his teeth as if he had bitten into something unpleasant. He rubbed his hand over the stubble on his chin and said, "Look—it's no secret I've been a jerk here and on Earth."

"I am not familiar with your conduct on Earth," Bialig replied.

"But you had a pretty good taste of what I was like when I first came here. I'd like to think I'm changing for the better since hanging out with you guys. Not that I had a choice. About the hanging out, that is."

"Given the right opportunities, you will excel."

"But that's not enough, is it? When I'm having a run of bad luck, I must be strong and do the right thing even if no one is watching, right?"

The Leader parsed the comment, deciphering the unknown phrase.

"The individual is responsible for his or her own deeds, words, and thoughts in the face of adversity. This requires a lifetime of seeking wisdom that leads to maturity. And someone is always watching."

"No running with the crowd, rise above, and all that stuff?"

"You are making light of a serious conversation?"

"I'm sorry, really. It's just that I heard all this growing up in the orphanage, and I'd like to say my life is the result of my circumstances. But it's not. I made bad decisions, did wrong, and hurt people in the process. I convinced myself it was okay because I was just doing what I needed to survive."

"But you did not sow seeds of discord or act out in violence?"

"Life on Earth is all about violence. Especially condoning it as an acceptable response to something you disagree with. But I don't have to tell you. As long as you guys live, you've been watching us for centuries. You know what it's like."

"I am not without compassion for the *umane*, Rogue."

"Let's try something new, okay? We're called humans."

Bialig snorted. "That is one word for your people. I prefer *gradol*."

"I know what that means you jack . . ." The insult died on Rogue's lips when he sensed Bialig shaking with soundless laughter. "So can I see into Earth or what?"

"Yes, Rogue, if Nish is willing, you have my permission to look for your woman."

The gambler's steps faltered at the words "your woman." Raine had never been his, and in her mind, she probably did not belong to anyone. She possessed deep familial connections, but they were all dead, and Rogue certainly did not measure up as a replacement. Still, he needed to see her even if he could not touch her.

* * *

EVEN THOUGH ROGUE HAD PERMISSION to see into Earth, he waited another week to see if the terrain would provide privacy such as he had in the forest the first time Nish shared her second sight. He tried to convince himself this was a regression to his clandestine habits acquired while smuggling. Closer to the truth, he feared his reaction to seeing Raine and did not want any witnesses in case his emotions took over.

He knew his friends understood when Talj pointed out the return of waterways producing lush greenery that led into a forest of grasses resembling trees.

"The grasses here allow for concealment and solitude in case one needs to meditate," the old Healer said as he ambled along. "We may also find a source of the *yorit* needed for your cure in the caves on the far side of the forest."

"Is that why we're taking this route? I noticed we're no longer walking toward the sun," Rogue asked.

"It is not the most direct route to the *Avboeth*, but it will get us there," Bialig said.

The fact that his friends had diverted their journey just for him weighed heavy on Rogue's mind. He took a deep breath and made another request.

"I know you guys aren't supposed to learn each other's skills, but what if I taught Misko some basic self-defense? You know, just in case we run into Kolbian again."

The Leader sighed, his jaw working for several moments before he replied.

"It is not our way. Nevertheless, it may be what he needs to restore his interest in the *Doh s'Ima*. Talj and I are unsure how to help him through this difficult time."

"A little self-defense wouldn't hurt. Would it get you in trouble with the High Council?"

"The circumstances under which we have traveled necessitated improvisation in the way I protect my *Doh s'Ima*. If that means teaching self-defense to the members, then I will accept responsibility for the outcome with the High Council. But understand that the perfection of individual skills must be maintained to prevent their being lost."

Misko quivered at the prospect of learning basic maneuvers until he tripped over his own feet. When they stopped for the night, he did not unroll his bedding or unpack his instruments, questioned Rogue endlessly throughout the evening meal without eating, and almost pressed his luck when he asked Bialig if he could have his own weapon.

"C'mon," Rogue said, setting his bowl on the ground and heading toward a moonlit clearing in the woody grasses.

The Artist jumped up to follow, then froze with his hand over his forearm. He tugged on his long sleeve, hoping it would not ride up during the training.

Bialig moved as if to stand, hesitating when he felt Nish's hand on his arm. He faced her and his posture relaxed under her gentle gaze. Both blushed from close contact, laughing but not moving away from each other. If he could have unhinged his tongue, he would have complimented her hair.

The sound of running feet and uncoordinated thrashing came from the clearing where Rogue and Misko practiced. Rogue's voice was patient but strained, punctuated with praise and encouragement. Bialig could tell the lesson was not going well when Rogue cried out in pain, swore, and quickly amended his comments so as not to hurt Misko's feelings. To the Leader's surprise, Rogue called for Nish instead of him; he could not resist following her to the clearing.

Unsure of how she could help, Rogue explained that she was closer in size to Misko. They would be equally matched for a lesson tailored for beginners since neither possessed any skill. He walked them through the technique which they rehearsed several times. Bialig stood with arms crossed and head tilted. The pair ended in a tangle of arms and legs with Nish laughing and Misko scowling.

Misko jumped up and shouted, "I should not be fighting a woman! Be serious, Nish. We may need to defend ourselves."

"I am sorry, *Mir*-Misko. I did not mean to ruin your lesson," she replied, unable to hide her smile.

Bialig's eyes narrowed as much from the disrespect shown to Nish as Misko's lack of ability. He kept silent and did not interfere with the lesson.

"Try again," Rogue said.

Several more times Nish played her part to Misko's growing dissatisfaction.

"This is not helpful at all," Misko complained. "You are the warrior, Bialig. I should be fighting you."

"Whoa—Misko—let's not get ahead of ourselves," Rogue said, laughing nervously.

The Leader uncrossed his arms and stepped back.

"I am serious, Rogue. You are too small, and Nish is . . . well, women are not meant for making war," Misko said.

"Obviously, you've never met Jedla." Again, Rogue's laughter was anxious as he shot a glance at Bialig. "I really don't think the big guy here could restrain himself enough to . . . his fighting instincts are just so . . ."

"You think because I am a *Paten* that I do not have inclinations toward fighting?"

"Working with you, Misko, is different than working with other potential Leaders, hunters, and warriors. You need the basic instruction you can get from me and practice with Nish."

"No—I will learn from my *Natamos*. I will fight you, Bialig, because after all, you are the best."

The arrogance in Misko's tone swept across Bialig's face, producing a frown of disappointment. The Leader's eyes held fathomless compassion, and he took another step backward to distance himself from Misko's foolishness. To his dismay, it came rushing at him anyhow.

A quick sidestep sent Misko lunging past Bialig instead of resulting in the tackle the young man had intended. He recovered and turned, lashing out with a wild swing that the Leader easily dodged. Misko threw more ineffectual punches at Bialig's head and chest only to have the big man dance out of his reach.

"Misko—*stop*," Rogue yelled. "I didn't teach you to attack."

Misko had dropped to all fours. He panted from his useless exertions and sweat beaded his forehead. In the shadows of the forest evening, no one saw that his sleeve had ridden up. His eyes alone fell on the red tattoo midway up the underside of his forearm. With as much stealth as he could, he reached for a length of woody grass lying among the debris on the forest floor and sprang toward Bialig wielding the culm like a club.

Nish screamed when Misko raised his weapon. As Misko's arms descended, Bialig stepped inside the attack and wrapped the Artist's arms in one of his own. His hold landed around the younger man's elbows. With fluid speed, the Leader bent Misko's trapped arms upward to cause severe discomfort; the young man dropped his weapon. Bialig stepped backward, pulling Misko off balance, and ended the Artist's attack with a swift punch to the stomach, leaving him breathless but not injured.

In battle, Bialig would have head-butted his opponent, slid his restraining arm upward around the attacker's neck, slipped in behind his adversary, and finished him by twining his other arm around the head to break the neck. Misko would never know this as Bialig dropped him to the ground. The most mournful sound Rogue had ever heard escaped the Leader's lips as he bent over the young man, his hands hovering above Misko's head.

"Get away from me," Misko snarled. He struggled to get up, refusing Bialig's outstretched hand. "I ask you to teach me, and all you do is humiliate me?"

"Misko, I had to stop you before you hurt yourself," Bialig said. "Please, let us rest a moment and continue the lesson more calmly."

"Continue?" The word shredded Misko's voice with the force of his rage. "I will not subject myself to you any longer, Bialig."

Misko turned from the Leader and ran into Talj, who had entered the clearing unnoticed when he heard the practice session escalate. The old Healer grunted but did not fall, nor did he release Misko from his unexpectedly strong embrace. He had heard the young man's declaration and understood it carried a threat beyond the current situation.

"You are trembling, *Mir*-Misko. Perhaps a warm drink to soothe your spirits is required?"

"I just want—I just want to go . . ."

"Come, my friend," Talj said as he led Misko toward the camp. "Let me tend the scrapes on your hands. I have something for you to take that will prevent bruising."

Talj supported Misko with an arm around his waist. The Artist, still shaking, leaned on the older man, resting his head against Talj's fuzzed, white hair.

Nish's soft voice came as a plea. "Let us return to camp. We all need to rest, to sleep this off."

"Go on, Nish. I'm going to stay with Bialig for a few minutes. We'll catch up, okay?" Rogue said.

She hesitated, looking to Bialig, who knelt with his hands resting palms up on his thighs, head bowed. Then she returned to camp.

Into the stillness the insects wove their blended voices. Minutes passed with neither Rogue nor Bialig speaking. The gambler watched the silhouettes of his three friends pass in front of the fire, their shadows looming large and fragmented across the timber-like grasses reaching for the stars.

Without facing the Leader, he said, "Don't do this. I can accept that I have a deadly poison stuck in my body and that I've been whisked away to some strange world. But I will never accept you like—like this."

Rogue flung his hand toward Bialig. He waited, watching Talj tend Misko. Nish prepared the warm drink the old Healer prescribed, and then all three rested on their bedding and sipped the beverage. Talj leaned over and sprinkled something into Misko's cup. *Probably the medicine for bruising*, Rogue thought. *I wonder what Talj has in his medicine bag for lifting broken spirits.*

Shadows concealed Bialig's face.

"You think I am defeated because of what happened here tonight? I have not given up; I am seeking guidance. My duty to Misko will be more difficult than I anticipated, but I will not back down from it."

"I don't understand why he's so out of sync with you guys. Isn't he part of the *Doh s'Ima* because he has these talents that make him different, special?"

"He is special because of the superior talents he possesses. How he uses his talents will mold the person he becomes."

"And you're afraid he's using them for bad or self-serving reasons?" Rogue nodded in answer to his own question.

"Mine is not an enviable position as Misko believes," Bialig said. Rogue leaned forward into the long pause to keep his friend talking. "If he only wanted to leave the *Doh s'Ima* to pursue a life of his own within the Clans, I would understand. It would be difficult and disappointing for our Clan, but we would survive until another *Doh s'Ima* emerged. But to reject all authority in his life, to believe that anything he wants to do is acceptable and without consequence, to fail to serve others outside of the *Doh s'Ima*? These are the destructive thoughts our Clans have been battling for many, many cycles of the moons."

"You think that's where he's headed?" Rogue asked.

"Before we left for the Assembly, Misko began missing teaching sessions with the artistic Students of our Clan."

"I always wondered what happened at Kolbian's camp before you showed up. What garbage did he fill the kid's head with?"

"*Sojabosne* attempt to define their morality apart from the Infinite One. My brother is trying to undo Misko's purpose in life."

"Which is?"

Bialig looked sideways at Rogue. "To imitate the Infinite One by creating."

"Well, he still has a mission if you can get him back on track. You know, I often think about stuff like this for myself. I lead a rather purpose-less life back on Earth."

The Leader stood and brushed dirt from his knees. "You have not yet answered your calling."

Then he walked away with his typical abruptness, leaving Rogue scrambling to catch up. They entered the camp and unrolled their bedding for the night. No one spoke as Nish offered Bialig and Rogue cups of the warm beverage she had prepared. Talj rummaged in his medicine bag until he found a sleep aid, which he stirred into Bialig's drink. Misko rolled over, turning his face away from the fire and Bialig, and pulled his fur entirely over his head.

Moments passed in which the tension of the night's activities eased from Bialig's shoulders. He blinked twice, took a slow breath, and said, "*Mir*-Nish, would you be willing to show Rogue into Earth again with your second sight? You have my blessing to do so."

"Of course, *Natamos*. We can see into Earth tonight if Rogue would like. Perhaps he has someone he would like to look for?"

"Ah, *Mir*-Nish," Rogue said, "I don't know which you are more, beau-tiful or subtle."

Bialig snorted and choked on his drink making Talj and Nish laugh. The gambler smiled into his cup, his eyes dancing above the rim.

"Do not go too far," was all Bialig could think to say as Rogue and Nish walked into the forest.

A gentle wind blew across the tops of the tall grasses, catching the leaves and clacking the hollow stalks together like wooden wind chimes. Nish and Rogue chose a spot where the towering grasses allowed them to see the camp yet provided seclusion from the others' view. They sat facing each other, and Nish held out her hands to Rogue. He placed his own on her palms, and her long fingers curled around his. Rogue shivered.

"Close your eyes, *Mir*-Rogue."

He already had, but her use of the affectionate term startled them back open. Like a child caught disobeying, Rogue scrunched his eyes shut. Nish breathed a laugh as Rogue felt himself drawn into a vortex of burning frost. A mighty, rushing wind took his breath. When the motion stopped, Rogue sat face to face with Jessica Raine.

CHAPTER NINETEEN

THE INFORMATION FROM CAMPBELL HASTINGS'S HoloMir was meant to help Raine maneuver past security systems within Blast Tower, dodge roaming security details in the form of moonlighting GEA agents, and access Blast's schedule so she knew exactly when he would be alone in his office when the time came to kill him.

What she found was so much more, so much worse.

Her initial shock faded to intense sorrow, first for herself and then for the inhabitants of Earth. Hope simply did not exist as they had been led to believe. Denial settled like concrete in the pit of her stomach, fortified by the belief that only Frank Blast would be devious enough to fabricate a lie that would tear faith from the inhabitants of Earth and replace it with despair.

Raine sat immobile in the spotless air ducts of Blast Tower, knowing in her heart that the data she had stolen from Hastings was the truth. Blast had created a lie that masqueraded as truth to deceive and control the masses, to channel power to a select few, and to eliminate anyone perceived as a threat to this plan. Finally, she understood the similarity between the vocations of those whose names appeared on the list of people scheduled to leave Earth. She wondered how far this corruption went.

Heat flushed Raine's body. She ground her teeth as her finger swiped images off the HoloMir's screen, projecting a multitude of damning evidence against Blast that glowed in the dark confines of the ductwork. Everything from blueprints and advertisements for Mars Base Algernon and Space Stations Eden and Vista to bank accounts showing where the gold coin of those who had saved enough to buy their way off Earth had been deposited. Blast and his accomplices were growing filthy rich off the funds that were supposedly used to build and maintain destinations that did not exist.

The former GEA agent's eyes filled, blurring her vision, when she scanned a list of people—talented, intelligent people—who supposedly had already left Earth for a healthier existence in space. Their lives had been sacrificed for the greed of Frank Blast and others like him. If they had remained on Earth, they most likely would have figured out the truth.

The first thing they would have discovered was that the actual sun, moon, and stars were once again visible in the sky because conditions outside the domes were not as horrible as humanity had been led to believe. They would have discovered that the reddish-brown UV protectant sprayed on the domes once a month was nothing more than opaque camouflage meant to convince people that the atmosphere was still polluted beyond all hope. They would have discovered that Nutri-Synth was a genetically modified food source created for the purpose of shortening the human lifespan by altering the structure of human DNA.

People were not dying because of pollution and poor filtration. They were dying because they were being genetically rewired to do so.

The poor were the easiest targets, but they were not the only targets. Anyone with potential to discover what Raine had just found received the promise of a better life. They were strapped into space transports, administered lethal gases before launch, and their dead bodies were burned in furnaces on Moon Base Tarigo, their ashes blown into space to become cosmic dust.

Warring within her was the desire to expose Blast and his co-conspirators versus following through with her goal of killing Blast tonight. Who would believe her even if she did present documentation outlining the conspiracy? Blast controlled the media in Quadrant One, and no doubt his tentacles extended throughout the Northern Hemisphere. Once she came forward with the truth, she would be dead before the first news report aired. Was there anyone on Earth she could trust? Anyone who would care?

Raine fought down the desire to scream and pound the flexible metal sides of the air ducts. *Think this through, Jess,* Theo's voice whispered in her head. *Blast is powerful, but not everyone has yielded to him or others like him.* She could feel Theo's fingers sifting through her mind, culling information she had gathered and stored, sorting through the important pieces, and discarding the useless. Her eyelids fluttered. Her eyes blinked open.

Sector 48 of Quadrant Three in the Northern Hemisphere. Raine shoved the document images hovering in the space around her to one side, compressing them into a file for later use. Her finger swiped across the HoloMir screen looking for the information she knew existed. She opened and closed file after file as she searched for clues. Images and words scrolled by almost too fast for her to decipher. One word jumped out at her, and she brought the scrolling information to a standstill with a single touch. *Recovery.* Among all the other file names and reports, recovery was the only positive word that stood out to Raine. It must have been a thorn in Frank Blast's side.

With trembling fingers, Raine opened the file and read:

FROM: Dr. Jacob Lassalle, PhD, Environmental and Climate Research

Dr. Leah Breslau, PhD, Atmospheric Science

TO: Citizen Council of Sector 48, Quadrant Three, Northern Hemisphere

CC: B'nei Sinai University Faculty, Economic and Social Commission, and GEA Administration

DATE: Third Quarter, 3038

RE: Project Recovery Status Report

Research during the past year has confirmed that life within the CRBR-1 and the MR-2 Regions is sustainable outside a bio-dome. Our counterparts in Sector 39, Quadrant Three, Southern Hemisphere noted a 19% and 28% increase in flora growth and a 10% and 15% increase in fauna resurgence for the regions respectively.

Our field agents recently discovered falsified documentation in all four Quadrants of both hemispheres detailing how hazardous atmospheric and environmental conditions outside the bio-domes have been greatly exaggerated for at least 900 years. We believe the unchecked human-sourced pollution in the wake of global economic collapse that led to conditions requiring life inside the bio-domes is no longer a threat to Earth or humans.

A detailed report of our findings is ready for presentation to the above-listed addressees. We highly recommend recalling our field agents, inviting allies in close proximity to the presentation, and preparing a defense strategy in the likelihood that this information is leaked.

Raine leaned back against the air duct, processing what she had read. She closed her eyes and shook her head. Her whole world shrank with the realization that this was bigger than her desire to kill Frank Blast. Removing the crime boss might put a small crimp in the greater plan playing out across Earth—and it would definitely satisfy her need for revenge—but what then? She could think of several powerful snakes that would slither out from beneath the rock of self-serving greed to take Blast's place without a hitch.

Fear's icy fingers crept along her spine and lingered on her shoulders, paralyzing her with the weight of indecision. Doubt told her she was only one person, she had forfeited her life for a foolish vendetta, and she should probably start looking for a way out of the Quadrant. Theo's voice reminded her that the tears coursing down her cheeks did not compromise her strength. Raine sniffed hard and dragged the sleeve of Arusi's sweatshirt across her dripping nose, leaving a trail of viscous disrespect that made her smile.

A deep breath cleansed Raine's mind. She retrieved the file floating to her left and whisked the memo into it. Then she opened a new message to Drs. Lassalle and Breslau, using the university address on the memo. A downward swipe of her hand placed the electronic data into the message on her HoloMir screen. A tap of her finger sent the doctors everything they needed to know.

Raine forced her weary mind to memorize the route to the top of the skyscraper. She also committed to memory the times in which the two-person security teams would patrol, their routes, and their shift changes. Holes appeared in their routines, slivers of time through which she could slip. Ideally, she would do so without having to kill another person. She must be quick and efficient; no second chances existed in this scenario.

A small sense of satisfaction and revenge came with applying Hastings's security clearance to open as many files in the entire system as possible. Having done everything within her power to help the people of Earth, it was now time to find and eliminate Blast. The urgency of her mission throbbed at the back of her skull as did her awareness that the biodome's artificial environmental system would be lightening the skies within the next two, two and half hours. She avoided looking at the HoloMir time display to confirm what her internal body clock told her: Blast's employees would soon be arriving for work.

When nothing in any of the files indicated where she could find the crime boss, Raine exhaled through gritted teeth and rethought her approach, returning to the information she had specifically pulled off Hastings's HoloMir. Surely his calendar would have a meeting with his employer occurring in the next twenty-four hours; Blast micromanaged his upper echelon employees. But an appointment with Blast did not appear on Hastings's calendar. There was, however, a meeting with Yureed Santos of the Southern Hemisphere taking place at Santos's private mansion.

Santos's reputation in the Southern Hemisphere rivaled that of Frank Blast. Raine sometimes thought they competed in cruelty just for the fun of it. But there was no love lost between the two of them. For Hastings to have a meeting with Santos on his work calendar indicated that he believed he would be in the Southern Hemisphere before his employer discovered his betrayal. The e-mail she found reinforced this fact:

> Santos, Yureed <yureed.santos@SHQ1skymail>Yesterday, 13:42
>
> Hey, Campbell. Looking forward to seeing you tomorrow. We have lots to discuss about business. Hope you enjoyed the little present I sent your way. Her name is Chantal, and she's a real pleaser. You can toss her when you're done with her. Plenty more where she came from.
>
> Santos

Blast's statement of "I want to know that the man who conspired against me is dead" refuted Hastings's assumption that Blast was unaware of his plans.

The once-encrypted message had sailed past security and now sat in an inbox for anyone to find. Raine had no doubt that Blast knew of its presence the minute it arrived. He had probably been waiting for it. But Hastings had doubly messed up because he was still partying with the prostitute in the early morning hours of the day he should have been traveling to meet Santos. Raine quickly checked his itinerary to see if his passage to the Southern Hemisphere had been cancelled.

It had not been, which in a twisted way, made sense. Raine thought through the situation from Frank Blast's perspective. He would take Hastings's place, show up in the Southern Hemisphere, and either eliminate Santos for attempting to infiltrate his business or somehow use the incident to force Santos into an alliance in his favor. Raine's heart sank when she saw the passage was scheduled for eight that morning. She chewed her thumbnail while reexamining her plan to locate Blast.

Again, she put herself in the criminal's mind. Most likely, Blast would have his secretary put Hastings's trip on the calendar she kept for him. She would not have questioned the request even though she knew Santos was a rival. Blast's reputation would keep her mouth shut. Whoever had a calendar with the Hastings/Santos meeting would surely be his secretary. She would also be in possession of his itinerary. It was a long shot, but it was all Raine had.

The hacking and decryption program on Raine's HoloMir tablet was GEA issued and had probably been created by someone within Blast's empire. She had been fortunate to have not needed to employ it thus far. She felt no shame in using it against the crime boss to locate his secretary. Still, it took the high-tech software an hour to produce the profile of Clarice McNamara. The woman's pixelated picture slowly rose from the screen and gibberish characters turned into recognizable words. Raine could not care less about Clarice's job description or work history; she scrolled directly to the calendar the secretary kept for Blast. Sure enough, the Hastings/Santos meeting appeared as expected. And then it disappeared.

Raine flinched as letter by letter a blinking cursor deleted the Hastings/Santos meeting from the calendar. She sat immobile, watching the real-time image flip to Blast's itinerary as someone highlighted the block of his day that included travel as well as the meeting. The words "To Be Rescheduled" appeared in glowing red letters. The next obvious action would be to cancel Blast's passage to the Southern Hemisphere. That did not happen.

The alarms going off in Raine's head drowned out Theo's voice of reason. She knew exactly where Blast would be except for a large chunk of time. Why the change? What would possibly keep the crime boss from attending a meeting with one of his biggest rivals, especially when Blast held all the cards? *Nothing,* Raine thought. *Nothing would keep him from decimating Santos once he had him in his sights.*

Raine's mind replayed this new development to the suppression of all other thoughts. Tiredness crept along the edges of her concentration, crowding out Theo's voice in her head. It made no sense to change the calendar and itinerary but not cancel the passage. She mulled over the fact that perhaps Blast would send someone else to do his dirty work and just as quickly discarded the idea, knowing it would take too long to obtain new travel permits from the Southern Hemisphere. Had Blast's secretary simply messed up?

Too many variables and too many questions existed for her comfort. The grains of time kept slipping away from Raine while she sat motionless, trying to decide what to do, where to go. Ideas refused to come to her, yet she knew she had to keep moving forward. Her GEA training and survival instincts rose to the surface and took over. She moved mechanically, but at least she moved.

Raine ditched the sweatshirt and drawstring knapsack to allow for ease of movement. The shotgun had already been removed as she navigated the ductwork and to give her quick access in case of emergency. Transferring from the ventilation system to the elevators required that she reprogram the security cameras to swivel away from the elevators a moment after a GEA security team rounded the corner. She also needed to request the next available empty car.

Execution of the plan succeeded, but something nagged at the back of her mind. She was no sooner inside an elevator car than she heard the electronic scrubbers passing in the air ducts. It was the sort of preprogrammed service that should have taken place hours earlier. Raine could not help but believe they had been set in motion for another reason, and she was that reason.

Shaking off the suspicion that someone knew she was in the building, she took the car headed to the eightieth floor, double checking the connection between her HoloMir tablet and the mainframe on the ride up. She had to find Blast before he disappeared into the block of unaccounted for time. Her attention was still focused on her computer screen when she realized the elevator should have already stopped. The numbers eighty-three, eighty-four, and eighty-five lit up before her tired mind grasped what was happening.

Panic seized her heart. She fought the inclination to hit the emergency stop, which would draw attention to her. The elevator continued to race upward, passing floors ninety-five, ninety-six, and ninety-seven. Only three more levels stood between her and Frank Blast's private domain. Raine switched the safety to off on the shotgun slung across her back and the GEA blaster strapped to her thigh. She did not know what to expect when the elevator stopped, but she knew it would not be good. Right before the doors opened, Raine took a deep breath, exhaled half, and braced herself against the back wall with her GEA blaster held in front of her. The redundant HoloMir tablet lay at her feet.

No hail of bullets or pulses of light greeted her. No noise and no movement. Raine stepped from the elevator, her boot soles squeaking on the polished floor. As if in expectation of her arrival, the recorded sound of a waterfall began to emanate from unseen speakers, the track punctuated with the distant call of rare birds. Exotic wood from decimated forests paneled the walls of the one-hundredth story. Marble imported from across the ocean—the quality of which used to be reserved for mansions, churches, and museums—paved the floor.

She ventured farther into the reception area, passing between three rows of black leather wingback chairs where Blast's business associates usually waited like mendicants for the bestowing of a few precious minutes of the crime boss's time. All were empty.

Other examples of opulence in artwork, furniture, and window dressings begged for Raine's attention. She noticed nothing save only the empty chair behind the desk where Blast's secretary should have been sitting as she took calls and rerouted them to the crime boss's lackeys. The other detail to garner her attention was the recessed lighting down the hallway to her left. Each light came to life one at a time as if illuminating the direction she should take. Raine holstered the blaster and unclipped the shotgun from the strap, tightly snugging the weapon against her shoulder.

There was no reason not to follow where led. With her eyes focused down the length of the shotgun, Raine crept as quietly as possible along the halls. When she needed to round a corner, she used the highly polished blade of Theo's knife like a mirror. Two turns to the right deposited her in front of twelve-foot double doors carved with gods and goddess locked in timeless battle. She kicked the doors open where they met, banging them against the walls inside. Frank Blast sat at his desk, reclining with hands folded on his lap. He stared at her.

"My God you're hard to kill."

CHAPTER TWENTY

THE METAL SIDES OF THE ventilation system at Blast Tower enclosed Rogue's conscious presence. He simply folded himself into a cross-legged position beside Raine. His hands reached for her with an urgency checked only by his fear that they would pass through the vapor of a ghost. That he found himself crammed into an air duct in the building owned by his worst enemy did not trouble him. Realizing that he had been correct about Raine's intentions to infiltrate Blast Tower and trying not to torture himself with that fact mattered more.

The blue luminescence from the holographic documents cast by Raine's HoloMir provided the only light in the ductwork. Rogue assessed the former GEA agent's expression first, leaning between her and the multiple projections. To his surprise, the weird glow across her face disappeared, throwing her features in shadow, and he wondered how the incident would play out on Earth in her time.

Despite the stillness of Raine's body, her eyes still radiated vibrancy. Yet he felt no physical warmth between them; they were still worlds apart. Nish's gentle urging in his mind reinforced their separation, and Rogue leaned away from Raine. He did not need to be close to read the loss of hope etched on her face. He could not help but believe he bore some responsibility for what he saw there.

Again, Rogue sensed Nish compelling him to be observant past satisfying his emotional needs. Without words, the *Jiltraos* guided him by impressing her own thoughts and experiences with second sight upon him. He felt a gentle appeal leading him mentally to see what Raine saw. Rogue turned his attention to the flat holographic pages that required him to place himself in Raine's point of view. She had many documents open in the space around her. Some were layered one atop the other but not concealing so much of the text that he could not read most of it.

It did not take him long to understand the anguish drawing the corners of Raine's mouth downward. His anger reverberated off the metal ductwork at the loss of all his dreams as he read the reports revealing the truth—or rather the lies—about Mars Base Algernon and Space Stations Eden and Vista. Nish's mental presence started to pull him back when she sensed his distress and heard him cry out.

"No—Nish—please wait. I won't lose my head again. Just give me a few moments, please."

Her grip on his senses eased, and Rogue felt himself slip back into place beside Raine. His mind tried to reject her next plan of action, but there was no denying her objective as she sat in the ventilation system of Blast Tower, well-armed and having discovered the truth behind Frank Blast's vast wealth. Rogue also read the documents detailing the quality of life outside the bio-domes, and his thoughts drifted back to the night he stood beside the dome wall looking at the real moon. With all his being, he wished Raine would escape to another Sector, another Quadrant, or at least slip beyond the shelter of the bio-domes to attempt life in the outlands of Earth.

Ultimately, the moment came when he realized there was nothing he could do to help her. The duct wall produced a single note of metallic complaint when he slumped against it. Again, he felt Nish wrap him in silent words of comfort and gently tug his consciousness back into the Realm. He did not resist, and Raine began to fade from sight. Before they were completely separated once again, Rogue placed his fingers on her wrist. He gasped when he felt a single beat of her pulse.

Nish still held Rogue's hands in her own. Her grip lightened, but he reacted by tightening his. He had not yet opened his eyes and did not want to. They sat together in moments carved from the time between two worlds, serenaded by the night insects. He heard Nish draw a slow breath.

"Much time will pass here, and we will find the cure for the poison in your body. Then you will return to Earth and be with your woman."

Rogue noticed she did not say "rescue your woman." She also did not mention his desire to bring Raine into the Realm where they could lead a safe and healthy life, but she had to be aware of his wish. His opened eyes beheld the darkened forest floor, then rose to take in his hands engulfed in Nish's. A barely perceptible smile eased the uncertainty on his face as he marveled yet again at the color of the Realmer's skin, now smoky lavender in the shadows of night.

"That's my only hope, isn't it?" Rogue said.

"Is not restoring your life and your place among your people what you desire?"

"Could you see what I saw, Nish? The documents I read?"

"I can read your thoughts not your language, but I sensed how much harm was done to your spirit."

"Finding the cure isn't just about me anymore. Raine is in danger, and I have to do something."

"I know. But again, we have the benefit of time moving faster here. Trust me, *Mir*-Rogue, when I tell you to rest tonight, clear the images from your mind, and in the morning, we will figure it out together."

"Can you promise me she'll be safe until then?"

"You know I want to. That I would if I could."

"I know."

"You just want to protect those you love. Believe me, Rogue, I understand."

Nish's head turned toward the camp where Bialig, head bobbing from the medicine Talj gave him, forced himself to sit sentinel until she and Rogue returned to the safety of the fire. Rogue's gaze followed hers.

"Is there anything else I can show you?" Nish asked without looking at Rogue.

"No, thank you, *Mir*-Nish. You've done more than enough for tonight. As you said, we'll figure it out in the morning."

Morning arrived with its own set of problems. The turmoil of the previous evening lingered with the cold dawn mists. As beautiful as the tall grass forest was, the travelers longed to be in the open where sunlight could engulf them, and everything seemed clearer. Nish did her best to follow her morning routines and rouse her drowsy companions. She brewed tea for Talj and Rogue, who awakened at the sound of her activity, but she allowed Bialig and Misko to rest. Her hand on Rogue's shoulder eased the frown on his face when the Leader did not awaken first.

Spears of crystal sunlight sliced through the foliage of the woody grasses and blazed directly above them before either Bialig or Misko awoke. The Leader moved first, drawing a deep breath and groaning its release, stretching his arms and legs in a most ungainly manner. Nish smiled with pleasure when the big man threw his sleeping fur back and continued to roll his neck and shoulders. She presented him with tea and the simple porridge she, Talj, and Rogue had enjoyed.

Before he accepted the food from her hands, Bialig's eyes fell on Misko's sleeping form still hidden beneath his fur. Concern raised a ridge between the Leader's snowy eyebrows and tightened the muscles along his jaw. He rubbed his hands upward over his face, dislodging sleep and anxiety from his visage. Although desirous of pressing on, Bialig was not without compassion for the young man he thought of as a brother; he would allow Misko to sleep until he woke up on his own.

Bird calls like the sound of tinkling glass dropped into the spare warmth of morning and competed with the trills and snorts of small foraging mammals. A few unnatural notes accompanied the animal noises. Bialig looked up from his breakfast to see Rogue leaning over something he held across his lap. The *uma* plunked at the strings, hunting for familiar notes and chords, improvising a song as his fingers worked their way up the neck of the instrument.

The three wakened Realmers stopped mid-bite as they stared at Rogue. Appreciation for his abilities vied for embarrassment at his lack of understanding; one simply did not handle instruments belonging to the *Doh s'Imalo Paten*. But their friend coaxed a song from the instrument that, although made for a Realmer, rested comfortably across Rogue's legs. He smiled to himself, humming the song as he composed on the spot.

They resumed eating, and before they finished, Rogue had perfected the tune in the short time he had been working on it. This time when he smiled, he looked directly into Bialig's eyes, then Talj's and Nish's, seeking approval and acceptance. What he saw made him withdraw his fingers from the strings with the quickness of one burned.

"I thought a little music might lure Misko from his bad mood," Rogue said.

Bialig finished eating, scraping his bowl clean before he spoke.

"I am sure if *Mir*-Misko was awake, he would have given you permission to play the *tegil*."

Rogue understood his gaffe and silently cursed himself. To his surprise, the Leader spoke again.

"Your gift will no doubt be welcomed by our *Paten*. I am sure you would succeed under his direction."

As long as Rogue had been in the Realm, Bialig still needed to make allowances for him. At least the gambler no longer resented the grace the Realmers extended him. Not wanting to press his luck, he stood and walked to where Misko lay. Gently, so as not to disturb the young man, Rogue returned the *tegil* to its cloth covering and placed it next to the other instruments. He stood and hesitated for a moment, caught off guard by the sensation he used to experience when another card player bluffed during a poker game. Forever afterward, Rogue would wish he had said something right then.

* * *

THE NIGHT HAD BEEN PLEASANT, but the morning felt unwelcoming as the cold winds blew across Misko's face, whipping his long hair. Wine-colored clouds gravid with rain lumbered across the flat steel sky, and he wished he had been able to bring his outer cloak. Walking faster and rubbing his arms did little to alleviate the chill that originated from deep within. He shook his head to dismiss his doubt, instead returning his mind to the thoughts that had propelled him forward thus far. If only his head and his heart would not battle over his decision.

It still amazed him that Kolbian had been able to get a message to him through the *Damirg* Clan. He had not spotted a red tattoo on any of their members, but then neither had anyone seen his. The *Damirgne* probably did not know Kolbian had like-minded members among their families. How easily the young woman who supplied his *Doh s'Ima* with new sleeping furs had passed Kolbian's invitation for Misko to join him along. And after Bialig's treatment toward him, Misko could no longer resist.

He had been walking all night after slipping away once he heard Bialig's slow and even breathing, a result of the sleep aid in the beverage Talj had served him. Twice he lost his way, but once Misko reached the river cutting a swath through the grass forest, all he had to do was follow it to a natural landing where Kolbian would be waiting with a boat. Then there would be rejoicing and celebrating as he started down the true path of his life, answering a higher call than that of the *Doh s'Ima*.

Misko spotted Kolbian twenty paces away. The absence of other *sojabosne* startled him for a moment, but the Artist concluded their escape would be easier with fewer people. He shouted a greeting and waved his arms as he ran to where Kolbian waited.

The *sojabosnelo* leader, who crouched over the boat they would take, whirled around at the commotion and delivered a sharp smack to Misko's head as a welcome.

"You *fool*—is it your intention to alert the whole world to our presence?" Kolbian hissed.

"I am sorry, Kolbi—"

"You address me as *natamos* from now on. Do you understand?"

Misko nodded and hugged himself, willing the stinging in his eyes to disappear.

Kolbian's expression softened as he said, "Understand, Misko, we have worked too long and too hard to gain our freedom from the oppression of the *Dohne s'Ima* and the High Council of Elders to ruin it by alerting others to our escape. We will begin a new regime, a pure one that surpasses that of the weak-minded."

"Should that not begin with a purity of language, *natamos*?" Misko asked, hugging himself tighter when Kolbian's eyes widened.

The *sojabos* reigned in his reaction and chuckled. "You are wise, my young friend, but you still have much to learn. The language of the *umane* will unify us for when we join our brothers and sisters on Earth."

Now it was Misko's turn to be shocked, but he did not press the false leader any further. He stepped into the boat and sat in the bow as Kolbian pushed off. The tiny craft dipped dangerously low from side to side, then righted itself and drifted with the current. To his dismay, Misko was expected to paddle, a skill he knew nothing about. Soon, his back and arms ached with the exertion. He never knew freedom could be so painful.

* * *

BIALIG'S ROAR COULD BE HEARD over that of the rain-swollen river. Rogue, under the weight of his own pack and Misko's instruments, wondered if the Leader would plunge into the torrent to continue his pursuit. He tried to say something to assuage his friend's frustration, but Bialig refused to be consoled. Already an argument had broken out between them when Bialig had insisted he look for Misko alone.

"What do we do now, *Natamos*?" Nish asked.

The difficult choices played out on Bialig's face, resulting in a frown indicative of their undesirability. Rogue knew the Leader would not abandon them at the river to follow Misko alone, even if it did mean he would be able to travel faster. He thought about suggesting they walk back to the *Damirg* Clan for help, but that would give Misko an even greater lead, and none of them knew where he was headed.

"I have been able to track him this far, but he has taken a boat from this point on," Bialig said.

"I don't even know how you tracked him in the rain, so how can you be sure he took a boat from here?" Rogue asked.

"Because it is what I would have done if I wanted to kidnap someone and transport them quickly."

"What do you mean 'kidnap'?" Nish asked. "We would have heard someone come into camp, *Natamos*, and his belongings were still there."

Bialig lifted his face to the spit of rain falling from scattered clouds.

"I should not have taken the sleeping draught, then maybe I would have heard him get up and leave."

"So, you're back to thinking he ran away?" Rogue asked.

"*Mir*-Misko was tempted away. I am not only pursuing a member of my *Doh s'Ima*. I am chasing my enemy."

"*Mira*," Nish said, "Misko is not your enemy."

"No, but Kolbian is, and this is his work," Bialig replied.

Light flashed in Rogue's eyes but not from the dwindling storm. A vision of a raised arm and a red tattoo raced across his mind. When he fitted the pieces together with Bialig's statement, Rogue knew the Leader was correct in his assessment.

"He's gone to join Kolbian and the *sojabosne*," Rogue said.

"But why would Misko do such a thing?" Nish asked.

Talj put his arm around her to calm her trembling and pulled her hood forward to keep the rain off her face. His voice—worn coarse by his years, the rain, and the forced march through the grass forest—encouraged them as he said, "We will follow you, *Mira*-Bialig, to save our brother from those who wish to do him harm."

"Me, too," Rogue said. "Where you guys go, I go."

The Leader nodded once. "It is enough."

* * *

MISKO'S ARMS HUNG LIMP AND his back and shoulders burned. Even if he had brought all his gear, he would not have been able to unroll his bedding or play his instruments. Abandoning his things to slip away had been his greatest regret, but Kolbian assured him there would be quality instruments of greater worth among his new Clan to play. Now, as he and the false leader dragged the boat ashore, the young man's only thought was toward collapsing into a deep sleep. Kolbian had other plans.

Setting up camp fell to Misko as did making a fire and cooking food. The young man pondered Kolbian's apparent lack of preparedness when he realized there was only enough bedding for one. His new *natamos* covered his mistake by declaring the weather mild enough for sleeping without a fur. He finished with the observation that perhaps Bialig really had not prepared Misko for all life's struggles as well as the Leader had thought. Kolbian used the poorly made meal to drive his opinion home.

"If you had cross-trained in the skills of the *Doh s'Ima*, this meal would be edible."

"I am sorry, *natamos*. Nish did all our cooking," Misko replied.

"That is weak thinking, boy. Ask yourself: what has Bialig and the *Doh s'Ima* really done for you besides oppress you?"

"Well, I used my skills as the *Paten*—"

Kolbian waved away his answer. "Bialig does not have your best interests at heart. He only wants you in the *Doh s'Ima* to lord it over you; he craves the prestige of opening the portal between worlds."

"It is a talent that requires all our skills."

"*Mir*-Misko," Kolbian said, applying the affectionate term and moving closer to the young man, "I perceived your dilemma from the time you spent in our camp. Did Bialig hear your voice when you tried to stop his unprovoked attack? Could anyone hear you as you cried out for peace? No, my friend, you are a mere *Paten*, but you have the potential to be so much more."

Misko wrapped his arms around his drawn-up knees and rested his chin on them. He stared into the fire, immobile as a stone ready to be carved.

"But you took the mark of our people, the red tattoo, showing your willingness to think and choose for yourself. In our new world order, I shall give you a place by my side from which you can rule those who refuse to conform to our way of life."

"But why did you kidnap us, *natamos*?" Misko whispered.

Kolbian stiffened momentarily. A honeyed smile spread across his face as he poked the fire with a stick.

"I had no choice but to bring Bialig to me. He is headstrong, resistant, but it was for his own good." Kolbian took Misko's chin in his grip, commanding his attention. "It pains me to tell you this, Misko, but Bialig did not come for his *Doh s'Ima*. His only interest was in saving Nish."

"I know."

"Bialig's Leadership is suppressing your talent, and in effect, you, Misko. Next, he will censor your art to keep the truth from coming out."

"And he has already replaced me with another," Misko said, his voice a wisp of breath.

Kolbian's mind raced to grasp Misko's meaning. He knew Bialig would never do as the young man suggested, but something had occurred to make Misko believe this. Had his spies among the Clans missed a detail when giving help to his brother? The young woman among the *Damirgne* had mentioned nothing.

"With whom, Misko?"

"Rogue, the *uma*."

"The *uma* has not been sent back?" demanded Kolbian.

To keep the *uma* in their world was to break the ruling of the High Council of Elders and went against everything Kolbian believed he knew about his brother. Perhaps turning Bialig would not be as difficult as he had originally thought.

CHAPTER TWENTY-ONE

ANOTHER SCRATCH IN THE LEATHER strap of Rogue's pack added up to ten days of travel along the river upon which Kolbian had escaped with Misko. Even the gambler could tell their route took them far from the direction of the *Avboeth*. Every second or third day, they encountered cold ash of abandoned campfires, scrapes along the riverbank where the boat had been dragged ashore, and two sets of footprints in the soft mud. Bialig took comfort from the prints; his brother had not killed Misko outright. Yet the proof of life also tortured the Leader as every day his brother outstripped the distance he could travel on foot.

Rogue came to his assistance by keeping lookout from either the head of the line or the back. He requested a weapon from Bialig in addition to the knife Jedla had given him and received the Leader's shortest knife. When questioned about the extra weight, Rogue insisted that carrying the extra weapon as well as Misko's instruments posed no hindrance. The other three had divided Misko's pack between them; they were confident their *Paten* would return to the *Doh s'Ima*.

Much rode on Bialig's shoulders, and no single aspect took priority. He must rescue Misko, but in doing so he could not put the others at risk. He knew Talj had been consuming large doses of pain remedies to allow his aged body to keep up with the arduous journey on the rocky, slippery riverbank. Nish prepared food they could eat during the journey to compensate for the stolen moments Bialig required for hunting. They walked far into the evening and arose well before dawn. No one complained.

The Leader also considered Rogue, who clearly had his own set of problems. Besides the poison in his body, something he had seen during the second sight left the *uma* talking quietly to himself as they walked. Rogue sighed frequently and shook his head with an air of hopelessness. Guilt flooded Bialig when he prayed the gambler's problems would not interfere with his mission.

The group spent another five days in silent pursuit. Their spirits, already dampened by the intermittent rains, sank lower as the terrain became rockier and more difficult to navigate, forcing the four friends to take a trail not directly following the course of the river. Although Kolbian would have to cover longer distances looking for a safe place to come ashore, his faster mode of travel would continue to widen the gap between them. On the sixth day, the trail curved sharply back toward the river, but Bialig feared Kolbian had far outdistanced them.

That night the weather seemed even colder than usual to Rogue. He felt the chill more than the Realmers, and he did not know how to interpret the brittle, yellow leaves falling from the tall grasses. Nish wrapped him in Misko's sleeping fur and placed a leather bag of fire-warmed rocks at his feet. When they awoke to frost on the ground the next morning, the gambler finally understood the season was changing.

Rogue blew on his hands to get his fingers working. Stiff from the cold, he was the last to have his pack ready to go. The added weight of Misko's instruments required him to kneel on one knee to hoist the pack before pushing himself upright. From this position he observed footprints in the soft ground he had not seen the night before. He knew by their shape and size alone that they must be addressed. Bialig had already started leading the others down the path when Rogue called to him, waving him back.

"Hey, you need to see this. What in the Realm leaves that kind of track?"

"A *mojar*. I heard it come close last night," Bialig said.

"You heard it? Did you ever think about waking me up?"

"To wake you would have startled it. If I heard it, Rogue, obviously I was ready with a weapon drawn. And it was only one."

"Yeah, well, one of whatever it was looks big enough to finish me."

"*Mojarne* send one out to scout for food. You must not have appealed to their tastes."

"Oh, that's funny, real funny."

Nish's and Talj's eyes met across the comments slicing the air between their comrades. Without further remark, Bialig turned and walked down the path.

"We must move on from this area quickly," Nish said. "I will scatter *uketel* behind us as we walk. *Mojarne* cannot stand the scent, and they will be unable to track us."

Bialig slowed when he heard Nish's statement.

"I will walk at the back of the line and spread the *uketel*, *Mir*-Nish. Rogue, take the lead. Are you able to travel at an adequate speed?"

The gambler's jaw clenched before he said, "Just make sure you don't fall behind."

By midday, light rain added to the group's discomfort. The dropping temperature froze patches of the wet ground, requiring Talj to take Bialig's arm for support. The old Healer repeatedly mumbled his apologies, to which Bialig said nothing in reply. Nish secretly wished Rogue would make one of his awkward statements or strike up a conversation of endless banter. Anything to shatter the veneer of calm hiding the Leader's true feelings. Other than the rain falling harder, nothing changed, and no one spoke.

When it became apparent that Talj practically slept as he walked, Bialig ordered them to make camp for the night. Nish scouted a location away from the cold winds blowing off the river. The rain had diminished, but a fine mist collected on the leaves and dripped on the travelers, further souring their moods. Rogue helped Nish search for dry firewood.

"You should be tending Talj, and Bialig should be out here looking for wood. He is the Leader," Rogue said.

Nish smiled without looking at Rogue.

"I get that you're the Gatherer, but he's stronger and can carry back larger pieces. Then we'd have a good fire tonight. Talj could use the heat."

Nish continued collecting wood.

"What's up with him anyway? He acts like he's the only person with problems around here."

"Then perhaps you should share yours with him," Nish said. "Ask him whatever it is that has been on your mind."

"What do mean?"

"It is apparent to everyone that your thoughts are elsewhere."

"I said I'd help find Misko, and I meant it."

"No one is questioning your commitment."

"You sure about that?"

Nish faced Rogue who held a piece of wood in each hand while her arms were full.

"Have you not noticed *Mir*-Talj scratching at every rock within reach, searching for the cure he lost in our flight from Kolbian? Or how Bialig returns from hunting with pieces of *yorit* in the hope that it is the elusive ingredient?"

Rogue clacked the two pieces of wood together and blew out his cheeks. His expression held penitence, his words rebellion.

"What's the chance you could show me into Earth again tonight? I'm sure the big guy won't mind since he gave his approval once already."

"Very well, Rogue. Tonight, after we are settled."

The weather prevented the pair from slipping away to fulfill Rogue's request. He would not make eye contact with Nish, who would gladly have shown him into Earth in the presence of the others. She could not leave the old Healer, whose sore throat benefitted from the soothing drink Nish prepared him. Despite his pain, Talj spoke of things they all needed to hear; his hoarse whisper obliged them to sit quietly.

"Our brother Misko is young, but the light within him is strong. He is in our *Doh s'Ima* because of his skills as a *Paten*, but it is service toward others that truly solidifies one's role within the group. This is why it pains me that Misko has allowed his light to be dimmed by Kolbian's lies. But lies are all Kolbian has, so perhaps our brother will see through them.

"Misko not only battles evil forces from without, but he also fights those from within. He possesses abundant skill as an Artist, but his dissatisfaction compels him to pretend to be something he is not, such as a warrior. Or a *Natamos*."

Rogue hid his expression by taking a drink of his warm beverage. Nish's hands worried her cup, almost spilling her drink. Talj took a sip and continued.

"Misko has chosen to see a reality that does not exist. His inner self—his life force—emerges as the person he wants people to believe he is. But he cannot maintain this unhealthy obsession with becoming something that he is not. It will end in failure.

"From the dawn of our world, the standard of conduct for our people was set by the Infinite One, written and heard in the stars for all. It is up to the individual to decide how he or she will respond to this paradigm, not to create a new one."

"Then are we not accountable to each other, *Mir*-Talj?" Bialig asked.

"And *for* each other, my friend. When we see a brother or sister going astray, we speak with them and encourage them by setting a good example. We take others as witnesses to implore our fellow Clan members to turn from their errant ways. If needed, we present them and ourselves before the High Council, seeking guidance regarding the situation. And yet, in the end, each of us will answer for our own actions. This knowledge must be balanced with the truth that we do not live for ourselves alone. It is a hard thing, but it is not impossible."

Logs glowing from within crackled and fell apart, tossing a handful of sparks skyward. Nish jumped up to tend the blaze. She stacked pieces of wood to direct the heat toward them and the smoke upward. Rogue used her activity as cover to disengage from the group and prepare his bed for the night. Made uncomfortable by Talj's discourse, he had trouble falling asleep while trying to convince himself that his motives were not selfish.

* * *

ROGUE ROSE WITH THE DULL morning sun as it waged a losing battle against the wine-colored clouds. He wasted no time building a fire, choosing instead to roll his bedding and pack his few belongings. The Realmers awakened to the sounds of the gambler cursing softly under his breath while jamming items into his pack, emptying everything to retrieve his food stashed at the bottom, stomping around camp, and making more noise than necessary first thing in the morning. When Rogue noticed Bialig watching him, he lifted his chin toward the Leader but did not speak to him.

"Hey, Nish," Rogue said. "Do you think we could take a few moments for you to show me into Earth again?"

The three Realmers, still rubbing sleep from their eyes, sat up in their rumpled bedding to observe Rogue. Nish and Talj looked at the Leader.

"We do not have time this morning," Bialig said.

"I'm pretty sure I wasn't asking you," Rogue replied.

Bialig stood and rolled his neck and shoulders, stretched his arms and back. He looked everywhere except at the gambler.

"Nevertheless, our *Jiltraos* will not be taking time to share her second sight."

Rogue pulled the drawstring on his pack and stood to face him. "You know, I have things I need to take care of, too. I've practically put my life on hold for this little mission of yours, so some help might be forthcoming."

"Rogue, you willingly agreed to help find Misko," Nish said. Her voice held entreaty.

"What I need will only take a few seconds. Moments even."

"I said no," Bialig repeated.

"I thought you might, but that's okay. I know my way back, and I'm sure I can find the *Damirgne.* If Jedla and her hunting party were friendly toward me, why not other Clan members? I don't really need you."

Rogue picked up his pack and left Misko's instruments lying on the ground. He walked away from camp in the direction they had come last night. Two strides put Bialig in the center of his path.

"You do nothing without my approval, *uma*."

"I don't need your approval. I'm not a member of your *Doh s'Ima*. I'm not even supposed to be here, remember? Now get the hell out of my way."

Bialig raised his hands in what Rogue interpreted as an aggressive move. The Leader pulled them away when his and Jedla's knives were drawn against him.

"I said get the hell out of my way. You're not the only person with someone to save."

"You cannot even save yourself, *uma*. Remember the *bargelnelo* pit and how I rescued you from the *sojabosne*? You are weak, helpless, and destructive, just like every other *uma* who ever set foot in our world."

"Is that why you're so afraid of me? Because I'm weak and helpless?"

Bialig stepped closer to Rogue. "If that is what you believe, then make your first strike your best because it is the only one you will get."

The gambler sighed and turned back toward camp, letting his pack slide off his shoulders. It hit the ground with a thud that masked the whisk of steel through air as Rogue whirled to attack Bialig with his own weapons. Never having engaged a foe so small, the Leader's initial instinct was to hold back as he would with a child. Rogue, however, showed no restraint and lunged for Bialig's lower legs, delivering twin slashes to his calf with a duck and roll that put him behind the big man. Rogue miscalculated the speed with which Bialig would respond.

Nish's scream smacked the air with more force than the blow the Leader delivered to Rogue's stomach. He knocked the wind out of the gambler, sending him sprawling. Bialig pulled the weapons from Rogue's limp grasp, tossing them aside and waiting for the *uma* to stop coughing and catch his breath. Rogue looked up with defiance in his eyes, and Bialig took it as a signal that he could endure a much-deserved thrashing.

Little effort was required to pick up his diminutive attacker, yet Bialig was impressed when he felt Rogue's biceps tighten beneath his grip. He mistakenly brought the *uma* closer and took a kick to his chin, prompting him to throw the gambler against a thick stand of grass. Rogue crashed into the hollow culms, rattling them, and breaking off the older pieces. A dangerously sharp fragment tore through the gambler's tunic and raked across his ribs. He did not have time to contemplate the injury as Bialig whisked him upward by his ankle and shook him like a dusty rag.

The Leader held Rogue upside down at arm's length, taking care not to bring him too close. The gambler trapped Bialig's wrist between his ankles and curled upward to throw both hands around the larger man's elbow. Rogue pulled with all his might, throwing Bialig off balance. When the Leader stumbled and fell, he took Rogue with him. Both released the other and rolled away. They sprang to their feet and assumed postures of attack.

Rogue advanced first, driven by blind fury and the belief that he had nothing to lose. When Bialig tried to sidestep him, Rogue adjusted by crashing his full weight into the side of the Leader's knee. The Realmer's shout of pain deafened Rogue to his own cries as Bialig palmed the gambler's head, his fingers clamping on Rogue's ears and eyes, and ripped him away. Rogue landed close to where Bialig knelt with one leg extended.

Talj wrapped Nish within his arms. He meant to shield her from the fight taking place but quickly realized her strength was more than he could contain. She extricated herself from his embrace and ran to where Bialig stood swaying over Rogue. She calmly picked up two broken stalks and handed the smaller to Bialig and the larger to Rogue.

"Now you look equally foolish in this senseless battle," she spat. "Go on and beat each other to death."

When neither man moved, she yanked Rogue up by the arm and shoved Bialig toward him. If they had noticed her trembling, both would have laid down their useless weapons. Neither could see past his own palpable rage masking fears and frustrations.

Nish never knew who flinched first. She jumped between the men with one arm raised and the other held downward to fend off blows of splintered wood.

The accusations began the second Nish cried out. Bialig and Rogue dropped their weapons as the old Healer rushed forward. His crooked fingers gently searched Nish's arms and shoulders for the bruises he knew would appear. His strained voice outshouted the other two as he reprimanded them for their stupid actions. Then he led Nish away, urging her to sit on her pack as he rummaged through his own for salve.

"You see what your self-centeredness has done?" Bialig shouted. "For once in your life, would you think about someone else first?"

"I am thinking about someone else—Raine. She needs me, and come hell or high water, I'm not going to abandon her now."

"You cannot go back, you ignorant *gradol*. How are you going to save her when you will die the second you return to Earth? Not that I plan on sending you back."

"I told you before, I don't need you. I know from Misko that any *Doh s'Ima* can send me back. Besides, you're a coward—"

"*I* am a coward?"

"Yeah, you idiot. You're too afraid to admit how much you love Nish."

Rogue screamed the last two words. The ensuing silence held only the crash of whitewater. The gambler knew he possessed a tendency toward social tactlessness. This time, he surprised even himself with what felt like a personal admission. He panted a laugh and shook his head, staring into Bialig's face as if seeing his own reflection.

"I cannot abandon her," Rogue whispered. "Please . . . help me save her."

Bialig's jaw worked, and he looked over Rogue's head. In a soft voice he said, "To send you back would mean immediate death."

"Then open the portal—*please*—and save her yourself. Just like you did for me."

"Rogue—"

"You want me to beg? All right—I'm begging you. Save Raine."

"Rogue I cannot—"

"Why? Because she's an *uma*? Because the High Council forbids it? I'll take the blame at the *Avboeth*. They can punish me however they want. Just please don't let Blast kill her. Not Raine. She doesn't deserve this."

Bialig placed his hand on Rogue's shoulder, ready to withdraw it should the gambler lash out.

"My friend, I cannot open the portal without Misko."

Dawning widened Rogue's eyes. Disappointment closed them.

The Leader continued. "Help me find Misko first, and I promise when I can open the portal, I will save your woman."

"Can you guarantee me we'll find him in time? Raine is already so close to danger."

Turning to Nish, Bialig asked, "Will you show me the *uma* woman in her current situation?"

"Of course, *Mira*," she replied. Supreme composure kept Nish's features from conveying anything other than the ultimate respect for her *Natamos* despite Rogue's blunder moments ago. Not even a blush crept across her beautiful face.

Nish took Bialig's hand and Rogue's. She nodded once to indicate they should join hands to complete the circle. The familiar rush of wind took Rogue's breath away, leaving him with just enough to say, "Oh, God, no . . ."

CHAPTER TWENTY-TWO

DON'T ENGAGE THEM IN CONVERSATION, Jess, and don't lower your weapon. This is not a negotiation.

Theo's voice in Raine's head. Her first mission with her older brother. A smuggling ring busted in the very act. Forty arrests in one night except for the crime boss. Now she stood before the man in charge, a fact they could never prove, but what did that matter? Frank Blast would die tonight.

Raine allowed herself one blink as Blast moved with the fluidity of a snake from behind his desk to stand at the windows overlooking the city. She had the shotgun trained on his back, her eyes on the reflection of his face. His focus went far beyond the walls of the dome neither could see. A bank of gray clouds rolled in and deposited another layer of pristine snow over the filthy city. From this height, one might almost believe in the purity of the scene.

Their standoff pulsed with the tensity of a steel cable about to snap. She tried not to wonder what passed through Blast's mind as he stood there, ignoring her. Tried not to allow her emotions and exhaustion to blur her eyes with tears. She battled down the justification she had for killing the man in cold blood. She did not even entertain herself with the truth that he deserved death. But she waited too long and became lost in the void of inactivity.

Raine thought the muzzle flash from Blast's .380 would have been preceded by a warning rattle.

* * *

ROGUE FELL TO HIS KNEES when Nish ended the session of second sight into Earth. He had stood between Raine and the bullet from Blast's gun, and he felt her impending death more sharply than his own. His lungs burned from the mouthfuls of cold air he inhaled to keep from passing out. He could not control his breathing. Lightheadedness overtook him. Peripheral blackness encroached upon his vision. The last thing he saw was the Realmers' anxious faces crowded above him.

* * *

IT WAS HARD TO TELL who led the expedition to rescue Misko. Bialig tracked from the front of the line while Rogue set a relentless pace from the back. The gambler's determination to make things right for himself and the Realmers dominated his every thought since waking from his faint. He understood that their fates were too closely aligned. To disregard one would be to the peril of the other.

Rogue inserted himself into the *Doh s'Ima* wherever he was needed. He started by assisting Talj in dressing the wounds he inflicted on Bialig and willingly submitting to being tended as well. Then he helped Nish resize some of Misko's clothing so he and she would have extras layers of warmth; the rain had turned into steadily falling snow. The one fortunate turn for all of them occurred when Bialig announced that Kolbian had left the river. They would no longer be blasted by cold, wet winds.

However, the landscape had also changed and provided less shelter in the form of trees or grasses. Sharp boulders, the evidence of ancient landslides from the bordering mountains, dotted the plains through which they traveled. Bialig pressed on with unwavering resolution, and yet Rogue sensed something in his actions that sent up a red flag. Around the campfire that night, he sat close to the Leader for a private conversation, waiting until Nish and Talj drifted off beneath their sleeping furs.

"You're not tracking Kolbian anymore," Rogue said.

Bialig stared into the flames as clusters of snowflakes drifted into the heat and died in a sudden hiss of fire.

"How long have we been away from the river?" the gambler continued.

Bialig thought for a few moments and said, "About seven moon/sun cycles."

"You know exactly where he's going, don't you? And you're following."

"Would it surprise you to know there are days when I wish I had five more of you, *uma*?"

Rogue covered his concerns with a chuckle. "It's going to be that dangerous? I suppose I should take that as a compliment. I might be some real use if I was your size." Another pause of whispering winds followed. "Nish and Talj don't know where we're headed, do they?"

"*Mir*-Talj probably knows, but he has never been here."

"And you have?"

"Once. As a young man." Rogue watched the memories surface in Bialig's eyes. "Kolbian and I came with our father. It was the last time the Clans tried to make peace with the *sojabosne*. They launched a surprise attack. Many died. I never thought I would track my own brother to this place of death and desolation."

"But you'd even come here to rescue your little lost sheep, wouldn't you?"

Bialig regarded the gambler for several moments. "And you would return to the abyss that is Earth to save yours."

It was Rogue's turn to observe the Leader. "Does it ever strike you as strange how many similarities there are between us?"

"I had not noticed."

"Really? Because sometimes I feel like all this . . ." Rogue swept his arm across the view and the Realmers. ". . . isn't real or something. Maybe I really died in that warehouse, and this is my consciousness going on somewhere outside my body. Or I'm in a coma or a dream."

"Or perhaps you do not want to face reality?"

"Tell me you wouldn't want to escape all your problems for just a few moments."

"It is true. There are times when leading the *Doh s'Ima* is harder than I imagined. We are responsible for the success of the *Shlodane* Clan. But there are moments when I look up to see Nish smiling at me or Talj nodding his head in approval. Even Misko, when he stands close to me, unaware he is seeking guidance, provides moments of peace. And then I can go on."

A mass of clouds blotted out the triple moons, and the night blackened with a darkness Rogue had never experienced. He and Bialig sat quietly again, searching the sky for hidden stars.

"I've been calculating about how long I've been here, and I figure it's been about six months, give or take," Rogue said. "When I saw Raine on Earth, I noticed the date on her HoloMir."

Bialig shook his head at the last word.

"Her computer. Anyhow, I saw six days have passed for her. And I'm guessing if one month here is approximately one day on Earth, then maybe I can figure out how long she has before that bullet . . ." The heat in Rogue's face did not come from the fire. "Why won't you help me save her?"

"*Mir*-Rogue, you have been counting days as if you were on Earth. But we do not know the exact amount of time that passes on Earth when we are here because we do not cross over often or stay long enough to determine this. I promise you I will open the portal and save your woman as soon as Misko is returned to us."

"And trying to reach another Clan wouldn't matter because all the *Dohne s'Ima* are either traveling or at the *Avboeth*."

"There would be no one to open the portal."

"And no guarantee they'd help an illegal *uma*."

The Leader hummed a non-answer deep in his throat.

"Bialig, what if she runs out of time because we took too long?"

"Then I will destroy the man who hurt her."

A mighty blast of wind rushed through their camp, almost whipping the flames out of existence.

"That may not be enough," Rogue said.

* * *

RAIN TURNED TO SNOW, TURNED to slush, and turned the ground sodden beneath their feet. Kolbian and Misko trudged on toward the mountain range where the *sojabosne* lived when they were not roaming the Clan territories looking for unsuspecting travelers to harass, kidnap, rob, or kill. They had been granted the *Thetol* Mountains territory long before Kolbian's time. They became dissatisfied with their perceived banishment during the years when Talj was a young man. By the time Kolbian and Bialig had accompanied their father to the mountains, the *sojabosne* had perfected their technique of forced conversion upon anyone unfortunate enough to cross their path.

Against the ruling of the High Council of Elders, the *sojabosne* refused to stay within the boundaries of the land they had been given. They used the excuse that the surrounding plains no longer yielded adequate food. In truth, they had failed to apply basic agricultural practices, depleted the soil of any nutrition, and denied the land time to rest and repair. In their urgency to create their new society, the *sojabosne* lived in disharmony with the environment by allowing their livestock to destroy the vegetation with overgrazing. When their animals died off, they began depending on the roaming herds until they had been hunted out of existence.

Pollution of resources added to the deterioration in the quality of life for the *sojabosne.* They never properly disposed of the waste they left behind. Their rivers and lakes became undrinkable, and the aquatic life died, further fouling the water. Whole forests were felled to meet their needs no matter how frivolous, yet new trees were never planted. Everyone among their self-indulgent community had an opinion on how things should be done, but no one could ever agree on what that was. They pointed fingers, argued and fought, and ultimately destroyed themselves. At their worst, they made their sufferings the fault of the Clans they believed had wronged them. Now they wanted the peace and prosperity the Clans enjoyed, and they wanted it without working for it.

All this Kolbian, as the new leader of the *sojabosne*, refused to see as he marched his unsuspecting pawn through the barren landscape toward the mountains. He trained his vision on making the Clans—specifically his brother's—pay for what he believed were evils done to those who chose to embrace the ways of the *umane.* No longer would his people remain in slavish existence to those who oppressed them with ancient observances. Kolbian would never give up until the High Council integrated everyone's belief system into the instructions of the Clans.

Every day he traveled with Misko, Kolbian expounded upon his dreams for the *sojabosne.* The false leader's first plan of action was to rename his people. No longer would they be known as thieves or *Kidtiana Tagne*, Abandoned Ones. Misko received another smack to the back of his head when he pointed out that stealing had become the chief practice of the *sojabosne*, and they alone had been responsible for referring to themselves as Abandoned Ones. The young man never asked what Kolbian planned on calling his people.

Kolbian soon lost the lead he had upon the river. He had to spend his time teaching Misko basic tasks he assumed the young man knew how to do. Too late the false leader realized that beyond Misko's enthusiasm for joining the *sojabosne*, he possessed no skill as a hunter. Providing food fell to Kolbian alone, and he knew there was precious little on the plains. At least Misko was better at making camp, although the fires he built were as unimpressive as the rodents Kolbian snared for their dinner.

"This is forbidden for us to eat," Misko said as he shivered under the thin cloak Kolbian had finally provided. The young man knew better than to question the source of supplies when the false leader returned from hunting.

"Then find your own food," Kolbian snarled. "You will not be pampered among your new Clan, Misko. The opportunity to make a life of your own and lead it as you choose does not come without a cost."

"I am sorry, *natamos*. Please forgive my ignorance." Misko paused, searching for the right words. "When we encounter the game herds, would you please teach me how to hunt?"

"I have something better than animals for you to kill."

* * *

BIALIG TOED THE ASHES, UNCOVERING the bones of a small animal. The ground around the remains of the fire bore the footprints of two people, but the tracks disappeared before the trodden earth gave way to sparse turf jutting through patches of frozen snowmelt. The Leader scanned the terrain in every direction, his eyes sweeping back and forth. He brought his attention back to the area immediately around the campsite. When Rogue started to advance past, Bialig held his hand up. Talj and Nish huddled together against the cold winds.

"They were here," Bialig said. "We are gaining on them."

"The ground's too soggy to tell which way they went. We might have been able to see their tracks if it was still snowing," Rogue said.

"Could this be the campsite of other *sojabosne*, *Natamos*?" Nish asked.

"Yeah, why haven't we seen the others by now? With us being so close to their territory, I thought they would have attacked us or something." Bialig shot Rogue a familiar look of annoyance. "What? They were going to find out anyway," Rogue said, casting a glance at Nish and Talj.

Rogue's comments mingled with a scene from Bialig's past. Another time arose before his eyes, and he saw the slaughter of Clan members who had journeyed to the *Thetol* Mountains to make peace with the *sojabosne*. Bialig could barely suppress the memory of bodies impaled on logs studded with branches sharpened into spikes.

In a voice hoarse with remembrance, the Leader said, "This is a trap."

Bialig pulled his spears from his pack and tossed one to Rogue. The gambler gave a small grunt when the giant weapon landed against his chest.

"Use the blunt end to test the ground in front of you. If it feels soft or the shaft goes through, stop immediately. There is a pit with stakes below," Bialig said. "Nish, Talj—you walk behind me about ten paces back. Rogue, stay to my right. Leave five paces between us."

"My paces or yours?"

The Leader huffed a small, derisive laugh as he and the gambler started their trek over ground more dangerous than they originally believed. At least the extreme deforestation on the mountainsides left no place for the *sojabosne* to hide. This fact gave little comfort to Bialig when Rogue prodded the terrain twenty steps into their walk only to have the spear sink halfway in. He lunged and grabbed Rogue by his pack before the weight of it forced the *uma* into the pit with all the dirt and rocks cascading over the edge.

"*Sonofa—*," Rogue yelled. "Pull me back, *pull me back—*"

Teetering on the edge of a pit with wooden teeth bared hungrily at him was like looking into the mouth of death. The bones of people of a greater stature littered the spaces between. Rogue saw all this in the moments before Bialig yanked him away from the lip of the hole.

"I dropped your spear," Rogue said between pants. The side of his face pressed into the cold, damp ground.

Nish and Talj rushed to the men heedless of Bialig's order to stay back. They helped both to sit up and check for injuries.

"We can reach the spear over the side if we are careful, Rogue. It is not lost," Nish said as she wiped dirt from his face with her sleeve.

"And you are worth more than many spears," Talj added. "Even those made by the *Damirgne*."

"I'll get it," Rogue insisted when he intuited the value of the lost weapon.

Bialig and Rogue resumed their place ahead of the other two.

"Reach as far as you can with the spear before taking a step," Bialig said.

"Do you really think Kolbian and Misko had enough time to make so many traps?" Rogue asked.

Rogue's inclusion of Misko in a plan meant to hinder or kill them cut the Realmers to the heart.

"These traps were made long ago when the High Council sent the Clans to offer peace to the *sojabosne*."

"You mean when you and your brother came here with your—"

"Yes, Rogue, that is what I meant."

"So, the skeletons in them are—"

"These traps were reset once something or someone fell in. Kolbian has lived here long enough to know where they are placed. Now please—concentrate on what you are doing."

The travelers made their way step by step over the barren ground sloping up toward the mountain pass where they hoped to overtake Kolbian. All around them the mountains closed in, funneling them toward an uncertain outcome. If Kolbian reached the pass, he would take Misko into the heart of the *sojabosnelo* territory, and without help, there would be no way the Realmers could recover their friend.

Massive arched pillars leading to the *sojabosnelo* stronghold loomed in the distance. Carved out of the mountains and etched with words of glory for the *sojabosne* and conquest for those who opposed them, the tops of the stone sentinels disappeared into the blood-colored clouds lowered upon them. Rogue's breath came hard in the thinning air. The higher they went, he felt as if he could reach up to touch the dome of the sky.

Darkness heightened the danger of their efforts. With the appearance of the triple moons, the four agreed it would be best to stop and make camp. Nish and Rogue scrounged for any shred of dry wood. More grass went into their fire that night, requiring them to work in shifts to keep it burning. They sat beneath their sleeping furs, gnawing on dried meat, and drinking tea. Cold radiated up from the ground, drawing them together to conserve heat.

"Rogue, are you in pain?" Nish asked when she noticed the gambler fidgeting.

"My back feels funny. Probably from sleeping on the cold ground. I'd kill to be back in my crappy apartment right now."

"You would kill for this?"

"It's just an expression. Means I'd really like to be there right now."

"Let me see your back," Talj said, waving the gambler toward him.

"Right now? It's kind of chilly to be stripping down," Rogue replied.

Talj pulled Rogue closer and roughly shoved the sleeping fur away. Then the old Healer lifted Rogue's coat and tunic, palpating his lower back.

"Does this hurt?" Talj asked.

"More like the muscles there are numb."

"There is a strange dark red discoloration. You did not injure yourself when you almost fell in the trap today, did you?"

"Don't think so. Can you do something for it?"

"For pain, yes, but I need to determine what this is."

"What about Nish and her second sight?"

"What do you mean?" asked Bialig. "Nish's ability is not for frivolous uses."

"If she can see into Earth, why not into a body? Kind of like an x-ray."

"I have never seen inside an *umalo* body before," Nish said. "I only know Earth because another second-sighted person showed me."

"But I know what a human looks like inside. I had a little schooling at the orphanage before I split. If you, me, and Talj hold hands, couldn't we see together?"

"*Mira*?" Nish directed at Bialig, nodding hopefully.

"This is most unusual," Bialig said, "but you have my permission."

Nish grabbed Rogue's hand and Talj's.

"You must think about the inside of an *uma* for me to see it, too. Our connection will be shared with *Mir*-Talj."

"I understand, Nish. Let's do this."

Rogue closed his eyes and remembered.

CHAPTER TWENTY-THREE

ROGUE CLOSED HIS EYES AND turned his face into the wind blowing snow at an angle; a dusting of lavender flakes collected on his lashes and hair. He was not supposed to be frozen in this moment with his gloves off, catching snowflakes. Not so long ago, he had won a very prestigious poker game that was the first step to securing his dreams of a better life. That life no longer awaited him. Now he questioned whether he truly existed in this world through which he traveled, no longer knowing where he belonged.

The airstream rose and fell with the same song as the river they had departed, only slower and colder. Rogue felt lulled into a grave slumber. The crunch of snow underfoot faded as the three Realmers walked into the gauzy lavender curtain. Without pause, Bialig called back over his shoulder to Rogue, warning him about the dangers of becoming separated. The Leader's words snagged Rogue's thoughts. His tone set the hook and reeled the gambler back to the present.

Rogue brushed the snow from his hair and pulled his hood forward. He slipped his gloves back on and fell in line behind Talj, jogging to catch up. For the past three days, ever since Nish had used her second sight to see into Rogue's body, they walked toward the *sojabosnelo* stronghold nestled between two mountain peaks. Their trek had been silent except for the sound of weather. The Realmers could not conjure words of consolation for what Nish had seen. Rogue tried to pass it off as insignificant compared to the gift he had given the Realmers. Now the *Thedanosne* could join with the *Jiltraosne* to use second sight for diagnosing internally with accuracy.

As a distraction from his worsening condition, Rogue focused on the curved pillars they had spotted three days ago. The stone fingers beckoned like the devil's own hand. They were magnificent in size when the travelers first noticed them, but every day they grew taller and more ominous the closer they came. Rogue shivered in his many layers, thankful for Nish's nimble fingers and the generosity of the *Damirgne*, but still cold from the knowledge that the poison had begun to creep forward.

He longed to be back on the path to the *Avboeth*. Rogue did not know when it had happened, but somehow, the trek to the Assembly of the Groups of Four had become his journey, too. The Realmers might already be there if they had not been waylaid by so many detours to their plans. Between the problems that came with rescuing Rogue and Misko's decision to follow Kolbian, his friends would have much to tell their fellow *Dohne s'Ima*. He wondered if he would still be present when they arrived at the Assembly and imagined the surprised looks on the faces of the other Realmers.

He always believed the *Avboeth* would be the place of his healing. Potential repercussions for his presence in the Realm melted before his fantasy, which was reinforced by the Realmers' commitment to life. Sometimes, Rogue allowed himself to envision Raine in the picture with her slim hand held safely in his own as if tethering them both to a better, safer life.

Rogue sensed Bialig was equally anxious to resolve the situation with Misko and resume their journey to the *Avboeth*. He watched his already cautious friend scrutinize their every move, reach for a weapon at any sound, and not only arm Talj and Nish with small knives but demonstrate techniques for self-defense and attack. When the gambler tried to discuss the Leader's actions, Bialig masked his concern with the admonition to focus on the mission at hand.

And so, they pressed onward and upward. Toward what none of them knew for sure. The terrain turned unfriendly with the appearance of more rocks and less turf. The blackened mouths of caves yawned at the travelers from the walls of the ever-encroaching mountains. The promise of a surprise attack lurked within. The fact that Kolbian's forces had yet to do so further unsettled the friends. All four assumed the false leader had a reason for withholding an assault, never doubting his reason would include a heavy dose of personal retribution.

When the food stores they carried became increasingly low, Talj suggested they search the caves for edible *yorit* and *pludar*. Rogue had no idea how to translate the words but decided they meant bland or acidic plant growth that tasted like dirt. His stomach turned as he watched Talj and Nish scrape the gray and green substances from the cave walls. The smell of it simmering into a thin soup reminded him of the docks at low tide. When it came to taste, Rogue would have traded his share for a Nutri-Synth hamburger.

"May I explore the cave after our meal, *Natamos*?" Talj asked.

"Take Rogue. He can carry a torch for you, *Mira*," the Leader replied.

Talj slurped his soup and scraped the bowl clean of the gritty residue. Then the old Healer groaned as he pushed himself up and ambled toward the back of the cave. Rogue set his soup aside, grabbed a burning piece of wood from their meager fire, and followed.

The pair did not stray far beyond the glow of the campfire. Rogue held the torch aloft as Talj ran his crooked fingers over the cave walls. The old Healer sniffed deeply at the cold, damp rock. He rubbed his thumb over a scaly patch of light green fuzz growing in the deeper crevices.

"I did not think I would find it at such an altitude and in such a cold environment," Talj mused to himself. "This one usually prefers dry warmth."

"What are you talking about, *Mir*-Talj?" Rogue asked.

"Please fetch my knife and medicine bag."

"I can't leave you in the dark by—"

"Go, go," Talj ordered, his voice rough with command.

Rogue darted back and grabbed the requested items, returning to Talj before Bialig could reproach him for leaving the old Healer. Then there was more scraping and digging of strange looking matter off the cave walls. Talj muttered to himself in private consultation, asking and answering his own questions and gesturing wildly in explanation. Finally, the *Thedanos* settled down to nodding his head in agreement with himself. A satisfied look entered his one good eye, which he turned on Rogue.

Talj dropped to a squat more gracefully than Rogue would have thought possible. He motioned for the gambler to follow suit, directing him to hold the torch closely. Then Talj pulled a wooden bowl from his medicine bag into which he poured small quantities of powder from several different packets. A thin piece of horn with a stone stopper served as a vial from which an aromatic, oily liquid emerged drop by golden drop. Into this mixture he added the newly found ingredient from the cave walls. Talj worked the concoction with the tip of his knife, grinding and smearing it into a thick paste, adding more liquid as needed to make it bind. When the stuff in the bowl resembled dark green tar, Talj scraped it into a neat ball and offered it to Rogue.

"The *swijan* will make it palatable," the old Healer said.

Rogue's laugh preceded, "Everything you've offered me tonight has tasted horrible. What makes you think this will be any better?"

"Because the oil is from the *maharkia* tree, and the taste is beyond compare."

Rogue handed the torch to Talj and took the bowl, inhaling a pungent, sweet scent. He dabbed his finger in it and touched it to his tongue. The spicy flavor lingered, but it was not unpleasant.

"Shouldn't we share this with the others?"

"No, Rogue. This is for you alone." The old Healer paused. "I will take responsibility with Bialig for any delay this may cause in rescuing Misko."

The gambler's eyes rose slowly from the bowl. Talj placed his finger before his lips and shook his head once. Everything and everyone faded away until Rogue's senses were trained solely on the dish in his hands. He swiped two fingers through the paste and placed it in his mouth. From far away Rogue heard Talj instruct him to swallow slowly, allowing the medicine to melt away.

Rogue did not realize his eyes had been closed until he opened them. His mind raced to comprehend exactly what he had done. Guilt flooded his conscience for fear that he had acted in selfishness. Talj had always talked of side effects that might make travel impossible. Time could have been worked into their journey to the *Avboeth* for such an occurrence. But now, how would Bialig receive the news that Rogue might be too weak and nauseated to continue searching for Misko? Regret crept closer along with the understanding that he may have placed his friends in danger should it be necessary that they remain in the cave until any symptoms passed.

"How do you feel?" Talj asked.

"It tastes like some stuff Mother Jean once gave me for a sore throat," Rogue said.

"That does not tell me how you are."

"Good, so far."

"Let us return to the others."

"Fine, but I'm the one who's going to tell Bialig." Talj started to protest. "No—this is on me, okay?"

The old Healer nodded and pushed himself up with one hand, the other still holding the torch. Together, they approached the campfire and took seats among the other two, pulling their sleeping furs around their shoulders. Nish offered everyone tea, but Rogue spoke before they could take a sip.

"I need to tell you something."

All eyes looked to Rogue. When he returned the gaze of Bialig alone, the Leader said, "Go on."

"I took the cure for the poison in my body. So now I guess we wait to see if there are any side effects."

"You did what?"

"I took the cure—"

"Yes, I heard that. Where did you obtain medicine to cure yourself?"

Rogue watched the glowing embers for a breath before looking back to Bialig.

"It was my decision, *Mir*-Bialig. Please don't be mad at Talj."

"Why would I be mad at *Mir*-Talj?"

"Well, clearly, I didn't find and make the medicine on my own. But I did choose to take it now when we're looking for Misko."

"*Mira*," Talj directed at the Leader, "we could not take the risk of losing the cure again."

Bialig's eyes burned into Rogue's. He threw off his sleeping fur and jumped to his feet.

"You selfish *melfet*—what were you thinking? Why would you do this now?" the Leader shouted. "Yet again you have shown complete disregard for my authority as *Natamos* of this *Doh s'Ima*. Have you no concern for what we are going through? Our brother is on the path to ultimate destruction. I have had to jeopardize the safety of my *Doh s'Ima* by bringing them to this place of death. I am still responsible with the High Council for your life. And you do not even have the respect to consult me before taking medicine that may delay any attempt to secure Misko's safety."

"Bialig, my friend—"

"No, Rogue—not friends."

"Dammit, I'm still here." Rogue stood directly in front of the Leader. "I can't go anywhere until we find Misko and open the portal. I told you I would help find him, and I meant it. Absolutely nothing has changed."

"Except now you might be too sick from the cure—"

"Listen, I don't care if I'm sick in the snow every two seconds. I'll drag myself to the *sojabosnelo* fortress before I let you accuse me of bailing on my commitment. I got your back on this one, okay?"

Nish edged next to Bialig and slipped her hand around his fist, working her fingers between his.

"*Mira*," she said. "*Mir*-Talj and I are here because we want to be, not because we must be. I would rather die fighting beside you for the preservation of our *Doh s'Ima* than cower somewhere safe while you deal with this alone."

The Leader turned to her, taking in the soft white tresses framing her face. He had not noticed that her hair had grown back considerably. He brushed a lock from her warm cheek, humbled by the strength and compassion shining in her eyes.

"I should have sent the three of you to stay with the closest Clan and finished this on my own," Bialig said.

"No—that's not your way. Not really," Rogue said. "We do this together."

"And if it does not end well, then what of your woman?"

"Focus on the task at hand, remember? I can only save one person at a time, and I choose to save Misko first."

"Are you sure?" Bialig pressed.

"What is this, a test? All I know is that there's no guarantee for anything we do. But we have to try. If Raine is . . . if she's lost to me, well . . . I'm going to need you guys to make it through, to keep an eye on me with the second sight. My life won't be worth squat on Earth without her. I'll even be the High Council's slave if they let me stay. Besides, I'm starting to feel like I belong here."

"That is strong medicine. It is affecting your reasoning," Nish said, laughing.

Bialig relaxed beside her and leaned his arm into hers without letting go of her hand.

"How do you feel, *Mir*-Rogue?" Talj asked.

"Kind of jittery. Like I've had too much sugar."

"We should try to get some rest. It has been an exhausting day, and I want to keep an eye on Rogue during the night," Nish said.

"I have something to help with the agitated feeling, Rogue," Talj said.

"Give him anything that will put him to sleep," Bialig added. "It is the only time he does not cause me any grief."

Rogue ignored the jest and helped Nish scavenge outside the cave for any scrap of wood to stoke the fire. Bialig stood watch, positioning himself close to the mouth of the cave. Once they were settled for the night, Talj and Nish fussed over Rogue, much to his embarrassment. He relented when nausea and a light fever set in.

Bialig checked on the others periodically, often bringing bowls of fresh snow to melt for drinking or handfuls of twigs to toss on the fire. Delirium plagued the gambler's rest, and he tossed all night, keeping Nish and Talj awake with worry. With dawn came another candy coating of lavender snow and peace enough for Rogue, Nish, and Talj to finally drift off. Bialig kept watch while his friends slept.

* * *

NISH'S INTERNAL BODY CLOCK TOLD her she had overslept. The alarm could not compete with the warmth of the fur drawn tightly around her neck. And yet as her senses came awake, Nish registered the slap of extreme cold against her exposed cheeks. Her eyes popped open followed by her ears recognizing the sound of a deafening roar overlaid with an unnatural howl. The twin voices of a snowstorm challenged each other for dominance.

She threw back her covers, instantly regretting the loss of heat. Drawing her coat tighter around her, Nish hastened to the fire, where she shoved in the last few scraps of wood. All her blowing and fanning barely withstood the onslaught of wind coming from the cave opening.

"Bialig," she called in desperation.

The Leader appeared with his hood drawn forward, the fringe of fur encrusted with snow.

"The storm hit without warning. We must move to the back of the cave," he shouted as he grabbed their gear. "*Mir*-Talj—"

"I am awake, *Natamos*," the old Healer yelled over the raging storm. "Carry my things, and I will bring the *uma*."

The Leader did not have time to question his friend as the old Healer grasped the ends of Rogue's pallet and began dragging it backward, taking care to look over his shoulder as he shuffled along. Snow began to spill into the cave, narrowing the opening and driving the travelers deeper within.

"We need a burning piece of wood for the fire," Bialig said to no one in particular.

Nish raised the flaming wood in answer. She wished she had saved some of the kindling in case they could not find any deeper in the cave. No time existed for the luxury of regret; the beast of the blizzard chased the four into the cold blackness. Its growl echoed off the walls and mocked the frail beings trying to escape its icy grip.

"Lead us, Nish," Bialig said, pointing at the glowing stick of wood in her hand.

The Gatherer took up the foremost position—a place she had never occupied—and walked steadily into the darkness. Her devotion to the men relying upon her for guidance lent purpose to her actions. She placed one foot in front of the other, scanned the flickering shadows for harm, flushed with exhilaration as she drew her little knife from its inner pocket and directed her charges to safety. Anticipation made her bold, and Nish knew she would defend her family from whatever lay ahead.

About twenty paces along, her bright mind and quick ears picked up a change in the song the storm screamed at them. She sensed a shift in the ground beneath her feet and realized the left wall of the cave had come closer.

"We are going around a curve," Nish called back to the men. "It bends to the left enough to keep us out of the wind. There is sand under our feet, and I believe we are going upward."

The group walked on until the cave ballooned outward and ended. Nish's assessment proved correct, and the natural curve lessened the impact of wind grasping at their backs. The men set down their burdens and felt along the walls for any piece of wood. Surely if they had found the cave, someone else might have once used it and left a small supply. And small it was.

The shafts of Bialig's spears, Talj's medicine bowl, and Nish's cooking utensils were sacrificed for the sake of heat. The Realmers could not bring themselves to burn Misko's instruments since the young *Paten* was not there to make the decision himself. To do so would be to tempt fate, as if gambling with Misko's life.

CHAPTER TWENTY-FOUR

ROGUE'S FEVER BROKE WITHIN ONE moon/sun cycle, but his nausea and dizziness persisted during the two days the unexpected blizzard trapped them. He tried to stand upon waking, insisting that he be given a useful task, but ended up staggering around like a drunk, crashing into the Realmers, and nearly falling into the fire. Bialig pushed him into a seated position against the cave wall, wrapped him in a fur, and ordered him to entertain himself with Misko's instruments.

Misko. Always at the forefront of Bialig's mind, troubling him more than a sick and headstrong *uma*. He wondered if Misko was cold and hungry, regretful or satisfied. The Leader vacillated between his desires to discipline the young man for the crisis he had caused and to shelter him from every evil influence, starting with his own brother. Against his will, Bialig's mind wove thoughts of Kolbian into the tapestry of his concern.

He could barely admit to himself, let alone the others, that he still cared for Kolbian and still felt pain from the wound to their filial bond shredded by betrayal. He could not reconcile his emotions, and so he often suppressed them. He knew only fools avoided confronting an enemy, even one from within, but the component necessary to repair the rift between them eluded Bialig. He worried this detail exposed a flaw within his own character.

Kolbian's choice to live among the *sojabosne*—to embrace their lawlessness, disorder, and complete lack of structure—plagued Bialig every time he thought of it. No explanation existed for how two men raised by the same parents could turn out so different. The memory he struggled with the most was the day their father died, the day Kolbian swore he would take care of Bialig and their mother by adhering to the instructions of the Infinite One. Only then had their father been able to release their hands and allow them to escape.

The dark memory merged with the moonlit shadows of clouds drifting across the snow, rendering the frozen swells mulberry, orchid, or wine depending on where he looked. Bialig had hoped to be lodging with the *Holaped* Clan for the cold season before pressing on toward the *Avboeth* with the return of the growing season. Still, as he stood at the mouth of the cave, he enjoyed the beauty and respite in the wake of the storm.

Talj coughed as he approached to announce his presence to the Leader.

"*Mir*-Talj, why have you strayed from the warmth of the fire?" Bialig asked.

"To bring you this, *Mira*," Talj replied, handing Bialig a cup.

The two men stood side by side for several minutes, sipping hot tea. When Bialig thought perhaps Talj really had joined him for the company, the old Healer spoke.

"I have been reading specific portions of the ancient writings the *Damirgne* gave me after losing my own copies during our flight from Kolbian."

Bialig hummed a note of interest, so Talj continued.

"The High Council of Elders is truly wise. More so than the average man or woman of the Clans."

"Is that not why they serve on the Council?"

"Indeed, my friend. They are called by the Infinite One Himself. And yet in many ways they are ordinary members of the Clans, like any other man or woman."

"Are you contradicting yourself, *Mir*-Talj? What is your point?"

"My point is that we must look to the Infinite One's instruction for guidance first. The commentary produced by the Elders is good, full of wisdom and knowledge, but even they are sometimes in disagreement regarding the approach toward and application of Divine instruction."

"But never done in deception or for seeking fame."

"Of course not. Everything the Elders do is for our spiritual protection and maintenance. Still, they sometimes enacted additional rules to safeguard perfect obedience to an original command."

"Can you give me an example, *Mir*-Talj?"

"With pleasure, *Natamos*."

Talj took a deep breath and smiled at what he was about to reveal to Bialig.

"You know that everything the Infinite One wants us to know about Him is written and heard in the stars. He teaches us how to relate to Him first and to each other second. But if we do not have access to His instruction, then we make the mistake of relying solely on the Elders' enactments which, although good, are based on interpretation and tradition. There are stars in the *sojabosnelo* territory that we have not encountered in so many cycles of the moons that the original command has been lost to us. It is these stars I have been reading and listening to every chance I have while traveling here."

"What have you discovered?"

"I compared what I learned from the stars to the ancient writings, and the problems within *Dohne s'Ima* that led to the ruling prohibiting marriage between members was not what the Infinite One ever intended."

"What?"

"Discouraging unions between members was probably the easiest way to solve the envy that sometimes arose when two married. The ruling certainly settled claims of distraction to duty by married members and kept *Dohne s'Ima* from constantly breaking up, but this practice was not the best way. We should have addressed the issue more closely and arrived at a better solution."

"*Mir*-Talj, are you saying—"

"Yes, my friend. There is no reason why you should not spend the rest of your life with the one you love. It pains me to think how many *Doh s'Ima* members needlessly renounced marriage for the sake of duty. Not only are we allowed marriage within the Group, but we may also marry non-members within our Clan."

Bialig's eyes screwed shut, and his breathing came as hard blasts that fogged the cold air. He tempered his next question with the same strength that made him a good Leader.

"How could we have lived in error for so long, *Mir*-Talj?"

"At the end of the Great War when the Clans honored the Serving Elder's oath to allow the *sojabosne* to possess the *Thetol* Mountain Region, we cut ourselves off from the commands established in these stars. The territory was vast enough to keep us from encountering the *sojabosne*, but again, the Clans denied themselves a wealth of instruction in the process.

"And we did not apply our wisdom well. It was during this time of upheaval as we dealt with the aftermaths of the war that the prohibition against marriage in the *Dohne s'Ima* was hastily put in place.

"Further compounding this problem was the fact that many *Thedanosne* familiar with the instruction written in these stars died in the Great War and the younger who ascended to the position never traveled here. The knowledge was lost to us. But do not rely on my words alone, *Mira*. Read the truths for yourself."

"I know the Infinite One concealed things to keep us seeking His glory and our own, but it is to our shame that we allowed this instruction to be excised from our awareness."

"We should have dealt with the *sojabosne* completely as instructed by the Infinite One. If we had, this would not be an issue today. Also, they would not have risen to attack us throughout the ages."

"Is there anything else we missed?" Bialig asked.

"Yes. I was correct when I said you did not break the Infinite One's commands by bringing the *uma* here. We were not supposed to cut ourselves off from interaction with the *umane* but rather work toward contacting them after we left the scrolls. I suspect Kolbian knows this, and that it is the true reason he wishes to open a portal to their world."

"We have much to address at the *Avboeth* once we recover Misko." Bialig glanced toward Nish. "Have you mentioned any of this to anyone?"

"No, *Mira*. I thought you should be the one to tell her the good news."

Bialig lowered his eyes. "As soon as this is over."

Talj chuckled, patting Bialig's shoulder as he turned to rejoin Nish and Rogue.

* * *

NO GREETING REACHED ACROSS THE snow-blasted landscape to grace Misko's and Kolbian's ears with welcome, not an advance party nor a single scout. They slogged through the well-packed banks of lavender flakes, weighed down by the snow with every step. They had never sought permanent shelter during the storm. Rather, they scurried from place to place, taking refuge between boulders thrown down in landslides or unoccupied dwellings whose dilapidated condition Kolbian refused to explain. Through it all, Misko trudged on without complaint.

All the hardships he had endured on their trip would be worth it in the end when the *sojabosne*—or whatever they chose to call themselves—rose to form a glorious new society of free thinkers where all would be welcome despite their abilities or lack thereof. To know that he, Misko, a *Paten* from the *Shlodane* Clan, would witness the origination of this event gave him a sense of accomplishment unlike any he had ever known. Never again would he be in submission to another's attempt to rule over him, and the only thing inhibiting him, or any member, would be their own inability to envision greatness.

Misko held fast to his beliefs not because he doubted Kolbian and his harsh ways, but because the ideal life of which he had always dreamed now lay within his grasp. He knew deep inside that he would fulfill the roll of peacemaker and bridge builder. With gentle yet firm persuasion, Misko would change the minds of Clan members like Bialig, whose adherence to the ancient ways were commendable but archaic. He trained his thoughts on methods to accomplish this without violence or bloodshed.

The mantraps he had helped Kolbian reset or repair sprang to mind. Misko shook his head to sweep the thought aside, deeming them necessary to prevent anyone from hindering their goal. In time, when the Clans joined or at least accepted them, the need for such deterrents would cease to exist. Until then, he would glean what he could from Kolbian to ensure he survived, as well as help the *sojabosne* thrive in their land.

The work could take many cycles of the moons. Even under the blanket of snow, Misko observed the barrenness of the land. He chose to interpret the lack of food and potable water as a testimony to the strength of the *sojabosne* to endure instead of assigning them responsibility for the destruction. With the guidance of the new instruction he planned on writing, he would shepherd the people through the restorative measures required to heal the land. Then as a single, benevolent force, the *sojabosne* would offer unity and prosperity to the Clans. Even as he imagined this, he agreed with Kolbian that a new name would be necessary.

"You have been silent since we started traveling again," Kolbian said, breaking into Misko's reverie.

"I was wondering why this village was destroyed, *natamos*," Misko replied.

Kolbian looked around at the wooden dwellings. "This is the result of being abandoned by the Clans."

"You mean they did this?"

"They are not completely without responsibility for what happened here."

Misko pondered the statement and thought of the future he had envisioned. "What are your plans for me, *natamos*?"

"I told you before. You will rule by my side."

"And I will guide our Clan with the new instructions I write?"

"Instructions? What did you have in mind, Misko?"

"Freedom through the expression of one's talents whether it be artistic or useful. Everyone will be welcome to join us and pursue their desires. Nothing will be withheld or considered improper just because it deviates from a standard designated by someone else."

"And how will you oversee the people along this path to enlightenment?"

"They will not require governance, *natamos*, not in the old ways of the High Council of Elders or the Infinite . . . I will provide the writings, but the natural inclination to do good will encourage them toward selfless service and sacrifice."

"You know the Clans will not receive us willingly."

"Are you suggesting the need for confrontation?"

"Misko, I appreciate your desire for peace, but you must be realistic. Only when the Clans have been subdued will we ever know any real concord."

"You believe violence is necessary?"

"For rooting out those who oppose us? Yes, absolutely. It is the only way to guarantee our success."

"I admit I struggle with that portion of your plan, *natamos*."

"I am not asking you to relish the prospect, Misko, only to accept that it is essential."

"You believe we must attack first."

"A preemptive strike is the only way to identify the persons who are detrimental to our way of life. Think of it like curing an illness. The results justify the actions."

"And under your leadership—"

"Under my leadership, we will create a new order. You will be my mouthpiece, the voice of a new generation. This time, with both of us working toward the goal, we will triumph."

Misko ran his hand through his long, unbound hair as he pondered Kolbian's comment of "this time." The young man walked in silence, and the snow-laden clouds above shifted to allow a single finger of pale sunshine to touch the ground below.

* * *

ROGUE YAWNED AND FORCED HIMSELF to stay awake, scrambling yet again to catch up to the Realmers. The daze caused by Talj's cure had lessened, but he still overlooked the fragments of burned timbers and discarded weapons poking through the layers of snow. He tripped over one and landed face first. The light purple snow muffled a bevy of swear words. His spitting and coughing attracted Bialig's attention. The Leader looked back and signaled Nish and Talj to pause.

"Are you all right?" Bialig asked.

"I'm fine," Rogue replied, brushing snow and ashes from his coat. "What is all this?"

"Are you walking in your sleep? We have entered a *sojabosnelo* village."

Bialig swept his arm to the right and upward, indicating large, two-story dwellings built into the mountainside. The homes lining the pass bore the fingerprints of fire around the open doorways that looked as if they were gasping for breath. Heat-shattered windows gazed vacantly upon the detritus of life strewn about in charred piles: clothing, furniture, bedding, and toys.

"What the hell happened here?" Rogue asked.

"From the broken weapons and burned homes, I would say a battle. This could be why we have not seen any *sojabosne*."

"Who attacked them, *Natamos*?" Nish asked.

"If I had to guess, I would say they turned on each other." He pointed to a curved sword embedded in a charred beam and picked up an axe blade separated from its handle. The quarter moon-shaped slice of metal still looked deadly. "These are the weapons favored by the *sojabosne*, and I see no others."

"And the knives and spears?" Rogue asked.

"Also fashioned in the style they prefer and carved with words proclaiming discord and anarchy."

"But why?" Nish asked. "What more could they possibly have wanted than the beautiful land they were granted by the Serving Elder and the freedom to live as they chose?"

"It was not enough that our Clans agreed to let the *sojabosne* have their own place. They would never stop until we not only condoned their beliefs and behavior but endorsed and celebrated them as well."

"That answers the 'what more' part of the question, but I'd still like to know why they turned on each other," Rogue said.

Snow crashing through the roof of a house gutted by fire checked any answer. Bialig's eyes narrowed as he set down his pack. He drew his sword and swept Nish behind him with one arm. Rogue prepared to defend Talj with his two knives.

"Someone is in there," Bialig said.

"Could it be the weight of the snow?" Rogue asked.

"I saw a shadow. Movement brought the snow down." Bialig lifted his chin and called out, "*Uhrshues flod*."

Jagged laughter echoed off the mountains walls and dripped like acid from the amethyst icicles clinging to the scorched eaves.

"Yes, yes, I am coming, young Leader."

Bialig startled to hear the language of the *umane*. The voice rasped in a sing-song manner, taunting as the form that possessed the hideous tone shuffled from the shelter in which it hid.

"I throw myself on your mercies, *Natamos*."

The bedraggled heap—whether bent from age or infirmity the friends could not tell—lumbered into view. It made a strange progress of approaching with its left side forward. Filthy rags hung in tatters around its body, and a tangled beard dragged along the ground.

"They are gone. They are all gone," the voice cackled, its hands grasping at the air. "And doubtless, my Master wants to know why."

The creature turned wet eyes upon the friends. Eyes glazed over with the evidence of unspeakable horrors. Bags of flesh drew the lower lids downward, revealing the reddened lining and broken veins.

"Stop, demon, and state your name," Bialig commanded.

"Not know me?" the voice whined. "How could that be? Did I not serve your father well? Will I not also serve the son?"

"Who the hell is this guy?" Rogue asked.

"I do not know," Bialig replied.

The monster threw back its head and howled its ire, pointing a wicked finger with ragged nail accusingly at Bialig.

"How quickly the son forgets my faithfulness to his father. When Jogo lay dying and beyond help, who told him about the hidden passage in the walls of stone? Who saved the sons that they might live another day?"

"Ojatam," Bialig whispered, loath to speak the fiend's name.

"Yes, Bialig, it is I."

Nish pressed herself against Bialig's back and slipped her arm around his body. She placed her hand on his chest drawing him toward her, eliminating even the air between them. He took strength from her presence.

"Tell me what happened to the others," the Leader said.

"Death came as sickness. A plague of the skin that emerged from within. And hunger, always the hunger. No crops, no animals. Everything taken, nothing replaced. Fear spread like disease, and the people fought each other for lack of an enemy on which to expend their frustrations. They died in a polluted land."

"There were many *sojabosne*."

"Once that was true. The numbers dwindled over many cycles of the moons, but our current *natamos* would have you believe we are still many."

"How is it that you cheated death, old one?"

Cackling preceded Ojatam's answer.

"Because I knew the ways of the *Thedanosne*. I may not have been a member of a *Doh s'Ima*, but I studied as a student. I bartered healing for food until the food was gone. Then I used my medicine and skill to save myself."

"You are a traitor thrice over," Bialig shouted, extricating himself from Nish's protective embrace. "You betrayed the Clans when you joined the *sojabosne*. You betrayed your people for profit when they were sick. You betrayed your leaders when you helped me and my brother escape."

"But I saved Jogo's sons—"

"*Never* speak my father's name again."

Life drained from Ojatam's eyes. The traitor was dead before he knew it himself. When the body slumped forward, the head fell to the ground and rolled away. Bialig wiped his sword in the snow, unwilling to further contaminate the blade on the betrayer's cloak. Then he sheathed his weapon, retrieved his pack, and resumed walking.

"Wait a minute," Rogue called after him. "What the hell was all that?"

"It is over. We must move on," the Leader called back.

Talj and Nish shared a worried look before falling in behind their *Natamos*. Rogue ran to catch up, jogging beside Bialig to match his stride.

"Who was that guy?" the gambler asked.

"You heard him."

"What I heard was that he helped you and Kolbian escape that day the Clans came to make peace and the *sojabosne* ambushed them."

Bialig whirled on Rogue and grabbed the front of his clothing. "What you heard was the confession of a traitor. That worthless *gradol* did not save us out of kindness. He refused to do anything without payment first. My father lay dying, and with his last breath he bartered his sword for our freedom. That sword had been in our family since the formation of the *Shlodane* Clan."

When the Leader stopped shaking Rogue to emphasize his statements, the gambler wrapped Bialig's fist in both his hands. Rogue stood on tiptoe, looking through the fog of Bialig's breath mingling with the snow. From the corner of his eye, he saw Talj and Nish fixed like statues.

"I'm sorry you lost your father," Rogue said.

The muscles in Bialig's jaw bulged. His breathing came hard, but he would not allow any more of his emotions to spill forth.

"You were worth more to him than many swords."

Bialig set Rogue on his feet, but he did not relax his grip.

"I wish I'd known my father," Rogue said. "Or my mother. I used to wish I had someone who would have my back no matter what. Funny how I ended up here with you, huh?"

Bialig released Rogue's coat and brushed roughly at the front of his clothes. Then he looked skyward and inhaled deeply, held the burning cold within, and released it into the diminishing veil of snow.

"Why are you here, *uma*?" the Leader asked.

Rogue parsed the comment. "You think everything went bad the moment I entered the Realm, don't you?"

"You are not responsible." Bialig shook his head and looked at Rogue. "*Umane* from long ago corrupted our people with lawlessness and selfish ways. The seed of helping others for profit was planted in Kolbian's mind the day our father gave his sword to Ojatam. Misko decided to join the *soja-bosne* long before you arrived. It would be so easy to believe these events occurred just to undermine my position as *Natamos*. But I know better.

"When Kolbian and I were to fight at the *sojabosnelo* camp, he had the sword of our father. He fled before he had the chance to use it, but he made sure I saw it. It is his right as firstborn to have the sword. I do not begrudge him that. What angers me—what I deal with every day since he left the *Shlodane* Clan—is how he came by possession of it. He traded a life of freedom and peace for the opportunity to own the sword. He reduced it to a mere piece of property, and he forsook the values our father taught us to do so."

"Then let's go get it back," Rogue said.

CHAPTER TWENTY-FIVE

THE QUESTION LINGERING ON MISKO'S lips as he and Kolbian approached the *sojabosnelo* stronghold disappeared the closer they came. The carved pillars through which they had walked were impressive, and the size of the stone dwelling looming in front of them inspired awe. The double doors intrigued Misko's artistic sensibilities, and the young man could not take his eyes off the elaborate bas-reliefs.

Beneath the word "freedom" spanning the lintel, Misko viewed life-sized male and female warriors rising from the polished surface of what he recognized as rare and valuable wood. The figures, locked in battle with their doomed counterparts, were both magnificent and frightful. The graven images grasped for the stars as they trampled the High Council of Elders and the ancient writings underfoot, thus liberating themselves from a belief system and social structure that had existed from the beginning of time.

Such monuments to rebellion could never be opened by two people alone. Misko shivered as he imagined the doors swinging wide to reveal people from every walk of life uniting to form a single Clan. He saw them standing in camaraderie before large hearths ablaze, dancing and singing to the music provided by an ensemble of musicians, feasting and drinking in merriment and welcome.

Expectation blinded his mind's eye to the reality of gaping windows darkened with neglect, drifts of snow banked against the massive doors, and the absence of ebullience pulsating on the currents of glacial air.

As a result, Misko's question slipped a little further from being spoken as he and Kolbian cleared piles of snow from in front of the entrance. They kicked away chunks of ice that had wedged the unlocked portal open enough for them to slip through. The pair removed their few possessions from their backs and turned sideways, stepping into the emptiness of the hall. The interior, comprised of black stone blocks hewn from the surrounding mountains, radiated cold that penetrated their cloaks.

Misko trod like a sleepwalker to the center of the circular foyer and pivoted slowly, taking in the torn tapestries, broken furniture, a dangling chandelier, and candle stumps strewn across the flagstone floor. Fresh snow blew past the jagged teeth of stained glass clinging in the window frame high above. The young man closed his eyes, but the room still spun as his question resurrected on his lips. The answer to where the others were only emphasized the fact that he did not know why they were gone.

Misko pressed the heels of his hands against his temples to keep the shreds of his fantasy from escaping. His lips moved with whispers of encouragement meant for his ears alone. Shivers of excitement turned into tremors of fear, and for the first time since leaving his *Doh s'Ima*, Misko's doubts appeared as tears in the corners of his eyes.

Kolbian observed Misko's response and shook his head at the transformation taking place before him. He brushed past the young man, knocking his shoulder, and walked toward a high-backed, wooden chair placed on the dais at the end of the long room beyond the foyer. Kolbian cleaned snow and debris from the throne of the self-appointed leaders of the *sojabosne* before seating himself upon it.

"I did not tell you because I wanted our vision to remain the focus of this endeavor," Kolbian said. His voice echoed throughout the hall.

"But *natamos*, we are the only ones." Misko's voice limped across the space between them.

A snort burst forth from the false leader. He bared his teeth and said, "Did I choose wrong when I set my sights on you, Misko? Where is the greatness I witnessed as I trailed your *Doh s'Ima*, waiting for the right moment to liberate you from Bialig's tyranny?"

"I fear this will require more than a new name by which to call our people. Do we even have any people?"

"Ah, Misko. Why do you persist in thinking small? Has life under Bialig's domination crushed your passions, your spirits? Yes—we must rebuild. Yes—we must recall those who would think for themselves and live free from among the Clans. But this is why I chose you. This is the purpose for which you were born. You are the only one I need."

The pounding of Kolbian's fist upon the arm of the throne punctuated his every word, making Misko jump. But the effect worked, and the young man felt hope flow through his body. He no longer saw the rubble at his feet as the wreckage of lives gone off course but rather as the building blocks of a new civilization. One in which he would play a guiding role.

Misko knelt to pick up a fragment of broken pottery. The design painted on the piece marked it as the work of an artist from the *Bedok* Clan. The lightness of the strokes indicated the hand of a woman, and he wondered if she was dead or had abandoned her true purpose to slink back to her Clan. The young man shook his head, unwilling to harbor anger toward this unknown woman. As Kolbian said, he must reach out with patience and compassion to the disenchanted among the Clans. Their decision to leave the *sojabosne* would be forgotten, and all mistakes would be forgiven.

With head held high and shoulders squared, Misko stood to face Kolbian and the challenges that lay ahead. He was drawn forward by the charm in the fixed expression of the imposter seated upon the throne.

"What do we do, *natamos*?"

"We wait for them to come to us."

"The people who would join us?"

"No, Misko. Those who would try to stop us. They will come first."

"You mean my *Doh s'Ima*. I know they are following."

"Think, boy. Would Bialig put his precious *Doh s'Ima* in danger? Would he risk the life of Nish, Talj, or even that worthless *uma* to come for you?"

"No, but what are you saying, *natamos*?"

"I am saying that my brother will come alone, and the fight will be in our favor. He is coming, Misko. Make no mistake, he is coming."

* * *

ENDLESS EXPANSE OF SKY, ENDLESS stretch of snow. The mountains closed in from every direction. The elevation rose with every step. Rogue pressed forward, putting one foot in front of the other and willing himself to not succumb to the dizziness, whether it be from height or the medicine coursing through his body. Today of all days, the sun sliced through the clouds to blind him with unusual clarity. At least the winds had stopped roaring in his ears so he could hear Nish lament the fact that they had no darkened glass to place before their eyes. The lifeline of Bialig's barked commands to stay together, keep your head down and your hood pulled forward, and do not lose sight of the others superseded the black spots dancing before Rogue's eyes.

They had spent the night on the far side of the *sojabosnelo* village. Bialig had paced the fire-blackened building where they sheltered. Rogue did not bother to worry about Bialig's lack of sleep as the big man roused everyone early the next morning and insisted on a quick breakfast before they resumed their travels. What did concern him was the conversation he overheard when the Realmers thought he had been sleeping.

The ruins of the *sojabosnelo* village provided abundant firewood. Much of what they found bore the charred inscription of death. Still, Nish had a better fire going than they had enjoyed in a long time. The heat and warmth lent a sense of security despite the cold seeping through the gaps in the walls; the friends huddled close by choice rather than necessity. Rogue stilled first, and with his face turned away from them, the Realmers assumed he had drifted off. Talj's voice began the dialog.

"Have you given any thought to what we discussed about our *uma* friend, *Mira*-Bialig?"

Rogue knew the Leader would simply nod as he collected his thoughts to answer. He also wondered when his friends had had the opportunity to talk about him without his knowledge.

"We have all been in close contact with the *uma* since his arrival. Nish first brought her suspicions to my attention after we sought refuge from the flood. She sensed something about Rogue when using her second sight."

"Tell me, *Mira*."

"Nish looked for the woman from the warehouse, and she felt Rogue seeing along with her."

"Seeing as we do when Nish shares her second sight with us?"

The lengthy pause in conversation conveyed the answer as clearly as if Bialig had spoken.

Again, Talj's coarse voice breached the silence. "I, too, sensed Rogue when he and Nish and I joined hands to see into his body. His thoughts, although *uma* in nature, were strong and clear. I had no trouble locating the poison within."

Nish, who had been silent until then, spoke for herself and Bialig. "And when you and Rogue and I were joined to see the *uma* woman on Earth, *Mira*, you, too, were aware of his presence. We not only saw the same images, but we also saw it through the mind of Rogue alone."

"Let us not forget the talent Rogue displayed with the instruments belonging to Misko," Talj added. "It was beyond the skill of a Mentor."

This time the Leader drew a deep breath and exhaled with the steady force of the winter winds. The fire crackled, the wood ticking in anticipation of Bialig's response. His words, dancing at the forefront of everyone's mind—Rogue's included—refused to leap from his tongue unbidden. He was not prepared to address the suggestion burning in Nish's eyes, and so he looked to Talj instead.

The old Healer's laugh ground the silence between the millstones of his wisdom and amusement. He clapped Bialig on the shoulder. "Do not be afraid, my friend, to consider what this discovery may mean for us, for Rogue, and for the *umane* and our Clans."

"But what do we really know, *Mir*-Talj?" the Leader asked.

"That we are never too old, and it is never too late, for us to learn something new."

Bialig chanced a look at Nish who nodded in agreement with Talj. Her smile warmed the Leader more than the fire she had built, but still he shivered and looked away. When he returned his gaze to her, Bialig saw worlds of promise in her soft, gray eyes. He could have lived there forever, abandoning his mission to rescue Misko and return Rogue to Earth if his honor would have allowed. Nish blinked once, communicating her pledge to wait until all their duties had been fulfilled.

All this Rogue missed except for the words spoken between the Realmers. He debated with himself the significance of the late-night conversation and whether it had any bearing on his presence in the Realm. He sensed that something had changed, and yet he could not pin down exactly what it was. So, he held fast to his agreement to help Bialig rescue Misko in exchange for his return to Earth and assistance with saving Raine. These thoughts raced through his head as he drifted off, infiltrating his dreams until he could no longer differentiate between what he had heard and what his mind conjured while he slept.

* * *

REPRIEVE FROM THE BLINDING SUNLIGHT came as a blanket of clouds unfolding across the sky. The billowing masses heralded the arrival of more snow. Rogue rubbed his eyes, thankful for the reduced glare. He squinted up through the falling snow, still unused to the strange color, and wished himself and his friends safely en route to the *Avboeth* instead of passing beneath the curved pillars marking the entrance to the *sojabosnelo* stronghold. As long as the bowed columns had appeared in the distance, he could put off his anxieties about what would occur once they arrived. Now the four of them stood just within the enemy camp, facing an uncertain future as they walked headlong through the gates of hell.

Unlike any other time since coming to the Realm, Rogue and the Realmers walked in a tight cluster. Bialig occupied the foremost position with Talj walking behind and to his right, Nish to his left. Rogue hovered near Talj, sometimes straying ahead of the old Healer, sometimes hanging back to prevent attack from behind. Bialig stopped without warning, unmoved by the other two stumbling against his back.

"What is it? What's wrong?" Rogue whispered as he crouched low with both knives drawn.

Nish placed her hand on Bialig's arm. Her eyebrows rose when she felt him tremble.

"*Mira*?" she said.

"I should not have brought you to this place," Bialig said. The other three crept closer to hear his voice over the moan of the storm headed in their direction.

"It's a little late for that," Rogue replied. He cringed at his comment, wondering if he would ever learn to think first, speak second. "What I meant is, we're all here because we want to be. I can see it on your face, but don't even think about sending us away."

"You would not do that, *Mira*, would you?" Nish turned Bialig toward her, reading the answer in his eyes.

"My foolish pride has placed all of you in danger." Again, Bialig's voice came softer than the winds, and regret stole into his tone. "I compromised your safety for the chance to restore my *Doh s'Ima*, to correct my mistakes."

"That is not what happened," Nish replied. She placed her hands on either side of his face. "The bad decisions Misko made belong to him. We all know it, and so do you."

"Even so, *Mir*-Nish, I must ask you to respect my authority as *Natamos* and leave this place."

"Then what? You take on Kolbian and Misko by yourself?" demanded Rogue. "You're letting your ego get the better of you and making a big mistake."

"I do not expect you to understand, Rogue—"

"Right—because I don't have anyone to care about and nothing matters to me but me, so how could I possibly comprehend what you're going through? Only we both know that isn't true, is it, you selfish ass?"

"I am not going to explain myself—"

"Why now? That's all I want to know—"

"Enough!" Bialig's command echoed off the pillars, the mountains, and the tombstone of his father positioned just off the path they walked.

Talj's one good eye, although dimmed with aged, had spotted the name of his deceased friend cut deep into the polished black stone right before Bialig's pace ground to a halt. The old Healer had intended to move within the Leader's line of sight before the monument came into view. His legs failed him in the deepening snow. He had not known the marker would be there, but he was not surprised to learn of its presence. The gravestone mocked the righteous with words of praise for those who had defeated

Bialig's father, Jogo, in life. Concern for keeping the son from facing the same defeat flushed the old Healer's face.

Rogue, still unaware of the reason for Bialig's decision to carry on alone, followed Talj's gaze to the obelisk serving as a headstone.

"What is it?" the gambler asked. He stepped forward and ran his gloved hand over the inscribed symbols, unable to read the words.

"The resting place of a great man," Talj said.

"And the words?"

"Lies told by those who would subvert peace and truth."

"Please, *Mir*-Talj, just tell me whose grave this is."

"My father's," Bialig said.

"And this word here, the biggest letters. His name?" Rogue asked.

"Yes."

"*Jogo s'hel Shlodanene*?"

"I thought you could not read our language."

"I guessed. If this is his name, it made sense that the other words would identify his Clan. As for the rest of it, you know the truth. We all do, and nothing changes this fact. You're his greatest legacy, *Mir*-Bialig, not his sword."

"Who placed the stone, *Mira*?" Nish asked.

Bialig addressed the question on all their minds. "Not Kolbian. This is the work of a stonemason from the *Adanet* Clan. His signature is at the bottom."

"It is time to walk on, *Mir*-Bialig," Talj said. "The sooner we return Misko to his proper position in our *Doh s'Ima*, the sooner we can leave this evil place."

"I am sorry, my friend. I will not be dissuaded from doing what I know is right." Bialig held his hand up to silence their protests.

"No—it is my decision as *Natamos*, and I expect you, too, Rogue, to abide by my command."

"That's not fair. I'm not from here, and you know I can help you."

A smile creased Bialig's face. "You keep telling me what I know today, and your argument, Rogue, is that of a child."

On Earth, Rogue would have been face to face and toe to toe with Bialig, asserting his strength of will to back the Leader down. He was unprepared for what the Leader said next.

"Will you take *Mir*-Talj and *Mir*-Nish back the way we came to the safety of the *Damirg* Clan?"

Rogue indicated with his hand and said, "We're only a hundred yards from the entrance."

"I know."

"Kolbian knows we're here. He's probably been watching the whole time."

"Again, I know. That is why you must take Talj and Nish and leave now. If I do not survive this—"

"*No*—"

"If I do not survive, then the three of you must be as far away from here as possible. Kolbian's intention is to destroy all of us, and I will not be present to stop him. Do you understand?"

"I understand you're delivering what's most precious to you into my care. But they don't need my protection. Talj and Nish are almost twice my size."

"This is not about protection, *uma*," Bialig said as he removed his pack and withdrew his sword. "It is about trust."

"Then trust me to help you rescue Misko like I said I would."

"I have something more important for you to do."

"I thought you were going to help me with Raine?"

"There was always a chance that my mission would fail, but yours does not have to. Even if I die today, you can save your woman by seeking another *Doh s'Ima* to send you back."

"I can't be seen by others."

Bialig scowled and said, "Do not be ridiculous. You will find help despite the law concerning *umane* in our world. Everything has changed since you arrived. The stars tell us so."

Nish removed items from Bialig's pack and placed them in her own. Then she helped Talj put the lightened load on his back. The pair acted in accordance with the Leader's wishes, but they could not meet his eyes. Rogue shook his head and clenched his hands.

"Why are you abandoning me?" the gambler asked.

The heads of all three Realmers snapped up at Rogue's words. Bialig replaced his sword in the scabbard and walked to where the gambler stood.

"What the hell has this whole journey been about if you make me leave now?" Rogue asked.

"Look for the Infinite One's hand in all that has occurred, my friend. We always knew our paths would diverge at some point."

Bialig turned to Nish. He rested his hand on the back of her head, drawing her toward him until their foreheads touched. Then he released her and walked toward the *sojabosnelo* fortress without looking back.

CHAPTER TWENTY-SIX

EVERY EXHALATION DEPOSITED MOISTURE ON the fur lining of the hood cinched tightly around Rogue's face. The dropping temperatures froze his breath into needles that scratched his cheeks and chin. Misko's instruments, along with his own pack, banged against his back, adding to his discomfort with each labored step. Whether he lifted his legs above the depth of new-fallen snow or plowed directly through, the gambler made little headway. Nish and Talj faired as poorly as he despite their size and strength.

Talj's panting turned into grunts, and Rogue suspected the cold wreaked havoc on the old Healer's joints. He made the decision to stop on the far edge of the *sojabosnelo* village to allow Talj to rest and soothe his pain with liniment from among his remedies. Nish also looked as if she could use a break. No doubt her distress leaned toward the emotional. Rogue caught her looking over her shoulder several times, waiting for a silhouette to emerge from the curtain of snow. Her countenance fell when none appeared.

Concern for his friends erased any thoughts for himself, and Rogue encouraged them from the back of the line. He exercised the patience he had witnessed in Bialig's actions, but he also urged them forward with as much strength of will as their *Natamos*. Compassion for his companions bound the two qualities in Rogue's heart and mind. Still, he did not envy

Bialig his responsibilities. How his friend balanced the various aspects of his Leadership both perplexed and impressed Rogue. That he had been given the opportunity to experience the Leader's role both terrified and humbled him. It also made him determined to succeed.

Shadows deepened across the landscape with the rapid approach of dusk, rendering the drifts violet. At least the snow had stopped, and the path widened, allowing for better footing. Rogue took relief from the fact that the mountain pass they had traveled through to the *sojabosnelo* fortress led directly back to the village. From there, he would tend his flock of two before pressing on. He wished he had more than weak optimism to offer them. Their blind faith in his resolution bolstered his courage. He would not fail them or Bialig.

Rogue's fur-lined hood hindered his peripheral vision. When the large, dark shadow trailing them made the mistake of stepping on a dry branch, Rogue heard the additional presence before he saw it. The sound of cracking timber shot through the air, causing the gambler to jump. The noise confirmed what he had sensed for the last twenty minutes of their journey. He mentally cursed himself for not acknowledging it sooner. All that mattered now was not alarming Nish and Talj. He swore aloud when the unwelcome visitor's growl rose above the blast of wind.

"We are being followed," Nish said over her shoulder without breaking stride.

"I heard it. Keep walking." Rogue listened for noises such as an animal would make. "Do you know what it is?"

"A *mojar*," she replied.

"You mean one of those things that left a paw print in our camp along the river?"

"Yes."

"It tracked us all this way?"

"No," said Talj. "*Mojarne* have a wide territory, but these are not from the river. We have traveled beyond their range."

"These? You mean there's more than one?" Rogue asked.

"Yes, and they are from the mountains. Bigger and hairier than their river cousins, although these look lean and starved. Why they are hunting here is a mystery. The game herds have been destroyed. There is no food."

"Well, there is now."

Rogue wondered if their scent had attracted the large carnivores. He possessed no skill for this sort of situation. He would have to improvise by drawing on what he learned as a gambler and smuggler by employing deception.

"Let's pick up the pace. We need to find shelter for you two. I'm going to look for the place where Bialig killed Ojatam," Rogue said.

Nish shuddered and made a sound of disgust in her throat.

"Why would you go there, *Mir*-Rogue?"

"I have an idea how to lose our four-footed friends."

Nish walked closer to Talj and lifted his pack from beneath to lighten the load on the old Healer's shoulders. Rogue called to both frequently, urging them to hurry with words harsher than he cared to use on his friends, but he had no choice when the *mojarne* grew bolder. They no longer skulked along behind the travelers, hiding among the debris of landslides. The promise of food drew them from the shadows, and Rogue saw two about forty feet to his left. Much to his dismay, he spotted a third beast twenty feet to his right. They hunted with deadly precision.

The winds blew the stench of the *mojarne* toward the three friends. Rogue dropped back from the other two presenting an easy target should the beasts attack. He picked up two charred pieces of wood, an indication that they were close to the *sojabosnelo* village and banged them together to startle the animals. Then he called to Nish and Talj as loudly as he could to further confuse the *mojarne* as well as explain his plan.

"If these things charge, I want you and Talj to run like hell. Understand?"

"*Mir*-Rogue, you cannot—"

"Nish—listen to what I'm telling you. I have my knives, and I'm pretty sure I can outrun these guys."

"Do not be deceived by their bulk, my friend," Talj said. "*Mojarne* are faster than they appear."

"I'll keep that in mind."

Rogue shot a glance at the single beast now walking a path to intercept and separate him from the group. The shaggy, black form lumbered along with its massive front paws turned inward. A small, low-slung head with a long, tooth-filled snout and short horns sloped upward into the swell of wide, powerful shoulders. Its body tapered downward into back legs naturally bent for jumping or propelling the animal at great speeds. Red eyes burned through the dusk with bioluminescence. Rogue had no idea where to land a killing blow on such a creature.

As if reading his mind, Nish said, "Bialig always strikes the horns first. I believe this leads to extreme loss of blood and damages the *mojarnelo* ability to think."

"You mean like nerve damage?" Rogue asked.

"Yes—that is the idea. The nerves in its horns are for sensing and lead directly to its head. When they are severed, a *mojar* is easier to kill."

"Too bad I don't have Bialig's height to swing down on this thing."

"The nose is also very sensitive," said Talj.

And dangerously close to the teeth, Rogue thought. Aloud he said, "We don't have any more time. This one is getting too close. I want the two of you to run when I say. Head for that building with the peaked roof. I can see a door from here. Close it and make your way to the top. Try to stay clear of fire damage so you don't fall through steps or floors."

"What will you do?" Nish asked. Rogue heard the tears in her voice. He did not answer.

Instead, he discarded one piece of wood and tucked the other into his armpit. Then he fished striking stones Nish had given him from the pouch around his neck. One, two, three sparks jumped from the clicking stones before a fleck of fire ignited the charred wood protruding from beneath Rogue's arm. A few gentle breaths encouraged the flame to explore below the scales of the crumbling surface. Rogue had a suitable torch to wave in the direction of the closest *mojar*.

"Okay, Nish. Talj? On my count—one, two, three—*run*."

The gambler lunged at the *mojar* closest to him, yelling and waving his torch as he charged the animal. Twin flames danced in the demon's red eyes as it stood stunned with one clawed foot in midair. Rogue whacked its nose as hard as he could with the torch sending sparks into its eyes and, much to his surprise, catching the beast's fur on fire.

A howl to rip the fabric of the night burst forth from the three-chambered throat of the *mojar*. Rogue dropped the torch and covered his ears, shaking with more fear than he had ever known. The torch hissed its last breath and plunged them into darkness. The triple moons were no match for the clouds thickened with snow.

Rogue sensed the two *mojarne* approaching from behind. Their strides shook the ground, but they were strangely silent in their attack. He took advantage of the cloak of night and bolted away from the burning *mojar* rearing up in pain and rage. Its companions crashed into it and added their growls to the cacophony when they realized their intended prey had escaped. Though laden with his pack and Misko's instruments, Rogue ran through the deep snow as if the hounds of hell chased him.

Nish and Talj were nowhere in sight. Rogue trusted they had made it to the burned-out dwelling for he could not hear their progress over the howling and snarling. The uninjured *mojarne* had turned their appetites upon their singed pack mate, eating it alive. The feeding frenzy escalated with the sound of tearing hide and muscle, but it afforded Rogue the time he needed to reach the far side of the *sojabosnelo* village. He stopped and turned in a circle, hoping to see a familiar landmark. A sword embedded in a beam provided the clue he had been looking for.

Layers of snow hid Ojatam's body. The telltale sign of a massive blood stain told Rogue which mound covered the traitor's carcass. His stomach churned as he brushed away frozen blood from where the betrayer's head had been and kicked at the wound to coax forth more blood. Ideally, a meal of fresh meat would satisfy the *mojarne*, but if Rogue had learned anything from Frank Blast, it was the fact that predators will never stop until they have killed their desired prey.

The gambler removed his gloves and untied his sleeping fur from his pack. He placed both on Ojatam's corpse. With one of his knives, he made a shallow cut across his palm and touched his bleeding hand to the fur, taking care to drip blood back along the way he had come. A strip of fabric torn from the lining of his coat served as a makeshift bandage. Rogue hid in the closest dwelling and waited.

Unmasked greed continued to stalk Rogue in the Realm as the two remaining *mojarne*, covered in blood and gore, sought him. As anticipated, the beasts sniffed the air and followed the scent of human blood to Ojatam's remains. They pawed at the sleeping fur and chewed the leather gloves with satisfaction for having secured their missing prey. A fight broke out between the pair as they devoured the bounty, the noise of which covered Rogue's escape. He located the building with the peaked roof and found Nish and Talj huddled in a corner on the second floor.

"*Mira*-Rogue," Nish exclaimed as she jumped up, sweeping him into a hug, pinning his arms and crushing all that he carried against his back.

"Nish . . . I can't breathe."

The *Jiltraos* held on for several more moments, her tears bathing Rogue's face as she rocked from side to side. He staggered a few steps when she plunked him on the floor. Nish grabbed the front of his coat to steady him. They laughed through their tears.

"Are you guys all right?" Rogue asked.

"We are," Talj replied. "What of the *mojarne*?"

"You tell me. Will they leave once they've eaten?"

"They should if they believe there is nothing more to hunt."

"I would think they'd be too full to hunt again."

"That is a fault with *mojarne*; they will gorge themselves to death if given the chance."

"Great. Will they at least sleep off this meal?"

"That is a possibility." Talj thought for a moment. "I have a poison among my medicines that if they eat it, they will surely die."

"What if we employ the poison by sprinkling it on the dead *mojar*?"

"The dead *mojar* is in the direction we just came from. Are we not continuing our journey to the *Damirgne*, *Mir*-Rogue?" Nish asked.

Rogue shook his head and looked away. "This really isn't working for me."

"Do you mean you do not want to lead us to safety?"

The accusation hung in the air, yet Nish's voice was devoid of any condemnation. Her eyes glowed from within, and she tensed, waiting for Rogue's next command.

"Will you reject Bialig's request? He trusted you with his *Doh s'Ima*," Talj said.

I'm still wondering why he took that gamble, Rogue thought.

Every decision, every move, resembled the holding or disposing of a card, the result of which was nothing more than a door opening or closing on an opportunity. You won, you lost, you lived to play the game another day. Only now every card held the face of someone Rogue cared about deeply. He knew how this hand had to be played, his gut told him so. It had nothing to do with flouting authority and everything to do with not folding in the face of extreme opposition.

"Tell me you don't want to be back at that fortress and put an end to this craziness. Kolbian has yanked our chain for far too long. It's time to show him the collective muscle of our *Doh s'Ima.*"

Nish tucked her bottom lip between her teeth and looked at Talj, barely able to make out his wizened face in the dark. Moonlight parted the clouds, reaching down to touch the old Healer through a hole in the roof.

"As I told Bialig before, he does not have to do this alone."

Talj stood with the assistance of a spear shaft minus the blade. He grasped it in both hands in front of him, twirling it once before jabbing an end at Rogue who jumped out of reach. The old Healer's lopsided grin appeared.

"All right then," Rogue said. "Let's do this."

* * *

MOONLIGHT GLINTED OFF METAL AS Rogue's hands moved of their own accord, digging through the snow to recover weapons lost or abandoned by the *sojabosne*. His fingers cramped with the cold. Nish and Talj worked beside him, locating knives and short swords they felt confident wielding in battle. When they had acquired enough, each stood with two or three extra handles sticking out of their belts. Talj laughed first, breaking the tension.

"I have not lived this much in many cycles of the moons," the old Healer said.

"I do not think you have spoken this much either, *Mir*-Talj," Nish added, her laughter returning like a forgotten friend.

Talj nodded in agreement. "Our *uma* has been the catalyst of much good since his arrival."

"I'm glad you came to see it that way," Rogue said.

Nish hummed and tossed her head. "We were willing to extend grace for your sake."

"Yeah, right." Rogue stowed his pack and Misko's instruments in the closest dwelling. Nish and Talj followed suit. "We'll return for these when it's over."

Talj had already applied a pain-killing liniment to his joints in preparation for the walk back to the fortress. Then he poisoned the *mojarlo* corpse in case the other two returned looking for food. Before leaving, he pulled small packets from his medicine bag and handed one to Rogue and Nish.

"Swallow this powder down with a handful of snow. It will taste bitter."

"What is it?" Rogue asked.

"Ground *depakat* antlers."

"Do I even want to know what that is or why we're taking this?"

Nish gagged at the flavor and broke an icicle from the eaves of the building. She cracked it in three pieces and handed one to each of the men.

"Lick this for water and to get rid of the taste."

"What's the point of this stuff?" Rogue asked.

"For energy on the hike back to the fortress and during the battle," Talj said. He paused in repacking his medicine bag to repeat, "During the battle."

The eyes of all three met in understanding. Rogue could not chance doubts entering their minds. There was no going back once they started.

"Like I said, we'll return for our stuff once we have Bialig and Misko with us. It'll be safe here."

The gambler walked with eyes straight ahead and listened for the footfalls of his companions. The hollow sound of wind echoed off his surroundings. Buildings weakened by fire groaned under the weight of the snow. An airborne predator shrieked as it scoured the land below for something to eat. Finally, Rogue heard the crunching steps of Nish and Talj. He did not slacken his pace, choosing to let them catch up to him.

"Did you think we had changed our minds, *uma*?" Talj asked.

"I knew you guys would come. I just needed a head start because your legs are longer than mine."

The *Thedanos* barked a laugh. "You have been good for my spirits, *uma*. Perhaps I should not have healed you so soon."

"Oh yeah? Why's that?"

"You would have made an interesting exhibition at the *Avboeth*."

"You're full of yourself tonight, aren't you, *Mir*-Talj?"

More coarse laughter receded into the silence of the cold, dark night. The trio walked on until Nish asked, "What is your plan, *Mir*-Rogue?"

"We're going to play the hand we've been dealt and bluff our way through the rest."

"That does not sound very encouraging."

"You're going to have to put on your best poker face, Nish."

"This is a useful tactic?"

"It's always worked for me on Earth. Won me some serious cred-coin by playing it cool."

"I do not understand 'poker face' and 'playing it cool.'"

"Gambling, Nish. We're going to take the ultimate gamble and pray it pays off."

"What is your back up plan?"

Rogue knew a round of cards never had a backup plan. One simply lost and left with his tail tucked between legs. But at least the opportunity to walk away existed. The gambler stopped and turned to face Nish.

"To not fail," he said in answer to her question.

CHAPTER TWENTY-SEVEN

PIECES OF BROKEN FURNITURE BLAZED to life in the hearth of the *sojabosnelo* stronghold. Candles, their bases melted before sticking them to the flagstones, lit a path from the foyer to the great hall. Shattered dishes and dented goblets were kicked into piles in the corners of the room. Tapestries huddled in soiled heaps along the perimeter.

"We are ready, Misko," Kolbian said.

"But *natamos*, will not the fire alert Bialig to our presence? Surely the light can be seen in the dark."

Kolbian pinched the bridge of his nose. "Misko, it is because we are present that Bialig has come. Not because he was lured by a fire."

The youth nodded, a smug smile spreading across his face as if he had known this all along.

"Are you ready to choose a weapon, boy?" Kolbian asked.

"Why do I need one, *natamos*?"

"Misko, what did you think was going to take place here?"

"I thought I came here to join in the *sojabosnelo* effort to guarantee freedom for all people."

"Yes, yes, besides that."

"To establish—re-establish—the *sojabosne*?"

"How can one person be so ignorant?" Kolbian shouted to the ceiling. "To fight, boy. To eliminate those who would oppose us, starting with my brother."

"That I understand, *natamos*."

"I do not think so, or you would comprehend the need for a weapon. You must finish this war launched against us by the Clans. Your place as a leader among our people must be secured by your participation in the initial battles. Understand me now, Misko, you are required to fight."

The young man's face took on an ashen appearance. "You want me to fight *Mira*-Bialig?" he asked, remembering his one disastrous encounter with his former *Natamos*.

The hair on the back of Kolbian's neck bristled at the honorific Misko granted Bialig. The false leader inhaled slowly, expanding his chest nearly beyond capacity, to check the anger boiling within.

"What I want is for you to be prepared. There are undamaged weapons in the room behind the dais."

The Artist peeked around Kolbian, frowning at the seamless paneling behind the platform.

"The room is hidden behind a false wall." Kolbian turned and indicated Misko should follow. "Come. You may choose your weapon while my brother wastes time assuring his precious *Doh s'Ima* of their safety."

Kolbian pushed Misko ahead of him by his shoulder. Once they stood on the raised floor, the false leader touched his fingers to two knots in the wooden panels. Mechanisms within the wall released, and a door opened with a soft click. A breath of stale air gusted past them.

"Fetch a candle," Kolbian said, drumming his fingers against his leg until the young man returned.

He took the wax stub and entered the room ahead of the Artist, lighting metal torches secured around the chamber. Neither spoke as the flames flickered off the walls gilded with armament. The breath Kolbian drew this time held awe for the shrine to death and destruction.

Misko shivered. His eyes roamed over his reflection in the multitude of sword blades and battle axes hanging on the walls. Spears and maces stood to attention among carved and painted shields bound in strips of hammered metal. Long bows, crossbows, and quivers teeming with arrows threatened from among the rows of short swords and knives. The weapons looked ready to spring from the walls, march forth, and conduct battle without the assistance of a living hand to wield them.

"These have been separated for a specific use," Kolbian said. His breath fell cold upon Misko's ear.

The Artist in Misko could not be suppressed. He sought beauty among the lethal functionality exhibited before him as he walked a circuit around the room, hanging back from the walls with his hands clasped in front of him. His eyes never looked above his own height to where the most ornate weapons rested in deadly display.

When Misko touched an oiled blade with one finger as if testing for dust, Kolbian realized he was losing the young man to his doubts and fears. His inclination to punish the *Paten* as he would a warrior resisting instruction lost out to the modicum of restraint he possessed.

"Misko, look. This sword belongs to you."

Kolbian reached for a short sword with a wide blade and faceted red stones decorating the pommel and cross guard. The false leader hefted the sword from the brackets securing it to the wall and presented it to Misko. A small gasp escaped the Artist when he alone bore the weight of the sword. His eyes did not meet Kolbian's for fear of seeing disappointment; brandishing the sword in battle would prove difficult at best for the *Paten*.

The false leader ignored the truth confronting him and said, "This sword belonged to your ancestor."

Misko cradled the weapon in one arm, taking care to keep the blade away from his torso. With one finger, he traced the letters spelling *Shlodane* etched along the length of the blade.

"How can this be? My family never spoke of an ancestor among the *sojabosne*."

"Of course not, Misko. They would not want you to know that you had a family member who sought freedom among those they feared and scorned."

Kolbian smiled as he watched Misko embrace the sword and the lie. He chose a counterfeit name to perpetuate the untruth.

"Teron was among the first who broke away from the tyranny of the High Council of Elders. He lived before the time of Talj. He was a great man, a great leader. You remind me of him, Misko." The Artist looked up at Kolbian's error. "Well, the stories about him remind me of you."

Again, Misko gazed upon the sword with longing to finish the mission his imaginary ancestor had set out to undertake.

"You must succeed, Misko, where Teron failed."

"What happened to him, *natamos*?"

"He was struck down in battle."

"Then his life was not a failure. He simply did not have the opportunity to finish what he started."

"You are very wise for one so young. Are you brave enough to pick up where your ancestor left off?"

Misko gripped the hilt in his hands, muscles bulging and wrists shaking, as he held the sword before him in acceptance of the mantle laid across his shoulders.

Footsteps outside the armory room sliced into Kolbian's awareness. He turned his head to listen for Bialig's approach. His eyes flicked back to Misko, who admired the short sword resting in his arms. The false leader's sword lay sheathed upon his pack. His brow knotted as he contemplated whether he could reach it in time. When he recalled his brother's sickening sense of honor, he strolled from the room.

"I would have brought your sword to you if it was not forbidden to touch the weapon of a betrayer."

"I have no fear of tampering where you are concerned, Bialig. In fact, I have no fear of you at all."

"Where is *Mir*-Misko?" Bialig raised his voice in the hope of drawing out his missing *Doh s'Ima* member.

"Misko is no longer your concern. He made his decision, and he will adhere to it."

Bialig stiffened, his hand reaching for the hilt of his sword when Kolbian shouldered past en route to retrieve their father's sword.

"It was pointless to send your *Doh s'Ima* and the *uma* away. After I defeat you, brother, I will kill them. Except for Nish. She will serve my pleasure for as long as I desire, and only when I tire of her—"

"Surrender while there is still time, *brother*."

Kolbian's sword hissed through the air like a serpent missing its target. Bialig did not even flinch at the attempted intimidation.

"I'll ask you again. Where is Misko?"

The Artist stepped from behind the door in the fake wall. He held the short sword before him in his trembling hands. Bialig recognized the weapon as one he had helped forge for a young *Shlodane* warrior led astray by *sojabosnelo* teaching. His expression softened at the sight of the sword in the hands of his *Paten*. Kolbian noted the concern on Bialig's face.

"It is true, Bialig," Misko said. "I have chosen a path different from the one you would force upon me."

"*Mir*-Misko," Bialig replied, "you were free to choose at any point in your life. No one decided for you."

"You know as well as I do that I had no choice. I was crushed under the pressure to join the *Doh s'Ima* once our abilities had been established. To decline—to bring disappointment to every member of the *Shlodane* Clan—is a weight that should be carried by no one. And I cannot live under the burden of fear that comes when there is no *Doh s'Ima*. Fear incited by those who would use it to control."

Misko raised the sword as he raised his voice. His breathing quickened and sweat filmed his forehead. Bialig closed the distance between himself and Misko.

"I hear you, *Mir*-Misko."

"As will the High Council of Elders."

"When they hear of your rebellion—" Bialig winced at his choice of words and started again. "Misko, consider this: will lawlessness stop if the ancient edicts are abandoned? People need the Infinite One's commandments as guidelines within which to function. How else will they know how to connect with Him and each other?"

"People know right and wrong without His interference."

"Yes, some know how to do what is right without being told. For others, the framework of instruction exists."

"And penalty." Misko's voice wavered.

"Only for those who break the commands."

Kolbian raked his sword across the flagstone floor, worried that his brother's words would loosen his hold over Misko. The grating sound breached Misko's doubts, and he again raised the sword against Bialig.

"The commands bind us under outdated, irrelevant laws," Misko cried.

"My friend, the Infinite One never abandoned His standard of righteousness just because the *sojabosne* did," Bialig said. "And you did not gain freedom when you walked away from Him. You lost it."

The Leader's words to Misko floated on waves of heat from the fire, singeing the edges of his conscience. Misko looked toward the cool dark of the weapons room. He looked at the sword in his hands. And in the warm light dancing around the hall, the *Paten* looked to Kolbian and said in a weak voice, "End this."

* * *

BLOOD POUNDED IN ROGUE'S EARS; adrenaline pressed him forward. His leg muscles burned, and his back and knees ached, but he continued to maintain as brisk a pace as possible through thigh-deep snow drifts. Nish and Talj fared a little better as their longer legs sought purchase in the steep drifts. Rogue stopped the other two with his raised fist when the *sojabosnelo* fortress came into sight. All three panted silver mist into the black of night.

"All right," Rogue said when he caught his breath, "this is where we split up. Ojatam was vague about how many *sojabosne* were still around, so we have to make this work. Do you remember what we discussed on the way back?"

Nish pulled her striking stones from her pocket and patted the bundle of charred bow staves, salvaged from the *sojabosnelo* village, under her arm. Talj followed suit. Then they slipped away without a sound to place the wood around the perimeter of the stronghold. Rogue did the same, reaching as high as he could to give the impression that many Realmers from among the Clans stood in unity against the *sojabosne*.

Rogue had about half his bundle placed when he saw the first flames appear on Talj's and Nish's torches. He rushed to finish and barely had the last one lit before the other two began the war chants. Rhythmic cries punctuated with the clash of weapons and stomp of feet reverberated off the stone walls of mountains and fortress. The challenge went out in the soft voices of the *Jiltraos* and *Thedanos* but returned with the strength of a mighty force. Rogue added his deep voice to the fierce harmony, repeating the words Nish had taught him.

The battle cries had been used to intimidate enemies as they were driven from the land during the formation of the Clans at the dawn of time. Now they were taught to young warriors or potential Leaders for use in skill games or to repel the *sojabosne*. Nish, who inadvertently learned the words while watching Bialig instruct the *Shlodane* Clan children, never dreamed she would be called upon to speak them aloud in preparation for war.

The three shifted the torches forward, each repositioning between ten to fifteen burning staves in the snow to give the appearance of a large contingent advancing on the stronghold. Their unified voices faded or intensified depending on where they stood in their forward progress, but their relentless cry never ceased. They kept up the pretense as much for their own encouragement as to threaten those within. The possibility of a direct attack still existed, although the trio silently prayed any *sojabosne* inside the fortress would retreat in the face of a perceived assault.

The battle had begun.

* * *

BIALIG FELT AS IF HE watched the fight from far above. Two combatants moved with power and grace, their swords arcs of liquid metal slicing the air to within a hair's breadth of the other. Death waited patiently in the shadows for an invitation to their dance.

A lifetime passed with every moment. The goal of each burned brightly in their eyes. Blade crashed upon blade as bodies drenched in heat denied place to the cold. Their individual choreography melded until finally first blood was drawn, staining their weapons, their clothes. The battle raged beyond the confines of time.

Their steps never faltered as they lunged and feinted to the music of war cries coming from outside the fortress. The sound of labored breathing filled every remaining scrap of space in the chamber, hard breaths meant to keep muscles moving, hearts pounding. Hand over hand, Bialig climbed the lifeline of his own consciousness back into his body. His need to protect overwhelmed even as vulnerabilities were exposed.

The Leader did not know how long he had been fighting, but he knew he could not go on forever. Despite what else his brother may be, Kolbian was a formidable opponent, his skill honed by preying on the best warriors from the Clans, killing them off one by one as he made his name in the *sojabosne*. He fought without fear. He fought like one with nothing to lose, whereas Bialig battled to preserve the lives of those he loved. Starting with Misko, for whom he had left the path to peace and walked headlong into this den of thieves.

Exhaustion forced its way into Bialig's mind, robbing him of concentration. Multiple figures blurred past him, and he feared he was losing focus. He forced down the urge to stand still and regain his footing, both physically and mentally. Another attack from Kolbian re-engaged the Leader's will, but he finally recognized Rogue charging into battle with knives drawn. Against whom Bialig could not say until his brother cried out in pain from an unexpected wound to his lower leg. Kolbian crashed into Bialig, too close for their swords to cause any damage. They grappled and slipped in their own blood as Rogue continued to inflict damage where he could.

Talj and Nish confronted Misko. The pair, as inexperienced in combat as Misko, had their hands full when the Artist swung wildly with a superior weapon. The youth no longer saw his former *Doh s'Ima* members but only the loss of his dreams. He wanted vengeance upon those who stood in the way of his path to greatness. He would sacrifice whatever and whomever it took to achieve it, and so the lie thundered on.

Nish stumbled backward over a broken bench, crying out when Misko's sword cut through her sleeve, drawing Bialig's attention. Talj pounded the young man's back with a spear shaft, his arms tiring from the effort. Misko whirled on the old Healer and wrenched the crude weapon from Talj's hands. He would have plunged the splintered end into the *Thedanos* if Rogue had not launched himself at Misko's back, landing with one hand in his hair and yanking his head backward. The gambler placed his knife against the Artist's exposed neck, but the killing stroke never came.

"*No*—" Bialig screamed with every ounce of breath he had left.

The moment for which Kolbian had been waiting arrived just as he knew it would. His brother's concern for others could not be arrested even in the middle of battle. How glorious that moment of distraction would be as he thrust his sword into Bialig's turned back. He secured his grip on the hilt of his blood-soaked weapon, prepared to strike, and completely underestimated the ferocity with which Nish, Talj, and the *uma* would defend their *Natamos*.

Rogue's knives left his hands the same moment Talj hurled his recovered spear shaft like a javelin and Nish sprang up to whip her knife across the room. Their weapons flew past Bialig whose knees bent until his upper body was parallel to the flagstones. All four missiles found their intended target, penetrating Kolbian's chest.

Braced by one arm, Bialig twisted and pushed himself upward. He knocked Kolbian's sword aside but not out of his hand. The false leader shuffled backward yet managed to stay upright, his sword arm twitching with desire. A cough brought blood to Kolbian's bitter smile as he tore his eye patch from his face.

The Leader looked directly into his brother's eyes; one soft gray, the other strangely reptilian, yellow with a black scar bisecting it vertically. Bialig could not reconcile the man who stood before him with the brother he once knew. The two halves would never make a whole, and they could not be separated, could not co-exist.

Kolbian died a warrior. He kept his sword and lost his head. Bialig cried out in heartbreaking agony with the final blow, but he did not step forward to catch Kolbian's falling body. The traitor had been shown enough dignity.

Silence fell over the battle, yielding to the whistle of cold winds sifted through the broken windowpanes high above. Pieces of tapestry bore the blood from Bialig's sword. He turned at the clatter of a weapon dropped to the floor.

"Misko?"

The last excruciating moments of the battle burned away like fire receding before the rains that extinguished it. From the ashes, the *Shlodane* Clan *Doh s'Ima* would reemerge stronger than before for having survived their trials.

Rogue watched Bialig walk to where the fallen Artist prostrated himself. The young man's long, white hair hid his face but not the sound of his sorrow. Misko covered his head with one arm. The other he stretched out before him, palm up. The Leader knelt, placed his palm on Misko's, and grasped his hand.

Gashes in need of bandaging crisscrossed Bialig's arms, legs, and body. A laceration on his head left a crimson trail, and blood from a cut across his eyebrow blurred the vision in his eye already swelling shut. None of the Leader's injuries prevented him from helping Misko to his feet and embracing the Artist.

Misko's arms hung limp at his sides. He shrank away from Bialig when the Leader released him, wiping at the blood transferred to his clothes and staring at his hands in horror.

"We won, Misko. You are free," Bialig said, his voice etched with fatigue and relief.

Misko's visage reflected nothing. The hand of uncertainty wiped from his face all traces of his initial reaction to Kolbian's defeat. The Artist was clay waiting to be molded.

Nish stepped forward, oblivious to the wound on her arm, and wedged herself between the two men. Her fingers lightly grazed Misko's face as she searched for traces of her friend. Talj also crowded his way into the company of his *Doh s'Ima*. The old Healer was eager to restore balance to the group as well as the individual.

Only Rogue held back. Time still spun around him like a roulette wheel, his mind bouncing like the little ball seeking a place to rest. Rogue hated roulette. He thought it lacked skill. There were no faces to read, no ticks to discern. But the gambler did not know which cards had been dealt in the current situation, so he did not know which ones he held. He looked to Misko to supply the answer.

CHAPTER TWENTY-EIGHT

"YOU'RE BLEEDING."

Rogue stated the obvious to break the spell that had fallen over them, to force the hand of fate.

"*Mira*," Nish said, shifting her attention to Bialig.

The hands of the *Jiltraos* skimmed over the Leader's body, her eyes taking in the severity of his wounds. She pressed her palms to his face and felt him lean toward her, letting her support his weight.

"Sit him down," Rogue said. The gambler rushed to his friend's side, helping Nish and Talj ease Bialig to the floor. "Are you dizzy?"

"Just tired," Bialig said.

"We have no medicine," Nish said. "Our packs are hidden at the *sojabosnelo* village. We have nothing with which to treat your wounds, *Mira*."

Talj crouched beside the Leader and worked at a leather thong around his neck, untying it and pulling a small pouch from beneath his tunic.

"I always have a little something with me. Take this, *Mir*-Bialig, for the pain. You must rest here while we fetch our supplies. Then I can bandage your wounds."

"He needs water," Rogue said as he retrieved a battered goblet from the floor and ran to fill it with snow. A few moments in front of the hearth reduced the snow to a slushy consistency. "Here, sip this."

Bialig coughed on the first swallow of ice and water, drinking fast and shivering as his body cooled.

"Thank you, Rogue."

"I don't want you going into shock. You're really pale, and Talj is right. You need to lie down while Misko and I get our stuff."

The Artist had retreated into the shadows beyond the fire's glow. A small gasp escaped him upon hearing his name. He edged farther away until his form became one with the darkness clinging to the corner of the room.

"Misko?" Rogue assumed the young man had closed his eyes as he could not see light reflecting from them. "Let's get our stuff. Your things, too. I brought your instruments."

"My instruments?" Misko repeated as if he had no concept of what Rogue mentioned.

"Yes, now let's go."

"What use do I have for instruments now?"

"What?" Rogue stopped halfway to the door. "What are you talking about? Of course you need your instruments. You're part of this *Doh s'Ima*, and as the *Paten* you play the damn instruments. Now quit simpering and let's go."

"*Mir*-Misko." Bialig's voice, though weak, reached a place where Rogue's words could not. "Sit with me until you are able to go with Rogue."

The corners of the gambler's mouth turned down. He took a deep breath and exhaled with force, but Bialig only nodded at him. The Leader's wounds required immediate attention. Rogue knew his friend would use his remaining strength to care for Misko's needs first, whatever they may be.

Misko approached with his eyes cast down. Long, white locks covered his face. He hesitated when Nish touched his arm and guided him to sit beside Bialig. Talj pounded the Artist's shoulder with his typical gruffness.

Rogue tensed as he watched his friends. He shifted from one foot to another, braced against any harm that would befall them. The expectation of loss played at the periphery of his mind, and he glanced at Kolbian's body, too near for his liking. The betrayer's sword hilt lay within his slack hand, and Rogue half expected the headless snake to strike.

"Misko," Bialig said, "do you understand that all is forgiven?"

"Forgiveness? I do not think that is possible. Not now, not after you—"

Bialig groaned and grabbed his side, slumping sideways into Nish. He ground his teeth until the pain forced him to gasp. His breath came as desperate pants, and his head fell forward.

"*Mira*," Nish cried, holding him by his shoulders.

Misko scrambled away. Rogue hurried to Bialig's side.

"Lay him down, Nish. Easy. He took some nasty hits and may have internal injuries," Rogue said.

"No, please," Bialig whispered. "Help me stand to relieve this pain."

"Are you sure?"

Rogue held the Leader's hand and supported his arm, taking his full weight as he gathered his legs beneath him to stand. Nish pressed close to Bialig with her arms wrapped around his waist, his arm around her shoulders. Talj stood behind the *Natamos* with his arms spread wide in case the big man fell backward. The Old Healer's hands rested on Nish and Rogue on either side of the Leader.

Only Misko saw the shimmer around them. Only he witnessed the circle completed.

"No," the young man hissed.

Energy surged through Bialig. His weakened body drew strength from the other three; they received his pain without notice. The Leader took a few tentative steps and smiled, recognizing the familiar sensation of perfect connectivity.

Misko rushed the Leader, brushing Talj's hand away from Nish and shoving Rogue aside.

"*Natamos*, you are well enough to walk. Now we can all return to the village for our packs."

"Let's not rush things," Rogue said. "He's lost a lot of blood, Misko."

"We are a hearty people, are we not, *Natamos*?"

Bialig gave a lop-sided smile and nodded his head.

"Then let us go," said Misko. "The sky is lightening, and the snow has stopped."

Misko hustled Talj toward the door, fastening the old Healer's coat and pulling his hood up to muffle his complaints. Nish, too, was hurried away from Bialig and made to wait beside Talj. Her protests went unheeded.

"Misko, stop it," Rogue said, grasping at Misko's arm as he whisked past, returning to Bialig. The gambler stood torn between calming Nish and Talj or staying close to the Leader.

"Go on," Misko ordered the others with a wave of his hand. "Rogue, take charge of Talj and Nish as you are so apt to do."

"I said stop it."

Bialig swayed without anyone to lean on. Misko seized the Leader's arm, digging in his fingers. He spoke to the others, but he looked directly in Bialig's face.

"Did you not hear what our *Natamos* said? He has forgiven all. We are a complete *Doh s'Ima* once again." Pretense softened the hard lines of Misko's mouth, and his confident posture reinforced his words. "And I would follow him anywhere."

Years of dancing as the *Doh s'Ima Paten* lent Misko grace and agility. What Rogue did not count on was the swiftness with which the young man whirled and dipped and righted himself holding Kolbian's sword. A thousand possible outcomes exploded in the gambler's mind, the faces of cards all better than those he held flashed before his eyes. He was not ready when the Artist showed his hand.

Rogue watched in disbelief as the blade of Kolbian's sword emerged from Bialig's chest, driven from behind with the force of rebellion. The Leader grunted, his eyes widening with understanding, and cried out only when Misko withdrew the weapon.

"*Mira*, no—" Nish screamed, falling to her knees.

"Oh, no, Misko, no," Talj cried.

Words lingered in Rogue's open mouth; questions too painful to ask. He remained silent, pinned to the floor, when Bialig closed his eyes and crashed to the flagstones like a felled tree.

Nish reached the Leader first. She struggled to turn him over and pull him onto her lap, cradling his head against her breast. The *Jiltraos* rocked and wept. Her keening rose to the ceiling above. Her grief echoed throughout the fortress.

Talj knelt beside Bialig and pressed his gnarled hands over the blood blossoming across the Leader's chest. Nothing in the Healer's repertoire could reverse the damage wrought. He bowed low over his friend and spoke ancient words of intercession on his behalf.

Maddening Rogue most of all was the complete lack of repentance on Misko's face. And the realization that everything from the moments before had been a lie. And the look of shock when the *Paten* beheld Kolbian's sword in his fist as if he had no idea how the weapon had come to be in his possession.

Rogue almost smiled at the young man. Misko was an Artist, but he was not that good of an actor. Too late the gambler learned that evil is not always apparent; he would not make that mistake again.

It gave Rogue no pleasure, no satisfaction, to end the Artist's life. He charged Misko to make the young man wield the weapon in his hand, for there was no honor in killing an unprepared opponent. The judgment and justice were swift and painless. Rogue stayed near Misko, who ineffectively applied pressure to twin wounds on his neck.

"Don't fight it," Rogue whispered. "It's already too late anyhow."

The gambler closed Misko's eyes and wiped his sleeve hard across his own. Then he laid down his knives and joined Nish and Talj in their grief.

"Rogue . . . take my hand."

"Bialig," Rogue cried. "How the hell—"

"Listen," the Leader forced between pale lips.

Rogue took his friend's large, cold hand in both of his.

"I'm listening."

"I promised I would help you . . . save your Raine . . ." Pain gripped the Leader, and he reared up against Nish who held him tightly. "It must . . . be now."

"Bialig, save your strength. We can't open the portal, but I can go for help. I know the way."

The Leader closed his eyes and shook his head vehemently. Then he looked to Talj to make Rogue understand. The old Healer took Rogue's chin and turned his face like a child.

"*Mira*-Rogue, we can open the portal. The four of us. Do not make me explain, only trust. You have the abilities of a *Paten*. Rough and hidden but worthy of inclusion in a *Doh s'Ima*."

"That can't be."

Talj sliced the air with his hand and growled his frustration. "I tell you, the portal can be opened. And it must be opened now."

Deep within Rogue knew it was true. He, too, had felt the inexplicable connection between himself and the Realmers. But his soul cried out for time. Time to stay with his friends because they needed him. Time to make things right. A moment passed and with it an eternity.

"But I'd have to leave you. Nish's arm is cut, and Talj—you're too old. There may be other *sojabosne*. We need help, Bialig needs help. I can't leave you—not like this—without knowing what happens to any of you."

"Rogue," Bialig mouthed, the unspoken word silencing the gambler.

The Leader coughed wetly, bringing blood to his lips. Nish's tears coursed down her cheeks, falling softly on Bialig's as she brought her face close to his. With her thumb she wiped the blood from his mouth and pressed her lips to his, delivering a pledge of her love until death parted them.

Rogue closed his eyes and held tightly to Bialig's hand. The hard decision had been made.

"Now," he said. "Do it now."

Talj took one of Rogue's hands and reached for Nish's.

Nish felt the *Thedanos* take her hand, but her eyes never left Bialig's. She held the Leader's free hand against her heart.

Bialig's hand rested securely in Rogue's.

The bond was complete.

Light danced around the *Doh s'Ima*, refracted into a million rainbows. Images wavered in front of Rogue, and he saw into Earth as if looking through deep water. A mighty wind rushed between worlds, and Rogue held on.

The gambler heard the encouragement to go in the voices of those he loved. He knew once he released them that they would be lost to him forever. He may never know what happened to them, although he was sure of the destiny of one. And still Rogue held on.

Time meshed between the Realm and Earth. A single bullet flew past the four friends, harmlessly embedding in the stone wall of the *sojabosnelo* fortress. Bialig struggled to find his voice. It came to Rogue as if across space and time.

"Find . . . your *Doh s'Ima* . . . and return to us."

Rogue launched himself through the portal, finally finding the courage to let go. He felt their fingers slip from his own, but he never saw the celestial gateway close.

The gambler somersaulted across Frank Blast's office, bounding up to grab the terrified criminal's gun hand and his throat. Rogue forced the crime boss against the windows and slammed his hand on the glass until the .380 clattered to the floor. Then he vented his wrath upon Blast until the broken mass in a business suit no longer resembled a human.

Small, strong fists pounded Rogue's back, and a voice both familiar and frightened begged him to stop.

"*Rogue*—stop it! Oh God, help me please—" Raine screamed.

Instinct told him to throw off the person trying to pry his hands from Frank Blast's dead body. And Rogue did with much force. Raine returned the courtesy by sweeping his legs and placing a knee to his chest when he fell. She cocked her arm to deliver a punch that would have dazed the gambler if he had not pulled her forward by her shoulders, looked directly into her eyes, and kissed her.

Something shifted inside Raine. Her body resisted even as her heart yielded. Nothing and everything made sense. The seconds ticked by and still explanation and understanding did not come to her. All she knew was that a missing piece had been restored.

"Hello, sweetheart," Rogue whispered as their lips parted.

Raine's half-hearted punch to Rogue's jaw made the gambler swear and roll from beneath the GEA agent.

"What was that for?" Rogue asked, rubbing his chin.

"Who are you? Where the hell have you been? And what are you wearing?"

"You know who I am, or you wouldn't ask where I've been. We can discuss my clothing later. We need to get out of here now. I'll explain everything. I promise."

Rogue took Raine's hand to lead her from Blast Tower. She yanked it from his grasp and backed away from him.

"No. I am not going anywhere with you until you tell me what's going on."

"Raine, I can't right now. Blast is dead, and we need to make ourselves scarce. Just please, trust me."

"Why should I trust you?"

Rogue picked up the discarded shotgun and Blast's .380. He turned to answer Raine and stepped away from the GEA blaster pointed at his face.

"Whoa, Raine—easy does it."

"Give me one reason why I shouldn't end you right now."

"How about the fact that I just saved your life?"

"Not enough. You have one chance to make me believe you really are Rogue."

"What can I say?"

"The choice is yours."

"Okay, okay. I saw you in the ductwork when you found the memo that said Mars Base and the space stations are fake."

"How does that prove anything?"

"Damn it, Raine—I don't know what you want me to say."

"Tell me something only Rogue would know."

"I know you hate it when I call you sweetheart."

The tip of the blaster dropped a fraction. Raine shook her head then righted her weapon, sighting down the barrel.

"But that never stops you from doing it, does it, jackass?"

Rogue held up a weapon in each hand to show he meant no harm. He approached Raine as if walking toward a lioness of dubious tameness.

"I promise I'll never call you sweetheart again if you please come with me now."

Alarms blared outside the office and Blast's HoloMir screen glowed to life.

"Too late," Raine said as she shot the screen before the face that appeared could ask her who she was. "How the hell did they know?"

"Blast is probably wearing a bio-sensor that triggered the security systems within a certain amount of time after he died."

Rogue ran to shut the office doors and barricade them with as much furniture as he could stack in front of them.

"I thought you wanted to leave," Raine said.

"Well, obviously we're not going out that way."

He pressed his ear against the door to listen for the footsteps he knew were coming.

"Rogue, how exactly are we getting out of here?"

"Didn't you come up with a backup plan for this little escapade of yours?"

"It was a one-way mission, you jerk."

Rogue smiled with appreciation. "That's my girl. But now it's time to think on your feet, sweetheart."

The gambler dodged another punch and made his way toward Blast's body.

"Is he really dead?" Raine asked.

"'Fraid so. Let's hope I didn't smash his eyeballs too much."

"What are you doing?"

Rogue struggled to lift Blast's lifeless form and position his face in front of a scanner while prying one eyelid open.

"I'm going to scan his retinas—"

"Here, you idiot. I have a BioMet Card."

The gambler dropped Blast's body in a heap at his feet. "What else you got stashed in that tight suit?"

Raine ignored his comment and stepped over the crime boss. Her hand hesitated above the bloodied face, and she took a deep breath. She chewed her lip while waiting for the card to copy the dead man's retinas.

"I got nothing. It just keeps beeping," she said as the march of many feet exited the elevators.

"Try his other eye."

Blast's security forces advanced in calm precision, heralded by the blaring alarms.

"Nothing."

"Let me see," Rogue said.

Raine offered him the BioMet Card, but he waved it away.

"Here's the problem," Rogue said as he swiped his finger across Blast's unfocused eye. "Anti-replication lenses."

"How did you know?"

"Only criminals use them," Rogue said with a shrug.

Pounding that could not budge the office doors preceded, "Mr. Blast, are you all right?"

"Come on, copy, damn it," Rogue said as he retried the BioMet Card. "Got it."

"Open these doors," ordered the voice outside.

Rogue held the duplicator card in front of the scanner and a panel in the otherwise flawless wall slid open.

"An elevator," Raine said. She moved to enter the car.

"Raine—no!"

The GEA agent stopped with her toes on the edge of the small car. Rogue tossed a paperweight from Blast's desk into the elevator and watched it disappear. They heard it bounce against the shaft as it dropped.

"It's a hologram—a safety feature in case—"

"I don't care why," Raine said over the sound of splintering wood. "Just tell me how we escape."

"Listen," Rogue said. "The real car is coming up."

Blasters ripped through the last few inches of wood between the security forces and Rogue and Raine. Energy pulses burned fabric and furniture until smoke and fire filled the room. The gambler returned fire with the shotgun and .380, emptying both. Raine used her blaster until it was depleted. The security forces rushed the room, kicking aside burning material and calling for Blast. Several members stepped on the criminal's body while others employed the fire and ventilation systems to clear the room.

"There's no one here, sir," said a team member.

The young man received a backhanded slap from his superior.

"Well not anymore, you fool. Clear this room and . . . never mind. I found Mr. Blast."

* * *

THREE BUILDINGS DOWN FROM BLAST Tower, a buzz-cut blonde in a black bodysuit and a man wearing a fur-trimmed coat, leather pants, and strange boots exited. The pair held hands and hurried away from the building with a stiff-legged gait. Anyone watching would quickly discern that the two were guilty of something they wished to leave far behind. But it was Earth, and no one took notice, let alone cared about two strangers among the crowds of thousands.

CHAPTER TWENTY-NINE

SISTER MARY JOY OPENED THE door, and her welcome froze on her lips. Her mind simply could not process what her eyes beheld. Instinct took over as she grabbed Raine and Rogue, pulling them inside by their arms. She placed a finger over her lips and hustled them downstairs, pushing them into a small room. Only when the door was shut and locked did she speak.

"Did anyone see you arrive?"

"Lots of people saw us as we walked here," Raine replied.

"Yes, yes—but did anybody recognize you?"

Raine's fingers grazed her shorn head. She looked at Rogue and his strange clothing.

"No?" Raine said.

"No matter. We must get you out of these clothes and into something that will help you blend in. Stay here—I'll be right back."

Sister Mary Joy returned within twenty minutes with clothes borrowed from the poor box and two flimsy cots.

"These are worn but clean," the nun said of the clothes. "You'll have to stay in the furnace room because I told my fellow sisters you have tuberculosis. It was the only thing I could think of to keep them away. I'll burn your clothes in the trash barrel in the alley to reinforce the fear of contagion."

"This was the first safe place that came to mind," Raine said. Her voice held apology, her expression entreaty.

"I know. I understand." The nun bit her bottom lip and looked away.

"Are you sure it's okay we're here?" Rogue asked. It was the first time he had spoken since escaping Blast Tower. His strained voice sounded strange to his ears.

The nun made a soft noise of uncertainty in her throat, looking at Rogue's boots as she spoke.

"Get some rest, and I'll check on you after midmorning prayers."

Sister Mary Joy left without further comment as Raine and Rogue turned their backs to give each other privacy while they undressed and donned their new outfits. Sleeves were rolled up and pant legs tucked into footwear, and then they carefully sat on the cots.

"Good thing we're in the furnace room. She forgot blankets," Raine said.

Her attempt at conversation failed to draw Rogue out. The gambler stared at a spot above Raine's head where pale winter sunshine crept past a filthy window in the basement's block walls.

"Where are you right now?" Raine whispered.

"You tell me." Rogue's eyes searched the room, her face, the lines of dirt and blood in the creases of his palms. "I mean, clearly I'm here on Earth, but everything within me still feels like I'm supposed to be somewhere else."

"Can you tell me where that is? You promised an explanation."

"I wouldn't know where to begin."

"Let's rest like Sister Mary Joy suggested. You don't have to sleep, but try to unwind a little, okay?"

Rogue stretched out on the cot where sleep overtook him much against his will. He would have sworn he had slept without dreaming if he had not woken to Raine and Sister Mary Joy trying to contain his flailing limbs and calm his frantic cries.

"Breathe, Rogue. Just breathe," the nun said as she pressed her hand against his heart trying to pound its way out of his chest.

One of his fists grasped the black fabric of her habit while the other was locked in her restraining grip. Raine sat across his legs, and he almost laughed aloud, wondering how the cot bore their weight.

"I'm going to let go of your arm, but I need you to stay calm," Sister Mary Joy said. "Would you like to sit up?"

He nodded, and for the first time he heard his own ragged breathing. "I'm not crazy."

"No one's suggesting you are."

"I need you to believe me."

"We do, Rogue. Now drink this." Sister Mary Joy placed a cup to his lips. Fragrant steam curled upward, and the whole act of sipping the warm beverage soothed him with familiarity.

"This will take the edge off a little," Sister Mary Joy said.

Rogue pushed her hands away. "I don't want to sleep anymore."

"It won't make you sleepy, but it will relax you."

The nun offered the drink again, and Rogue finished it in tentative sips. A pleasant heat suffused his limbs, but as she had promised, he did not become drowsy.

"It's a little something I brew myself from things I grow in the garden," Sister Mary Joy said in answer to the question in Rogue's eyes.

Raine sat on the cot opposite and observed Rogue. Her interrogation skills surfaced, and she recognized guilt on the gambler's face. More surprising was the deep sorrow etching lines around his eyes. She knew from experience that whatever burdened Rogue would soon spill forth.

After years of hearing confessions, Sister Mary Joy also intuited what Raine saw. She sat on the cot beside the ex-GEA agent. "Say whatever it is you need to say, Rogue."

Rogue did not know where the Realm ended and Earth began. He nodded once, twice, and began speaking.

"My only request is that you let me tell you everything before you ask me any questions."

And then Rogue's time in the Realm spilled forth in vivid detail. He spoke without interruption, amazed at his powers of retention, reliving it all. The looks on the women's faces when he finished speaking reflected the complexity of his incredible adventure. He almost did not believe his own story.

"I thought you were dead," Raine said, breaking the long silence.

Sister Mary Joy nodded.

"So did I," Rogue said. "But I started to really live for the first time in my life. I didn't think I'd ever fit in, and I was a real ass at times. But eventually I learned to appreciate what I have in front of me, to stop running from my problems, and to fight for what I care about."

The old furnace that dominated the room stopped blowing, and the tick of cooling metal filled the silence. The taste of dry heat lingered on their tongues, competing with the flavor of mildew in the air.

Into the stillness Rogue asked, "Do you believe me?"

"I can't explain why, but I do," the nun said. "For some reason, I just do."

"Me, too," Raine said.

The nun smiled at the blush creeping across Raine's face. She would have liked to leave the pair alone to sort through their feelings. Impending danger necessitated that she break into their moment of peace.

"The reason I asked if anyone saw you arrive was because bulletins about Frank Blast's death have been scrolling non-stop across every HoloMir and billboard in the Quadrant," Sister Mary Joy said.

"We didn't even notice as we walked here," Rogue said.

"That's understandable considering what you've been through. But the fact remains unknown persons are being sought for questioning in the matter."

"Who would have the power or authority to do that?" Raine asked.

"Let me show you," Sister Mary Joy replied.

The three convened in the nun's tidy but crammed office with the door closed. Raine and Rogue sat stunned in front of a first generation HoloMir as they watched news reports covering the arrival of Yureed Santos in Quadrant One of the Northern Hemisphere. Ambassador Santos, as he had labeled himself, descended the stairs from his private air transport twice when the screen glitched. The man raised his arms in benevolence over what was undoubtedly a crowd of paid performers surging against the glass doors on their side of the airlock between the docking-dome and the bio-dome.

Santos and his entourage waited patiently in the airlock during the decontamination procedures before submitting to a GEA delegation that went through the motions of verifying travel and identity documents on a HoloMir tablet. Lights flashed among those in the crowd, and several hands shoved recording devices in Santos's face when he cleared the safety checkpoint. Two armed giants in black suits and black sunglasses with listening devices evident in their ears pretended to push the throng backward.

The farce continued with Santos answering questions that had not been asked and reassuring citizens who could not have cared less that he would personally make it his mission to discover Frank Blast's killer. At least the man had the good sense not to eulogize Blast.

"Why do I suspect his first priority is actually taking over Blast's enterprises?" Rogue said.

"Funny how that worked out for Blast considering what we know," Raine added.

Rogue shook his head in disgust. "I can't watch anymore."

"Good, then let's talk," Sister Mary Joy said as she sighed and slumped into her wooden desk chair, causing it to swivel. She removed her glasses, letting them dangle from one elegant hand as she massaged the bridge of her nose with her thumb and forefinger. "There's an increased presence of GEA agents on our street. It may not seem like a big deal, but I have spies in the neighborhood, and one in particular tells me an ex-GEA agent is being sought for questioning."

"That could be anyone," Rogue said.

"Except my spy said he detected surprise in the agents' voices because they thought *she* was already *dead*."

"You trust this source?"

"With my life. He doesn't look like much, but Ping is more honest and loyal than anyone I've ever met."

The ghost of a memory darted through Rogue's consciousness at the name.

"We need to brainstorm solutions," Sister Mary Joy continued. "I've been trying to come up with something since you arrived, but I got nothing. How did they track you here?"

"Facial recognition on any screen we passed while coming here. Not to mention we left our DNA all over Blast's office," Rogue said.

"Then why didn't they swoop in once they located us?" Raine asked.

"Santos is probably trying to decide if we're friend or foe. I'm in the GEA databanks as a person of interest, and you're supposed to be dead, Raine. Then again, we did Santos a favor."

Raine pressed her fist against her mouth, her eyes reviewing the list she mentally compiled. "We need cred-coin to buy safe passage to another Quadrant. We can purchase fake identities, travel passes, lenses and fingerprints to fool scanners, the total package to reinvent ourselves."

"That's going to take a ton of cred-coin," Sister Mary Joy said. "And the type of people you'd have to deal with only take payment in gold coin."

"I know. The kind of coin a person trying to buy his way off Earth would probably have stored in several extremely secure locations known only by him."

Rogue turned his best poker face on Raine, who felt the dashing of her hopes with the rise of her doubts.

"I'll admit I have the resources to buy our way out of here. But Raine, you have to know that if Santos has amassed the GEA against us, there's no way we could get to it, let alone take time to buy passage for three out of the Quadrant."

"What do you mean 'three'?" Sister Mary Joy asked.

"You have to go with us. I'm sorry but harboring us has put you in their crosshairs."

"I can't leave. I have responsibilities here to the homeless and the sisters."

"Let me help you understand. Santos will have you tortured just because we were here, and I don't want to think about what he'll do if he believes you know where we've gone. And not just you. You must leave for your sake as well as the homeless and the sisters."

Anger distorted the nun's reddening face, and tears rimmed her eyes. "This is my life's work, Rogue."

"I know. But you can be a nun anywhere."

"It's not that simple. These people trust me."

"Then you have to trust that you've trained the sisters well enough to care for them in your absence."

Sister Mary Joy cast about for something to anchor her to the convent. A soft rap on the door disrupted her thoughts.

"Sister?" said the unusual, lilting accent.

"It's Ping," the nun said, jumping up from her chair and opening the door far enough to grab the boy by his arm and drag him inside.

Sister Mary Joy's odd behavior caught Ping off guard but more so the presence of two additional people in her office.

"Hey, you're that kid that hangs around the bar down by the canals," Rogue said.

The thin boy shook his head and backed toward the door. "No, sir. That kid not Ping."

"It's all right, Ping," Sister Mary Joy said. "Tell me what's going on."

"He's your informant?" Rogue asked.

The nun waved him off and waited for the boy to speak.

"Many more GEA come. It look like war zone outside."

Rogue stood and looked between the broken slats of the vertical blinds. Eight GEA air transport vehicles descended on the buckled pavement of the road, knocking into surrounding buildings as they landed. A battalion of GEA Special Forces poured out with half the personnel taking up position in the abandoned buildings across from the convent while the other half cleared the street of pedestrians and set up barricades. Three armed drones hovered over the building opposite.

"So much for doing Santos a favor. He's going overboard covering all his bases. We're definitely not going out by the front door. Is there another way out of here?"

“The other exits lead to easily blocked alleys,” Sister Mary Joy said. “What about the roof?”

“We’d be picked off by a drone in seconds,” Raine said.

The nun put her arm around Ping and drew the boy close. She gasped when the image on her HoloMir became the face of the officer commanding GEA forces outside. The voice coming from the screen was half a second ahead of the same voice booming from loudspeakers on the drones now over the convent.

“By order of Ambassador Santos, all persons are to exit the building in a swift, orderly fashion—”

Rogue ripped the screen out of hover-lock and smashed it on the desk. The shattering was accompanied by the stampede of frightened people bailing out of every door and window on the first floor. Raine peeked out the fifth-story window to see GEA personnel rounding up homeless people and nuns into groups for identifying and possible imprisonment. An explosion from behind rocked the building and rained plaster dust on the office, cutting all power to the convent.

“This is it,” Raine said. Unwilling to go down without a fight, she grabbed shards of the broken HoloMir and handed a knife-like piece to Rogue.

“Ping—find us a safe place,” Sister Mary Joy said. The nun rummaged her desk for her first aid box, jamming it with bandage rolls, packets, and bottles stashed in the drawers. “If we survive this, we’re going to need medicine.”

Raine positioned herself by the door to receive the first onslaught and waved Rogue into position opposite her, knowing their efforts were futile.

“Get under the desk now,” Raine ordered the nun and boy. “Stay away from the window.”

“Hurry, Ping,” the nun said.

Rogue turned to see Ping kneeling under the desk with his eyes screwed shut. The boy rocked back and forth, wringing his hands as if trying to work something out.

"I see safe place, Sister, and way out."

"Let's go," Sister Mary Joy said as she stood to exit the room.

Rogue caught her by her habit. "What the hell are you doing?"

"Ping scouted a way out of here. He can lead us to safety."

"Are you insane? That kid doesn't know anything."

"Rogue—listen to me. I don't know how, but Ping can see things in his head if he's seen them before." Another explosion removed the front doors of the convent. "He sees a path out that the GEA isn't covering."

Rogue felt as if the nun's words were puzzle pieces dropped in his lap, but he could not make the pieces fit, could not paint the complete picture.

"They're coming," Raine yelled over the rhythmic march of boots.

"We go now," Ping replied. "I take care of us, I promise."

"It's going to be all right, Rogue," Sister Mary Joy said.

The GEA forces ascended the steps in the old building, advancing three abreast up the sagging stairs. An impenetrable wall of death for the four in the office. And still Rogue stepped back in the remaining moments to see Raine ready to lead them into battle, Ping prepared to guide them to safety, and Sister Mary Joy equipped to treat their wounds in the event they lived.

"You never said anything frivolous, did you Bialig?" Rogue whispered. Saying his friend's name aloud broke through a barrier in Rogue. "You're second-sighted, aren't you?" the gambler directed at Ping.

"I no understand."

"Yes, you do. You're second-sighted. Have you ever tried seeing through someone else's vision?"

Ping's eyes shined because he knew somehow the gambler understood what he had never been able to explain to himself.

"Take each other's hands—now," Rogue ordered the others.

"You want to pray?" Sister Mary Joy asked.

Rogue smiled at the nun. "Our prayers have already been answered. Raine—let's go."

The ex-GEA agent looked at the door one last time before joining the other three.

"What are we doing, Rogue?" she asked.

"Hold tight and see, sweetheart."

Peace descended on the foursome when they joined hands. Sister Mary Joy's mouth moved in silent supplication as Raine leaned toward Rogue, their lips meeting in the middle. Ping closed his eyes and marveled at the others' visions racing through his mind.

Rogue had only seen pictures of Sector 48 in Quadrant Three when he had read the documents over Raine's shoulder in the ductwork of Blast Tower. The second-hand memories would have to be enough to show Ping. But first, Rogue sought a tree in another world meant for signaling direction under whose branches they would take momentary sanctuary. He shared that vision with the boy.

Light enveloped the Group of Four within a crystal orb. Rogue had some idea of what to expect, but the other three cringed at the fire flashing outside the calm sphere of radiance that moved like water.

"Don't let go," the gambler charged them, tightening his grip.

A mighty breath blew through the leaves of the tree that materialized before them, and the building shook with the thunder of a great army. Rescue from the malevolence rushing to overtake them came as a cool wind through an open door. They stepped forward, seemingly into the same space. A cloud of dust rose at their backs when the old convent, weakened by assault, collapsed upon the horde streaming upward into the building. The four were undaunted by the destruction that could not touch them.

"Hold tight," Rogue called over the tumult. "And now go here, Ping."

Ping closed his eyes and saw Rogue's thoughts again. He quickly scouted their next safe location, one devoid of people on the shores of a small, freshwater sea where it was already evening. One more time they stepped forward holding hands and crossed over into their haven. Rocks shifted beneath their feet, and water lapped at their heels. Only then did they break the connection and close the portal.

The few who witnessed what took place in Sister Mary Joy's office lay buried under five stories of rubble. Yureed Santos, privately deeming it a small price to pay, would publicly eulogize the GEA Special Forces team members lost in the operation. He would never know that those closest to the open portal had been scorched by a fire not of Earth. Or that four civilians had survived the attack. Bulldozing the site to create a mass grave ensured he remained ignorant.

Santos ordered all records of the two people wanted for Frank Blast's death deleted from any databank in the Quadrant along with that of the nun who sheltered them and her teenaged informant. They simply ceased to exist, rendering them beyond the need of an acknowledged death.

And yet the four had never been more alive.

THE END

REALM WORD KEY

Mir – a term of affection between two people engaged in a deep friendship

Mira – same as above but with the added qualities of respect for authority, honor for position, and ultimate admiration

Doh s'Ima – Group of Four

Avboeth – Assembly

Natamos – Leader

Thedanos – Healer

Jiltraos – Gatherer

Paten – Artist

Example of how words are made plural and/or possessive:
Sojab – verb meaning *to steal*

Sojabos – the addition of *–os* to any root verb is equivalent to adding *–er* to a word, thus *sojabos* means a stealer (one who steals, i.e., a thief)

Sojabosne – the addition of *–ne* makes the word plural (thieves) *(–ne* can be *–s* or *–es* depending on the English translation of the Realmese word)

Sojabosnelo & *Sojaboslo* – the addition of *–lo* makes the word possessive, thus *sojabosnelo* is thieves' whereas *sojaboslo* is thief's

PRONUNCIATION GUIDE FOR LANGUAGE OF THE REALM

A – /ah/ as in father, short a

E – /ay/ as in date, long a

I – /ee/ as in bee, long e

O – /o/ as in rose, long o

U – /u /as in dune, long u

Y – /y/ as in yellow, never long i (as in thyme) or long e (as in candy)

G – /g/ as in good, never soft g (like the second g in garage)

J – /j/ as in jump

S – /s/ as in sand

K – /k/ as in kitten

S and K are included as a reminder that there is no C except in the Ch sound construction.

Ch – /ch/ as in church

Sh – /sh/ as in show

Th – /th/ as in this

H – /h/ as in hello

> H sounds very much like a standard English H except when following a vowel, in the middle of a word, or at the end of a word in which case it is pronounced a little breathier. The exception to the rule is the Ch, Sh, and Th sound constructions.

s' (which means of) is blended with the following letter of the word if the word begins with a vowel. If the next letter is a consonant, the S is pronounced as a separate sound.

Every letter of the language of the Realm is pronounced except in the double letter sound constructions listed above.

Letters are never repeated as in English words (cookie, summer) with the exception of some vowels in a few verb conjugations.

ACKNOWLEDGMENTS

BARUCH HASHEM FOR HELPING ME grow this spark to its fullest potential. Thank you to my husband, William, for supporting me along the way, and to my son, Joshua, for challenging me to finish. Much appreciation to Doug Nelson for asking all the right questions. Many thanks go out to Heath Smith, Priscilla Smith, and Grant and Robin Luton for finding the little flaws that needed to be fixed. I am forever grateful to my editor, Kori Frazier Morgan of Inkling Creative Strategies, who polished the rough stone of my manuscript until it became the multi-faceted diamond that is *Realm*.

ABOUT THE AUTHOR

HL GIBSON, A NATIVE OHIOAN, is a lifelong lover of books and storytelling. She credits her mother for instilling her passion for reading, which led her to cultivate a vivid imagination as a writer and inspired her to finally put her stories on the page. As a member of the Beth Tikkun Messianic Fellowship, her faith plays a significant role in crafting her fiction. HL has a vast and growing personal library, loves tea and classical music, and is a self-proclaimed bourbon snob. She is married with one son and five high-maintenance cats.